Th

Gil lowered his shoulder and leaned forward to dive through the window.

His feet went out from under him. He lurched forward, reaching out, and landed with his right arm on the windowsill, his head out the window, his left hand entangled in the curtain. Hands dragged him back into the room . . .

One of the men planted a foot between his shoulder blades and shoved him back down. He lay quietly, willing to accept the respite, no matter how brief. There was something sticky under his right hand: Pombal's blood . . .

The officer knelt, shoved a pistol before his eyes. "You will do nothing, say nothing, unless we wish it, Señor," he said. "Is that understood?" He rotated the gun for emphasis. Gil recognized the model: a Browning 9-mm automatic, powerful enough to sever an arm or a leg at close range . . .

Tor Books by Harold A. Schofield

A Private Kind of War
Red Light Red Light

A PRIVATE KIND OF WAR

HAROLD A. SCHOFIELD

TOR

A TOM DOHERTY ASSOCIATES BOOK
NEW YORK

A PRIVATE KIND OF WAR

Copyright © 1990 by Harold A. Schofield

A TOR Book
Published by Tom Doherty Associates, Inc.
49 West 24 Street
New York, NY 10010

Cover design by Joe Curcio

ISBN: 0-812-50365-1

First edition: August 1990

Printed in the United States of America

0 9 8 7 6 5 4 3 2 1

For Emily,
with love

PART ONE

·

CHAPTER 1

June, 1938

The hot, wet air discouraged movement, thought. Andre Duchesne could hear the rain splatter against the tin roof. A flash from above caught his attention. He looked up to where wall and ceiling joined, saw a lizard the color and size of a Cuban cigar. He turned back to Ellen.

She was restless. It was uncharacteristic; usually, she seemed so composed. He opened his mouth to ask what was bothering her, then paused. Ellen was not one to reveal her thoughts unless she wanted to. He could wait.

He kept watching her, aware she was oblivious to his presence at that moment. She twirled a loose piece of thread—fugitive from an old doily on the arm of her chair—in her fingers. Her eyes kept darting back and forth, as if she sought something which eluded her. She was a strange woman, he thought. Jamaican-born and raised, with only five of her twenty-nine years spent in England, yet so damnably English—living proof that the nation's brand of snobbery grew as easily in tropical climes as it did at home.

She had been distracted even during their lovemaking. That was uncharacteristic, too. He watched her lift a cigarette from his case and light it. She held it between the first two fingers of her right hand—as would an American—and put it to her mouth. She drew lightly on it, squinted as if the smoke irritated her eyes. At last, she met his gaze. Her blue eyes were so dark they seemed almost violet. "What is it?" he asked.

"My husband has found out," she answered, breaking the cigarette's thin column of smoke with her words.

The revelation stirred conflicting emotions. He tried to sort them out, select those which seemed most real. "But that is marvelous," he told her. She was not receptive. The words fell flat. He rose from his chair, intending to put an arm around her.

Clad only in a pink slip which clung to her hips and outlined her small breasts, and with her dark hair down, curling in damp waves around her face, she had an earthy look: basic, sensual, warm, and wet. Her lower arms were tanned. The tanned skin seemed darker in the glare of artificial light than it did by day, as if she were wearing gloves. Andre lifted his gaze slightly: her neck and face were also tanned, but the definition was not as sharp—a hint of a V below the neck, nothing more. The contrast of that golden skin with the creamy tones elsewhere added to the intimacy of the scene.

"Don't be absurd," she said matter-of-factly, "there's nothing marvelous about it."

The impertinence brought him up short. Whatever her attributes, he thought, she had never accepted certain attitudes as unfeminine. His own impulse was to reprimand

4

her, but he checked it. That could come láter. He began anew. "He had to find out sooner or later," he said. "Now that he has, you are free to leave him. We can be married."

Her look turned from critical to probing. She set the cigarette in the oyster shell which served as an ashtray, toyed with it for a moment, then snuffed it out. "How did he find out? Did you tell him?"

The question stung. He had considered doing so many times, but he had not. "You know better than that," he replied.

She nodded.

He reached for her, felt her stiffen at his touch. He pulled her from the chair. Slowly, as if shifting a statue, he managed to turn her until he looked in her eyes. Long eyes, with heavy, dark lashes, such as those one might find painted on the walls of ancient Egyptian temples. Isis would have had such eyes, he thought. She was beautiful, even with the worry that showed in her face. "You don't love him," he whispered. "You said you never did."

"Yes," she agreed.

Her flesh under his fingers was soft, pliant. He tightened his grip on her upper arms. "Then this is for the best," he assured her. "A few months of unpleasantness and it will be all over." He saw a glint come to her eyes.

"And then you will marry me?" she asked. The spark had kindled a look of mocking humor. Her words carried the same tone, mixed with a hint of malice.

Andre ignored the sarcasm. "Yes," he answered.

"What will we do then?" she continued, emphasizing the pronoun.

The question was soft-spoken, but the edge remained. Might she be on the verge of hysteria? Not Ellen. She was above that sort of thing. He paused, recalling something he had once heard about Englishwomen: how, unfortunately, they always acted regally in the bedroom and whorishly in the salon. He had never believed it fit Ellen. Now, he was not so sure. She might be more like her other countrywomen than he had assumed. "What we have talked of. I will quit the foreign service. We will go to Paris."

"It will ruin your career."

He almost smiled. So that was it; some of her husband's timidity had rubbed off on her. "I should have done it long ago," he assured her. "The Foreign Office is controlled by my enemies. It is they who have kept me here. Resigning will make, not hurt, my career."

As always, mention of Paris excited him. He released her, began to pace, filled with his own thoughts, his own dreams. He would have left the Dominican Republic long ago had it not been for Ellen, he told himself, aware it was a lie, but content to accept it as the truth. He picked up his cigarette case from the table, took out a cigarette, tamped it on the gold cover, put it to his mouth, and lit it. A Gaulois Bleu. Its pungent sweetness reinforced memories of Paris. It was as if he were already home. He glanced at Ellen. She was looking at him, her eyes quizzical, her mouth half open. A wide mouth, indicative of a generous personality, and sculpted lips. She had spoken; he had been too preoccupied to hear her. He raised an eyebrow.

"I said, 'What if I don't want to go to Paris?' "

"But we must!" he answered. "What would you prefer? That we remain in this stinkhole? Let others take advantage of the changes which will take place?"

"I do not understand."

"That is because you pay no attention to affairs in France," he said. "Spain, the question of rearmament, have split the Left from the Center. Daladier's government cannot last. When it falls, it will be the Right which will profit. I want to be there when it does."

"You sound eager," Ellen said. Her voice was even softer than before.

"Why should I not be?" Andre agreed. "Tell me one good thing that has come out of our so-called Republic." He gave her no time to respond. "You cannot. No one can, except for the Jews and atheists. Everything France once stood for is gone—sold or stolen by pimps like Blum." A warning sign flashed in his mind, but his words galloped on, as if possessed of a life of their own. "If France is ever to recover its greatness, it must duplicate the German experiment," he concluded.

"You still support the Nazis?" Ellen asked. The disapproval in her voice was evident.

Andre was not surprised. They had talked of it before, had disagreed before. He paid little attention to her disapproval. Politics were alien to women, he believed. They adopted their husband's principles, as a sort of protective camouflage. Ellen was only spouting the views of her English diplomat husband. Those would change once Ellen was with him. "The only thing I dislike about the Nazis is that they are German," he spat. "Their ideas are right, it is their methods which are wrong—as usual. What would you expect? The *boche* are too crude to develop a great idea without brutalizing it."

Ellen shook her head. The gesture irritated him. He did not like it when women disagreed with him. "What is wrong?" he asked.

She continued to shake her head. Her hair swayed back and forth with each head shake, sending light and shadow at play across her face. The act made her seem all the more beautiful. Andre suppressed the feelings the sight inspired, awaited her answer.

"I will not go to Paris."

How could she refuse? She was about to be cast aside by her husband. She had nowhere to go, no other man upon whom to rely. And she was getting older, had a child to take care of. It was her pride, not her good sense, which spoke, he concluded. He had to reassure her. "But why not?" he pressed. "Paris is made for women." He saw a frown beginning to crease her forehead and automatically switched his argument. "Are you afraid you will no longer be able to work? I have no objection, as long as it does not interfere with our life together. I remember your saying how much you would like to work at *L'Institut Géographie Physique* or *L'Académie Maritimes et Océanique*. Now you can do it."

"It is not because of my work that I will not go with you."

A knot formed in his stomach, his throat grew tight. "Then what? Religion? That is silly. Neither of us takes it seriously. You would have to give some attention to my church in the beginning, until we get you an annulment, until we marry. After that, it is only a matter of form."

He stopped, looked into her eyes. He could not read them. "Tell me," he urged. "Is it because of your child? Think of the opportunities she will have in Paris. Her education!"

The last had made an impact. "Conditions are unsettled in Europe," Ellen countered. "I do not think I would like to take her there now."

She had become specific. Was she weakening? "But that is all the more reason for us to be there," Andre responded. He settled into what Ellen used to call his diplomatic voice: persuasive, melodic, soothing. "This crisis with Czechoslovakia will amount to nothing. The *boche* have their hands full assimilating Austria. And we have an alliance with the Czechs. Hitler will do nothing. Meanwhile, we will soon have a new government. My friends will come to power. They will take steps to see that Germany will not risk war. And we will be there when it happens—you, me, your daughter. We will be a perfect family for the new France. We will take Paris by storm. No one will be able to resist us.''

Ellen shifted to face him squarely, a look of amazement in her eyes. Slowly, she nodded. A feeling of triumph spread over him. He smiled.

She did not return it. ''Yes,'' she began, trailing out the sibilant, ''I believe you might care for me after all.''

What did she mean by that? Had she thought it had been only the sex with him? There were many in the Dominican Republic who would have been only too happy to supply all he wanted and have given him far less trouble than she.

''No,'' Ellen continued, ''we won't go to Paris with you.''

The pain numbed him. ''Why not?'' he managed.

She stood silently, as if mulling over which answer to give him. It made him angry. He was about to repeat his question when, finally, she spoke. ''Many reasons.''

''Give me one.''

Her gaze was calm. Its steadiness angered him. The muscles of his forearms twitched. He clenched his fists to stop them. ''Very well,'' she said at last. ''I will not jump from one bad marriage into another.''

It was as if she had struck him. How could she compare their relationship to that she had with her *con* of a husband? He glanced over to the mussed bed, as if to give the lie to her assertion.

She followed his eyes. "No, not there," she admitted. "There, you and George are different."

"Then why—?"

"Poor Andre," she said. "You really don't understand, do you?"

Her patronizing tone infuriated him. He fought to control himself. "No," he said through tight lips.

"And you want me to tell you?" It was like a warning sign.

He ignored it. "Yes."

She signed. "Very well. You may care for me, but you don't like me."

"How can you say—"

She waved her hand to stop him. He obeyed, suppressing his rage. "Not me, personally, perhaps," she explained, "but us: women, I mean. You don't; neither does George. What you call love is only a desire to dominate. I came to hate that in George—his smug tolerance, his assumption always that he knew what was best for Sara and me."

He detected hesitation in her voice. "There is something more," he said. "What is it?"

"There is nothing more," she insisted. "Everything else stems from that—the way you try and lead my life for me, your politics, your—"

"My politics?"

"Yes." Ellen began to speak more rapidly, as if anxious to get it all over. "Your stupid anti-Semitism, your elitism, the way you strut and swagger. You're a Nazi. I had not realized the extent to which those horrid ideas have poisoned you. I suppose it shows how little I actually knew you. After all, we never talked much, did we? Fucked a lot, yes, but—"

"Do not be coarse," he commanded.

"I forgot how much my *petit crudités* upset you," she responded. "Very well, it doesn't alter my opinion. What are you people called in France: *Croix de feu? Camelots de roi?* Whatever, French Nazis aren't any more palatable than German ones, only more polite. And more comedic, like your Italian confederates."

The energy which impelled him toward her seemed to come from outside him. He raised his hand to strike, then stopped, hand still outstretched. Other than to narrow her eyes in anticipation of the blow, Ellen had not moved. He lowered his hand. It was as if, in that instant, all his love for her was snuffed out. Hatred replaced it. It burned. "I believed you different from the rest of your race," he said through clenched teeth, "but you aren't. You English are so superior, so sure of yourselves. I'll tell you what you don't like about men like me: we don't automatically accept the English as rulers of the world. Do you know what I really think of you people?"

He spat out his question, as if the words themselves were noxious, to be expelled quickly. The rapidity and the completeness with which he was engulfed by the new emotion surprised him, but he knew it was as real and compelling as that which it replaced. "Parasites, all of you: pimps and whores, living off the labor of the rest of the world. And you accept it as your right, as if God had created you on the seventh day to rest along with Him. Well, the day of accounting is near. When it comes, France will be among those who decide what price you must pay for your arrogance." Andre stared at her. The hatred was now complete. How could he have ever thought the English cunt worthy of his love? He spun on his heels and left without looking back. The hallway shook when he slammed her door shut behind him.

* * *

With a sigh, Ellen twisted in the chair, rested her fore arms along its back, folded one leg under her, and looked outside. The rain had nearly stopped. A little moonlight penetrated the cloud cover. She turned down the kerosene lamp in an effort to see better. Not that there was much to see: a line of tin-roofed shacks; puddles filling the ruts of the dirt road, like lines of broken canals. The smells, stronger now that the rain was done, made her crinkle her nose: decaying vegetation, nightsoil, garbage. La Palma was hardly a metropolis, she thought, even by Dominican standards. How long had she been here? A week? No, more. Not quite two weeks. The length of time it had taken to chart the nearby coastline, take soundings of the offshore waters. Soon, the job would be done. The team would move farther along the coast, toward Haiti.

All but she. She would have to quit. George's letter had made that clear. He was leaving his job at the consulate in Ciudad Trujillo and returning to London. She had to return to the Dominican capital to collect Sara and make arrangements for their future. She sighed again. The work with the Dominican-German Scientific Institute had been enjoyable. It had helped provide an identity separate from her husband's. It had also given her the chance to jump into bed with Andre, she thought guiltily.

She craved another cigarette. She did not know why; she rarely smoked. *Only when I lose a husband and a lover on the same day,* she told herself. She picked up what remained of the one she had recently put out, straightened it, brushed away the charred end. As she lit it, she could feel the flame's heat against her nose. The smoke was hot, burned her throat, but it satisfied her need. "Ellen Bainbridge, née Cooper," she muttered, "when you screw up, you do it royally."

Andre and George were gone from her life: a package

deal. She wondered which she would miss the most, decided it was a stupid question. George had been missing from the day they married. It was funny, the difference between what one imagined married life would be like and what it turned out to be. No walking hand in hand, no real sharing of life and its excitements, no mutual facing of problems. Instead, it was like being locked up, treated as a second-class citizen.

She picked a shred of tobacco off her tongue with the nail of her little finger. Not that it had been all George's fault, she admitted. He had been forced into his role, too. But what had angered her from the beginning, she recalled, was the ease with which he accepted their roles. God-given, beyond debate, that had been his attitude. She grew angry all over again, visualized herself penning a response to her husband's letter: *I didn't take a lover because you were such a frightful bore,* she saw herself writing, *but because the prison into which you threw me had neither windows nor doors. I couldn't see out; you wouldn't come in.*

She took another puff on her cigarette, felt its glow on her fingers, then ground it out. The tobacco's smell reminded her of Andre. She saw him clearly: his hair—dark and wavy—without a trace of oil, such as George used, his clean and sharp jawline, the chicken pox scar high on his cheek . . .

But Andre was gone. And for good. Ellen rose, turned off the lamp, and threw herself on the unmade bed. The sheet was rough, wrinkled. Her fingers found a damp spot. That and the butt in the ashtray across the room were all she had left of him.

Her eyes felt dry. It hurt to close them. In the dark, she peered sightlessly at the ceiling. Andre was more political than George. It came from his being French, she supposed. It was why he accepted nothing as beyond his grasp. That another possessed what he wanted meant only that the other had grabbed it first; it did not sanctify the possession. He had seemed like a pirate when they had first met—daring, wicked. That was what she had found so hard to resist. To be honest, she was not sure which of them had been the more zealous in pursuit of the other. "What a tramp I am," she said aloud. The words frightened her. They sounded alien, as if a stranger had accused her.

In the new silence, she heard the scuttering of a lizard's feet. Outside, a dog growled. *Who but a tramp would hold back news of discovery from a lover until they had made love one last time?*

A new question struck her. Would she miss either one? Her answer was like a secret shared with only the closest of girlhood friends: *No.* She turned onto her right side. She knew what she would do. She and Sara would return to Jamaica to live with her mother. Her mother would like that. She had lived alone since Ellen's father's death, and she had never really cared for George. Money?

No problem. There was her father's legacy, and George would help provide for Sara. She could get back to work. She would revise her monograph on the Greater Antilles, expand the section covering Hispaniola. Not that it would bring in much money, but it would enhance her reputation. It might enable her to get a position at an American university. She backed off from the last thought. She was not prepared to think of leaving Jamaica, not before she had even returned. It did not matter. There would be opportunities in Jamaica. She might never have to leave the island again.

Life without men. She was ready to try it. Did they all insist on dominating, controlling? She thought it likely. It was in their genes, had something to do with their hunting instinct, their compulsion to defend the cave from outsiders: a behavior pattern run amuck in a civilized state. It made them fight wars, act like bullies. *Shits, that's what they are, all of them.* She was well rid of them.

Was she rid of them? Even if George did not divorce her, he was gone forever. Moral outrage, justified umbrage—phrases like those defined him. George was implacable when it came to sin. He might forget; he could never forgive.

Andre—he was the one she was not so sure of. He believed he loved her, and she knew how obsessive he was. Andre always played by his rules, acted according to his needs. He might try to get back in bed with her, if only to prove how wrong she had been in rejecting him. What was worse, she was not sure of her resolve—firm enough for now, but what about next month? God, she hoped he would not try.

CHAPTER 2

March, 1941

A scraping sound issued from the loudspeaker, then a loud, electric whistle. Andre looked up from his newspaper in anticipation of the broadcaster's voice. It came, high-pitched, but authoritative: *"Attention! Attention!"* More squeaks, then *"L'express de Paris arrive dans cinq minutes."*

He checked his watch. The train was only three-quarters of an hour late. That was fifteen minutes better than usual. The delay came at the demarcation line, he knew. The German inspection was always thorough, time-consuming. As always, thought of the occupation angered him. Sixty percent of the land, including Paris, under German military occupation and control, with only a handful of dirt left for Vichy to govern. Forty percent, the rump of France. In Caesar's day, Andre reflected, Gaul had been divided into three parts. Two thousand years later and the country was again divided. The former government bore full responsibility for it. Andre was not sure which he hated more: the *boche* or those former leaders.

Why didn't the SCNF drop the pretense that the train was an express? That, or change the estimated time of arrival in Vichy to something closer to reality? The same answer satisfied both questions—it was necessary to maintain the myth that the German occupation had not changed life. An express is an express, even if it is stopped and searched; a time schedule is a time schedule. He folded his journal and stuck it in his pocket, threw his cigarette on the floor and ground it underfoot, then rose from the depot bench.

It was cold on the platform. A bitter wind blew along the track. Andre turned up the collar of his woolen overcoat and faced away from the wind. He did not like Vichy. He never had, not even as a child, when his parents had come for the water. There was no more reason to like it now—a once sleepy town bursting at the seams as the temporary capital of the new French state.

Temporary! Even that was a laugh. It had been the capital for almost a year. Unless there was progress in negotiations with the Germans, it might even become France's permanent capital. A horrifying thought.

The wind penetrated his coat, stabbed like a thousand cold needles. He wished he were back in Martinique. Why had he been recalled to Vichy, anyway? He could not understand it. In the month since his arrival, he had seen no one of importance, had done nothing. Nor could he get an explanation for his recall. "Orders," that was all he was told, as if orders appeared mysteriously, like Moses' tablets. This assignment seemed the final humiliation: meet the courier from Paris on the morning express. It was beneath him.

He heard the train, turned to view it. White steam, trapped under the iron and glass shed, swirled around the engine and its cars. Slowly, the train came to a stop. The car doors slammed open. The platform, nearly empty a few seconds before, suddenly was filled with grim-faced men hurrying into the station. Andre stood his ground, brushing shoulders with the passersby. He kept watching for the Colonial Ministry courier.

He felt something hard jam into his back, was about to protest. "Don't say anything, don't turn around," came a voice from behind him, "I have a gun in your back. Do you understand?"

Andre nodded. He started to lift his arms, an involuntary reaction to the feel of the pistol's snout against his kidney. He was not frightened, only confused. The voice whispered a new command, "Keep your hands down." The man's mouth was close to Andre's ear. He could feel the warm breath. He let his arms fall back to his sides.

"*Bon,*" whispered the man. "Now, come with me. Say nothing, do nothing. I have a colleague. *Comprenez-vous?*"

Andre understood that he was being kidnapped in full sight of hundreds of train passengers. He understood also the implied threat in the man's words. "Yes," he whispered.

"*Bon,*" the man repeated. Andre felt someone slipping an arm under his. There came a tug and a quiet "*Allons.*" It was as if he had been asked to dance and his partner demanded to lead. They turned, arm in arm, and went with the flow of passengers. He glanced at his captor, saw a man shorter than he, clad in a dark blue overcoat and brown hat. Was there really another behind him? Memory of the gun jammed against his kidney discouraged him from finding out or shouting for help. He would accompany his captor without protest. What else could he do?

He was propelled into the station, then out through a side door to the Avenue des Célestins. The man pulled at his arm, growled, *"Vite, vite."* He was steered toward a car at the curb—a black Renault. The car lacked the characteristic tank and converter of the few autos still on the street. That meant it still burned regular fuel. Whoever his captors were, they had enough influence to obtain a gasoline rationing card.

A man opened the car door, pushed the front passenger's seat forward, then waved Andre into the back. The man was bulkier than the other, with heavy jowls and a small mustache. Andre stooped to enter, felt his captor push him. "Sit on the floor," the bulky man said.

He obeyed. There was not much space; his shoulders were pinched between the front and back seats. His hat had been knocked awry. Above him, looking at him from the front passenger's seat, he saw his armed captor, the pistol in evidence. It was of blued steel, an automatic, like those army officers carried, but smaller. Andre straightened his hat. "Now," the man told him, "make yourself comfortable and be quiet. We are not going to harm you."

The assurance did little to stem Andre's anxiety. "Where are you taking me?" he asked.

The door on the driver's side opened, and the second man slid into the auto. The other merely shook his head.

Andre opened his mouth for another question, but waited until the car's ignition caught and the Renault was in motion. "Who are you?"

The man looking down on him smiled, then reached into his coat. He pulled out a wallet, flipped it open, and held it for Andre to inspect: a lieutenant of Internal Security. *Jesus,* he thought, *I've been kidnapped by the po-*

lice. He had heard rumors of such things—men suddenly disappearing without a trace. Was it going to happen to him?

The driver turned right, then left. Originally, their car had been heading down the avenue. Now, Andre was not sure where it was going. He lifted his head to look out the window.

"Careful," his guard said in warning. "Keep your head down."

Andre sank back, felt the rear window handle on the back of his head. The auto had an ashtray embedded in the back of the front seat. It was close to his nose. The smell of old cigarettes was strong, like dried orange peels. It awakened a craving for one. "Mind if I smoke?" he asked, shifting so that he might reach his cigarettes.

The guard shook his head. "Not until we get to where we're going," he said. "Then you can smoke all you want."

It didn't sound as if death awaited him. Why this kidnapping, then? Might he be suspected of having liked the Americans too well during Vichy's recent negotiations with them? Surely not. He tried to relax, failed. The uncertainty of what awaited him kept him on edge.

The auto slowed, then halted. Andre shifted, prepared to get out, was told to sit still. It was easier said than done. His left foot had gone to sleep. His discomfort was acute.

His captors seemed to be waiting for something. Then one muttered, "All right, let's go." Both doors opened. The seat was pulled forward. A gruff command: "Come, quickly." Andre extricated himself one foot at a time, crablike. At last, he managed to stand. His left foot felt heavy and tingled. He looked at the building before him with surprise; it was the Petit Casino, a gambling establishment that had always reminded Andre of a Viennese torte.

Now, with gambling made illegal, it had become a rarity—an unused structure with boarded-up windows in a city where nearly every square centimeter was occupied. For some reason, no government agency had taken over the premises. The front door was unlocked. He was hurried through it, into a large, empty room, filled with tables all draped with white cloths, like a morgue.

"This way," one of his guards said. Andre obeyed, threaded his way around the covered tables. Was he at last going to learn why he had been recalled from Martinique? He suddenly felt sure of it. The lead guard began to ascend a flight of marble stairs. Andre followed, noticing that the staircase was free of dust. The handrail, too, had been recently polished. The building might look vacant, but someone was using it.

They came to the top of the stairs. One of the men rapped on a door, then opened it. "Enter," he said as he stood aside.

Andre looked into his eyes, saw nothing in them to provide a clue of what awaited him. He took a deep breath, stepped inside, and heard the door click shut behind him. Before him, two men, seated on straight-backed chairs, looked up. Andre recognized them, Marcel Pic, his superior in the Colonial Ministry, and Major-General Jean Hibbert, one of the delegates to the Franco-German Armistice Commission. Quickly he glanced around the room. A large desk or table, covered as those downstairs had been, filled one corner of the room. Two empty chairs helped frame a coffee table between the men. There were two glasses on the table. Hibbert's looked half empty, Pic's hardly touched.

He detected the scent of apples and sought the source,

relying as much on his nose as his eyes. On the mantel above the fireplace, an open bottle of Calvados, its unmistakable bouquet all the sharper for the fire which burned in the hearth. The pair of empty glasses beside the bottle confirmed his earlier impression: a fourth was expected. The occasion, if not social, was at least not immediately dangerous.

Pic stood, a broad smile on his face. He was a tall man, with beefy shoulders, blond hair, and a thin mustache. The mustache seemed to snap in half with the smile. "Ah, Duchesne," Pic said. "It is good of you to come. Do you know General Hibbert?"

Andre was tempted to click his heels as he bowed. Hibbert looked more like a Prussian general than anything the Prussians had produced in this war: a small man, thin, with close-cropped gray hair—everything but the dueling scar and the monocle. "We met once, years ago," Andre acknowledged. "At Verdun, at a ceremony commemorating the tenth anniversary of that battle. My father introduced us. I imagine the general has forgotten the incident."

"I remember your father," the general replied, as if that had been Andre's point. "I was grieved to hear of his death. He was a brave man."

Andre accepted the statement with a nod. "He once told me that serving under you was the most rewarding period of his life."

"They were hard days. Like these. One had to be bold, had to accept the consequences of command and carry on. Audacity, that was the key. Audacity and courage."

The remark seemed more than a commentary on the past. Andre glanced at his superior, expecting to hear why he had been summoned.

Pic went to the hearth, lifted the bottle and one of the glasses from the mantel. "Calvados?" Pic asked, turning.

Andre remembered Hibbert had been born in Normandy, assumed that was the reason for the choice of drink. Pic held the bottle by the neck, as a butcher might display a goose. "Yes," Andre said, "thank you."

He took the proffered glass. Pic topped off his and the general's glasses, straightened, and turned first to Hibbert, then to Andre, with his glass raised. "To audacity and courage," he said. They drank. Andre half expected the others to dash their glasses into the fireplace.

"Please, sit," Pic said, motioning to one of the empty chairs. Andre obeyed.

"I hope you will forgive the melodrama, M. Duchesne," Hibbert said.

"General?" Andre responded.

"This meeting," Hibbert continued, waiving his arm in a broad sweep. "Not telling you why you've been recalled, abducting you at the station as we did. I assure you we have good reason for all of it."

Andre let his glance swing over to his superior. Pic was nodding and smiling. "May I ask what it is?" Andre asked.

It was as if Hibbert donned a mask. The general was not used to being questioned. "In time," he replied. "You have been recently posted in Martinique. You know, of course, of the demands America has made on us, telling us how we must govern our Caribbean possessions."

He was referring to the most recent round of American negotiations, where Andre had assisted Admiral Robert. The highhanded manner of the Americans still rankled. He nodded.

"Your superior here," Hibbert continued, nodding toward Pic, "told me he had a devil of a time convincing you to remain with the Colonial Service because of those demands. Obviously, America is interested in what we do in the Caribbean. It fears we might make concessions there to the Third Reich. It does not want that. It wishes to keep those waters safe for its own use. It goes without saying that that also means Britain's use.''

If it went without saying, why had Hibbert mentioned it? Andre had the impression the general was not the sort who used words idly. The Americans' favoritism toward Britain, the humiliation Andre had suffered from his treatment by them, irritated him all over again.

''The American ambassador in Vichy—Admiral Leahy— is doing all he can to make sure we live up to our Caribbean agreements,'' Hibbert continued. ''He has a large staff. Most of them are spies. You have been followed since your arrival. That is why we spirited you away. It is important you are not seen in the company of the man who will soon arrive.''

''Who is that?'' Andre asked.

Hibbert closed his eyes. Andre knew he had again gone too far. ''Courage and audacity,'' Hibbert said. ''Your father had both. Do you possess them as well?''

It was an insulting question. ''If my country is involved,'' Andre responded, ''I think you will find I lack neither virtue.''

''So I have heard. We are going to give you—''

There was a knock on the door. Hibbert turned toward it. Andre followed his gaze. The fourth man walked in, wearing a heavy, belted overcoat. He took it off, revealing a gray suit, and threw the coat on the sheeted desk. Andre continued to stare. The newcomer was young, but his skin was weatherbeaten, and his light blue eyes had lost all appearance of youth. Clearly, the man was not French. German! He was certain of it.

After brief nods at Pic and Hibbert, the new arrival turned to Andre, staring at him with great concentration. Andre returned the stare. In some way, he knew, his destiny was tied to this man.

The silence was broken by Pic. "Ah, yes," he said, "Andre, let me introduce you to our guest. Andre Duchesne, *Fregattenkapitän* Heinrich Schatz; *Kapitän* Schatz, M. Andre Duchesne." Then, as if further clarification was needed, "Heinrich was an officer aboard the *Atlantis* until recently."

The *Atlantis* was a raider, Andre knew. Such service marked Schatz as a particular kind of navy man, one experienced in the type of warfare which depends upon surprise, camouflage, the ability to operate without close support. Schatz stuck out his hand. Andre took it. The grip was firm. "Delighted," Schatz said.

Andre stumbled slightly in returning the greeting.

"And now," Pic said, gesturing once again toward the chairs, "I think it best if we sit."

"The captain left his ship in Japan," Pic continued after all were comfortable. "He has met with naval and political figures in Tokyo."

Andre gathered that special importance should be attached to Pic's revelation. But what? That two military allies should have occasional talks? That could not be it. The fact had to having meaning for France—and, by extension, for him. The Japanese figured strongly in French thinking these days, due to their recent occupation of Indochina. France continued to administer the colony, but there was fear the Japanese occupation might become permanent.

That would be disastrous, especially as it would obviously encourage Mussolini to step up his demands on French North Africa. With half the country under German occupation and without an overseas empire, how could France pretend to greatness?

The others were gazing at him. He did not know what to say, or if he was expected to say anything.

Schatz filled the vacuum. "You have been recommended to us," he said. His French was flawless.

"For what?" Andre asked.

Schatz did not answer. He spoke instead on why he believed Andre was eminently qualified: ". . . excellent record . . . a true patriot . . . devoutly loyal to the new regime . . . a correct ideological bent . . . a thorough knowledge of the Caribbean . . ."

The German's listing of Andre's qualities evolved into a geopolitical monologue. Andre had some trouble making the transition, but caught up with Schatz as he said, "Britain is unable to resist much longer. It has but one hope—for America to soon join her."

The speech paralleled the French government's assessment, Andre realized. If conquered, Britain, not France, would be forced to pay for the war. The Axis could carve up the British, not the French, empire. And if France could convince Germany it deserved to become its ally, it too would participate in the redistribution. So far, neither former Premier Laval nor Admiral Darlan, his successor, had managed to persuade Hitler to grant ally status.

Andre caught his breath. Whatever he was wanted for, it had to do with just that. The thought grew into a certainty. He could feel his heart pounding. Schatz paused, a little smile on his lips. "Go on," Andre requested. His voice sounded strained.

The smile broadened. "As I said, Britain's only hope is America. But this time Japan is our ally. This time, when America enters the war, it cannot concentrate all its strength in Europe. It will have to fight also in the Pacific.''

Schatz clearly regarded America's entry into the war as a foregone conclusion. Germany's aim, therefore, seemed to be not to prevent the inevitable, but to negate its power when it happened. ''What do you want of me?'' Andre asked. He did not know how loud his voice was, but it seemed to echo like a clap of thunder.

''I want you to help me blow up the Panama Canal.''

Blow up the Panama Canal? Assemble a force strong enough to do it in waters dominated by the Americans? How? Sail some pirate-laden yachts from Martinique? It might have worked two hundred years ago, but not today. ''Why?'' Andre asked. He was stalling for time. The enormity of the task!

Schatz's gaze grew hard. He turned to Pic and Hibbert, as if accusing them of wasting his time with this presumptuous dunce. Pic, but not the general, shrank from the ferocity of his look. Schatz turned back to Andre. ''Do not ask,'' he said. ''It is enough that we want it done. We want to stop all traffic in the Panama Canal for a minimum of six months. You French have been telling us all along how much you wish to help. This is your opportunity. We cannot operate in the Caribbean. You can.''

Six months, Andre pondered. At least Germany didn't want it totally destroyed. But why had they picked him? He had no idea of what would have to be done. It was impossible, he told himself—a suicide mission, a fool's errand. He wished he could tell the German to go to hell. Pic's and Hibbert's presence made that impossible. For some reason, they approved the plan. That meant that France, somehow, would benefit. But why did Germany want it done?

An answer came to him. Schatz had been in Japan, Pic

had said. It was not the Germans, but the Japanese, who wished the canal destroyed. Was that how the Third Reich planned to negate American military power? It didn't sound right. There must be something more. "And France," he asked, "what can our country expect of this?"

He glanced around, saw Pic beaming. Schatz, too, broadened his smile. Only Hibbert maintained his composure. The general was a stoic. He would not show his emotions under any circumstances.

It was Pic, not Schatz, who answered. "France obtains what *Maréchal* Pétain has sought from the beginning," Pic exclaimed, arranging his face to match his grandiloquence: jaw thrust out, eyes narrowed. "An alliance with the Third Reich. We will help define the New Order; we will sit alongside Germany and Japan at the peace tables. From defeat, France will rise to become more powerful than ever."

A cautionary note sounded in Andre's ears. He could not afford to let jubilation sweep him away. He had been picked to do a job. He must approach it soberly. "How will it be done?"

Schatz blinked his eyes. "That is why we have picked you. You have been trained as an engineer, you worked with the Dominican-German Scientific Institute in '38, you know the Caribbean well. The plan will be your responsibility; with my help, if you need it. We can supply you with a few men, if you decide they are necessary, but it is to be largely a French operation." Schatz's ice-blue eyes were haughty. "There it is. Your government has been clamoring for such a chance; we are offering it to you. Our only request is that you be prepared to strike by mid-October."

"Seven months! It is not enough time!" Andre blurted.

28

"An exact schedule has not been set," Schatz said. "You might have more time than that."

Seven months . . . even eight, he would have to move fast. "It will be expensive," he said. "Where will the money come from?"

Schatz rolled his eyes and looked to the others for support. All acted as if Andre had committed some social gaffe and wished to distance themselves from him.

Their attitude did not deter him. He had been asked to do a task. He would need money, and Germany had sucked France dry of funds. He remained silent, waiting for an answer.

Pic cleared his throat. "There is our gold in Martinique," he suggested. "The Bank of France shipped most of its reserves there last June, remember, just before Pétain's request for an armistice."

"It can't be touched," Andre protested. "The Americans monitor it closely. If we try moving even an ounce of it, they'll occupy the island and grab it all."

Pic stuttered, then said, "My point is that the gold is there. We know it, so do the Americans, and so does everyone in the Caribbean. We might not be free to spend it, but there is nothing to prevent us from using it as collateral."

His superior had lost him. "Collateral?" Andre asked.

"There is an old, time-tested method, used in the days of freebooters," Pic began. "Issuance of letters of marque against that gold, redeemable at the end of the war. You will find someone to assist you. In the Dominican Republic, that should not be too difficult. Whoever agrees must bear the burden of expenses for the project. We will promise to reimburse this ally for all legitimate expenses after the war. In addition, we will give him our letter of marque for $1,000,000 in gold. That should enable you to get the support you need."

Andre wondered whether Pic truly lived in a dream world or merely pretended to. He stifled the protest which sprang to mind, adopted a more sober approach. "The promise of reward is well and good, *Monsieur le Directeur*, but I cannot expect whoever helps me to bear the entire expense. I will need operating funds, to 'prime the pump,' let us say. How much will the government allow me?"

Pic's face went blank, as if he had not expected such a question. He looked to Hibbert. The general leaned forward, cleared his throat, and began to speak. "You are aware, I am sure, of our country's present financial straits." He glanced at Schatz before he continued. "We pay the Third Reich 400,000,000 francs a day. The Germans have agreed to let us funnel some of that back to support our project. Prepare an estimate of your needs; I will present it to the Armistice Commission. I think I can assure you the Third Reich will accept your proposal, as long as it is within reason." At that, he looked again at Schatz. Andre saw that Hibbert was not as sure of his ground as he pretended. It was humiliating, France's total subservience to Germany.

"How much of what France gives Germany is in dollars?" Andre asked.

That got the attention of all three. Their heads snapped back to him. "Why do you ask?" said Pic.

"Because the currency of exchange all over the Caribbean is American," he said, displaying some impatience at their ignorance. "The British pound sterling is not as good nowadays—because of the war. French currency, German currency, or letters of marques—they are all the same in the Caribbean: worthless bits of paper. I will need either American dollars or gold.''

It was as if Andre had placed his demands before a group of dead men. Finally, Schatz spoke up. "This is a matter which does not need my attention, I think. I will leave you to talk it over." He rose abruptly, turned to Andre, and clicked his heels. "M. Duchesne," he said, "I look forward to working with you." He swung back to the other two and added, "Gentlemen."

There was an awkward silence after he left. Then Pic squirmed in his chair and sighed. "The money—" he said.

"Forget the money for now," Andre interrupted. "I want to know what I am getting into."

Hibbert extracted a pair of pince-nez glasses from his vest pocket, polished them, and set them on his nose. Andre and Pic waited. At last, Hibbert was ready. "You are being asked to do something beyond the line of duty," the general began. "I suppose you have a right to know why we want you to do it."

Andre nodded in full agreement.

"Our information has come to us in roundabout ways, of course. Never would the Germans let us in on their inmost secrets." Hibbert's sarcasm was evident. If given a choice, Andre thought, the general would have preferred to march against, and not with, the Third Reich. "Still, we have picked up bits here and there." He paused. "Britain has held out longer than Hitler believed possible. He is impatient to get on with the rest of his program and needs peace. He wants to end the war quickly—not just the conflict with the British, but the whole war. He wishes to finish off *all* his enemies. Do you follow me?"

Andre was sure he did. He whispered, "Russia." The mere mention of that hated nation set his nerves on edge.

"Exactly! But Hitler is not so foolish as to try knocking

out Russia and Britain—and America, too—without aid. For that, he needs the Japanese.''

"It is what Schatz meant when he spoke of neutralizing the Americans,'' Andre interjected.

He got the kind of smile schoolmasters reserve for pupils who have grasped part, but not all, of the problem. "Yes, and more. Our officials in Hanoi have noted an increasing presence of Japanese naval officers there. Construction of facilities for submarines has begun. Normally, we would conclude that Nippon was only strengthening its position vis-à-vis Singapore, but for one curious fact.''

"Which is?'' asked Andre. His excitement was growing. It was as if Hibbert had provided a crystal ball to permit him to gaze into the future.

"The Japanese have approached our embassy in Tokyo about undertaking similar construction in Madagascar; the Germans are pressuring us to accept. As we interpret it, the Hanoi facilities will simply be a transit station. Their submarines are destined for the Indian Ocean. Think about that: If the Japanese stop British shipping in the Indian Ocean, they would, at once, halt the flow of Persian Gulf oil to Britain and isolate all British Middle Eastern forces. Then, if the Germans stepped up their U-boat campaign against oil from America, how long might Britain last? Three months? Not much longer. The Germans then could attack the Russians through the Middle East as well as along their Eastern front. Undoubtedly, the Japanese would join in the attack through Manchuria and Mongolia.''

Andre had caught the magnitude of the scheme. "Then, my role . . .'' he said.

The general nodded. "Is crucial to the plan. We believe the Japanese have insisted the Panama Canal be closed for six months as the price of its participation in the Russian attack. They must figure they can sweep the American fleet from the Pacific, as long as no reinforcements arrive by way of the canal. The rest you know: We have agreed to help Hitler in return for his accepting us as a full-fledged and independent ally. You have the honor of being picked to lead us back to the position that is rightfully ours. Will you do it?''

Andre wanted to scream acceptance, but kept a rein on his enthusiasm. "The October deadline worries me," he cautioned.

"That has already been considered," Hibbert said, smiling. "It will be taken care of. I think I can promise you another sixty days. Would that make it any easier?"

Nine, not seven, months. "It still is not much time."

Hibbert shook his head. "Don't be greedy. Our bargaining position is weak. Take what you can get."

The project was possible, if only barely. Already one part of his mind began to focus on what he would need to carry it off. "The money," he said now. "As I told you, I will need some American money for operating expenses."

Hibbert and Pic both shook their heads. "We will do what we can," Hibbert promised, "but our supply of American funds is limited. You must make do with what we scrape up." He paused, took off his pince-nez, and added, "There is one thing which will please you: the promise of the million for your ally. I have been told to assure you an equal amount if you succeed in this. Nor, I think you will find, will that be the end of French gratitude. You will see. Young man, your father was a brave man. Will you be as brave as he?"

That was what it came down to, Andre realized: country, family, personal reward. And the gratification of striking a blow against the British and against the Americans.

Let them squirm, grovel in the dust. Let the Anglo-Saxon race come crawling to France for favors.

An image of Ellen's face came to mind. Why did that happen every time he thought of the British? When it was all over, he vowed, he would again seek her out. She had once turned him down. He would return the insult. The thought was sweet.

"Well?" Hibbert prompted.

Andre's answer was enthusiastic. "Yes, I will do it."

CHAPTER 3

July, 1941

Gil shifted his lunch from tray to table, then set the tray on an empty chair. He moved slowly. His headdress made him feel top-heavy. He slid the plates and coffee cup to his left, clearing a space in front of him, and pulled a copy of the *Los Angeles Times* from his tunic. That section which had been next to his skin was damp from perspiration. It didn't matter. He had no interest in the front page. He thumbed through the paper until he came to the Classifieds, turned two more pages to find the Boats for Sale section, then folded the paper, set it on the table, and groped for his bologna sandwich.

The ads looked the same as yesterday's—a few small sloops and schooners, the kind one took for a weekend's sail to Catalina. Nothing like what he was looking for. He wanted a forty footer, maybe longer, ketch-rigged, something big enough to take to sea, yet not so large that he couldn't handle it alone, if he had to.

Back in Florida he could easily find what he wanted. Six thousand; that's what it would cost. He pulled a paper napkin from the tin holder, took an automatic pencil and a crumpled package of Chesterfields from his pocket. He tamped a cigarette down on the table, shoved the firm end between his lips, lit it, and threw the match on his plate.

On the top of the napkin, he wrote $6,000. "Sixty dollars bus fare," he muttered as he wrote down the figure, "and fifty per week, living expenses, for, say, ten weeks."

He put $500 on the paper under the $60. "License, charter, docking fees, starting-up expenses, miscellaneous: figure another two thousand." He added the column up: $8,560. The computations hadn't been difficult. He repeated them nearly every day, like a ball player calculating how 0 for 4 at the plate has affected his average.

He glanced at his sandwich, saw the match and some ashes on it, reached instead for his coffee. He didn't much care. As usual, the sandwich had been terrible—stale bread, wilted lettuce. He drew two lines under his figures, to separate his dreams from his reality, and set to work anew. "Six hundred and fifty a month," he said, writing it down. The words slipped out from between tight lips. Smoke got in his eyes. He ground out his cigarette and continued to work on the budget, adding the new column up at the bottom of the napkin. It came out the same as always. The most he could save was $150 a month. Even that was stretching it. It would take five years before he had the money he needed.

It was like being an indentured servant. His eyes went back to the $2,000 incidental expense item on the top half of the napkin. Slowly, he crossed out the two, substituted a one for it. It was stupid, he knew. Halving the estimate would reduce his servitude by only a year or so. It would also guarantee failure. Income and savings, those were the areas that needed improvement, not capitalization.

Would the studio give him a new contract? He grimaced. The only reason he had a contract at all was because Mona had insisted on it. Still, his wife had influence with the front office. She might be able to get him a better deal.

Gil put his pencil back in his pocket and crumpled the napkin in his fist. He'd be damned if he would ask. She wouldn't do it if he did, he concluded. She had said as much—many times. Maybe not in so many words, but that was what she had meant.

So what was better? Remain at a job he hated and try saving enough to do what he wanted, or leave and give up all hope of ever having a boat of his own? Neither course was very appealing.

There was another tack: to become even more dependent on Mona than he was. The thought was like a faithful friend; it always popped up when he was most discouraged. But, if he did, he could save what he needed in a year. An obvious solution—if he could stick it out. It would reduce him from indentured servant to slave; a gigolo kept to bed an aging ingenue on demand.

Face it, he told himself: that was what he already was. It had been a mistake to marry Mona. He didn't love her, was no longer sure he ever had. And she did not love him. From what he'd heard, she was already looking for his replacement. That was okay. If she got the divorce, it might void their prenuptial agreement. Then he could get the money he needed through community property. "Christ," he whispered, "I'd be swimming in dough."

Fat chance. Mona's lawyers would find a way to cut him out. His scheming chilled him. Three years in Hollywood and he was figuring angles like an old-timer. What would another five years in town do to him? He ground out his cigarette, looked at his pack, reluctantly decided against another. He didn't want her damned money. He wanted nothing from her. What he wanted was $8,560 of his own.

He glanced at the clock: fifteen minutes before it was time to get back to the set. He shoved his earlier scruples aside, reached for a Chesterfield, and lit it. The cigarette smoke suddenly made him feel grimy. It was hot and muggy in the cafeteria. His monkey suit had begun to ride up on him. His crotch felt as if it had been rubbed raw. He arched his butt off the chair and tried to adjust the trousers. He had to be careful. The wardrobe assistant had fitted them to him with pins.

Maybe his agent hadn't been kidding when he claimed there was a chance for a second lead in the pirate film Paramount was going to shoot. He snorted, blew smoke from his nose. And maybe his agent wasn't an idiot. It was another Hollywood pipe dream. Still, if he managed to land it, he'd have his money, and then some.

Gil looked around. The commissary was filled with its usual assortment of cowboys, Indians, dancehall girls, spacemen. At the entry were two who didn't belong—men in ordinary dark suits. Gil took them for the vanguard of a tour group, then changed his mind. Not gawking tourists, something else.

Feds. He could still spot a G-man when he saw one. He choked down his uneasiness. There was nothing to indicate they were looking for him. If they were, he had done nothing wrong. Not recently.

The two approached Nick, the commissary manager, and began to talk. Gil saw Nick nod, then turn to scan the cafeteria. Gil sat stiffly, pinching his cigarette between thumb and forefinger. Nick's eyes met his. The glance held for a second before the manager turned to the men and nodded. *Shit!*

The men approached. The one in front was older. The other seemed like a kid his first time at Minsky's; his eyes were as big as cue balls. They stopped at Gil's table.

"Gil Brant?" said the first.

Gil nodded. "You?"

The man pulled out his wallet, opened it, and handed it over.

Gil took it, looked at the identification card. Federal, but not FBI. He was with something called the Office for the Coordination of Information. Gil had never heard of it. He returned the wallet.

"We've got a few questions for you."

Damned feds are all alike, Gil thought. "What if I don't want to answer?" Gil asked.

"You'll answer," the man said, "one way or another; here, or somewhere else."

Gil fought down an inclination to tell them to go to hell. The studio wouldn't like it. "I'm not in any trouble, am I?" he asked.

Both agents smiled. "No," the older one assured him, "you're not in trouble. And it's nothing to do with taxes, either."

Gil felt better. "Sit down," he offered. The men accepted his offer. The young one had transferred his stare to Gil's headdress. "I'm one of Emperor Ming's minions," Gil explained, pointing to it. "We're shooting a *Flash Gordon* serial," he added when he saw no sign of recognition. It didn't seem to help. "So what can I do for you?" he asked.

The older man grunted, pulled out a notebook, and thumbed through it. "You once worked with a Ned

Walker," he said at last. It was a statement, not a question.

Gil thought all that had been forgotten. "Why do you want to know?"

"We want to make sure you're the right Gil Brant," the agent explained.

"You're not trying to nab Ned?"

The other shook his head. "He died in '35."

Gil hadn't known that. He'd liked Ned. "We ran rum together during Prohibition," he admitted.

"You worked out of the Dominican Republic?"

"Santo Domingo, back then," Gil amended. "Not always, but sometimes. The hootch didn't cost as much as it did in Cuba or Jamaica."

The man wrote something in his notebook. "You did time," he said when he had finished.

Gil nodded. "Eleven months," he agreed.

"How'd you get out so quickly?"

One way or another, the man had said. He believed him. "It didn't seem so quick to me," he responded. "Roosevelt's election did it. They figured it didn't make a lot of sense to keep rumrunners in jail when the next president had already promised to repeal Prohibition. I wasn't going to argue with them."

The man checked his notebook, looked back at Gil. "Early in '37, you went off to Spain. Mind telling me why?"

Gil shrugged. "Times were tough, in case you don't remember. They were especially tough for ex-cons. I was in New Orleans, looking for work; not finding any, as usual. Anyway I got to talking to some guys. One said he was thinking of going to Spain. That sounded better than starving to death in New Orleans, so I went along."

"You were wounded there."

"Hit in the leg."

"Any permanent effects?"

"You helping Selective Service out?" Gil asked. He'd not taken his physical yet, but was certain he'd be classified 4F. That was what he wanted. If war came, a 4F classification would be worth a lot of money in Hollywood.

The man shook his head. "Not that, either." He looked directly at Gil, awaiting an answer.

"Not really," he finally answered. "A frog doctor put some screws in it. It's as good as new, almost."

The agent nodded and slipped his notebook back into his pocket, saying, "I'm satisfied." He looked back at his colleague. "You?"

The young one nodded, looking surprised to be consulted. The first turned back to Gil. "All right, Mr. Brant," he began, "it's this way. We need someone to go to the Dominican Republic to look into something for us. We thought . . ."

Gil raised his hand to stop him. "Just a minute," he said. "By 'we,' you mean whoever it is you work for: the OCI?"

The man blinked. "Yes."

"Forgive my stupidity," Gil continued, "but I've never heard of it. What is it?"

"We're new, an intelligence-gathering outfit," the agent responded, then hurried on as if to forestall any more interruptions. "As I said, we need someone to go to the Dominican Republic. It struck us that a man with your qualifications would fit the bill."

Gil felt his pulse quicken. A job in the Caribbean? And for the government? That would be a switch. The other continued, "You have a contract with Federal Studios

41

which pays $650 a month. That's a bit steep, but I think we can match it—''

He could keep still no longer. ''You mean the government's offering me a job at my present salary?''

The agent frowned. ''Not exactly offering it to you. Not yet, at any rate,'' he cautioned. ''For that, you've got to go to Washington, D.C. But we will clear everything with your studio so that you can go. If we take you on, it won't be for long. You'll be free to return here and get back to acting.''

Gil's slide back to reality had begun at the sight of the man's frown. It picked up speed as he heard the qualifiers. ''Return? Come back here?''

''That's right. We would need you for about two months; six months, tops.''

''What if I don't want to come back?'' Gil asked. ''Could I stay with whatever-it-is you work for, the OCI?''

The agent's smile was not friendly. ''Studio not renewing your contract, or something?''

Gil ignored the sarcasm. ''What about it?''

''You'd have to ask about it in Washington,'' the man finally replied. He had been unable to hide the doubt in his voice.

Gil had known it was too good to be true. Six months, then back here. Just long enough to miss whatever shot he had with Paramount. ''I'm sorry,'' he responded, ''but I can't do it. Find another ex-rumrunner.''

The agent seemed shocked. ''It's important to your country,'' he said.

''I'd like to, but I can't. I'm up for a big role. Tell you what, come back in a month. If I don't get it, I might take you up on your deal.''

Gil could hear the drum of the fan as the blades turned overhead. The commissary was now almost empty, as if all but he had scurried out at the sight of the federal men. "You won't reconsider?" the man asked.

"I can't afford it," he answered. He was angry. Typical of the Feds. Ask a favor, but give nothing in return. He rose, put his lunch back on the tray. "I've got to get back to work," he said. As he walked out, he could feel their eyes on him.

"What's going on?" Gil muttered. There were picketers before the entrance to the Hollywood Bowl, protesting the evening's Aid to Russia Rally. The fact annoyed Gil. When he promised the organizers he would attend, they had assured him there would be no trouble. Now he was staring at a crowd of America Firsters, other isolationist types. Gil wondered how many were Bundists. Last month, Germany and Russia had been the best of friends. Nazi sympathizers and Communists had gotten along fine then. Tonight, they'd be at one another's throats.

Gil shrugged. A promise was a promise. And the demonstrators wouldn't know him—unless they went to Saturday matinees. He took a deep breath and strode on toward the entrance. Somewhere in front of him and off to his right, he heard a woman shouting: "This is a free country. You can't keep me out." He recognized the voice. It belonged to Gayle Sonders. He'd met her once at a party and had liked her. He shouldered his way toward her, wedging those in front out of the way with his arms.

By the time he reached her, she was surrounded. She seemed to be keeping the men at bay by swinging her purse whenever one threatened to move closer. Her pillbox hat was askew. Shredded wisps of lace hung from it, like Spanish moss. Her face was streaked with red, as if someone had struck her, and she seemed to have dislocated a shoulder. Then he saw it was lipstick which was smeared across her face and that one of her shoulder pads had somehow been torn loose and had slipped down. ". . . free country," she screamed again. "Let me through."

He broke into the circle. Gayle raised her purse to swat him, then lowered it. "Gil," she said, "help me."

The crowd looked mean. There had been police out by the curb, but none were in evidence nearby. One thing: Gayle's screams weren't helping any. Gil turned to the crowd, smiled, began to pat the air in an effort to calm things down. "All we want is to go into the Bowl," he said in his most soothing voice.

The crowd grew tighter, not looser. Gil heard one ask: "Who's he?" The reply: "Another Red." Then, a shout: "Go to Russia if you love it so much."

He turned back to Gayle. Her teeth were bared. She was in a fighting mood. She screamed, "Slimy, fascist bastards! You—"

The crowd surged toward them. Once, in a storm, he remembered being on deck when a huge wave crested over the ship. Tons of water had fallen on him. It had crushed him to the deck, knocked the breath from him, nearly washed him overboard. This was like that. He tensed as the men approached, swung at the closest face, and felt his knuckles crunch against a cheekbone. Then, he fell in a jumble of knees and fists and bodies. With his face pressed against asphalt, he heard Gayle still shouting obscenities.

Gil opened the newspaper, flipped through it. He wanted to find why he had been forced to spend the night in jail. There—on the front page of the second section—a photograph of Gayle and him. He gazed at it. His hair was mussed and his suit torn, but anyone could tell it was him. *My fucking luck,* he thought, still concentrating on the

44

picture. Over it, a caption: FRACAS AT HOLLYWOOD BOWL; under it, a short explanation;

Film stars Gil Brant and Gayle Sonders were among those arrested at Hollywood Bowl last night. They purportedly attacked a group of demonstrators who had come to protest the Leftist-sponsored rally. Both have been charged with disturbing the peace.

At least he had been called a star. He found the theatre section. *Shit!* Hedda had led off her column with him.

Beautiful Mona Langer revealed to this reporter that husband Gil Brant's relationship with actress Gayle Sonders is "only the tip of the iceberg." My heart goes out to poor Mona. She deserves better. As for the philandering Gil Brant, all I can say is that he has bitten the hand that feeds him once too often.

He let the paper fall. It was evident why his agent hadn't bailed him out and why the studio hadn't done anything. He'd been dumped. So much for Mona; so much for Paramount; so much for his career.

The block door clanked open. Gil looked up. The jailor approached. "Man to see you," he said, then stepped aside. Gil wasn't surprised to see the OCI agent standing there.

"You're in trouble," the man observed.

"Tell me something I don't know," Gil returned. He had to talk softly, slur some of his words, in order not to open his mouth too far. His jaw hurt.

"Maybe you won't be so busy for the next six months, after all."

Jesus, had he been set up? If he had been, was there

anything he could do about it? Not a thing. Gil nodded. That hurt, too.

"We can help straighten all this out, if you'd like. Interested?"

Gil stared. The notion that the fracas had been arranged grew stronger. "You'll take care of Gayle, as well?" he asked. One thing he knew: she had not been a part of any frame.

"Already done," the OCI agent assured him.

"It's not enough to spring her," he said. "You've got to square everything—with her studio, the police, the press."

"It's been done; I guarantee it."

Gil knew when he was licked. He nodded again, this time a single, gentle tip of the head.

"I'm glad you're so reasonable," said the other. He thrust a sheet of paper through the bars. "Here, sign this. Then we can talk."

Gil examined it. It was an application form. Everything had been filled out. All that was left was to sign it. He did.

CHAPTER 4

Maria Gainsley paused in the lobby. The entry to the Columbus Yacht Club's dining room loomed ahead. She needed a little more time to think. What did this man Andre Duchesne want with her? She had found out all she could about him, but still had no idea. A former foreign service official with a short stint in the Dominican Republic, now with the French colonial office; conservative enough to approve of his new government; from a good, but depression-poor family; thirty-four years old, engineering degree from the École Polytechnique, a bachelor, a cynic. The bare facts pointed nowhere. She put the question in a different way, as if a change in wording might provide the answer. What did a Vichyite want with a British subject who ran a small shipping line out of Ciudad Trujillo? She sighed. Even the question sounded ominous.

Out of loyalty to her husband, she should not meet with

Duchesne. One of the drawbacks to marrying an Englishman was that you were expected to acquire his prejudices.
Her husband hated Vichy, believed there was no fouler a
foe than one who had once been a friend. She passed a
mirror in the foyer and was struck by the intensity of her
frown. It was silly. The Frenchman's note had said he
wished to discuss business. She was here out of loyalty to
her husband, even at the risk of incurring his ire. The
Gainsley Estates needed all the money she could find. She
wiped the frown away, then looked into the mirror once
more. Her husband was right: the sea-green gown ac-
cented her eyes nicely. She lifted her long skirts and
mounted the stairs.

Carlos, the maître d'hôtel, met her at the entry. "Señora Gainsley," he said, flashing a smile. "Welcome back
to Ciudad Trujillo. Will you be dining alone?" He stood
on tiptoe, to seem taller than he was, and tapped a menu
into the open palm of his left hand. He had the smallest
feet, the pudgiest fingers of any man Maria had ever
known.

She liked Carlos. He was one of her few friends from
the old days who was not jealous of her rise in fortune.
"Not tonight," she responded. "I'm dining with a
M. Andre Duchesne."

Carlos's smile grew even broader. He lifted an eyebrow.

"Nothing like that," Maria assured him. "This is
strictly business. Is he here yet?"

She couldn't tell if Carlos's look conveyed doubt or
disappointment. "*Sí*," he replied. "He told me he was
expecting a guest, but did not tell me it was you. I will
take you to his table." He turned, started into the dining
room.

"*Momento*," she whispered.

Carlos swung back and looked quizzically at her.

"I have never met him. Can you point him out?"

Carlos grinned. "Stay where you are," he suggested, "so he won't see you spying on him." He waited until no one was paying attention, then, "He is to the left, by the window. Can you see him?"

Maria parted the lacy leaves of a fern and peered between them. He was seated alone, staring at nothing, apparently deep in thought. Dark, wavy hair, with sharp features and a trim body—all added up to something her informants had not told her: Duchesne was handsome. She sucked in air, expelled it softly. No wonder Carlos had jumped to the wrong conclusion. It had been a long time since she had been with someone like Andre. Not since her marriage. She kept staring. Not before then, either, she concluded. *Holy Mother,* she thought, *why couldn't Eric look like that?* The thought made her visualize her crippled husband in Jamaica. It sobered her. This was business, not pleasure. "All right, Carlos," she managed, "let's go."

She followed the maître d' across the dining room. The sharp tap of her heels against the tile floor was like a coded message. It seemed to dull her reason and appeal directly to her senses. She felt the slide of silk against thigh, saw eyes lift as she strode past tables. She was beautiful and knew it. Tonight, she envied those who stared. She wished she could leave her body to join them in their appreciation of her.

Andre Duchesne's eyes brightened as she neared. She liked that. He rose from his chair while Carlos seated her. The Frenchman said nothing until the other had left, then, in English, "I am delighted you accepted my invitation." His voice was low, soft. His accent was not as pronounced as hers, she thought.

Maria paused before responding. "I nearly didn't."

His eyes showed disbelief. Dark eyes, nesting deep under thin, black eyebrows. She wondered if he plucked his eyebrows. His confidence irritated her.

"In that case, I am happy you reconsidered," he admitted, "although, from what I have learned, I did not believe you were one to let convention govern your behavior."

She shrugged. "Convention and good sense are often the same thing."

His smile was not as wide as before. "Sometimes, perhaps," he agreed, "but not tonight. I have already ordered for us. I hope you don't mind."

Maria shifted in her chair. "As long as it's not beans and goat," she answered. The band was playing. She thought she recognized the song as an American tune. The clarinet sounded like someone's fingernails rasping on slate.

Andre's face froze for a moment. Then, he smiled. "You can joke about your background," he said. "That is good. Wine?"

She accepted and leaned forward while he took her glass. The move provided a clearer view of her bosom within the V-neckline of her gown. By the glimmer of appreciation that showed in Andre's eyes she knew he had noticed. She paused briefly before putting up her hand to shield herself. He returned her glass. Their fingers touched. His hand was steady; Maria was not so sure of hers.

"*Saludos,*" he said.

Maria nodded in response. The champagne was crisp and tart. "Is there any reason to pretend I was not once poor?" she asked. "I sometimes fear what would happen if I stopped thinking of it."

His eyes were warm. "I don't understand."

Maria sought the right words. "To be poor in this country," she finally said, "teaches you what hell must be like, that is all. As long as I do not forget it, I will fight with all my strength not to fall back into it."

The silence was long. Not for a second did Maria lose eye contact with Andre. His revealed more than mere appreciation of her beauty. Selfishness, a touch of cruelty, she thought. She had seen them in men's eyes before. "Interesting," he said at last, "but I'm not sure whether any of *them* would agree." He swung his glass in a small arc to indicate the other guests. "They seem to have put their pasts behind them."

She snorted. "I was told you knew us well. Now I am not so sure you know us at all. None of them have ever been poor. They were rich before Trujillo came, they are rich now, they will be rich after Trujillo goes."

"Goes?" he said. "You had better be careful. That is dangerous talk." He had small ears and short earlobes. Her mother used to warn her about men with small ears. Maria couldn't remember why.

"I am British now," she said. "And they like my money. I can say what I want." Neverthless, she lowered her voice. "Yes, 'goes,' " she repeated. "Overthrown or assassinated—isn't that what happens to dictators? Even if he lives long enough to retire, someday he will be here no longer. But these people never change. They never grow old, never die. They stay rich forever."

"More wine?" he asked. Then, "You sound so emphatic. Do you not believe there are more important things than wealth?"

Were there? She had never considered it. Not seriously. What could be more important? Power and fame, perhaps. But they were wealth's partners. Love? She wasn't sure it was real. If it was, then, yes: it, too. "I once heard," she replied, "that if you ask a dying poor man what he will give to be restored to health, he will offer everything he owns, but if you ask the same question of a dying rich man, he will name a price. Does that answer you?"

His affirming nod indicated approval. Why should the anecdote have pleased him so much? Maria warned herself to be careful.

"Let us talk of something else," she said, with a shake of her head.

"Of course," he said. His right hand rested on the table, fingers on the stem of his glass, right shoulder thrust slightly forward. He moved easily, like an athlete: a polo player or swimmer, perhaps.

He looked perfectly relaxed, as if his sole aim for the evening had been to meet her. She wished it was so. It would be pleasant to think that all he wanted was her company. She tensed, as if someone had run a piece of ice along her spine. *Don't get involved with him,* she told herself. *He's like all the rest of his kind: one who takes and gives nothing in return.* "Is this your first time in the Dominican Republic?" she asked. She knew the answer, but it was safer to talk than to think.

"No," he replied, "I was stationed with the French Consulate here before the war. I left in 1938."

That had been the year after she married, she recalled. "And how long were you here?"

"Three years."

From 1935 to 1938. In 1935 she had been in training at the Sister Kenny Institute in Puerto Rico, with tuition supplied by a former lover. It had been worth it: her virginity in exchange for a future. Without the institute, she would never have met Eric Gainsley, would never have acquired the standing she presently enjoyed. Never had she regretted events. Until now.

It was nonsense, she told herself. Without Eric, what would she be today? A general's mistress? A whore? Whatever it would have been, a man like Andre Duchesne would have had no interest in her.

Food came, conversation continued: safe, easy exchanges. Maria found she was enjoying the evening, and shoved all questions concerning its purpose to the back of her mind. Eventually, the tablecloth was swept clean. A snifter of brandy was placed in front of her. The liquid picked up the light from overhead. She put her hand around the base, half expecting its reflected glow to shine through her fingers. There were fewer people in the salon than before. The music had changed, too. The band was playing Latin music. She glanced at her wristwatch—it was nearly half past twelve. It didn't seem that late.

"Tell me about Carib Shipping," Andre requested.

At last, his reason for wanting to meet her. "There is little to tell," she said, cautiously. "How much do you know already?"

He lifted a hand from the table and wiggled it, palm down. "Some." He smiled. "Still, I want to hear it from your lips."

"Why?"

"Because you and I might become business partners. I want to know how and why you formed the shipping line."

Maria rolled the brandy around in the snifter, lifted it, and breathed in the bouquet. His request begged the question. *Why* did he want her as a partner? That was the important point. "Where do you want me to begin?" she asked.

"Anywhere you like," he responded, then prompted,

"from the beginning." He lifted his glass. It hid his face from the eyes down.

Maria thought of a dozen places where she might begin, settled on one. "You know my husband had polio, is confined to a wheelchair?"

Andre nodded.

"It means he cannot attend to business as he once did. His family has been in the sugar business for nearly two hundred years. What do you know about the price of sugar?"

He shook his head. "Only that it is low."

"An understatement," she commented. "The price collapsed after the last war, was depressed even further in the thirties, then dropped to almost nothing after the war broke out two years ago. We lost our markets, you understand: Cuba has America sewn tight, the British are so desperate for shipping space they don't buy, and Europe is now closed to us. Jamaica is sinking under the weight of the sugar it can't sell. All our growers are close to ruin. My husband was in no better shape when we married. But he had some ships: small steamers. They had been losing money, too."

"Why?"

She rolled her eyes, laughed. "Mother of Christ! Why not? Taxes were killing him, the ships were too small for transoceanic trade, and because they were of British registry, we couldn't break into the West Indian–American trade. I thought—"

Andre was waving his hand, asking her to stop. "I'm sorry," he said after he had her attention. "Why couldn't you trade with America?"

"The Depression turned things upside down," she began. "What was bad to begin with grew worse after the Americans elected Roosevelt. The Good Neighbor Policy, it's called. I'm not sure when it began, maybe before Roosevelt, but it wasn't until around 1936 that most of it was in place. It gives preferential treatment to Latin American and Caribbean businesses—maybe not in so many words, but that's its net effect. When I realized that, I suggested we register the ships in the Dominican Republic in order to capture some of the trade with the United States. My husband agreed to let me try."

"But it was your decision?" Andre asked, as if he thought his question important. His ears weren't as small as she had first thought, she decided.

"Yes," she agreed, "mine."

"And that was your only reason?"

"Not the only one, but the most important one."

He pressed the issue. "What others had you?"

Was there any reason for not telling him? Maria could think of none. "We married in the fall of '37," she began. "Soon after that, there was more trouble in Europe. I was sure there would be war. Eric thought so, too. I was afraid that, if war did break out, the British Maritime Commission might commandeer our ships for carrying goods across the Atlantic. That didn't seem like a good idea to me."

"It would cut into your profits?" asked Andre.

She took a sip of brandy. "Yes. I told you about my husband's ships. They're small: 1100–1200 tons displacement. And they're coal burners. We'd have to use more space for fuel to cross the ocean than we could use for cargo—it would be like carrying a cup of sugar in a wheelbarrow. No money in that, that I could see. And we'd get no insurance against U-boats."

"But surely the British government was willing to guarantee your losses?" The question was not casual.

She raised the snifter to her nose, waited for the fumes

to clear her head. "All well and good," she finally answered, "but . . ."

"But what?"

"But such guarantees are meaningless if the British lose the war," she said. She met his gaze.

"Ah, I see. Your husband was willing to go along with the decision?"

"He was reluctant. He is a patriot. I convinced him." She stopped, then added, "I can always do that."

Andre nodded. "No doubt. And so you transferred Carib Shipping from Jamaica to the Dominican Republic. Has that led to any difficulty back home?"

Maria was not sure how to interpret the question. Had the move made her any more unpopular among her husband's friends? How could it have, when they had never accepted her? She shrugged. "Nothing to speak of. And it has saved us. Not only do we have some business now, but Jamaica has a new excess profits tax. That would have killed us had we kept the firm in Kingston."

"You are doing well, I take it."

She would bet he knew to the penny what Carib Shipping made. "Yes," she agreed, "the company is doing very well."

He laughed, shook his head. "Amazing," he confessed, although he did not say exactly what he thought amazing. "And so you do business with Trujillo and his government. How do you like that?"

"I was born and raised here, remember. It is a question of finding out who must be bribed and how much is needed to satisfy them. I don't mind that. It's cheaper than taxes, especially now."

"And your husband goes along with this?"

It was the second time he had asked this question. "My husband trusts my judgment. We are making

56

money." The band was between numbers. Maria realized she was speaking too loud. She smiled. "Not as much as I would like, of course, but I hope to correct that. At least we've kept the plantation. We almost lost that a few years ago."

"And that is important to you?"

Stupid. People who had never been poor did not know what owning land meant. "Very," she said. Andre leaned back at her answer. He seemed satisfied. "You have been quizzing me for quite a while," Maria said. "Let me question you for a change."

He waved permission.

"What is your business proposition?" she asked.

Andre laughed. "You are abrupt, I must say. Very well, I may wish to lease one of your ships."

She did not believe it. A Vichy agent did not approach a British subject merely to rent one ship. "For what purpose?" she asked.

"We will talk about that later. I might ask additional help from you, as well." Aha, thought Maria. "All I can say is that you will make a lot of money—more than you dreamed possible. And it will be all yours. There will be no need to share it with Trujillo's bloodsuckers. Are you interested?"

She nodded slowly, stopped, then nodded again. "I am willing to discuss it. I am always interested in examining ways to make money."

Andre's smile was warm, intimate. "I was certain you would agree. Now, Mme Gainsley, would you be offended if I suggested we go elsewhere to celebrate?"

"Where do you suggest?"

"I have let a cottage from the club. It is on the bay—very secluded, very quiet. We might go there."

Her senses grew more alert than ever, her brain was

cleared of all but the immediate. Everything about her registered with such clarity it was almost painful. She nodded acceptance, then waited for Andre to help her from the table. She accepted his hand, felt the other under her elbow. The evening was going to turn out better than she dared hope. The band was playing a merengue. Maria's hips swayed to its beat as she left the salon.

CHAPTER 5

Gil wrinkled his nose. The room smelled like a moldy basement; it was the calcimine, newly applied. There were wooden chairs running along two sides of the room. The windows were high in the wall, covered by venetian blinds. Some of the blinds' cradles were broken. A few slats angled down and rested an edge on those below, letting in long, thin triangles of light. Gil shifted. His chair squeaked on the linoleum flooring. He put out his cigarette in the floor stand ashtray, pushed the button to let the butt fall from sight. The button didn't work.

He leaned forward, took a handkerchief from his pocket and wiped his neck. He had forgotten how muggy Washington, D.C. was in July. As bad as the Keys. He heard a noise from inside the office to his right and turned toward it. The door opened. A man, wearing a vested gabardine suit, emerged. Gil had forgotten easterners dressed like that, no matter how hot the weather. The man looked younger than he.

"Mr. Brant? Roger McEachern," the man said, extending his hand. His grip was firm. "Good to have you with us," he continued. "Shall we go into my office?" He waved his arm at the door he had left open. A clanking noise came from inside.

The office wasn't furnished any better than the anteroom: an olive drab metal desk and chair, two file cabinets—one which more or less matched the desk, the other gray—and a brace of chairs for visitors. The noise came from a swamp cooler set in the window. Water dripped from one corner and fell into a coffee can on the floor. The office was cooler than the room he had just left; it was also wetter. *A few hours in here,* Gil thought, *and fungus will grow under my fingernails.*

"Go ahead, sit down," McEachern said from behind his desk. Gil selected a chair and sat.

"As you can see," McEachern offered, "our furnishings are a bit Spartan."

Gil nodded. "I'd say that was about the right age, yeah."

"We were established from whatever discretionary funds Roosevelt could scrape up. Unfortunately, he couldn't find much."

"This is the main office?"

McEachern laughed. "Donovan is in a temporary building over on Q Street, but it's not any better than this. We use this for briefings—out of the way, not as likely to attract attention."

The name was new to Gil. "Donovan," he asked, "is he your boss?"

McEachern nodded, picked up a file and began to look

at it. "Yours, too, now," he finally said, putting the file down and looking at Gil. "He's a good man."

Did that mean the job was already his? Gil said nothing, waited for the other to get down to business.

"I needn't tell you that your credentials aren't what the government ordinarily looks for in a new employee," McEachern began. "Lewisburg Penitentiary, Spain, a couple of friends in Hollywood we're not too sure about—the Sonders woman, for instance—"

"I thought all that was settled before you approached me," Gil said.

McEachern raised a hand. "I was about to say just that. Personally, I'm delighted you're with us. With Hitler's invasion of Russia last month, we're all ending up on the same side, anyway." He leaned back. His suit coat was unbuttoned, probably, Gil figured, to permit a view of the Phi Beta Kappa key stretching across his vest.

Gil took his Chesterfields from his shirt pocket, turned to screen out the swamp cooler's blast, and lit one. He offered the pack; McEachern refused. "What do you know about the OCI?" he asked.

Gil peered through a cloud of blue smoke. "It's an intelligence agency, that's all your men would tell me."

"Our agency collects, analyzes, and evaluates data on matters of national security," McEachern said. Gil nodded to show he followed the explanation. "There is something going on in the Dominican Republic which interests us."

Gil's pulse quickened.

"Normal sources down there have dried up. Our consulate in Ciudad Trujillo has learned nothing. Even the navy has come up blank. The matter's been thrown into our lap."

He was not sure he liked what he was hearing. "Hold

it,'' he said. ''I agreed to do something for you, I know, but I'm not exactly trained . . .'' He didn't know how to end his thought, suddenly felt foolish.

McEachern smiled. ''I shouldn't worry. What we want from you is simple. It doesn't involve sticking your neck out.'' He reached into his desk, pulled out a new file, and leafed through it until he found what he wanted. ''Here,'' he said, handing it to Gil.

It was a photograph, like the glossies Mona mailed to her fans, except it wasn't signed and it was not as clear. A man's face. He wore a fedora, and his coat collar was turned up. He was young, handsome, and—from what Gil could make out—had dark hair and fair skin. His jawline was clearly defined. ''Who is he?'' He set the photograph back on the desk.

''Name's Andre Duchesne,'' said McEachern. ''You'll get a copy of his dossier. Study it. He was in Vichy early this spring. That's when this photo was taken. We think he's in the Dominican Republic now, but we don't know for sure. Their police have suddenly become evasive.''

Gil picked the photo back up, focused on the man's eyes. They were deepset, seemed to have an unnatural glow to them. He had seen eyes like Duchesne's before, among those with whom he had fought in Spain. They were the eyes of a fanatic. ''So?'' he asked, looking back up.

''So, we believe he went to Vichy to see a certain German naval officer—you'll read about him, too. That meeting bothers us.''

''Why?''

McEachern rubbed the corners of his mouth. ''A lot of this stuff we'll give you later—after you've left Washington,'' he said. ''For now, let me remind you how hard we've worked to neutralize the French colonies in the West

Indies since the fall of France. When Vichy brings back an official"—he lifted his hand to tick off his points—"who is a recognized expert on the Caribbean, who probably knows more about the waters around the Dominican Republic than any man alive, and who has secret talks with a ranking officer of the German navy, that could add up to trouble for us." McEachern asked, "Any questions?"

Gil shook his head. "They can wait. Go on."

McEachern continued, "We're going to be at war soon. Hell, as far as the navy is concerned, we're already in it. When we jump in with both feet, a lot of people will discover what some of us already know: we're not prepared for a two-ocean war. We don't have the ships, we don't have the aircraft. Our defenses in the Gulf are inadequate now. When war comes, higher priorities elsewhere will strip them clean. Know what that means?"

Gil had a good idea. The sea lanes in the Gulf of Mexico had been crowded even back in the late twenties and early thirties. Tankers, mainly, out of Galveston and the mouth of the Mississippi, heading up through the Florida Straits. That trade would be much heavier in time of war. He said simply, "Oil shipments."

"Exactly," McEachern agreed. "A few U-boats in the Caribbean could wreak havoc. If they had a base on the Dominican coast, they could stop our shipments altogether, and we couldn't do a damned thing about it. It will take us two full years before we'll have enough ships and planes to control those waters. Who knows what could happen in that time? Hell, the Germans overran France in six weeks. From the way they're slicing through Russia, they might knock it out just as quickly."

"You think this Duchesne is trying to set up submarine supply bases?" Gil asked. He doubted it. The Santo Domingans with whom he once dealt might have been greedy, but they weren't stupid. Supplying submarines was a long-term proposition. As weak as McEachern claimed America was, it was still too powerful for them to risk it. If there was anything going on, it would be something the Dominicans could get in and out of quickly.

"We don't know," McEachern replied. "That's what we want you to do: get down there and find out."

"How am I supposed to do that?" Gil asked. Before his marriage to Mona, he had played a spy in a *Don Winslow of the Navy* serial. He had been killed off in the third episode. It was his impression that was how all spies ended up.

"We've a boat in Miami. We want you to sail to Ciudad Trujillo. You've got friends there. Talk to them. Snoop around; find out what Duchesne is up to. Then report to me. It shouldn't take long. You might be able to wrap it up in a few weeks: six months at most."

"Tell me about the boat," Gil asked.

McEachern dug into his folder and pulled out a sheet of paper. "Let's see," he murmured, raising his eyes to make sure Gil was listening, then lowering them again. "It's a ketch, sixty-five feet long, eight years old. It's moored at the Ponce de Leon Marina outside Miami. That's about all I can tell you."

"Sixty-five feet," Gil said. "I'll need another crewman."

"We can supply one, unless you have other ideas?"

"I do," Gil countered. "Anibal Dieudonné. We used to work together."

McEachern frowned. "A Frenchman? I'm not sure about that."

Gil smiled. "Not French," he said. "Haitian. He's knocked around the Caribbean and West Indies for forty years. What he doesn't know about the islands isn't worth knowing.''

McEachern stared at the ashtray as if he'd never seen it before. "I don't think—''

Gil did not let him finish. "Anibal and I were a team once. Back then, when a lot of people thought I was just a kid, he was the one they dealt with. He and Ned, more than me. They see us together—it will look natural. They'll be more willing to loosen up. Besides," he added, smiling at the man behind the desk, "you wanted a man with my experience. Get Anibal and you'll have another."

McEachern seemed to be searching for words. "But he's . . . colored!" he finally sputtered.

Jesus, so that was his objection. "So's Joe Louis," Gil countered. "And so are most of the people in the West Indies. Do you want me to just fart around or to find you some answers?"

"You don't understand," McEachern replied. "I've got nothing against them personally. It's only that I'm not sure I can hire one."

"Then don't hire him," Gil responded. "Just give me the money and let me do it. I tell you he'll be invaluable."

McEachern's face changed. He avoided Gil's eyes. Then, he turned back. "Can you trust him?" he asked.

"Totally," Gil assured him. "I can't count the times he saved my skin. And he's trustworthy. In the years we worked together, we must have carted a couple million dollars worth of booze and Anibal never took a bottle of it." Gil saw McEachern frown. Obviously, the man wasn't swayed by a parallel between serving the American government and dealing in bootleg liquor. "You're trusting me," he added. "I trust him. Like I said, he'll be invaluable."

"Tell you what," McEachern said, "I'll try and find him. Any idea where he is?"

Gil shook his head. "He was arrested with me," he offered. "I imagine he went to the pen, too. He didn't get sent to Lewisburg; maybe Atlanta. You could start from there."

McEachern jotted a note on a pad. "I'll see. If he's around, you've got him," he promised. "Now, money."

Gil thought that had been arranged. Was the government going to renege on its promises? "What about it?"

"You'll need some to hire your friend," McEachern said. "And you'll need supplies; there will be hotel bills; things like that."

Gil breathed more easily. "Yeah," he agreed. "I was going to ask about that."

"I'll arrange for a draft of $3,000. That should cover your expenses, and then some. You can pick it up in Miami, along with the boat's ownership papers and the dossier, other materials you must study. You will be held accountable for all you spend, so keep good records." He began to write something on a pad of paper.

Damned government, anyway, Gil thought as he watched. *Complains about what it pays you, then hands over a fortune for expenses.* He took the paper and glanced at it. It contained a Miami address, some other information. While McEachern told him how to identify himself in Miami, he folded the paper and stuck it in his wallet. The money could shorten his stay in Hollywood by as much as two years. One thing—he vowed—the OCI would never see a penny of it again. He looked at McEachern. The man was staring at him. "Sorry," Gil apologized. "What did you say?"

"I said, we want you to stop in Jamaica before you sail to the Dominican Republic. There's a woman there—Ellen

Bainbridge; you should talk to her. She was with Duchesne in the Dominican-German Scientific Institute for a while. Rumor has it they were more than colleagues. She might have some useful information.''

Jamaica! That would cost money and probably be a waste of time. "Tell me about that institute," Gil said. "If it was Dominican and German, what were an Englishwoman and a Frenchman doing with it?"

McEachern grimaced. "You know as much about it as we do," he said. "We assume their employment was for window dressing—to convince people the Institute wasn't up to anything sinister."

"But it was," Gil pressed. The more he thought of it, the less he liked this stopover. Why would the lady scientist talk to him, anyway? What could she tell him if she did?

"It charted most of the Dominican Republic's coast. That's why we worry about German U-boats in the area. They know every bend and bay, how deep the water is, and how strong the currents are."

"Duchesne, too?" Gil asked.

"That's how he got to be an expert. He was with the Institute until we got suspicious and forced Trujillo to shut it down."

"What about the woman? Does she know as much as Duchesne?"

"No. She quit before he did. Still, she probably knows more about what the Institute did than anyone outside of Germany—except for Duchesne, of course."

"That's why you wanted me, isn't it?" he asked. "Ex-rumrunners know a little about coastlines, too."

"It entered our minds," the man admitted. "Talk to the Bainbridge woman. Get her to fill you in on the Institute." McEachern continued, "You need to get a ton of shots. Go to a private physician for them. After that, get down to Miami. Whatever else you do, don't come here again. If you must contact me, use the telephone number and the telex number on your paper. So, Mr. Brant, unless there's anything more to talk about . . . ?'' McEachern put both fists on the desk, started to push himself up.

"What if I need help? Will navy intelligence at Guantanamo help? What about the American Consulate in Ciudad Trujillo?''

McEachern sat back down. "Not much hope of either helping, I'm afraid. The navy was as much opposed to our creation as the army was, so it's not going to volunteer aid. The consulate made a few inquiries for us, got nowhere, then backed off. It wants nothing to do with you. It doesn't want to give Trujillo any reason to complain if you're found out. Not that anything is going to happen,'' he added quickly. "This is only a straightforward fact-finding mission. It shouldn't be difficult.'' He stood and extended his hand.

It didn't sound that way to Gil. If it was going to be easy, he concluded, McEachern would have set one of his Phi Beta Kappa boys onto it. He took the hand, shook it, and left.

Outside his doubts faded. There was $3,000 and a sixty-five-foot ketch waiting for him in Miami; and he'd be working with Anibal again. *What the hell*, he reminded himself, *I've spent most of my life risking more for less.* He was happy.

CHAPTER 6

August, 1941

The late afternoon sun seeped through the louvers, slicing the room into strips of light and dark. Andre sat to the side, observing Maria. She was perched on the bed, a foot on the edge of the mattress, trimming her toenails. Her back was rounded, her head bent forward. He could not see much of her face—her black hair veiled it from view. It reminded him of a painting, something from the Flemish or Dutch schools—shadowed flesh, intersected by slashes of gold.

"I cannot understand why you spend so long on your toilette," he said. "Other women would have finished long ago."

She did not look up. "How many women have you watched preparing themselves?" she said. Her hair muffled the words.

"Enough to recognize you as the grand champion," he replied.

That brought up her head. She smiled at him, then returned to her task. She picked up a nail file in one hand, with the other grasped her big toe. "I do it because I must," she said. "People inspect me—the women especially. You should see them at home. They look at me as if I'm dog pee on a piano leg."

The Jamaican attitude toward her was a sensitive issue, he knew. Her husband had been accused of having betrayed his race for having married her, she had said. In their eyes she was a tramp.

She finished and slid off the bed, heading into the bathroom. As she stood in front of the mirror, a tube of lipstick in her hand, he tried to view her as the English Jamaicans did. How much black blood had she? There was an umber undertone to her skin. At night, Andre thought, it darkened quickly, as if it absorbed, rather than reflected, light—a sure tip-off of a *négrillonne*. There were other signs, as well: her high bust and dark nipples, also her large mouth and full lips. Her hair, too—smooth and wavy enough now—but when wet, it coiled into tight ringlets. All might be considered as much Spanish as African, he told himself—not that some Jamaicans would see that as much of a difference. Why not be honest? He believed as they. It was all right to bed them, but, he, too, would draw the line at marriage.

That she was a pariah in Jamaica made it all the more certain she would accept his scheme. He had moved cautiously. Still he held back. Twice before, he had almost brought it up, only to back off. Best, he thought, to wait. The most propitious moment would come; he would recognize it when it did.

She was done with her face, had started to roll a stocking up her leg. It was shapely, like the rest of her. She was lithe, supple as a sapling. The image stuck in his mind. Everything about her—the tautness of skin and muscle, the slimness of her limbs—reminded him of a young tree. She emerged from the bathroom, dressed only in robe and stockings. Her lips looked black in the shaded room. He smiled. "What is it?" he asked.

She came close. The waxy perfume of her lip rouge blended with the smells of the hibiscus and bougainvillaea outside the window. "Why don't we stay in tonight?" she whispered.

Andre reached up and pulled the robe off her shoulders.

"Yes," Maria agreed, "I can help you set up a company to lease one of our ships."

An hour ago, Andre reminded himself, they had been in bed. Now, Maria, pencil and pad in hand, was all business. How had the subject of business been introduced? He could not recall, but it had not been he who had done it. It was as if she had read his mind.

"I do not want my participation known," he cautioned.

She nodded, wrote something down. "In that case, others will have to be brought in. It will cost a little more."

He paused. Having come this far, he suddenly feared taking the next step. "That presents problems."

Her head jerked up. She stared at him, jade eyes sparkling. "Tell me about these problems," she said evenly.

Had the breeze died, or was it only her mood change which made the air seem as if all had grown still? "I am a little short of American money. British, too. I have French francs, however."

She shook her head. "American," she insisted.

Andre took a deep breath, held it for a second, then, "German? I might pay in marks."

71

Maria froze, then set her pencil down and rose from her chair. "I don't think we should talk anymore," she replied.

Andre stretched and grasped her forearm, catching her in mid-motion. He could feel the silk of her robe under his fingers, noted the contrast between its white and the tawny skin under it. "Hear me out," he pleaded. "At least do that."

She began to pry his fingers loose. "You are playing a game with me. I don't like that, especially not one like this. Let me go."

He peered into her eyes. The green was darker than before. Was she serious, or was this a game of her own? He could not tell, but he dared not let her leave. "I will tell you everything," he promised.

"You will hold nothing back?"

He fought an urge to squeeze her arm all the tighter, to make her flinch. He *had* to persuade her. His superiors might not buy him the additional time they promised. There was no time to find another ally. "Yes," he promised.

The muscles in her arm remained taut, but, slowly, she sank back to her seat. Her gaze was like a cat sensing danger. He told his story as persuasively as he could, working in references to Maria and her plight as he went: ". . . your husband's friends hate you . . . you have no reason to be loyal to Britain . . . the Germans will win the war, regardless . . . you need money."

Maria hardly blinked. Only once, at the mention of the Panama Canal, did he elicit a response: a short gasp and narrowing of the eyes. "Admit it," he finally said, "you have nothing to gain by a British or American victory. I am giving you a way to profit from their defeat, already assured."

"You want me to help blow up the Panama Canal, but you do not have much money. Is that it?" she said when he was done.

She had an irritating way of putting things, he thought. He nodded.

"How much American do you have?"

"It is a question of how much my government can find," Andre explained. "The Americans, as you can imagine, are not spending much in France nowadays."

"How much?"

"Nearly $50,000," he answered.

"That will not get you very far, I think," she responded.

Andre stood and walked to the window. With his back to her, he pulled his cigarette case from the pocket of his robe, and lit one. *In for a penny, in for a pound, as Ellen used to say.* He turned to her. "I want you to loan me the rest," he told her, then waited.

"So," she answered, "not only do you ask me to put my head in a noose, but you expect me to buy the rope."

"You have no love for the English," he reminded her.

"Never have I thought that a reason to kill myself."

But it was the expense and the danger to which she objected, not the deed, he noted. Money and love; they were his levers. He leaned closer to her. "There is no money now," he agreed, "but there will be a great deal when this war is over," he promised. "My government will pay back what you have spent and more."

"And what if your government loses the war?"

"Then you lose, too," he admitted. "It is a gamble; so is life. But we will not lose. We will be Germany's ally. You see how Germany is racing through the Soviet Union. In thirty days, the army is already beyond Smolensk. Russia will be crushed before the year is out. And when the

Reds give in, the British will be doomed. No country can stand against Germany if their generals can concentrate their full weight against it. How much of a gamble is it to help those who are going to win?''

Her eyes narrowed as he talked. He saw that she had begun to measure risk against gain. "How great a reward?'' she asked at last.

"You will receive a letter of marque for $1,000,000, in gold, to be delivered at the end of the war.''

"It is not enough,'' she replied.

Not *enough*? Andre wanted to grab her and shake some sense into her. He forced himself to calm down. A woman who had eaten only beans and goat most of her life could not appreciate what a million in gold would buy.

"That will be, in effect, doubled,'' he said, his voice low, smooth. He had her attention again. "I get the same,'' he told her. "Together, we will have $2,000,000. For that, you can buy half of Jamaica, if you like. We can live half the year out here, the rest of the time in Paris. We will be rich, honored, famous, respected. Heroes!''

"You are proposing marriage?'' She was staring at him.

"Yes.'' His response was unqualified.

"I am already married.''

"Yes, but it is a marriage of convenience, is it not? We will take care of it after the war. You will get an annulment. Then, we can marry.'' The words brought to mind the last occasion he had used them: the same promises, made in the same country. Back then, he had meant them.

There was no pleasure in Maria's eyes. "Money, marriage,'' she said, "everything is in the future. You are like the government you work for.''

"We are equally sincere,'' he responded.

"I don't know what that word means,'' she said, then looked away. "Sincerity and love, how does one know if such words stand for anything?'' she whispered. The question was directed to the far corner of the room.

He waited, hardly daring to breathe.

There was silence. Then, with a hint of fatalism or foreboding, ''I will help you.''

She had agreed; that was all that mattered. It had not been he who had talked her into the deal, he knew. Maria herself had done it. ''There are conditions,'' she warned.

He checked his gratitude, held words of affection in abeyance. ''What are they?'' he asked.

''One million is not enough. Since your government is willing to mortgage the future, let it give me $1,500,000.''

He wondered if she intended him to surrender half his share or if she wanted him to petition Vichy for more. ''I will see to it,'' he said, forcing himself to smile.

''And the $50,000 you have. I want that, too.''

''It is less than that,'' he protested, ''and I have expenses.''

''Keep $5,000,'' she conceded. ''If you need more, you can ask me.''

With hat in hand, he thought, begging for his own money. What could he do? ''Very well.''

She smiled, picked up her pencil, and began to doodle on the pad. ''Now,'' she said, ''I will help you found the company. But I will not lease it one of my ships.''

''What?''

Her eyes flashed. The halos around her pupils shone bright yellow: a dragon's eyes. ''It is too dangerous,'' she said. ''I want nothing to connect me to this. I will arrange for another ship.''

''We don't have much time,'' he told her.

''How much?''

She was extracting more information than he had wished to divulge. The woman should have been a general, he thought. France would never had lost with her in command. "I'm not sure," he confessed. "Initially, I was told all must be ready by mid-October, but I was assured I would be given more time."

"How much more?" she pressed.

"Another two months. We have five months at the outside."

Maria bit her lip and looked away. "Ask for all the time you can get," she finally said. "I can find your ship for you. What else?"

He had not expected the question. "What do you mean?"

"The night we met, you mentioned other work. What had you in mind?"

Once she got going, the woman was like a steamroller. Was there a reason to keep anything from her? None came to mind. "My government cannot transport war materiel into the Caribbean," he explained.

She looked puzzled. "What has that to do with me?"

"It means it would be too difficult to ship all the explosives from France within my time frame. To try would only invite American discovery. That would prove disastrous. We must get much of what we need here."

"How much?"

"Altogether I need four hundred tons of TNT. We can safely ship one hundred tons from France to Martinique. The rest . . ."

Maria's eyes widened. He didn't blame her. "¡Caramba!" she exploded. "Where can we get that much?"

Andre moved cautiously, like a lion tamer in the ring. "We must buy it in small amounts in order not to arouse suspicion. You can do it. You are, after all, a businesswoman."

Maria's face had grown masklike. Somehow, he had

insulted her. "I am sorry," he added hastily. "I only meant—"

Maria waved him to silence. "I know what you meant," she said. "I was thinking. Wait before you commence shipments from France. I'm sure I can find all you need."

He had misinterpreted the look on her face. "All?"

"All," she repeated. "If it works, it will be much safer than going around purchasing a few tons at a time," she assured him. "I will handle it."

Andre believed her. He began to relax. "One last point," he told her. "Nothing we do must arouse American suspicions. I must, after all, secure permission to enter the canal from them. Can that be arranged?"

"There will be no problems. I will begin work for you as soon as I have the letter of marque for $1,500,000."

"That will take at least two weeks," he protested.

"Then I will start in two weeks." She rose from the chair and strode to the bed. It was apparent she was done talking. Maria took off her robe. She slid her black panties over her garter belt, and picked up her brassiere. She put it on backward to hook it, then slipped it around to put her arms through the straps and nestle herself into the cups. What had she worn before she was wealthy enough to afford brassieres, he wondered. A ragged camisole? Or had she had nothing at all under her blouse? Thoughts of her young breasts rubbing against the rough cloth of a peasant's blouse excited him. Andre watched her pick up her skirt, shake it, step into it. Finally, she put her blouse on and went into the bathroom. This time she closed the door.

When she reemerged, he saw she had fixed her hair, but had not put on any makeup. She came to him and kissed him. "I must get back to my place," she said. "I do not think it safe for us to meet here any longer."

He rose and embraced her, saw Maria close her eyes as he did. Whatever else she was capable of doing, she was unable to feign or mask passion. "Are you saying we must not meet until this is over?"

She sank her head into the angle between his neck and shoulder. "No," she whispered, "I will find us a less conspicuous place." The words were breathed into his skin.

He suppressed the rush of excitement. The time was wrong. He walked her to the door of his cottage and saw her out. "Remember the $45,000," she told him as she left.

Andre returned to the table for his cigarettes. A sound from outside startled him; he realized it was only a hibiscus branch brushing against the window. When he turned back to the table, he spied Maria's notepad. The page was filled with hearts, dollar signs, and knives. Love, money, and what? Danger or distrust? Probably some of both. She had agreed, but she was still too independent for his comfort. He wanted her where she dared not move without his permission. He liked that thought, visualized her trembling, begging.

Maria could not sleep. What had been promised amounted to considerably more than £500,000. Andre had not been far wrong when he suggested that she could buy half Jamaica. The Crichley plantation, she remembered, was for sale. They were asking £50,000 for it, but would probably take £35,000. Four thousand acres of good land plus the sugar mill and other outbuildings for less than ten percent of what France would pay her. Even the $45,000 was a fortune. She was sure she could obtain all that Andre wanted without having to dip into her own money. There were way: corners could be cut, palms lightly greased. She would never tell Andre that, of course.

But thoughts of profit did not calm her. What bothered her? That she had agreed to betray her adopted country? What did she care about that? Next to security, loyalty to country or pride in nation counted for nothing.

The danger? Closer to the truth. Not that she disagreed with Andre's assessment—Germany probably would win. She had long thought so. So did her husband's friends, if only they dared admit it. But what good would a German victory do if she were executed for treason before it happened? The money would make no difference then. All a corpse needed was a rosary and a clean shroud.

Could she hide her involvement? Probably, if she brought in some Dominican officials. Who would dare unmask her if they would have to stand in the dock beside her? She could manage that. In a government like Trujillo's, the difficulty was not in finding a corrupt official, but in locating the one who would prove most helpful.

All those were business questions; risks against potential profit. One assessed the difficulties, then decided—one way or another. None caused her present sleeplessness, she knew.

It was Andre. Was his profession of love real? Men like him were never honest with women.

It made no difference. She knew how she felt about him. The intensity of those feelings, the ease with which they crushed doubt and caution, almost overwhelmed her. She had held out as long as possible, but she had given in, as she had known she would. She would have given in to him even if he had held out his golden apple on the hangman's platform. She would do what he wished. *Just don't be stupid about it,* she warned herself. She would tie him as tightly to her as she was tied to him. Then, it would be worth it.

She was fond of her husband Eric, but Andre had been right. She did not love him and never had. Eric knew that as well as she. He was old, crippled; Andre was virile, fit. Andre was all she had ever dreamed of. Wealth, respectability, honor, love—she would have them all. She could force Andre to live up to his promises. However he tried to cheat her, she would not let him. And she would make him love her. God would help her. She caught her breath, rethought the last. Let God help Eric; it was the devil on whom she must rely.

CHAPTER 7

Rivulets tracked down the bottle and soaked through the label. Anibal Dieudonné fingered the paper, then peeled it off. It left only a few sticky spots behind. He raised the bottle to his lips, tipped his head, drank deep, and felt the beer flow down his gullet, as cold as ice. Back when they had been working on the Panama Canal, his daddy had told him cold drinks cramped a body up on a hot day. That had been almost thirty years ago. He took another swig. The beer tasted good, regardless.

"Hey, old man!"

He looked up, saw the bartender leaning across the bar. "Want another Ruppert's?" the man asked.

Anibal rocked his bottle. There were only a few sips left. He nodded and watched the bartender bend to pick another from the cooler. The saloon had changed since he had last been in it. It had electricity now. The old windup

Victrola was gone from the far corner, a jukebox now in its place. And there were fans overhead. But strips of fly paper still curled down from the ceiling, jars of pigs' feet and pickled eggs still stood on the bar, the floor was still bare pine boards. The half-dozen customers hunched over the bar were probably new, but they looked just like the old ones. How long since he had last set foot in the place?

He couldn't remember, exactly. Before he'd gone to the pen, back during Prohibition. A tippling house, that was what the police called it when they used to raid it. He shook his head. *"Have ye tippled drink more fine/Than mine host's Canary wine?"* That was what old Ned used to say after he'd had a few drinks, only it was never wine, always bourbon. Thought of Ned brought on anger. It was a familiar response, had long since lost its power. He choked it down without much difficulty. What had happened had not been Ned's fault.

The bartender lumbered around the corner of the bar and headed toward him, beer in hand. Quickly Anibal emptied his bottle. He wadded up the wet label and stuck it down the neck.

"Ten cents," the man said. A scar ran down his left cheek from his eye to the corner of his mouth.

Anibal dug into his trouser pocket, found a dime, and gave it to him. "Satch still around?" he asked.

"Who?"

"The man who owned this place in the old days. Does he still?" Even as he said it, he knew it was futile to ask.

"Oh, him. No, he died," the bartender replied. The scar was smooth and shiny—like a piece of brown satin set in the black skin around it. The man picked up the empty and left.

Of course Satch was dead. Everyone from the old days was gone. Dead and buried. He took a sip from his new bottle and glanced at the clock. It was five after two. He'd been told that the man would come by at two o'clock, sharp. Anibal hoped he would get the job, whatever it was. He had less than three dollars in his pocket, and he'd have a hard time finding any other work around Miami. Liberty City was full of out of work geechees. He had seen hundreds of them idling in the streets on the ride to the saloon.

He clucked his tongue. Why he had been picked from the seamen's hall in Biloxi was beyond him. A peckerwood trick. They always acted that way. The G-men had said only that they had a job for him. He hadn't argued. Arguing with G-men didn't pay.

Not that there'd been any work in Biloxi. At least he had been promised a job here. He wondered what kind it was, shoved the thought aside. You took what you could get. He lifted his bottle, downed a mouthful, then wiped his lips with the back of his hand.

The front door opened. The afternoon sun's glare in the doorway blinded Anibal. All he saw was a man's outline. Judging by the sudden silence, he figured the newcomer was a stranger to the regulars. The man started toward him and a half-dozen hostile stares began to include him in their focus.

A chair's legs scraped against the floor, then: "Hello, Anibal. It's been a long time." The words were soft-pitched.

He did not have to look up to know who it was. It was as if a cold knife had been run along his spine. "Ten years, almost," he agreed.

"Another beer?" Gil asked.

Anibal shook his head, looking at Gil. He had filled out some—his chest was broader, his arms heavier. He might also be graying at the temples, but it was hard to tell for sure: Gil's brown hair was light enough to pretty well hide it. Otherwise, the man looked about the same. He watched Gil signal the bartender, then turn back to him. The man's grin was broad, genuine. *He doesn't know,* Anibal realized.

"Jesus, where you been?" Gil asked. "I haven't heard a word about you since we were picked up. I thought you'd disappeared from the face of the earth."

The bartender arrived, plunked a bottle on the table. "Twenty-five cents," he said.

Anibal's first impulse was to protest the price, but he didn't. Gil looked as if he could afford it. He waited until Gil handed over the money, then: "Felt like that myself. Doing time in Atlanta was kind of like disappearing."

Gil lowered his bottle. "I figured that was where they'd sent you. How long were you in?"

"Five years, ten months," he said. "Two months less than my minimum sentence. Got out in March of '38."

"Why so long?" replied the other. "I got out in a year."

Anibal shrugged. "Shines get treated different in this country, remember? I stayed in because the warden could make money off me—contracted out for building roads, working in jute mills. I only got out after I broke this," he said, lifting his left arm. "It would cost too much to feed me when I couldn't work, so they let me go. I should have broken it earlier."

"Tough," Gil said.

"Yeah."

"The family? How big is your son now? As tall as you, I'll bet."

Anibal lifted his beer and drained it. He'd been right. Gil did not know. "Dead," he said.

"Dead?" Gil repeated after a moment. "And Bettina?"

Anibal nodded. "Her, too. Both dead." He stared across the table, saw that Gil did not know how to react. At least that was in his favor.

"I'm sorry," Gil whispered. "When did it happen?"

It was only right he should know. After all, their deaths had been his fault. "Four years ago. They were killed." He felt his fingers tighten around the bottle, looked down, noted that his knuckles had turned white.

"Who did it?"

After holding the story in for so long, Anibal suddenly was reluctant to let it out. "Many people," he said.

"How?"

Anibal blinked. "They ran out of money after I was sent to Atlanta and—"

Gil interrupted. "Ran out? Why? Didn't Eric send your wife some?" His voice seemed tight.

"For a few years, he did. Then he stopped. Bettina had someone write me a letter. She said they weren't getting any more and she and our boy had to leave home to find work."

"That was the last you heard from her?"

"Last and only," Anibal agreed. "I had someone write her for me a couple times, but I never knew if she got them. Even if she did, she might not have found anyone who could read them."

"Go on," Gil pressed.

"When I got out, I went back home. I couldn't find them. Someone told me they had gone to Santo Domingo to cut cane." He stopped to let Gil draw his own conclusions.

Gil looked blank. "I don't understand."

"Remember what happened there in '37?" Anibal's voice dropped a notch. His arms and shoulders had begun to throb, as if he had been holding something heavy for too long.

Gil shook his head. "I was in Spain, then."

"Trujillo had all the migrants from Haiti killed. His soldiers attacked as they were returning to their own country. They slaughtered thousands."

"Why?"

Dumb, fucking question. "Because Trujillo's a crazy greaser, why else?" Anibal spat. "He claimed it was because the people were squatting on Santo Domingan land, but I think he did it to prove he wasn't black himself. Who cares? They were all killed. That's all that matters."

"God," Gil whispered. Anibal saw sympathy, but no guilt in the other's eyes. That would come, he promised himself. "Bettina and young Anibal were killed with the rest?" Gil asked. "You're sure?"

Anibal spat again. "If they were still alive, they would have come home. Even a dumb ofay should understand that. Unless he had a reason not to."

At last, awareness was growing in the other's eyes. "Good Lord—"

Annibal had often wondered how he would act at this moment. The anger had come, but there was no strength to it. That had been replaced by a void. The old emotions still bounced within the emptiness, but they had little life. They had nothing to cling to any longer. "*Le Bon Dieu bon* played no part," he replied. "You and Eric Gainsley were the ones." He thought he'd spoken softly, but was aware that, except for them, the saloon had grown as silent as a tomb.

"Don't say that," Gil protested. "You know I would have—"

"I know if it had not been for you, I would not have gone to jail," Anibal retorted. "If you had not believed

Ned's life was more important . . ." He paused, started again. "Did you figure it that way—one old cracker was worth two young niggers?"

"You blame Ned, too?" cut in Gil. "Was it . . ." His voice trailed off as he broke eye contact to stare at something behind Anibal.

"You need help, old man?" It was the bartender's voice. Anibal swung around and saw the razor he held. It looked as long and as deadly as the Baron Samedi's scythe. There were other faces behind the bartender's. All he had to do was nod, and Gil would be as dead as his wife and child.

He looked back at Gil, saw him slowly pushing his chair from the table. *He's getting ready to fight. Damned idiot hasn't changed a bit,* Anibal thought. He could hear his own heart beating. "Nothing serious," he assured the bartender. "A little disagreement, that's all." His words seemed to dissolve in the stillness. He wondered if the other heard him. At first, nothing happened. Then Anibal saw the razor being folded into its handle. How could anything so huge fit into something so small?

"Okay," the bartender said. "You two haul your asses out of here."

Anibal rose to his feet. When he looked across the table, Gil was also standing. At least the fool was not insisting on a fight. That was what he would have done in the old days. He grabbed Gil's arm and trundled him out the door.

A second later, they were standing on the street. The sun beat down. Anibal tried to shade his eyes with both hands. He turned and bumped against Gil's shoulder.

"You saved my ass. Thanks," Gil said.

Anibal squinted, saw Gil's hand extended. After a few seconds hesitation, he took it. "Let's get on the shady side," he suggested, nudging Gil across the street.

They walked. Here and there a black sat in a shop doorway, but no one seemed to pay them any attention. Maybe it was too hot for that. "I came to offer you a job," Gil said. His voice was low, subdued.

"I figured," Anibal admitted. "Doing what?"

"Did you mean what you said back there?"

Anibal looked out at the heat waves bouncing off the street. He nodded. "Every word."

"God, Ani—" Gil said.

Anibal felt as if he had just laid down a heavy burden. Wearily, he waved Gil to silence. They walked down the street, not looking at one another.

"How would you feel about the job?" Gil finally blurted out.

"You with the government now?"

"Sort of."

Anibal shrugged. "Let's talk about it."

"After what you told me, I'm not sure you'll want it."

"Why not?"

"We have to go to the Dominican Republic."

The Dominican Republic. "I'll take it," Anibal said.

CHAPTER 8

September, 1941

"**Y**ou made it at last," Andre observed. He hesitated, then held out his hand.

Fregattenkapitän Schatz looked seedy and dirty, and there were patches of blond fuzz on his chin and cheeks. The German let his seabag slip to the floor. He ignored the proffered handshake. "I said I would be here by early September. Here I am."

Con d'un frisé, Andre thought. He swallowed his resentment. It tasted like bile. "Of course. I referred to American and British surveillance. It is tightening, I have been told. Under what flag did you travel?"

The German went to the window and peered out. The late afternoon polo grounds were empty, except for three enthusiasts exercising their mounts.

"Swedish," Schatz said at last.

"The others—are they with you?"

"They come singly. It was best not to journey *en masse*."

"It makes no difference," Andre commented. "It will be two weeks, perhaps longer, before we have the ship."

Schatz's back stiffened, his head jerked back. He let the edge of the curtain fall, turned from the window, and sat in an overstuffed chair, throwing a leg over the arm: a pose of studied casualness. "Why so long?"

"I told you in Vichy: The project is taking time to set up."

"You said you wanted two dozen experienced seamen as soon as possible," he said, ignoring Andre's point. "I assumed that meant we could begin refitting immediately. What has happened?"

"Why do you ask?" Andre responded. "Are you worried that the ship will not be ready to meet your deadline?"

The German's easy manner was betrayed by a tic beside his mouth. Andre met the man's gaze and waited.

At last, Schatz moved his eyes. "The operation has been postponed for a month, probably longer," he admitted.

Hibbert had come through as promised, Andre thought. He wondered what Vichy had done to force the delay. Thrown obstacles in the construction of submarine pens in Hanoi? Dragged its feet on the Madagascar negotiations? Whatever it was, it had bought Andre some of the time he had asked for.

"There is a ship, I hope," Schatz said. Some of his forceful manner returned.

"Yes, a Cuban *paquebot*. It can take on the four hundred tons of TNT you will need."

The German glowered, picked his nose, wiped his finger on the fabric arm of the chair. "Four hundred tons does not strike me as much, considering the task."

Andre tried to set the criticism aside. "Would it not be better to wait for discussion until you have rested and changed?"

"Now," said Schatz.

Andre shrugged. "If you believe the amount is insufficient, it is because you are thinking of attacking one of the locks. That would not do." He rose, and took a chart from his portmanteau, unfolded it and dropped to the floor. "Here, come," he urged.

Schatz sank to his knees next to the chart. Andre moved it so that his guest would be able to read it easily. "The locks," he said, pointing out the four locks with his forefinger, "are invulnerable to anything but an all-out assault."

The German did not move. "Why do you say that?" he asked.

"Because it is so," Andre replied. "Each lock has two chambers, side by side, to permit the passage of ships in both directions. The chambers have double gates on both ends, plus restraining chains to prevent a ship—accidentally or deliberately—from ramming the gates. If we blew up our ship in any of the locks, we might well accomplish nothing."

"Explain," said the captain.

"It is a question of physics," Andre said. "The weight of the water in a chamber would be insufficient to hold the explosion. Its thrust would be mainly vertical, strong enough, perhaps, to kill the birds overhead, but not to knock out the double gates at both ends." He paused, then added, "There is more."

"Tell me." The captain's eyes were still glued on the chart. He resembled a sphinx with head bowed.

"Each chamber is separated from its sister by enough reinforced concrete that an explosion in one—no matter how powerful—would probably fail to knock out both. We've been ordered to stop traffic for a least six months, not merely to impede it. If we destroyed one chamber, but left its twin intact, the damaged one could be sealed off and the other could still be used. It would slow traffic down, but it would not stop it.'' He lifted himself up from the floor. "Excuse me," he said.

He went to get his cigarettes and an ashtray, leaving the arrogant bastard to ponder his words. If the man knew anything about explosives, the truth of what he had said would be apparent. And there was a better way. He had found it. He lit his cigarette, stood looking down at Schatz.

Schatz lifted his head. His light blue eyes looked remote. "Have you anything to drink?"

"Of course. Brandy? Rum? Or I can send for something."

"Brandy." The captain turned back to the chart.

Andre brought two glasses of brandy and the bottle. He sat, folding his legs under him, Buddhalike.

"You have an alternative plan?" said Schatz, sitting back on his heels, sipping his brandy.

"Yes."

"Let me hear it."

"It was an early French critique of the original American proposal for a locked canal which set me onto it," Andre commenced. "One criticism was the enormous amount of energy it would take to operate the locks and control the water level."

"Get to the point," Schatz said.

Andre collected his composure. "But that is the point," he said. "The proposal was made when electrical power was new. No one knew much about it. By the time the canal was finished, such knowledge had become commonplace; the earlier critique was forgotten. But the fact remains: The Panama Canal uses as much electricity as a small city. And all of it,'' he said, pointing at a spot on the chart, "comes from here—the Gatun Dam. That is the canal's weak spot, not its locks.''

The German signaled for silence while he traced the Caribbean side of the canal on the map with his forefinger. Andre watched the finger move from the town of Colon at the canal's entrance, follow from the lower, through the intermediate, then to the upper level of the Gatun Locks, into the lake formed by the dam, then linger on the dam itself, immediately adjacent to the locks. Andre waited until he was sure the man had a clear picture of the layout.

"The lake behind the dam is fed mainly by the Chagres River,'' he resumed, pointing it out for Schatz's benefit. "The Gatun Dam controls its flow into the Caribbean. The lake it has created is huge. For our purposes, what is important is that the dam's spillway generates all the electricity needed to operate the entire canal.''

Schatz said, "If the spillway is destroyed, the canal will be shut down until it can be repaired. But, surely, it would not take long to do that.''

"Correctly placed, the explosion would do more than destroy the spillway, it would carry away the turbines,'' Andre responded. "Let me ask: How long will it take to transport new ones from the United States, set them up, and resume producing electricity? Remember, there is no adequate alternative power source within 1,000 kilometers of the Panama Canal.''

"The canal could not operate without electricity?''

"It would be impossible.'' He glanced at the ashtray, saw his cigarette still burning there. He crushed it out and looked back at Schatz. "That is not all. Four hundred tons of TNT set against the Gatun Dam. Your job—'' he added, nodding at Schatz, "would not only lift the spillway off

93

its bed, but would also unleash the water backed up behind the dam.''

"And that would lower the lake to an unusable water level," Schatz said.

"It is possible, if not probable," Andre replied. "At any rate, the dry season will soon begin. Water lost would not be recovered for months. More crucially: What would this avalanche of water do to the dam? By my calculations, it would wash it away. And it would also erode the foundation for the Gatun Locks. We would take out the locks from the flank." It was his final point, one he was sure established the brilliance of his scheme. "Nature would complete what we began. The Panama Canal might be incapacitated for five years, not six months."

Schatz set his brandy down and resumed his study of the chart. Was he trying to find fault with the plan? Andre let him try. It had no weaknesses. "The Gatun Dam," Schatz finally said. "Tell me of it."

"Very well," Andre agreed. "The dam is just west of the Gatun Locks. It is over three kilometers long. The spillway is in its center. The water's depth decreases rapidly as one approaches from the lake side, due to the mounding of the earth—"

"Mounding of *earth*?" Schatz said. "An earthen dam? I do not like that. Earth can absorb the shock of an explosion without cracking."

"Let me finish," Andre said, then waited for Schatz to calm down. "The dam," he resumed "is anchored in the middle by a rock island. The spillway was built on that island. The rock, however, is weak, fractured in many places. Our explosion will break it. In addition, the rest of the dam is and is not earthen." He refilled Schatz's glass, poured more for himself. "The dam spreads out from either side of the rock island, like two arms. The arms are, as I said, essentially earthen, but the earth was mixed with concrete—to strengthen it, the idiots who constructed it assumed. So the dam is really a concrete sludge—not as strong as true concrete, not as absorbent as earth. It won't withstand the shock of the explosion. Four hundred tons of TNT, sunk against the lake side of the spillway, with the weight of Gatun Lake behind it to force the explosive thrust against the spillway and dam, will crack both open. It cannot fail." Andre was done. All he could do now was wait for the *boche* to react.

The German rose, walked to the window, looked out. It seemed an eternity before he turned back to Andre. "I salute you," he said. "Your scheme is superb."

Andre nodded. He did not need the German's approval to know that, but he was exultant, nonetheless.

"Now, for the rest of it," the German reminded him. "Your plan for the explosives." He stood with his back to the window, feet apart, his arms folded. The sun had set, leaving the sky awash in a red afterglow. Against it, in outline, he suddenly appeared menacing, satanic.

"My associate has located a source. She will obtain what we need."

"How?"

"We have worked out a scheme," he said.

"How will she get them?" Schatz demanded.

To hell with the fritz. "A reminder, *mon capitaine*," he replied, "I am in charge of the project's development. You have no authority until the ship is ready to sail. I believe the fewer who know of the details, the safer we all are. It is something you need not know."

Andre saw the word on the other's lips, rather than heard it: *"Franzosen."* Then Schatz's anger seemed to pass. The ensuing smile was hardly one of submission. "Very well, I leave it to you," he said. "Succeed, that is all I ask."

He paused, mouth half open, then continued. "This woman helping you has much responsibility. Is she *die Negerin* I have heard about?"

"Yes."

Schatz nodded curtly. "Was she a wise choice?"

Would the *boche* have preferred him to advertise? "I can control her," he assured him.

"You are good at that, I'm sure," the German agreed, smirking. "As long as she is here. But she also resides in Jamaica. Is she watched when she is there?"

It was a serious oversight, Andre realized, one the Germans, with their thoroughness, would never have made. "Not yet," he said lamely.

"Never mind. It has been done," the German snapped. "We have taken the liberty of contacting the Independent Jamaica Movement. An accommodation has been reached. One of their members has already been employed in her home; others will remain in its vicinity until the plan is carried out."

Andre felt sick. As always, he reminded himself, control belongs to the conquerors. "They will protect her?" he asked.

"Of course," Schatz assured him, smiling broadly.

Andre fought to return the smile, but wasn't sure he succeeded. "And I will watch *la chatte noire* while she is here."

"A pleasant enough responsibility, from all I have heard . . . Now, one or two more details."

It was a relief to change the subject. "Yes?"

"Once our ship is inside the canal, we might have to stay there for a short while before we actually strike."

It was not welcome news. Ships in the canal were monitored, Andre knew. If Schatz delayed too long, he would invite a search. "Why?"

"That is my business, not yours," Schatz replied. "All you need to know is that it must be done."

"How long a delay?" Andre said.

"Not long. No more than a week."

A week! Les frisés didn't know what they were asking. "It can't be done," he protested.

"I did not ask whether it could be done or not. It *must* be done."

The German returned Andre's stare, inviting him to argue. Andre felt a tightness in his stomach. "I will do what I can," he muttered.

"Do," Schatz replied. "I'm sure you will find a way: you and your little friend."

Andre ignored the jibe. "The other detail?" he asked.

Schatz smiled. "A minor point. Our governments have rejected your suggestion that you remain behind. You will accompany us into the canal."

"That . . . was not part of the agreement," Andre stammered. "I was to have nothing to do with the actual operation." Why was he wanted along? An answer suggested itself: They would leave no one behind who could reveal what was afoot. So much for Maria's "protection," he thought. What did it matter? *La con noire* could look after her own skin; he had his own to take care of.

Schatz's smile grew broader. "Nothing to do but obey, I fear."

A glance was enough to convince Andre the German was relishing his new role. Andre nodded.

"It is interesting, is it not?"

"What?" asked Andre.

"That you are my superior on land and I yours at sea. Come, it's not that bad," Schatz assured him, contempt dripping from every word. "You don't have to stay with the ship *bis der bittern Enden.* I will need help with the explosives. You are the expert at that. If you wish, once that last minute work is done, you can leave the ship and go off on your own. It would not be an impossible trek to Panama City. If you made it, you could hole up in the French Consulate." He paused, then added, "Or, if you choose, you could stay aboard. I, for one, would be delighted for your company."

The words sank into Andre's mind, numbing him. "I have no choice?" he asked.

"Other than to decide whether or not to stay with the ship, no."

Had he wished for danger, Andre thought, he would have accepted an appointment to Saint Cyr, as his father had wanted, rather than train as an engineer and diplomat. But he hadn't. He had wanted nothing to do with the military. His government had no right to demand this of him. It was one thing for Schatz and his men; they would be covered by the Articles of War. But he was a French civilian. The American military would treat him as a common criminal. He would be shot. He remembered General Hibbert's words: *courage and audacity*. Had Hibbert and Pic known all along it would come to this? Schatz's eyes were dancing with pleasure. "You find this amusing, don't you?" Andre asked.

The young German lifted his arms, as if inviting a search. "I assure you I do not," he said, still looking pleased. "In point of fact, I sympathize with what you are thinking. So do my superiors. They have arranged an honor for you which might help you make a decision."

His fright was gone, replaced by seething anger: at his own government, at all the *boche*, most of all, at Schatz. "What is it?"

"As of August 4, 1941—one month ago—you have been

commissioned a *Kapitänleutnant* of the German navy. A uniform will be provided for you.''

Briefly, Andre thought of smashing Schatz in the face, to remove the smugness he saw there. It helped him come to a decision: He would rather trek the length of Central America than remain with Schatz and his ship. ''Thank you,'' he said through clenched lips, ''I will consider your kind offer.''

''Do,'' Schatz advised silkily. ''Now I think I will leave you. You have found me a place to stay?''

''Yes,'' Andre answered, writing its name on a piece of paper, ''a hotel by the docks. It is clean. Here.'' He handed him the paper. ''I have given you instructions on how to get there.''

''It is clean, good,'' Schatz agreed, taking the paper, ''but is it safe? Will the officials give me any trouble?''

''Trujillo plays a double game,'' Andre told him. ''All his public speeches profess friendship with America. Privately, it is a different matter. Never fear, Trujillo sees that Germany is winning the war. You will be left alone.''

The assurance seemed to satisfy the German. He strode to his seabag, untied it, and rummaged through it. He handed a packet to Andre. ''Your orders.'' Then, something wrapped in an old Swedish newspaper. ''And your commission.''

Schatz shouldered the bag and walked to the door. ''We must not disappoint Trujillo. We will see to it that Germany does win the war, *jawohl, mein Kapitänleutnant*?''

''Germany *and* France will win it together.''

Schatz smiled and left.

Perhaps it would not be so bad to be commissioned a naval lieutenant. He might be able to make use of it in the future.

CHAPTER 9

Ellen Bainbridge was tired and hot. Her light blue linen dress clung to her, she could feel the dampness under her arms. She wanted to go home, take a bath, change clothes, have a cool drink. She wanted to tell the American what he could do with his proposal to take her to the Dominican Republic.

Instead, she sat still and pretended to be interested, as the second secretary had advised. She tried to tune out the painful memories evoked by the American's words and let her mind drift. The ceiling fan droned on with minimal effect—no air stirred about her, there was no cooling of her skin. She glanced up at it, saw the American's gaze follow hers. Perhaps it had been put in wrong. It wouldn't surprise her. Electrical power seemed incompatible with things Jamaican.

She glanced out the window. The tops of the palms that

lined Government House were swaying. She wished some of the breeze could find its way into the meeting room where they sat.

The American was done talking. She hadn't noticed him stop. A second ago, he had been jabbering away; now, he was quiet, peering at her under knitted brows. He seemed a little irritated, as if she had irked him. The man was handsome in a crude sort of way, she thought, like a newly cast bronze which has not had its rough edges smoothed over. She tried to dispel the observation. It was the wrong time, the wrong place for it. Most of all, she was the wrong person. "I am sorry," she began, picking her words carefully, "but I fail to see how I can be of further help. You have my monograph. It contains all I know of the Dominican Republic."

Indeed, a copy of *A Physical and Political Geography of the Greater Antilles* rested in front of him. Its pages were dog-eared and it had a crease along the cover, as if he had tried to bend the book double. Apparently, Mr. Brant confused reading with wrestling. She wondered if he also tore telephone directories in half. Small ones, perhaps, she concluded. He saw she had noticed the book's condition and grinned. "The sailor who said, 'A place for everything and everything in its place,' wasn't thinking of books; they don't fit easily into seabags." The grin left. "I have read it," he said, "more than once, but it does not give me what I want."

"What is that?" she asked.

"It does not talk specifically of your work with the Dominican-German Scientific Institute, for one thing. It's also too limited. I would prefer the book's author to the book."

"I prepared a report of my activities with the Institute.

It is on file downstairs. It is as complete as I could make it.''

"I have looked at it," he said, "but I have the same reservations about it as I do your book; even if I knew it by heart, it would not be the same as being with the expert who wrote it.''

"It will come to that?'' she queried, ''visiting some of those sites?''

"Possibly not, but I've a job to do; I might not have time to sail back if I needed to talk to you. I would like you to come.''

She thrust objections at him: her new job, her daughter and her mother. But there was another reason she did not use—a distaste for doing anything which might incriminate a former lover, no matter what the crime; a dread of possibly meeting him again. "I am sorry," she ended, "it is impossible.''

That made him sit up. She wondered how often he had failed to get women to do what he wanted. Not often, she concluded. "I assure you there is no danger, Mrs. Bainbridge,'' he said.

"It is not a question of danger. I cannot do it, that's all.''

"Not even for the war effort? Your husband died for his country. It seems the least you could do is give a little of your time.''

The blood rushed from her face. The thought had haunted her ever since she had been notified of his death: Had she not had her affair with Andre, George probably would still be alive—a consul in some remote corner of the world. This American had the impertinence to remind her of it. "Leave my husband out of this," she snapped. "And my country, too.'' She rose, felt her damp skirt peel from the chair's leather bottom. The American sat staring at her, as if transfixed. "I think we have nothing more to say to one another," she told him. "Please do not try to get in touch with me again." He said nothing, only opened and closed his mouth a few times. She turned and left, knowing his eyes were still on her. She wished she could feel the back of her skirt to tell how perspiration-soaked it was.

A sudden impulse shot through her mind, like a bolt of lightning disrupting a radio signal: *Go back*, it said. *Accept the offer.* Ellen recognized it as a desire to break from her shell, but she was not yet ready to try. Whether she would ever be ready was moot, but the arguments seemed heavily stacked in favor of the status quo. If there was not excitement or zest in life, there were also no sorrows.

"Damn," Gil muttered. He tapped a pencil on the table, alternating the lead and eraser tips. Ellen Bainbridge was an expert on the whole of the Dominican Republic, not just the docks and bars he and Anibal knew. And she knew people they could never approach—British diplomats, wealthy businessmen, men of influence. There was another point, too; never before had he met anyone like her. He dropped the pencil on the table, got up, and buttoned his coat. One way or another, he would get her to agree. Hell, he thought, he'd been shanghaied; why shouldn't she be?

Charles Strachey's suit was similar in cut and style to his, Gil reflected, as he entered the man's office. And both probably cost about the same. But the Englishman's looked as if it had just been pressed, while Gil knew his looked like it had been rolled into a ball and stuffed into a drawer for a week. The difference was not in the suit, but the wearer. He had noticed it before. It was a class thing.

Aristocratic types don't sweat like ordinary folks. Strachey smiled and waved him into a chair. Gil plopped down into it.

"From your look, I'd guess you got nowhere with Mrs. Bainbridge," said the head of MI6 in Jamaica. "I warned you. The poor woman is almost a recluse, I've been told. Her husband's death has upset her terribly."

There was no doubting the reclusiveness, but Gil didn't think widowhood caused it. Something else bothered her. Gil shook his head. "Struck out," he confessed. "I need your help."

"Be only too happy to give it," Strachey said. "As long as it's within my power."

"I want you to convince Mrs. Bainbridge to accompany us to the Dominican Republic."

The look on the other's face passed from guarded cooperation to distaste. "I'm not sure I could do that, even if I agreed to try. It's not as if she is one of us, you know."

Strachey presumably meant a fellow intelligence officer. Neither was he, if the truth were know, Gil told himself. "I know you can't order her, or anything," he persisted, "but can't you somehow persuade her?" He gave the man a comradely wink.

Strachey's eyes began to dart back and forth, as if seeking an escape route. The wink hadn't been a good idea, Gil thought. He leaned forward putting on his most serious mien. "See here, Strachey, you know that what I propose falls within the exchange of information and promise of support provisions contained in the UKUSA Agreement Churchill and Roosevelt signed after the Atlantic Charter meetings last month, don't you?" He had no idea what was in the UKUSA Agreement, or what the heads of state had promised: He hadn't really studied McEachern's brief on those points. But, one thing about his career at Federal

Studios, it had given him the ability to pretend to know what he was talking about when he hadn't the foggiest notion of what was happening.

Strachey sat back in his chair. He nodded.

"And also," Gil continued, "that your prime minister and my president have agreed to cooperate to the fullest extent possible in defense of this hemisphere?"

"Of course." Strachey's expression had begun to change into something resembling resignation.

"Well, good Lord, I'm not asking you to drug her and help me carry her off, you know. Talk to her, that's all. If you convince her, I'll mention it in my report. It will probably get you a commendation. If you fail, well, no harm done." He paused, adopted a conspriatorial tone. "Remember, my mission is as important for the security of your nation as it is for mine."

Gil sat back. He hoped he hadn't been too theatrical.

Apparently he hadn't. Strachey seemed to borrow some of Gil's sobriety. "What about our consular staff in Ciudad Trujillo? Cannot one of them help if Mrs. Bainbridge won't?"

"Not the same thing. None have her knowledge. And we prefer to keep regular government personnel out of it for the moment," Gil responded. "Too much noise and our quarry might drop from sight."

"Very well," Strachey said. "I will talk to her, but I make no promises, understand."

"Perfectly," Gil agreed. He stood up, prepared to leave. No promises, but, Gil thought, if anyone could succeed, it was someone like Strachey. How could any woman resist a man who didn't sweat?

Gil saw Ellen as soon as she stepped onto the dock. She was carrying a shopping bag in her right hand. From the length of her stride and the manner in which she was swinging the bag, it was evident she was angry. He waited until she was within hailing distance. "Ahoy," he shouted.

She stopped as if he had swatted her with a board, glared at him, said nothing. There was a breeze. It pressed her white skirt against her legs, outlining them. They were long, shapely. She held a wide-brimmed straw hat to her head with her left hand. She stood still, let her eyes run over the boat: a sailor's gaze. In the background, behind the town, stood the mountain peaks. The scene had a Spanish air, although the Spanish had left Kingston two hundred years ago. It served as a backdrop to Ellen's beauty. He shunted the thought aside. If there was anything he did not need, it was more woman trouble. "Come aboard," he said, beckoning to the gangplank.

The invitation set her in motion. Still clinging to her hat, she stepped lithely onto the deck.

"Welcome to the *Stardust*," he offered.

She was in no mood to accept his blandishments. "Where are the bunks?" she said. The words were sharp, capable of cutting anyone caught in their path.

Gil swore it would not be he. "Inboard," he replied, nodding toward the cuddy. She dropped the shopping bag on deck and turned away. He watched Ellen's head disappear as she climbed down to the cabin. After a few moments, he squatted and began to run his scraper over the deck again.

It was no good pretending he was not curious. He set his scraper down and returned to her bag. It was stuffed with books. He extracted one: *The Nature of Geography* by someone named Richard Hartshorne. Idly, he flipped through it. The work was well underlined, filled with marginal notations. *Her handwriting,* he guessed, holding the book at an angle to better make out what she had written in one spot. There was an exaggerated slant to the cursive, with overlapping letters. They made no sense, he thought, turning his attention to what she had underlined: "The other term introduced by Varenius, *'geographia specialis,'* has been largely replaced in Germany by *'Landerkunde,'* or more recently by *'Landschaftskunde,'* . . ." No wonder he had been unable to make out her handwriting. It wasn't the style, but the words, that had been beyond him. Was this her light reading?

"What's going on?"

Gil had not heard Anibal come aboard. He slipped the book back in the bag, looked up and said, "I'm not sure. We may have a new mate." He nodded toward the cuddy.

Anibal folded his legs, and sat beside Gil. "The woman?" Anibal asked.

Gil nodded.

"What is she doing below?"

Gil shrugged. "I was afraid to ask."

"Why don't you go find out?"

Gil paused, then stared directly at Anibal. "Why don't you?"

Noises came from below—clattering, rattling, rustling sounds. "You don't suppose she's cleaning up?" Gil asked. He wasn't very optimistic.

" 'Better to dwell in a corner of the housetop, than with a brawling woman in a wide house,' " Anibal offered.

Gil squinted at him. "What's that supposed to mean?"

"It seemed to fit."

They heard a grunt, followed by the sight of a faded blue seabag flying from the hatch. It came to rest beside the wheel. Gil looked at Anibal. "Looks like you've been dispossessed," he said.

Anibal frowned. "I don't think she's done yet."

Gil saw his own seabag plop next to the other. Ellen

climbed from the cabin, stood before them in stockinged feet, holding her shoes in her right hand. She took in Anibal's presence with a sweeping glance, but did not acknowledge him. "All right, Mr. Brant," she said, her eyes flashing, "let's get matters straight. When we're out to sea, the cabin's mine—all mine. You'll have to bunk on deck. The only time either one of you can go down there is to cook. We'll share that duty. Do you agree?"

"The head's down there," Anibal protested.

"Rig up a sheet aft, if you're shy. I don't care what you do, but you are not going below. Not as long as I'm aboard. Do you accept my conditions or not?" The remark was pointed straight at Gil. Her nostrils were flared, her eyes burned.

Slowly, Gil nodded.

"Then I'll come with you. For two months; not a day longer."

Gil sighed. He looked at Anibal—the black bastard was laughing. Gil wondered how long it would take before the pair joined to make his life even more miserable than it was. Whoever had written that thing about brawling women had known what he was talking about. It was going to be a stormy voyage, no matter how calm the sea.

CHAPTER 10

Maria wondered if Rosario could detect her tension. He was behind her, massaging the back of her neck. She rolled her head around, smiled, peered through half-closed eyes. "It feels good."

"You work too hard, my dear," the general responded. She submitted willingly, felt the pads of his thumbs under her collar, pressing against her vertebrae. The roots of her hair seemed almost painful where he disturbed them. "A woman as lovely as you was not meant to do man's work," he continued. "It is against your nature."

Maria did not have to stretch to guess what Rosario believed was woman's proper work. The way he initiated his caresses—as if it was his right to dictate, her duty to submit—made that clear. But she had not come to debate that issue. She stilled his hands. "Please," she whispered. "Come, sit," she said, making sure her skirt covered her knees and patting the space beside her on the sofa. "We have all night. Let us talk now, while our minds are clear. I want to know what you thought of my proposition."

She heard him sigh, felt his fingers leave her neck. From the regret which came over her she realized she had almost waited too long. Rosario rounded the sofa, sat down next to her. He was graying at his temples and on the tips of his mustache. She thought him handsome, but too fleshy around the middle. His eyes conveyed none of the surliness she might expect from a thwarted lover. "I must confess I have forgotten some of the details," he began. "Explain again what it is you wish."

Maria did not believe him. Men like Rosario forgot nothing that had to do with money. "It is relatively straightforward," she said. "I must set up a new trading company, one with which I will have no formal identification. Ultimately, I intend to sell it all ships presently belonging to Carib Shipping. I will, of course, continue to run it."

"Ah, I remember now. You wish to sell because of the British Maritime Commission, is that not right?"

"Exactly," Maria agreed. "British shipping losses are growing. As long as my husband and I are the ships' registered owners, the commission might try to commandeer them, no matter what flag we sail them under. I don't want to take that chance."

Rosario nodded. "But why do you wish me to become the firm's president?"

Maria shifted to face him without straining her neck, resting one arm on the sofa back. Their knees touched. "Let us not pretend," she said. "I can get little done here without assistance. I picked you because you have influence and because I hoped we would be doing business on that other matter."

"The purchase of explosives."

She nodded. She'd been right; he'd forgotten nothing.

"Let us talk of them first," he suggested. "To what use do you intend to put them? It would not be wise, after all, to let four hundred tons of TNT fall into the wrong hands."

How much did Rosario know already, how much could he guess? As head of the National Military District, as well as of the national police, he would, of course, have had her investigated. Did he know of her relationship with Andre? Probably. Beyond that? Little of which he could be sure, she thought, but Rosario did not need surety. Hints, innuendos, fears—those were his staples. "The entire cargo will be shipped out of the country," she promised. "Is that enough to satisfy you?"

There was a hardening of his eyes, as if steel doors had slammed shut behind them. "Let me tell you a story," he responded. "Not too long ago, someone from the American Consulate approached me. He wanted to know whether a certain M. Duchesne was back in our country."

She arched her eyebrows. "And what did you tell him?"

"I told him nothing. I thought it would prove more interesting to see what developed."

"Of what concern is that to me?" she said. A man like Rosario needed to probe, to weigh odds, to calculate. He was a chess player, always thinking three moves ahead. He wanted information. Very well, she would play chess along with him. He might be surprised at her endgame.

"What was it you said a moment ago?" the general asked. " 'Let us not pretend.' M. Duchesne is a close friend of yours, I hear. He is also an agent of Vichy. You wish to involve me in certain matters, yet you would keep me ignorant of them. That makes me anxious. I imagine the Americans are still interested in Duchesne's whereabouts. They might be even more interested if they learned one of the Frenchman's friends wanted to purchase explosives."

At heart, Maria was sure, Rosario was a fascist. Privately, therefore, she was certain he would be sympathetic to Andre's venture. But Rosario was a public figure before he was a private man. She had to make sure he was fully committed before she dared trust him.

She took a deep breath. "Friends keep secrets, don't they, general?"

"As do business partners." The look in his eyes remained severe, probing.

"My point exactly. So, if each held a secret about the other, we would be honor bound to remain silent, is that not so?"

"Would you care to explain?" he asked after a moment.

"A trifle," she assured him, "a matter of the '35 uprising in the province of Puerto Plata. You were commander of the military district back then, I think."

He had become very still. "Go on."

"Yes, of course you were," she continued as blithely as she could. She did not feel lighthearted, rather the opposite. "It was because you were so efficient that *El Presidente* promoted you to your present position. All the insurgents were killed; the evidence against them was presented after their deaths. The leader, Calderón, however, was a letter writer. Did you know that?"

His eyes had turned hard, all traces of the lover's warmth gone. It would not take much for him to decide to kill her on the spot, she knew. She believed he might actually be debating it. But he would do nothing. Not until he had heard her out. Rosario was a hot-blooded Latin, to be sure, but he was also a calculating one. He shook his head, his eyes fixed on hers.

She continued, "I have one of his letters. Back in Jamaica, not here. In it, he names a certain major as co-conspirator."

"A lie," Rosario said, hardly opening his mouth.

"I'm sure it is. The question is, would Trujillo agree with us?"

Maria could see the muscles in his neck and face tense. Suddenly, they relaxed, as if a key had turned somewhere inside him. "It is as you say," he told her, "friends keep secrets. That each has one cements our mutual esteem." He reached over and placed a hand on the elbow she had set on the back of the sofa. His stroke was light. "Now, tell me, to what use do you and your friend intend to put so much TNT?"

"It is a project designed to end the war more speedily."

Rosario gave a snort of impatience. "I hardly would have expected anything else. Against whom will it be used? The British?"

Why not let him answer his own questions? "Yes," Maria agreed.

"Where?"

"I should not tell you," Maria answered, patting the side of her nose with her forefinger, "but—"

"Yes?"

"Trinidad and Aruba."

"The oil refineries?" he asked.

She nodded and wondered how long the answer would satisfy him. Long enough.

"And this will expedite a German victory?"

"The British are desperately short of petroleum," she answered. "Once those refineries are destroyed, Hitler need not watch the southern route to the Atlantic. All his U-boats can be concentrated at the Florida Straits. It will dry up all petroleum shipments from the Western Hemisphere. Then, Britain must surrender or face invasion. Either way, the war will end.''

Rosario looked away briefly, then, his mind made up, returned his gaze to her. "And you are willing to pay me $30,000 for the explosives?''

Maria relaxed. "As a one-third down payment," she reminded him. "The remainder to be paid after the war.''

"I do not like to dwell in the future," Rosario told her, still caressing her arm. "What you offer me now is only seventy-five dollars a ton. You would pay ten times that for firecrackers.''

Maria had assumed he would demand more. But she had the letter. "Perhaps so," she conceded, "but the manufacturer would have to be paid for his firecrackers. The TNT cost you nothing.'' It was true. Trujillo had acquired it as a part of America's Good Neighbor Policy, supposedly for underwater harbor improvements.

"What it cost me has nothing to do with what you would have to pay if you went elsewhere.''

She smiled. "There is no place else to go. You know that as well as I. At the same time, if you wish to sell, I am the only buyer to whom you can go. And I have only a limited amount of American currency.''

"You will pay $30,000 now and $60,000 later," Rosario mused, rubbing his chin.

"I can have the first installment in your hands tomorrow," Maria promised.

"And the letter?''

"Surrendered with the last installment. Is it a deal?''

He smiled, stroked her arm. "Yes.''

The release which swept through her was complete, exhausting. "And you agree to become president of the company, as well?''

"Let me ask," the general countered. "The transfer of

your ships—do you plan to begin it immediately, or will it take some time?''

He knows I have no intention of ever doing it, she thought. "That must wait until later," she acknowledged.

"I gather you will not use one of your ships in the adventure?'' he pressed.

"It would be too dangerous,'' she admitted. "I am making other arrangements.''

"In that case, I think it would also be too dangerous to accept your offer of the presidency.''

His refusal jolted her. He had all but agreed. "Does that mean you will have nothing to do with the firm?''

"It means just that,'' he affirmed. "But I have a nephew—on my wife's side, a good-for-nothing dolt. Why don't you offer him the job?''

"At the same salary?''

"He is a young man. He does not need much money. Give him half what you offered me: $500 a month.''

"And the rest?''

Rosario closed his eyes, then opened them. His smile became beatific. "A monthly finder's fee, shall we say? To me, of course.''

Maria calculated. She would have $15,000 left after Rosario got his $30,000. The Cuban owners of the steamship demanded a $5,000 advance, plus $1,000 a month rental for the ship. Rosario and his nephew would split another $1,000 a month. Andre had said the operation would take place no later than December—three more months of payments, at most: another $6,000. It left $2,000 for other expenses. There was a chance she could do all Andre asked without dipping into her own capital. She returned Rosario's grin. "I think we have become partners,'' she told him.

"It is so,'' Rosario said. "It should be sealed with

something more than a handshake, do you not think?'' He
lifted a hand, brushed her breast with the back of it.

If the feeling which took hold was not sexual, it came
close. She leaned toward him, put her hand on his jaw,
felt only a slight stubble of beard. He had recently shaved.
She liked that. They kissed. She could smell his perfumed
breath. Sen Sen, she told herself. The hand on her turned,
cupped her. She relaxed against him.

PART TWO

CHAPTER 1

Gil sighed. The tension that had been building since they had checked into the Hotel Independencia was so heavy he could feel it. He snuck a peak at his watch. It was past nine. They had been in the hotel for less than four hours. It felt like a week. "Okay, spill it," he said.

She looked at him, opened her mouth as if to speak, then closed it. Gil waited.

"What I don't understand," Ellen said, "is why you demanded I come along. Obviously, you're going to go out and do what you bloody well want, whatever I say."

"Let's get something straight," he retorted. "I wanted you along to advise me, not to head the venture."

"All right, you wanted my advice; I gave it. You cannot do what you are suggesting," she responded fiercely. "Conditions have changed in Ciudad Trujillo."

Gil stood with his back to the window. Behind him

stretched the blackness of the Caribbean. Ellen was still wearing what she had donned for dinner—blue skirt and jacket, pearl-white blouse, the latter noticeably creased from packing. The skirt fell well below her knees, at least two inches longer than present fashion dictated. He tried to visualize Mona going to dinner in an outfit that was not up to the minute. It would have been unthinkable. "You may be right," he conceded, "but I've been instructed to uncover what your friend—"

"Please don't call him that." Ellen's words were softly spoken, but had a burr around their edges.

He pulled his Chesterfields from his shirt pocket, tipped the pack to shake a cigarette free, and got one, along with a palmful of tobacco shreds. He lit it and set the still-smoking match on the windowsill. The act gave him time to think. What term would she have preferred? Lover? That would have been more honest. He was certain of that by now. How had Duchesne broken through the wall surrounding her? An answer suggested itself: Duchesne was not a dumb ex-rumrunner pretending to be something he was not. "I've got my instructions," he repeated. "I must find what I can, as fast as I can. All I'm doing is looking up some of my old associates to see what they've heard." It looked like she was about to interrupt again. He held up his hand to stop her. "My boss in Washington told me to do it. Once I see what these people have to say, we can start digging more deeply. I don't have the time to go as slowly as you want."

"You may not have time to do anything but," Ellen countered.

"That may be," he acknowledged, "but I've still got to try. Trujillo can't have gotten rid of all the crooks. They're like rats—you reduce their numbers so far, then they start multiplying again." He waved the cigarette in the air for punctuation. "It's a law of nature, or something. Don't worry, I'll find some I know." He went to the table, picked up an ashtray, and carried it back to the window.

"If I'm worried, it's because I'm sure you will find them," she replied.

He looked at her. "What's your point?"

"I've told you before: The Dominican Republic has changed. Everything about it is different: the players, the rules, even the games. When you were here last, Trujillo had only begun."

She paused. Her eyes glowed, the pupils large and round as bull's-eyes. "Go on," he said.

"By now, he's had the time he needs. He's organized everything, and that includes the underworld. Police spies: the docks, the underworld, are filled with them. You won't be able to say hello to one of your old friends without the police hearing of it."

That was where she was wrong, he thought. She didn't know those with whom he had worked. A police spy couldn't last five minutes among them. One or two might hang around the outside, but none could ever get into the center. He flicked the ashes from his cigarette, then took a deep drag. Nothing: no reassuring rush, no pall of smoke behind which to hide. Glancing down, he saw the ember smoldering in the ashtray. He had knocked it off. So much for *savoir-faire*. "I may be an upstanding citizen now," he said, "but I can still spot a fink when I see one."

Ellen looked steadily at him. "There's nothing I can say to discourage you?"

Gil shook his head. "Nothing. We don't have the time."

"I can't argue that," she responded. "I wish you luck."

Her concession pleased him. It was a good way to end

the discussion. "I'll be back before you know it." He went to the door.

"Perhaps before I know it," she warned, "but not before the police do."

"Thanks for the advice," he said after a moment's pause. He opened the door and left.

Damn, but she's stubborn, he thought as he walked down the corridor. *Attractive, though.* An image of her as she'd been on the *Stardust* came to mind: wearing canvas ducks and a sweatshirt, with her dark hair pulled into a bun and a cricketer's cap on her head. She'd looked like a twelve-year-old boy. *Almost like one,* he amended. Black hair, dark blue eyes, creamy skin. She might be English, but there was an Irish ancestor somewhere in her family tree. He would bet on it.

He spotted seven men in the lobby, including the clerk behind the desk. The clerk showed no interest in him. Nor did anyone else. The revolving door swished as he passed through it. He stopped outside, took a deep breath. No mysterious men lurking about. So much for police spies skulking behind every corner. He continued on, turning into the *avenida*, heading toward the old town.

He passed by shacks built of packing crates and patched with pounded-out oil cans and signs advertising soft drinks or beer. Trujillo called himself the builder of his country, Gil recalled. Obviously, he hadn't yet got around to helping the poor of his capital. Statues and broad thoroughfares seemed more his style. Gil heard footsteps behind him, turned, saw no one. He wished Anibal were along, but he had not yet been given his papers. It meant Anibal had to stay aboard ship.

He entered the old city and breathed a little more easily. Much was as he remembered it. This part had not been as devastated by the hurricane of 1930 as that to the west.

Older, sturdier buildings; they had withstood innumerable hard blows before, would survive as many after. The Calle El Conde was crowded, as always. That, too, was different from the area around his hotel. There, the streets had been almost empty. His confidence came flooding back. Police spies? Ridiculous! He stopped under a gas lamp to look at his watch. It was after ten o'clock.

"Americano!"

He peered into a doorway, saw a broad-hipped, buxom woman, her mouth and eyes black slits in the shadows. His pause encouraged her. She stepped into the dim light, lowered her blouse and showed off a large, dark breast. Its expanse startled him. "Want a good time?" Her voice was husky.

Gil shook his head, *"No, gracias,"* he said, and resumed his former pace. How had she known he was American? He remembered he had never fooled them before, either.

Gil found the corner he sought, saw the stairs leading down from the cobble-stoned street. He descended. They were worn unevenly; he had to be careful not to twist an ankle. At the bottom, he knocked on the heavy wooden door.

A hatch opened. A square of light, then a pair of eyes. Gil moved to let the light catch his face. "Pombal," he said softly.

The hatch was slammed shut. For a second, nothing happened. Gil heard sounds within—muffled shouts, laughter. Then the bolt was thrown back and the door opened. He stepped in, moved to the side so that the attendant could close the door.

Gil was on a landing. The room below was windowless, the smoke as thick as swamp fog. Through the haze, Gil made out a crowd of men. The laughter he had heard outside had died down. The men stood and stared into a pit, as if transfixed. A cockfight was about to begin. Two men crouched in the pit, holding their birds, teasing them into fighting furies. He could not see Pombal. He took a deep breath and started down the creaking steps. The haze grew thicker, seemed to cling to his head. It was foul, fit only for beings who needed something other than oxygen for life.

Slowly, he circled the crowd, peering into their midst, then looking off into the corners of the room. Pombal must be there. Why else would he have been let in? Suddenly, shouting. He did not have to peer into the pit to know what was happening. The fight had begun. The cocks, freed by their masters, were flying into each other, slashing away with steel talons, grabbing and poking with their beaks.

In one corner, seated on a tier of earthen benches, was a group of men apparently not interested in the fight. And there was Pombal. How had he missed him before? Gil approached the group, saw men turn to him, most of their gazes heavy with suspicion, dislike. "Carlos," Gil called when he thought he could be heard above the crowd's roar, "I would like a word."

Pombal eased his bulk off the terraced embankment, scratched his crotch, pulled at his trousers. If Pombal had not gained any weight since they had last met, he hadn't lost any, either. Under the fat, however, there was strength. Gil had once seen him lift a man and fling him into a wall at least ten feet away. The man had been knocked senseless, or worse; no one had stayed around to find out.

The crowd's noise increased: cries of anguish, screams of triumph. The cockfight was over, or nearly so. It had lasted hardly longer than a minute.

Pombal ambled toward him with the seafarer's roll fat

men use to stop their thighs from chafing. Through the smoke of the thin cigar stuck in the corner of his mouth, Pombal's eyes were dark pinpricks peeking out from under folds of fat. The man nodded as he neared and said, "Brant, you are back. Have you taken up smuggling again?"

Pombal acted almost as if he had expected Gil to come walking in. Ellen's warnings came to mind. He shook them off. However much Ciudad Trujillo might have changed, this cockpit was inviolate. It was its own world. Gil smiled, shook his head. "Those day are done for. I've got something else. Can we go somewhere?"

"What is wrong with this?" Pombal sounded insulted.

Gil grinned. Pombal had grown up here. He worked here, lived here and even—back in the twenties—had predicted he would die here. "Your air is a little thick for me, that's all." He fanned a hand before his face.

"You get used to it soon enough." Pombal pointed toward an empty corner. "Over there. You want rum? I'll get some."

Gil nodded. His host jerked his head. A four- or five-year-old boy appeared, as if from nowhere. Pombal said, "Rum." The lad left as quickly as he had come. "So," the fat man said. "Why have you come back after so many years?"

"I want information," Gil admitted.

Pombal nodded. They reached the empty corner and sat on the embankment.

"There's a Frenchman in the country—Andre Duchesne's his name. I'd like to know what he's up to."

The little boy returned, a bottle in one hand, a glass in the other. He handed both over to Pombal, then retrieved a second glass from his trouser pocket and gave it to Gil. It was smudged with fingerprints, lip prints. Gil wondered how many had drunk from it since it had last been washed. He suppressed the question. It came from having lived too long in the antiseptic cleanliness of Hollywood. Anyway, alcohol killed germs. He held out the glass, let Pombal fill it to the brim.

"Saludo," Pombal said, extending his own glass.

Gil nodded, imitating his host by downing the rum in a gulp. It tasted like raw alcohol over a cup of sugar. Had what they smuggled into the States been as bad? Pombal was watching him carefully. "Smooth," Gil said, blinking his eyes. Angry voices rose among the crowd. Gil glanced that way, wondered whether there would be a fight. It had been common enough in the old days.

Pombal paid the noise no attention. "You still work for Gainsley?" he asked.

"No. I haven't heard from him since Prohibition ended."

The affirming jerk of Pombal's head seemed more a confirmation of what was already known than an indication of new information. "Then who you working for?" he asked.

In Pombal's cockpit, all governments were suspect. "Let's just say I'm employed by people who are interested in what the Frenchman is up to," he responded.

"How much money they got?"

Pombal never did anything without a price. It was the reason he had been trusted in the old days. He was an honest crook who never pretended an interest in anything but money. "Enough."

"Enough that you could afford two hundred, American?"

"Fifty," Gil countered.

"Fifty now, fifty when I get what you want," Pombal suggested.

A look in Pombal's pig eyes made Gil doubt he could get a better price. "Done," he agreed and pulled out his wallet, handing Pombal a pair of twenties and a ten. The money disappeared in the man's fat hand.

"I've heard of the Frenchman," Pombal admitted. "I don't know what he's up to, but I can find out."

"When?" asked Gil.

"I'll have the information by two o'clock this morning. Meet me then."

Only three hours away. How could Pombal find out so fast? A mental warning sounded. *He knows already.* "Two it is," he agreed. "I'll be back."

"Not here," the fat man said.

Not here? Pombal hated leaving the pit. "Where?" Gil asked.

"Remember La Casa Azul?"

The brothel just off the Modelo Marketplace where rumrunners and sellers used to cut deals. He and Anibal had been there a dozen times. It was close by. Perhaps Pombal was planning to spend some of the money he had made. Sex was one of the few things that ever got him to leave his establishment. "I'll meet you there," he agreed.

Pombal nodded. "Don't forget the rest of the money."

"I get the information, you get the money." Gil headed for the stairs. It would be nice to breathe real air again. Why hadn't Pombal seemed surprised to see him? How had he remembered his name so easily? He shrugged it off. How could he kill three hours? Return to the hotel? That would give Ellen another shot at trying to talk him out of the meeting. He shuddered at the thought. *Best to keep her out of it,* he concluded. *After all, what she doesn't know won't hurt me.*

* * *

Who was Pombal? Maria had never heard of him until his call. She had almost hung up on him, would have, had he not shouted Duchesne's name. That had caught her attention. It had also convinced her she would be wise to see him.

Maria picked yesterday's blouse off the chair—white crepe, slightly yellowed under the arms. She shrugged, slipped it on, shook out the black skirt she had worn with it, then donned that, too. She went to the mirror behind the door. Not good, but it would do, she thought as she retrieved her black pumps from under the bed and put them on. She glanced at her watch: eleven-forty-five. Pombal wanted money, obviously. What did he have that was so important he assumed she would give him some?

She went to her purse, opened it, and extracted a pistol. It smelled of oil. She set it under a copy of *Elle* on the table next to where she would sit—in case Pombal proved something other than a purveyor of information. She returned to the mirror, fluffed up her hair, waited for the knock at the door.

When it came, it startled her. The second knock seemed even louder. She opened the door. The man in the hallway was a mountain of fat. His shirt had gaps between the buttons, revealing slits of the dirty skin underneath. He held a grimy cap in his hands and had bicycle clips snapped around his dirty, white trousers. Maria tried to imagine that big ass on one of those tiny seats, but failed.

If she had never met Pombal, she had known others like him—men who sold whatever came their way to whoever would buy—lottery tickets, whores, stolen goods, or information. She relaxed a little. Men like Pombal were harmless to all except those they could bully. "Señor Pombal?" she said.

The fat man nodded, clutched his cap a little tighter. "*Sí,*" he responded.

"Come in. Please sit," she said, pointing out the chair she wished him to take.

He wedged himself into it. She sat across from him, the butt of the pistol against her elbow. "You said you have some information about Señor Duchesne. What is it?"

"Have you ever heard of an American named Gil Brant?" He was sweating. Was he nervous, or was it his normal condition?

She shook her head, annoyed at the man's deliberate manner. "Should I have?"

"I know him from ten–fifteen years ago. He worked for your husband then. He is here now, asking questions."

"In Ciudad Trujillo?" she asked. "Asking questions about me?"

He shook his head. "No, señora, not about you, about Andre Duchesne. I know that you and the Frenchman . . ." He did not complete his statement. "Forgive me, señora," Pombal began again, "but, since Brant once worked for your husband, I thought he might still. It would mean your husband was having you watched. I hope I did the right thing in coming to you."

She was numb, had hardly heard the last of Pombal's speech. "Yes," she agreed, "you did the right thing. What exactly did this man want? What did you tell him?"

The soft look in his brown eyes disappeared. He grinned, revealing a gold premolar, then wiped his smile away. "I will tell you, of course," he began, "but . . ."

Maria nodded. "I know; you need money."

"I am a poor man, señora."

"You will be rewarded," she agreed. "Tell me."

There was a second's hesitation, then, "Señora Gainsley's generosity is well known," he said and began. When, finally, he finished, she wished the fat man's assumption had been true. How much simpler if she had only to deal with her husband. "You say Brant claimed to be with the American government?"

"He said only that his employers had money."

She nodded. "And you knew of Andre and me," she said. "How?"

Pombal made a circle of his forefinger and thumb, then pretended to spy through it. "One person sees, tells another," he said, lowering his hand. "Eventually, word comes to me. That is what happens."

It was not a convincing speech. "You did not hear it from the police?"

Pombal shuddered, as if he had a sudden chill. "No, I swear."

She wasn't sure she believed him. Whatever it might mean, it was not good. Someone from the American Secret Service wanted to find out more about what she and Andre were doing. "And you will be meeting the American at this brothel in a few hours?" she asked.

"At two o'clock," he agreed.

Much had to be done before then, she told herself. "I am pleased you came with your information, Señor Pombal." She rose from her chair. "I reward well those who work with me."

Pombal smiled. "I am pleased to have been of service," he responded. Maria could feel his eyes on her as she went to her purse. She pulled out a few pound notes, looked at him. "I assume you prefer British currency," she said.

He nodded.

"Very well. All I have now is fifty pounds. Keep your appointment. Report to me tomorrow and tell me what he said. I will have more for you then."

Pombal extracted his bulk from the chair with considerably more ease than he had displayed in sitting down.

He took the money, jammed it into his trouser pocket. "I will do that," he assured her.

"I am glad," she said, steering him toward the door. She opened it, saw him out, then leaned against it once she had shut it. *Madre di Cristo*, much to be done and less than two hours to do it.

CHAPTER 2

Andre listened at the door before he entered. Nothing. Had Maria gone? The note had told him to come immediately. He inserted his key, turned it, and went inside.

Maria was seated on a sofa by the window. She had on the same skirt and blouse she had been wearing when he had left her earlier. A man sat beside her. Emilio Rosario. Andre fought the temptation to back out of the room and leave. Bringing Rosario and him together was dangerous. The realization that Maria knew that as well as he, yet still did it, meant the business was serious.

"You're here," Maria said. "Come in." The glow in her eyes intensified the imperative.

Andre approached. "General Rosario," he said with hand outstretched, "it has been a long time."

"Not since '38," Rosario agreed.

The general's fingers were meaty, powerful. Andre had

never liked the man, had regarded him too grasping, too blatantly corrupt. He broke the handshake, sat in a chair opposite the sofa, and glanced at Maria. The look in her eyes was suspicious. He pretended not to notice it. "What is so urgent?"

Maria glanced at Rosario, then looked back. "An American has arrived. He has been asking questions about you."

Andre felt all his energy flow from his body. He struggled to regain it. "How do you know?" he asked. "Who told you? Was it you?" He turned to look directly at Rosario.

The general shook his head.

"A cockpit operator named Pombal came to me a little while ago," Maria said. "He and the American used to do business together. Earlier tonight, the American approached him and asked him about you."

Andre's adrenaline had begun to pump, reversing the flow of energy. Ideas leading in all directions were flooding his mind. "A government agent?" he asked.

"What else?" Maria responded sarcastically.

Let the black bitch have her fun, Andre thought. She would pay for it. "Why did Pombal come to you?"

"It is like I said earlier. We shouldn't have been seen together so much. Pombal said he had heard about us."

Maybe, Andre thought, but he would bet there was more to it. "What did he know? What did you tell him?"

"I told you," she responded wearily. "He knew only that you and I . . . have been together. As for the rest of it, do you think me a fool? I told him nothing. I gave him money and asked him to try to find out exactly what the American knows."

Andre nodded, then looked at Rosario. "Is Pombal one of yours?"

"Hardly," Rosario said. "He does us favors now and then. In exchange, we let him run his business. That does not make him one of my men. He did not hear of it through me."

The man was holding something back. "You've got more to say," Andre prompted. "What is it?"

"Nothing," Rosario replied. He waited a beat, "Except that we have learned the American is not working alone."

Andre glanced at Maria. She seemed as surprised at Rosario's news as he. There was a narrowing of her eyes, a tension around her mouth to confirm it. "Tell us," Andre said.

"I have checked the hotel registration cards," Rosario said. "He arrived from Jamaica on his boat. So did a woman. She is staying in the same hotel. The harbormaster tells me there is someone staying aboard the boat—a black."

The Latin glanced back and forth between Andre and Maria before he went on. "Curiously, neither is American. The woman is English, the—"

"Does that mean the British are also suspicious?" Andre interrupted.

"I think we must assume that what the Americans know, the British also know," Rosario answered. "I doubt the woman is an agent, however, if that is what you mean."

Had a smile flickered across Rosario's lips? Andre wondered what he had found humorous. The Latin's voice suddenly sounded far away. A new, unidentifiable fear gripped him.

Rosario continued, "The other is Haitian. Both have specialized knowledge. The American and the Haitian used to work together. We have a file on the Haitian." The general met Andre's gaze. "As for the woman, I believe you know her. Her husband was with the English Consulate here. Her name is Ellen Bainbridge.''

It was as if Andre's lungs had been emptied. He sucked air and glanced at Maria. She was looking at him. Gradually, her eyes widened. The bitch had guessed about Ellen and him, he knew. He marshaled bits of strength where he could find them. "General, it is almost time for Brant's meeting with Pombal," he managed. "What do you propose be done?" His stomach muscles had tightened.

"That depends on you," Rosario countered.

"What do you mean?"

"You have an agreement with Maria; she has one with me. Neither of us anticipated this kind of difficulty." Rosario looked at Maria for confirmation. Maria nodded in agreement.

"Not only has this difficulty arisen," Rosario went on, "but, if I am correct, you will not be prepared to strike for at least another month. Surely, the odds against success have lengthened. Why risk all our lives for the sake of a few refineries?"

There was no problem reading the threat: Rosario was ready to bolt. And, if he did, Maria might, too. He shot a look at her. Her eyes were set, a darker hue than he had seen before. *A very good chance,* he thought. He would not let that happen. If the scheme collapsed, his dreams would tumble with it.

Audacity and courage. It was time to employ both. "As far as I can see," he said, "nothing has changed." They looked surprised. "Well, has it?" he pressed. "What does the American know? That I am thought to be on the island. Nothing more." He turned to Maria. "You said Pombal came to you only because he knew we were lovers." He paused, included Rosario in his gaze. "The

American is ignorant of our working relationship. Is that not so?''

Their nods were slow, uncertain. They had agreed, that was the important point. ''Then we must get rid of the American and this informer,'' he said. ''They must die.''

''The American government will send others.'' It was Maria who spoke. There was a hardness to her voice. Andre suddenly recognized it was she, not Rosario, he must convince.

''Then they must be killed, too.'' He had captured the pair's attention. ''Understand one thing,'' he told them through clenched teeth, ''there is no backing out. We are in it. All of us. To the end. Should you try to back out now, you would be dead in a week.'' An image of Schatz's glacial eyes came to him. At least four of Schatz's men had already arrived in Ciudad Trujillo. Enough to make sure none could ever guess from which direction an assassin's bullet might come. ''That is not a threat,'' he concluded. ''It is a certainty.''

''You would do that?'' Maria asked.

''Not I,'' Andre assured them. ''Others.''

''The Germans who have been arriving,'' said Rosario. ''I can have them picked up.''

''That would only give us a littler longer to live,'' Andre said. ''More would come. The Germans have long memories. We would be already dead, waiting only for the bullet to confirm it. And what would happen to us in the interim? Your hands, *mon général*, have already been muddied. Is Trujillo likely to forgive you? Or the Americans? *El Presidente* will throw you in a jail so fast you won't know what happened.''

Andre turned to Maria, spoke more softly. ''The same is true for you, I fear. It will become known: you conspired with a Vichyite. What will your husband say to

136

that? You try to get out now and you can kiss your plantation, your easy life, good-bye. By the time the Germans catch up with you, you might be happy to die.''

''And you?'' Maria questioned, her voice low.

Andre shrugged. ''If I fail, I die. I accepted the risk when I took the assignment.'' He paused, looked at Maria, then Rosario. ''And so did you.''

Their resistance softened. It was time for magnanimity. ''It is a question of keeping promises, isn't it? You do; we do. You fail . . .''

''Speak no more of it,'' interrupted Rosario. ''The question is, what to do about the American?''

Andre glanced at Maria. Her anger was gone, but a deeper resentment seemed to have replaced it. Had he gone too far? It didn't matter. Women like Maria expected to be threatened. A black eye or a swollen jaw made them feel wanted. His mind was again clear. He proceeded as if he had never questioned their loyalty. ''I think I have made myself clear on that. He must die.''

Maria: ''And those with him? They, too?''

He dared not weaken. ''They, too!'' He saw Maria's eyes cloud over, but had no time to puzzle out why. ''General,'' he said.

''Yes?'' Rosario snapped.

''We need time. Can their deaths be arranged to give us a few extra weeks?''

The officer hesitated, then nodded. ''Of course. It can be arranged that they simply disappear.''

''Good.'' He glanced at his watch. It was almost one-thirty. ''Then you had better get started.''

The officer glanced at Maria. ''I go,'' he said.

Andre rose with him. ''Remember one thing, Emilio. My country will not forget. You will see how grateful we French can be.'' He turned to Maria. ''And now—''

"Don't go," Maria told him.

The command halted both. As soon as Rosario saw her words were not meant for him, he left, slamming the door behind him.

"What is it?" Andre asked. He tried to read her eyes, but could not.

"The woman, Ellen Bainbridge. You knew her."

"Yes," he admitted.

"How well?"

"We had an affair."

"Did you love her?"

He paused before answering. "We were thrown together while with the Dominican-German Institute. She was reasonably attractive and had a husband who paid her no attention." He let the sentence drift. "That was all there was to it. It's been over now for three years."

"You do not regret ordering her death? Does that not bother you?"

It was not the question Andre expected. He had to scramble for an answer. "Yes," he confessed, hoping to turn her interest to his advantage, "but she has left me no choice. She stands in our way; no one can do that. Do you understand?"

Maria's nod was slow in coming. He reached over and set his hand on her cheek. "I know you are upset," he said, "would you prefer that I stayed with you tonight?"

Her reaction was quick. "No, it is best that you go," she said, taking his hand away.

"Perhaps you are right," he acknowledged. "I will leave now." He turned to go. She nodded agreement.

Andre sweated as he ran. Thank God Maria had not insisted he stay. He could not yet see Ellen's hotel ahead. He sped up. What would he do once he got there? Would he have to stand by while Rosario's thugs killed her? He was sure of only one thing: he must arrive before Rosario's men. A plan of action would suggest itself. It had to.

Three years ago Ellen had rejected him. Was this a second time? What other explanation was there? She was his Judas, destined to deny him a third time if she lived. She deserved death. He knew that, but could not still the protest which shrieked in his mind like an eagle's cry. *Not now; not now.* If she had to die, the decision as to when and how must be his.

He had to see her. He reeled like a drunken man past the botanical garden. The Hotel Independencia was only two blocks away. His shirt and coat clung to him, inhibiting his movement. Sweat poured down his face.

CHAPTER 3

The huts in the compound were of wattle, with thatched roofs. Coconut palms ringed them, black against the dark sky, their leaves clicking in the breeze. Anibal had not noticed any people. Then, as he moved closer, he saw them clustered in the shadows of the huts. The women rose and left, their white dresses reflecting the moonglow. By the time he stood before it, the congregation was solely masculine.

"*Bon soir,*" he said, then, to be sure, "*buenas noches.*"

"*Bon soir,*" one responded.

He could not make out who had replied, but, by the timbre of the voice, judged him to be a young man. "May I sit?" he asked.

Someone grunted permission. Anibal sank to the ground, folded his legs, and placed his hands on his thighs.

It had been years since he had sat that way; his muscles reminded him of that fact.

He had figured there would be some Haitians about. As much as Trujillo hated them, he needed their labor. The truth's corollary resounded as if in echo: *And as much as the Haitians know they are hated, poverty forces them to come for work.*

"You have broken the law by coming at night," the same man said. He used a Haitian patois which stamped him as from the region around Gonaïves. "If you are caught, you could be killed."

"Yes," Anibal agreed. A fire burned. Only now could he make out the embers, smell the smoke. He smelled something else: plantains roasting. The aroma triggered memories of his childhood. "I wanted to be with my own kind," he added.

The men nodded. Women began to rejoin the group. Anibal had not heard or seen a signal, but knew one had been given for their return. Others also joined them. He sensed people behind him, too. It was understandable. He was an outsider, an object of curiosity, perhaps a bringer of news. All were quiet. It made him self-conscious. He scratched his thigh.

"Why did you want to be with us?" asked the man.

Anibal leaned forward, then rocked back. "I had a wife, a child," he answered. "They were among those killed four—"

"We know nothing about it," responded the man.

All had stiffened, and one woman crossed herself. The last sat close to the fire. Its glow highlighted her bare forearm, black as polished ebony. "Please," Anibal said.

The group sat, stiff and still, like stones in a graveyard. Anibal took their silence as permission to continue. "Since their deaths, I have wished for death myself," he began.

There were nods.

"I do not want to make trouble for you," he continued.

"You have already done that by coming here," responded the young voice.

"It was not my wish," he repeated. "I want to know only one thing."

"What is that?" A different, older voice asked the question.

Anibal swung about to identify the source, was aided by the turning of heads among his listeners. All indicated an aged man to Anibal's left. "I want to know where it happened," he replied.

"Why?"

The question stopped him. Anibal had never asked it of himself. All he knew was that it was important to him. Now that he was in the land where their bodies lay, the need to know had grown. It knotted his stomach, pressed into his lungs and brain. Quickly he hunted for a reason his countryfolk would accept. "They lay where they died," he said, then stopped. There was a rasp in his voice. He cleared his throat and continued, "The ground has not been sanctified. Their *'tit bon anges* float free; they could be plucked by the *bokor*."

The gasp was tangible, a collective sucking of air. He had used the name of the evil priests, magicians who commune with the *baka*, or evil spirits. In combination, they can resurrect those who have not received a proper burial. They control the *zumbi*, as people of his village used to call them: zombies, to others. It was the dark side of voodoo. He did not believe in it, but these people would.

If he had frightened them before, some were now terrified. But, if it was bad luck to speak of the *bokor*, it was sacrilege to refuse an appeal for help against them.

"Once you learn of the place, what is your intention?" the old man queried.

It had been thirty years since Anibal had dealt with the rites of voodoo. "To build a *hounfort*," he managed, "an altar to honor Damballa and his wife, Ayida Oueddo. So that they can protect my wife and child."

His response evoked murmurs from the crowd. Some wondered whether the *loa*—gods—to whom he would dedicate his altar could protect his wife and son without the altar being sanctified by a *hungan*, or priest. Others wondered if the altar might protect souls other than those for whom it was built. To Anibal, the questions were as senseless as arguing over how many angels could dance on the head of a pin. Slowly, the conversations petered out.

"We will tell you," said the old man. He crooked a finger to beckon Anibal closer. Anibal moved until the fire was so close he could feel its heat. Stick in hand, the old man scratched a map on the ground. "The killing occurred in more than one spot," the man began, "but it was in a valley by the Lago Enriquillo that the largest number were slain."

Anibal felt tears welling in his eyes. An old woman noticed, leaned over, and wiped them from his left eye with her thumb—her way of showing she shared his sorrow. A feeling took root in Anibal, then grew. Bettina and young Anibal were in the valley by the Lago Enriquillo. He had learned what he had come to find out.

Anibal moved his eyes in a wide arc, meeting the gaze of all. "Thank you," he told them. "I will build my *hounfort* in the valley. I will pray for Damballa and his wife to protect all who were slain that day." He started to rise. He could not do it as smoothly as he would have wished. His knees had stiffened.

"Stay with us tonight," said the younger man.

The offer was tempting, but Anibal refused. He managed finally to get to his feet and stretched his spine.

"It is even more dangerous to try to enter the city at night than to leave," the man continued.

There was truth in that, Anibal privately conceded, but he was sure he could get back to the ship without being detected. He thanked them again, leaned over and patted the cheek of the old woman who had thumbed away his tears. Her skin was dry, soft. Again, it evoked memories long suppressed. He left.

CHAPTER 4

The doorman's evening jacket was too short at the sleeves, too large at the waist. He eyed Gil for a moment, then said, "We're closed for the night. Have you an appointment?"

"Carlos Pombal asked me to meet him here."

It had been the right thing to say. The doorman stepped aside. Inside, Gil felt as if he had just shed fifteen years. Impressions shaded into memories, brought back all his teenaged association of sex with sin and tawdriness. The parlor was to the left, the bar to the right. He had forgotten how striking was the winding staircase across the foyer. Along the balcony, under the balustrade, there ran a fresco with the plaster limbs of chubby cherubs jutting from it. Most of the extensions were broken off: angelic amputations leaving stumps with harsh, white ends. The building must once have been elegant, he reflected. He remembered he had had the same thought during his previous visits.

He paused at the bar's entry. Glasses and half-filled ashtrays stood on the bar and tables, but the room was empty. Gil's skin tingled. He half expected to hear the echo of laughter, the whisper of conversation, even see the thin trail of smoke from a not-quite-extinguished cigarette. He turned toward the doorman. "Is Pombal here yet?" he asked.

"I will see. One moment."

Gil waited until the doorman started up the stairway, then crossed to the parlor and slid open its doors. That, too, was as he remembered it: a large room, lined with black leather benches and an oilcloth strip over the benches. A shiny, dark, irregular smudge snaked the length of the wainscoting, the impressions of countless greasy heads which had leaned against it. Somewhere among them, Gil thought, might be marks he had made.

"May I help you?"

The voice startled him. Gil turned, saw a small woman with dark eyes. The eyes protruded, like a lizard's. The image was so vivid, Gil wondered whether each might move independently. "I'm sorry," he began, then halted, uncertain how to continue. "You are the madam?" he asked.

"No. She is not in. The Casa Azul is closed for the night, señor."

"So I was told," Gil said. "I am supposed to meet a man here—Señor Pombal. Has he shown up?"

"Yes, he is here."

Her response surprised him. It was not yet two o'clock. In the past, Pombal had rarely been on time and never early. "Will you take me to him?" he asked.

"I have my work. You must find your own way," she said. "He is in room nine, behind the stairs and down the corridor."

"*Gracias*, señora," he replied and took a dollar from his wallet.

She snatched the bill and was gone before Gil could replace his billfold. As he left the parlor she was scurrying back up the staircase.

A bare bulb burned in the middle of the hallway. The floor creaked underfoot, the tap of his knuckle on the wall seemed hollow. "Damn," he whispered. The expletive was absorbed by the darkness.

The room he sought was at the end of the corridor. He turned the knob, cracked open the door, then paused. No light, no sound. He peered inside and spotted Pombal's seated silhouette against the dim light from the window. "Hey," he whispered.

The fat man did not move. A warning to get out rang in his mind. Gil forced himself to ignore it and fumbled for the light switch. The overhead bulb lit the room like a flare.

"Shit," Gil hissed. He took a step toward the hallway, then checked himself. He could not run. Not yet. He turned to face the body, caught a whiff of blood: sweet and acrid.

The body was slumped in a wooden chair, hands tied behind it. Pombal's mouth hung open. His complexion was ashen gray—almost blue in that light. The man's throat had been slit. The gaping wound showed yellow fat under a filmy layer of blood. More blood had soaked into Pombal's clothing, had collected into a pool on the chair by his crotch. From there, it dripped onto the floor. A knife lay at Pombal's feet. Blood covered it.

"You didn't die in your own place, after all," Gil whispered. Reluctantly, Gil approached and forced himself to inspect the body. All the man's pockets were torn and empty. If Pombal had carried a message, he had it no longer.

A noise interrupted his inspection. He lifted his head. Three guardsmen were standing in the doorway, rifles leveled. An impulse to run caught at his muscles, but sight of the weapons stifled it for the moment. It would be suicide. One of the guardsmen motioned Gil from the body. Gil swallowed and obeyed. His mouth was dry.

At the sound of a voice coming from the hallway, the troopers shuffled aside, looking that way. Gil bolted for the window. Impressions, clear and distinct, registered: the confused shouts of the guardsmen; the window, faded curtains halfway drawn, only a few strides away; his heart thumping, that feeling of exhilaration when he knew he would make it. Gil lowered his shoulder and leaned forward to dive through the window.

His feet went out from under him. He lurched forward, reaching out, and landed with his right arm on the windowsill, his head out the window, his left hand entangled in a gauzy length of curtain. Hands dragged him back into the room. He peered over his shoulder. "Wait a minute," he said, then paused. He had been about to protest his innocence. It would do no good. One of the men planted a foot between his shoulder blades and shoved him back down. He lay quietly, willing to accept the respite, no matter how brief. There was something sticky under his right hand: Pombal's blood. From out of the corner of his eye, he saw one of the dead man's feet. It was that which had tripped him up.

Men shuffled around outside his range of vision. A boot of highly polished black leather stopped an inch from his nose. Gil could see his breath cloud the surface. He lay still. It had been a setup, he realized. Damned fool that he was, he'd ignored Ellen's warning, had ignored all the danger signs, and had walked straight into it. He relaxed as best he could, breathed deeply.

The booted officer knelt, shoved a pistol before his eyes. "You will do nothing, say nothing, unless we wish it, señor," he said. "Is that understood?" He rotated the gun for emphasis. Gil recognized the model: a Browning 9-mm automatic, powerful enough to sever an arm or leg at close range. If the man wished, he could turn him into something resembling the plaster cherubs in the foyer.

The hand which pressed his head to the floor made talking difficult. "Understood," he managed.

Her unfamiliarity with her hotel room increased Ellen's anxiety. In the dark, items beggared identification, seemed possessed of a life of their own. Strange noises contributed to her malaise; nor did her guilty conscience help. Why should Gil have heeded her advice? What had she done to win his confidence? She shifted to look at the alarm clock on the bedside table. It was hidden behind a water bottle and glass. She had to raise her head to get a glimpse of the glowing radium dial. It was not quite two. She wondered once again where Gil was. The echoed assurance that he was a big boy capable of taking care of himself failed to calm her.

The telephone's ring cut through the stillness. Ellen leaped to pick up the receiver. "Where are you?" she asked.

The silence on the other end told her she had erred. "Who—" she began.

A man cut in, speaking Spanish; his words were muffled. "Leave the country," he said. "If you don't, you will be killed."

"Who is this?" Ellen asked. "What's happened to Gil?"

"The American has been taken care of," came the response. "Get out." The telephone clicked dead.

Ellen kept the receiver to her ear for a few seconds, then slammed it down and fumbled in the closet for her robe. Barefoot, she ran into the corridor and rapped on Gil's door.

No answer. She rapped again, harder. Still nothing. She paused, prepared to knock once more, but refrained, realizing it would be pointless. Instead, she hurried back to her room. What had she fallen into? No violence, Gil had assured her. He had been wrong.

There seemed something different about the room. "More ghosts," Ellen whispered, trying to deny it. She closed the door and groped for the light switch, felt the fingers wrap around her wrist before she found it. In that split second, reality and imagination were entwined, as if the grip was yet another figment of her mind.

The message broke through. This was real. Ellen twisted and squirmed, sought to free herself. She opened her mouth to scream; a fist grazed her jaw and landed full on her throat. Her head flew back and banged against the door. She tried to scream again, but couldn't. Her throat seemed paralyzed. The next she knew, she was shoved into the room. Her knee banged against the bed as she fell onto it. Instinctively she twisted her body and heard a knife rip into the mattress beside her. Wildly scrambling, she knocked over the bedside table. She kept rolling until she was on the floor, with the bed between her and her attacker. Her eyes began to adjust to the dark.

Someone in the next room pounded on the wall and shouted for silence. Ellen opened her mouth to scream for help, but managed only a few squeaks. She prayed they could be heard. A man passed in front of the window, coming toward her. She scuttled backward until she felt the closet doorknob hit the back of her head. She had to fight for breath. It came in short gasps.

A gray bulk loomed over her. Ellen gathered her strength, concentrated it all in one violent thrust. She kicked hard, felt her ankle crunch into his groin. There was a grunt of pain. Ellen scrambled to the side. She needed a weapon. Anything.

The floor was strewn with broken glass. Something solid touched the side of her hand. She grasped it: the neck of the water bottle.

He was lumbering after her again. Her nightgown was tangled in her feet. She tugged desperately on the hem to free herself, bumped against a table, dislodging the telephone. It landed on her shoulder. She shoved it aside and cast a quick glance toward the door. She would never make it. She crouched, waited until he loomed before her, then sprang directly at him. She could feel his arms on either side, ready to pull her close, smother the life from her. The bottle caught him on the face. His hands flew up to his wound.

She thrust again. This time, the man parried with his forearm. The impact jarred her wrist, numbed her entire arm. A fist caught her in the chest. Ellen's knees gave way. She hit the wall and slid down it, landing amid broken glass.

From the hall, the sound of running feet. Fists rapping on the door; a key scratching against the lock.

"¡Puta!" her attacker snarled.

A wedge of light shone in from the corridor as the door opened. Ellen glimpsed a large man leaving by the window. She thought her neighbor was still knocking on the wall, then realized it was her own ears pounding. Someone switched on the overhead light. Its glare made her blink.

Her rescuer was the night manager. He pummeled her with questions. She answered as best she could, barely speaking above a whisper. Her throat was numb; it was difficult to concentrate on what he asked. She drew her robe around her, aware now of the state of her undress. Blood dappled the front of her gown. The sight sent shivers through her.

"*Sí*, señor," she answered the night manager, "the police must be contacted."

"It is the correct thing to do, señora," he assured her. "I, of course, will call them for you."

"I would be most grateful," she told him. She was not sure she could have managed it had it been left to her. She felt as if she were in a hall of mirrors. Whichever way her thoughts went, they reflected back on themselves. The telephone call and the attack—those were juxtaposed, like sentinels, in the front of her mind, barring entrance to all else.

The manager drew himself up to his full sixty-four inches. "It is my duty," he responded. "A guest has been attacked. I cannot pretend it has not happened." He seemed eager to show his concern and his empathy.

"I want to call the British Consulate," she said.

"Of course," the manager replied. "After you talk to the police. That comes first."

"Yes, all right." She nudged the little man from her room. "Thank you so much."

He retreated reluctantly. "There will be clues," he said. "You must not touch anything. You will need to be put in another room in any case."

"I must get dressed," she reminded him.

He blinked, then lowered his head. "Of course. Later, then," he conceded. She had backed him into the corridor. A few curious residents were congregated there. "In the meantime," he added, before she could close the door on him, "I will see that you get medical assistance."

"*Gracias*, señor," she replied as she shut the door.

Alone, she put a hand to her throat and massaged it. She heard the manager clapping his hands, shooing the curious away as if they were chickens. Her gaze swept the room: broken glass scattered across the floor, ripped mattress half off the bed, furniture toppled, a trail of blood, telephone lying on the carpet, the phone wire entwined in the legs of an overturned table. She shuddered.

Who had attacked her? Someone Andre had hired? Then why had he warned her? It had been he who had called. She was certain of it now, although thought did not come easily. It bumped against pain, panic, false trails, as if caught in a maze. Gradually, answers suggested themselves: tentative, but the best she could manage. The attacker had known which room she was in. Who could have told him? The night clerk? The police? If the police had spies, what prevented them from also employing assassins?

Suddenly her bruises and cuts were forgotten. The more Ellen considered it, the more certain she became of it: she was about to be handed over to men who had already tried to kill her. There was but one thing to do. Get out. The decision was sudden, certain.

She must act quickly. The physician would soon show up; a maid might arrive to take her to another room. If she waited, she was done for. *Like Gil.* She pushed off from the door and went to the bureau, scattering clothing, rummaging until she found a pair of underpants, a bra, and a white shirt. She put them on, padded to the closet for a pair of slacks. *Get to the docks*, she told herself as she buttoned the slacks, plopped on the bed, and donned her tennis shoes. *Find Anibal.* She reached into her purse, took out her money, lipstick, comb, and . . . *passport! It was still down at the desk. To hell with it*, she concluded as she thrust the other items into a pocket. *Get away.* Someone from the consulate could always retrieve the passport.

She went to the window. The ledge beneath it extended nearly to the fire escape off to her left. She looked down the three stories to the street. An electric light, like a tiny, glowing dot, burned over the entrance of the building opposite. "Don't worry about that," she muttered through clenched teeth. "You used to do this sort of thing all the time when you were a schoolgirl." Counter arguments bubbled up for consideration: that had been fifteen years ago; never had she done it while fifty feet in the air.

Don't think about it; do it, she told herself as she crawled onto the ledge. It was about a foot wide, with a downward slope. She pressed her back to the window, then—slowly—turned until her stomach pushed against it. The ledge's slant forced her up on her toes as she shuffled along, an inch at a time. She could feel her calf muscles knot up. At the end of the ledge, with her right hand cupped around the edge of the window well, she reached over to the fire escape. It was a few inches beyond her outstretched fingers.

She paused. How did she know whether Anibal was still alive? Would it not be better to return to her room and call the consulate? The call would go through the hotel switchboard. It would alert the manager.

It was as if another's voice screamed in her ear. *Don't trust anyone.* Dangling in midair at the end of a window well was not the best place for such a debate. "Gil Brant," she muttered, "if you are still alive, you won't be after I'm through with you." She took a breath, held it, and launched herself into the air.

CHAPTER 5

Anibal sat on the other bunk, nearly invisible in the dark cabin. "So what shall we do?" Ellen asked. She had told her story in short bursts. The intervals between phrases had sounded ominous, even to her, as if the words had had to forcibly break free from the silences surrounding them.

He made no reply. Waves slapped against the boat's hull. The craft rocked gently. Always before, the motion had soothed Ellen. Now, it had an opposite effect. The rhythmic tugs were reminders to act.

Anibal's knee bumped against hers as he shifted position. She saw his head by the porthole, blocking what little light there was, like an eclipse. "Only one thing to do," he answered, looking into the night: "Get out of here."

"Gil?" she whispered.

"Gil's dead," Anibal replied, still looking out the porthole.

Was it true? Even if it weren't, what could they do about it? Logic dictated flight. It was a decision men seemed to reach easily. Cutting losses, they called it; refusing to sacrifice the whole for the part. A tribal instinct. Men's logic, perhaps, but not women's. And particularly not hers. "We don't know that for sure," she argued.

For three years she had had to live with the thought that her husband had died because she had deserted him; no amount of rationalization had ever rid her of that guilt. If she deserted Gil without knowing his fate, the extra burden might prove impossible to bear.

Once again, she could make out the full gray circle of the porthole. Anibal was staring at her, she knew, even if he could not see her. "You want to find him?" he finally asked.

She opened her mouth. Her throat tightened. Was that what she wanted? "Yes," she answered, her voice firm.

"You'd do it whether I went or not?"

He was being unfair. Alone, she could do nothing. "If I must," she lied.

"How much money have you?" he said.

"I don't know. Whatever I had," she replied.

He got up and moved into the galley. She realized he was digging for the coffee can where they stashed their extra cash. "Give your money to me," he finally said.

She did. It wasn't very much.

"There's a flashlight under the bunk. Get it," Anibal ordered.

Action, movement: they signified life, hope. She crouched, found it, and pushed up from the deck. As she did, there was a flash of light outside the porthole. It came again: a searchlight playing on the harbor's outer waters.

That explained why Anibal had changed his mind so quickly: not her appeal; hard fact. They would have been unable to get to sea had they tried.

Perhaps it was her stillness which caught Anibal's attention. "You see it?" he asked.

"Yes." The light depressed and frightened her. The search had begun.

"Find yourself a change of clothing. Practical stuff. And be careful with the light," he told her. He was rummaging through another cabinet.

She knelt to search her seabag, pressing the torch close to it. Slacks, cotton shirt, socks, extra pair of underpants, and a bra. She looked up. "Shoes, too?" she whispered.

"Take off the ones you're wearing," he replied.

She took them off and added them to her pile. "All right," she said.

"Hand them to me," he told her.

He stuffed her clothing into a rubberized bag. "Gil was alive two hours ago, if that will make you feel any better."

Two hours was a long time. Still, she felt her heart pound at the news. "How do you know?"

"We haven't much time," he said, as if she needed reminding. She handed over the flashlight and turned back to the porthole while Anibal finished packing the bag. "Done," he said at last. He climbed from the cabin. Ellen bent low and followed him up to the deck.

The night was still. She saw a few lighted windows along the Malecon, but spotted no activity.

Anibal sat and took off his trousers and shoes and pushed them into the bag, too. His legs were skinny and black. Obviously, he meant to swim to shore. "Why not take the dinghy back?" she whispered.

"Too easily seen," Anibal responded. "Let them think

we're still aboard.'' He had tied the bag to his wrist and was holding it in his arms. "Ready?"

"As ready as I'll ever be," she told him.

He jumped. The splash cracked the silence. She took a deep breath and followed. There came the shock of water as it closed overhead. Then she bobbed to the surface. When her vision cleared, Anibal was beside her. "This way," he said and nodded to indicate an oblique angle to shore.

Ellen swam slowly, not letting her hands break the water's surface. She was content to concentrate only on the immediate, defer thoughts on the future until later. Swells caught her up, then raced on. Anibal was in front and to her right. She looked behind her, saw that the *Stardust* was farther away than she had figured it would be.

The hand on her forearm startled her. It was Anibal, treading water. "Careful," he warned.

One glance was enough to tell her why. On shore, to her right, there were automobile headlights: cars stopping at the harbor. Police; or the national guard.

After a few seconds rest, Anibal started swimming again, now heading directly for land. Fortunately, Ellen thought, the moon was behind a cloud. Otherwise they would be visible to anyone on shore, like a pair of beach-balls bobbing in the surf.

The wave crested and broke. Ellen tumbled ahead of it, then gained her feet and scrambled through the foam. Anibal had fallen behind her. She tried to wade faster, but the water prevented it. Sand pricked her legs.

From a short distance to her right, Ellen heard someone shouting orders—staccato phrases which sliced through the night air. Salt stung her eyes, but she could make out silhouettes among the palms. From the water, she heard the sputter of a motorized launch, heading toward the *Stardust*.

She came to a shelf of hard rock, its surface worn smooth by the waves. Without pause, Ellen scrambled onto it. The ledge was slick. Anibal was having a harder time making headway than she. "Hurry," she said, her voice an urgent whisper, and continued on.

The crashing and sucking of the waves had eroded the rocky shore. It was that way all along the southern coast, she knew. She squirmed under an overhang; Anibal was immediately behind. From above, there came the thud of feet, but no shouts or orders. They had not been seen, Ellen told herself. It meant they were safe. But for how long? They would have to move soon.

A wave curled in front of their ledge. It rose black and silver in the moonlight, like a mountain, high enough that the overhang hid its crest from view. She nudged Anibal in warning, then took a breath, and grabbed an exposed root. The wave broke and ran in on them. The water rose over her head, pushed her back against the overhang.

It ebbed just as quickly. Ellen glanced toward Anibal. In the blackness, all she could make out were his white shorts. "Are you all right?" she asked.

"I guess," he whispered back. "Let's get out of here."

It was good advice. Even if those searching did not find them, they couldn't take much battering from the waves. Her shoulder felt like it had been rubbed raw.

Without a word, she turned and started to crawl along the hollow, pausing now and then to listen for pursuers. Twice, waves found them and nearly flushed them from their warren. She kept crawling.

Ellen waited while Anibal slid out onto the shelf to peer about. She saw him straighten. "There's no one," he said. "Come."

She did not need to be told a second time. Anibal preceded her up the bank and held down a hand to help her. She accepted it, felt at once the lifting force of his arm and the water from yet another wave on her calves.

He did not let her rest, but urged her across the Malecon and into the shadows of a narrow street. She heard no whistles or shouts, no running feet. They had not been seen. Anibal knelt to open the bag and took out their clothes. They were reasonably dry. Ellen turned away from Anibal, stripped, and put her dry clothes on hurriedly.

"At least we're sure of one thing," Anibal whispered from behind her.

"What's that?" she asked.

"You were right in not trusting the police."

The statement reminded her of something Anibal had said on the *Stardust*. "You told me Gil had been alive a few hours ago," she said as she forced her wet feet into her shoes. "How do you know?"

"He came to the boat," Anibal answered. "He left a note when he couldn't find me."

Why had Anibal left the *Stardust*? It was not the time to ask. She turned back to Anibal, a wad of wet clothing in her hands. He was leaning against a building as he put on a shoe. "Where to?" she asked. He knew the city's back streets; she did not.

"We'll retrace his steps," Anibal answered. "The note said he was going to a whorehouse we sometimes went to. Maybe we can find out something there."

The blunt response was unlike Anibal. It brought to mind the way her mother criticized old beaux. By innuendo; never directly. Was Anibal doing the same thing? What did it matter? Carefully, she lifted the top off a trash can and dumped her wet clothing in it. "Let's go," she whispered.

"*¡Ea!*" came a voice. "Get up so I can see you."

A key turned in the lock. Gil raised his manacled hands for leverage and rose from the cot. The door creaked open, admitting light from a gas lamp outside. A uniformed guard with olive drab puttees stood in the doorway, waving him out.

Gil obeyed, came out to the arcade beyond his cell. The discomfort of his bruises, the weight of the manacles hanging from his wrists became secondary, replaced in primacy by the emptiness in his stomach. He recognized the feeling: fear. The jailor snuffed, spat into the bushes, then ordered him forward. Gil walked to the end of the arcade, then waited, silently gazing into the courtyard. There, bathed in moonlight, stood the squat Tower of Homage, citadel of Ozama Fortress.

"Out," the man said, motioning him into the square.

There was no choice but to obey. Gil stepped onto a stone walk. He was not optimistic about his chances, not after he had his first glimpse of the fortress. In the old days, "Gone to Ozama" had been a synonym for a mysterious disappearance. The odds against its having changed its function seemed enormous. Were Anibal and Ellen locked in other cells? Probably—if they still lived. The thought was like a weight against his chest.

A cloud hid the moon. It was like stepping into a chamber with a ceiling so high it was hidden from sight. He heard the flutter of wings. Bats, flying overhead.

Three troopers, armed with rifles, stood in the square talking idly. Their words rang dully in the open air, like counterfeit coins on a tabletop. They pretended to pay him no attention, but, more than once, he saw them casting furtive glances in his direction as he approached.

His firing squad. They would put him against a wall and shoot him. He wondered if he would be offered a cigarette and a blindfold. Probably not. If the old stories held any truth, a formal firing squad was not the Ozama way. A single shot in the head sufficed. Then his body would be dumped in the river to float out to sea. Shark food.

He vowed not to accept his fate passively. Far better to be shot while resisting. He paused, trying to remember why he had always thought that. He was no longer sure of the answer.

His jailor grabbed his arm and led him forward, past the troopers. Gil shook him off, indicated he would walk alone. The other accepted the act without comment. He was a corporal, Gil noticed. The others fell in behind. He could hear their shuffling feet. The corporal lit a cigarette. Someone behind him sneezed.

Again, the corporal prodded him, guiding him toward the parapet by the river's edge. The citadel and cells were behind him. Gil fought an urge to turn and look back at them, to reassure himself they were still there.

They came to the parapet. A gas lamp illuminated an opening in it, with narrow pebbled-concrete stairs, encased within stuccoed walls, leading down to the river. Gil halted; the corporal preceded him, descended two steps, then turned and waved him to follow. One of the soldiers behind gave him a push to set him in motion. Gil started down. The stairway was barely wide enough for him. Behind him, he heard the others stringing out to follow. Below, the Ozama River—broad, a black ribbon. Gil breathed deeply, had to fight against the realization that soon he might breathe no more.

The stairs led to a loading platform. Gil could make out

crates piled along its length. They stood silently, like tombstones: forbidding, menacing. He would be shot beside the river. The conclusion was reinforced by implacable logic. Why carry him to the river if you can get him to walk there on his own?

He felt cold. In a minute, maybe two, he would be dead. What was it like? Would his brain stay alive for a time? He remembered stories of severed heads winking after the executioner had lifted them for display. Might he feel himself sinking in the water? He tried to renew his vow to resist, but his mind had turned to mush.

Maybe he was wrong. Maybe they were not going to kill him. Maybe they were only transferring him to another prison.

Christ Almighty, he thought. *They won't have to kill me. I'll have done it myself.* It was automatic, spontaneous. Gil kicked the corporal. The cigarette flew through the air as the corporal shouted and fell. Gil stepped on his back and leaped onto the loading platform, running along the river's edge, seeking to keep the crates between him and his pursuers. His muscles were stiff. Running was difficult.

He began to run more rapidly, heard his feet slap against the concrete surface. There were shouts behind him. Would the soldiers have unslung their weapons by now? Were they driving cartridges into their rifles' chambers? He bent lower, wished he were not manacled, that he could freely swing his arms.

Ahead, a mound of sacks. The crack of a rifle. It did not sound as loud as he had imagined it might. The bullet thudded into one of the sacks. Gil saw the hole, level with his chest. Material dribbled from the hole. Cement, he thought.

He rounded the mound, leaning against it, panting, trying to get his bearings. The platform went on at least as far as he could see, but, except for some bales of sisal and a few small packing crates beyond them, there was nothing more behind which to hide. He took a deep breath and started running again. It was the worst of nightmares, as if he were running in molasses. The cadence of his pursuers seemed easy, effortless.

He passed the sisal, expecting to hear gunfire at any second.

"Keep going."

The command came from the left. Gil obeyed implicitly, as if God himself had whispered in his ear. He stumbled on. It had been Anibal. He stopped by a packing crate. It would not do to get too far from Anibal. His friend would need him. Gil turned.

The guardsmen hove into view, then slowed, as if it was now they who sensed danger. *"¡Ea! ¡Cueros!"* Gil shouted.

It focused their attention. They resumed their shuffling trot, the gait of men who knew their prey had no place to go. From their rear, Gil heard a muffled shout. He saw one, hands over his face, pull away from the others, then sink to his knees. The others halted, turning.

Gil ran toward them, scything his irons in front of him. He reached the first trooper; there was the sound of metal against wood as his chains wrapped around a rifle. Gil pulled the weapon away, swung again and smashed his manacled wrist against the guard's temple. The chains got caught under the man's arm. As he fell, Gil went down with him.

From three or four paces away, Gil saw the corporal leveling a pistol: too near to miss.

The bullet's crush never came. Instead, the corporal collapsed, facedown. Ellen stood over him, like an avenging angel, holding a length of steel pipe. Someone was shouting in panic: the remaining trooper, beating a hasty retreat. Gil extricated himself from the tangle of irons and arms, then joined Ellen beside the corporal. "In the movies," Gil said, "it's the guy who rescues the gal."

For a moment, she acted as if she had not heard him. Her eyes looked wild, seemed to shine in the dark: an animal's eyes, Gil thought. "I suppose you've got to decide what you are," she said as she went through the corporal's pockets, "an actor or a spy. Help me turn him over."

He knelt.

"The keys to your chains," she said. "He must have them. They would hardly have dumped you in the water with them still on you."

She had an uncanny ability to make him feel like an idiot. Gil flipped the corporal over, saw the keys on his belt. He tugged in vain, then loosened the belt. Anibal joined them. He held a rifle. "Hurry," he urged. From the courtyard above came the toot of a tin whistle.

Pulling the keys from the man's belt was difficult. Gil's chains kept getting in the way. Ellen pushed him away, slipped the belt from the loops, and handed the keys to Gil. "All right," she said, looking up.

"Let's get out of here," Anibal said.

Keys in hand, Gil followed his friends as they raced away from the fort. They could climb the embankment and get back into the city farther down the platform. He no longer felt tired.

CHAPTER 6

Silence, Anibal signaled. This squad of police probably had not yet heard of the escape, but it paid to take nothing for granted, even if they were a mile from the fortress. Gil and Ellen crouched lower, shoulders hunched.

The police neared. The wall behind which they hid smelled of urine; rats skittered in the trash, ignoring their presence. Why should the rats fear them? This was their world.

The voices trailed off, the click of boots against cement could no longer be heard. Anibal stood and peered up and down the sidewalk. "It's all right," he whispered. "They've gone."

"What now?" Gil asked, once they were back on the sidewalk. The words lacked inflection, as if their speaker did not much care what the choice was, as long as he did not have to make it.

Anibal looked at him, then at Ellen. "The police are watching both the American and British consulates," he said, reminding them of what they had already seen. "Escape by sea is out. What's left, but to head inland?"

Slowly, their eyes widened. "All the way to Haiti?" asked Ellen.

"We'd never make it," Gil chimed in.

"Yes," Anibal said to Ellen. "We will need help," he told Gil.

"That's how I got us in this mess in the first place," Gil said.

Anibal hesitated. "There's the old woman."

Gil let loose a soft whistle. Anibal assumed it meant he wished he had thought of her. That he hadn't was no surprise. Young men rarely saw the obvious.

"Old woman?" Ellen queried. "Who's she?" Then, in the next breath, "Don't you think we should get out of here?"

"She's right," Anibal agreed. "What do you say?" he asked, looking directly at Gil.

"If anyone can help us, it's her," Gil agreed.

"Who's the old woman?" Ellen repeated.

"You two lead the way," Anibal suggested. "I'll follow in a moment."

He watched them go. The sight of Gil walking beside Ellen brought back a flash of anger, a brief, flickering heat from dying embers. Ellen liked Gil, Anibal knew, although she might not yet recognize it. Anibal shook his head, hoped she realized how dangerous a man like Gil was. Who should know better than he? He had been like Gil when he was young: impatient, sure that he could make a good life for his family. It hadn't worked that way.

Think no more about it, he told himself. *The old woman. Madam Gamba.* She had predicted they would meet again, he recalled. It was looking more and more as if she had been right. If she still lived.

Of course she did. Women like Madam Gamba didn't die, not in one's own lifetime. Besides, she had never been as old as she pretended. Anibal smiled. La Gamba was a mystery, no denying it, but she could help them. And, unlike Pombal, she would never betray them. How could the old woman collaborate with government officials if she refused to admit the government's existence?

He turned the corner and almost stumbled against his colleagues.

"Everything okay behind us?" Gil asked.

"Yes."

"Gil says the woman must be dead by now," said Ellen.

Anibal shook his head. "She is like a lime on the tree. She may wither, but she won't die until she drops to the ground. Somehow, I don't think she is ready for that." He paused. "To Madam Gamba's?"

"As you say: Is there a choice?" Ellen responded.

Gil shrugged.

"Then let's get started."

"Who is she?" Ellen asked as they resumed walking.

Anibal shrugged. "You heard: an old woman."

"But what else?" she demanded.

He smiled and said nothing.

"Madam Gamba," Ellen growled after a time. "She sounds like a dance instructor."

That's because you've never met her, Anibal answered silently.

Anibal swung his eyes from one side of the street to the other. Lamps bracketed to the sides of buildings offered small islands of illumination. Nothing moved. The street was deserted, the buildings dark and silent. He tried to peer behind the brightly painted shutters and doors, sure that, somewhere, eyes peered back, but he saw nothing, only the tightly pressed, two-storied, stuccoed structures on both sides of the street. It was as if they were walking through a gulley. If they were discovered now, he thought, there could be no escape.

He tried to rid himself of such thoughts. No one watched; there were neither police nor guardsmen nearby. Their situation might be desperate, but it wasn't hopeless. They were together. Equally important, they were heading for the interior. Anibal could not have wished for more had he planned it.

Ellen stumbled on the narrow sidewalk, but caught herself before she fell. She was a woman of substance, Anibal thought, like Bettina. He hoped Gil knew how rare a person she was. He doubted it.

A piece of paper fluttered across the empty square. Beyond, by the Villa Mella Bridge, soldiers. He should have realized it would be guarded, Anibal told himself.

Gil and Ellen were staring at him, as if he were responsible for the guards' presence. Quickly he realized his friends were not accusing him; it was fatigue they displayed. There was a mouse under Ellen's left eye. She kept fingering her throat, as if something was wrong with it. Gil, too, had been worked over. They needed someone to think for them. Who, but he?

"So can we go around it?" asked Ellen, the weariness evident in her voice.

If the Villa Mella Bridge was guarded, the other bridges would be, too. And the river could not be forded. Its banks were too steep, its current too strong. He shook his head. "This is where we must cross."

He read the question in their eyes. "Not tonight. Tomorrow, by day. The bridge is always crowded. We will cross it then.''

"And tonight?" asked Gil.

It was certain they could not remain in the street until daybreak. "We have to get out of sight."

"The cemetery we passed," Gil said, finishing the thought for him.

Anibal nodded reluctantly. "Yes. We will be safe there."

"There will be a caretaker," Gil cautioned.

"What caretaker would bother us this time of night?" Anibal responded. "And what choice do we have?" He nodded at the bridge. "Which is it to be?"

"The cemetery it is," answered Ellen. She was rubbing her upper arms, as if cold. Yet the night was warm. Signs of fatigue and shock. Anibal wished they had brought blankets. The ground was liable to be damp.

"Sure, why not?" Gil agreed.

It was unanimous.

"Here," Gil whispered. The young man was straddling the fence, his hand stretched down toward them. Anibal did not move. Neither did Ellen. It was as if she shared his distaste for intruding on sanctified ground.

"Come on," Gil urged, wiggling his fingers for emphasis.

Anibal glanced up and down the street, saw nothing. "Go," he whispered to Ellen. She set her toe in a crevice in the stone post, gripped an iron pale, and boosted herself until she could reach Gil's hand. Gil steadied her as she climbed over the spiked pales, then helped lower her to the other side. She landed in some bushes, little more than an arm's length away, yet was nearly invisible.

"Anibal? Can you make it?" Gil asked.

"Yes."

Gil turned without another word and dropped beside Ellen.

Anibal was alone, his friends already out of sight. He crossed himself and began to climb, picking his footholds carefully. Thirty seconds later, he was inside.

Gil came back for him. "Let's go," he whispered.

Anibal hesitated. His idea or not, he did not relish disturbing the dead. Reluctantly, he pushed through the bushes and strode deeper into the cemetery. It was too dark to make anything out clearly: a suggestion of funerary forms, black against black, hard and cold to the touch. A winged insect kept fluttering near Anibal's ear. Then it brushed against his temple.

Gil was waiting for him to catch up. "Who watches over cemeteries?" the young man whispered.

Anibal's first response was anger. He relented; there was no malicious intent in Gil's question. "The Baron Samedi," he answered.

"So can't you appease the baron with a sacrifice? We'll get you a couple of chickens or whatever you need."

Gil was like a child who whistled as he passed a graveyard, Anibal concluded. "It's not me I'm worried about," he responded.

"What do you mean?"

"It's you two," Anibal told him. "The baron, after all, is *rada*, not *petra*."

"I don't know anything about that stuff," Gil responded. His bantering tone gone.

"He accepts only the flesh of white- or red-colored animals. As long as I'm with you, the Baron Samedi will pay me no attention whatsoever." He smiled and selected a spot next to a marble stela. Let his white friend chew on *that* for a while.

* * *

A mist limited Ellen's vision to a few hundred feet. At least it hadn't rained. A dove cooed, its call soft and sad: a migratory bird, separated from others of its kind. She passed a family plot enclosed by a low fence, as if the rules of cast which governed its inhabitants in life remained valid for the next world, too. The stones looked cold to the touch. Dew had collected on the fence—the cold sweat of the graveyard.

The reflection made her shiver all the more. She rubbed her bare arms, felt the goose pimples. Gil was sleeping, curled into a tight ball, but Anibal was gone when she waked. She hoped he would return soon. Sunrise was upon them and would burn away the morning mist. They should be out of the cemetery by then.

She looked down at Gil. He was a strange man, more like a clumsy puppy than a secret agent. The American manner: no subtlety, all energy. Still, if all that was wanted was proof of conspiracy, his methods were effective enough. Hard on the agents, though. She smiled. Gil lacked guile. She liked that. One always knew where one stood with him.

She winced as she knelt, still stiff from her hours on the damp ground. "Come on, tiger," she whispered, shaking him, "time to get up."

He twitched, paused, twitched again, emitted a series of snorts, like a locomotive starting up. Suddenly he sat up, eyes wide.

"Anibal's not here," she said.

"Where'd he go?" Gil rubbed his chin and looked around.

Ellen could hear the scrape of his whiskers, assessed the purpose of his staring. "Try the bushes," she said, then, "I don't know. He wasn't here when I waked."

Gil groaned as he pushed himself up and walked off. He was as stiff as she, Ellen thought. They had both taken a beating last night. The bruise under her eye was still tender, and her throat was sore, if not unbearably so.

What chance had they to escape? The futility of even trying suddenly overwhelmed her. By now, every policeman in the country would have been alerted. They would have to evade Trujillo's entire army. And all they had for help was an old woman of uncertain qualities who was probably senile. What indication had she that Anibal was any better a judge of character than Gil?

She heard her stomach gurgle, pressed her hands against it to try to suppress her appetite. That she could feel hunger helped lift her spirits. *One thing at a time,* her body seemed to be telling her. *Don't think too far ahead.* They had evaded their pursuers thus far. They would continue to do so.

The whisper of footsteps on damp grass broke her concentration. Ellen turned, saw Anibal. He held a bundle under his arm. "Where were you?" she asked.

He didn't respond, but looked at where Gil had been sleeping.

"In the bushes," she said.

He nodded, dropped the bundle and sorted through it. "Clothes," he said, handing them over. "We should disguise ourselves."

Ellen unfolded the articles: a poncho of rough wool and some cotton trousers. The trousers were large enough that both her legs would almost fit into one of its legs, with a waist to match. It had holes punched around the waist in place of belt loops. She leaned against a headstone, rolled up her slacks, and pulled the trousers over them, then stood again, pressing her elbows against the trousers to hold them up.

"Here," said Anibal. He held out a length of hemp.

She wove the rope in and out of the holes, then tied it in front. *One thing,* she thought, *they certainly hide my figure.* The poncho had a damp, pungent odor. She wrinkled her nose as she slipped it over her head, then stretched out her arms and pivoted around. "How do I look?" she asked.

Anibal grinned broadly. "You'll do," he conceded, then handed her a final article—a sombrero, woven from palmetto leaves. She put it on, stood still, awaiting his appraisal.

"Très chic, madame," he said, then cautioned, "Remember to keep your head low when you pass the soldiers."

She agreed, turned, and saw Gil returning. The mist had already lightened. Ellen sat back while Anibal repeated his instructions and handed him his new clothes.

"Eh bien, mes amis," Anibal said. "Soon, laborers will be crossing the bridge. Then is our best chance to slip by. We must break up, move singly. If one gets caught, that person is on his own, is that agreed?"

It seemed to Ellen that the last remark had been directed primarily to her. She nodded.

"Anibal's lifted our clothing from close by," Gil added. "Let's scram before the owners start screaming about it."

Men and women trudged toward the bridge in small groups. They walked silently, displaying no animation. There were not as many as Ellen had hoped. *So much for getting lost in a crowd,* she told herself. One hundred yards ahead, three uniformed officials stood on the bridge. They seemed to be carefully scrutinizing those leaving town. Gil was somewhere in front of her. He would be the first to encounter the guards. The realization made Ellen happy to be behind him. She lowered her head again and edged closer to a small group, trying to keep it between her and the officials.

The mist had turned to a fine drizzle. All the more justification for hunching down and walking with head lowered. Gil should be at the bridge now, she thought, and listened for shouts of discovery. What would she do if they came? Could she continue on or would she lose her nerve and try to backtrack? She tried to ignore her fears. It did not work. The tension mounted with each shuffling step.

Seconds passed. By now, Gil would have passed the guards. He had got through. Anger competed with relief. They should have let her go first. She lowered her head still more and moved on. It was not fair.

The bump would have knocked her sombrero off had she not reached up to hold it.

"¡Ea!" The voice was sharp, gruff.

She lifted her eyes and stared at a polished belt buckle. She dared not look any higher. She had run into a soldier. On his right boot, she saw the gritty tread of her tennis shoe. He had moved to the middle of the bridge; she had not noticed it. "¡Ay! Sargento," she wailed. "Dispensa—"

Her apology was cut short by a push from the rear. She was holding up traffic. "¡Anda!" the guard shouted and swatted her on the back.

Ellen stumbled and might have fallen but for the man in front of her. She grabbed the back of his poncho for balance. Fortunately, the other said nothing and kept walking. She snuck a peek behind her. The sergeant was paying her no further attention. Ellen felt elated, almost dizzy.

"The next time we tell you not to attract attention, think of another way to go about it," said a low voice from in front of her.

Ellen looked up, startled, realized she was staring at Gil's back. She knew what had happened. He had deliberately slowed to be of help in case she needed it. He was limping. She wondered whether she might have taken skin from his heel when she had stepped on it.

"It makes no difference. We all made it," came a voice from behind.

She turned back. Anibal was immediately behind her, grinning. All the warnings about being on their own, not helping in case of trouble: idle chatter; neither had meant it. Both had worked their way close to her, to help should it have been necessary. The realization warmed her.

CHAPTER 7

It wasn't like other structures they had passed. Most had seemed jerry-built, made from materials near at hand. This was of quarried stone and had a tin roof, painted red. There was a courtyard surrounded by a wall high enough to ensure privacy. It looked, Ellen thought, like a government official's villa. The observation made her hesitate.

She felt better when she peered through the rusty iron gate into the courtyard. Trees—*lignum vitae* with shiny, dark leaves—needed trimming badly; ferns seemed to grow wild; weeds poked everywhere through their yellowed and frayed fronds. Most assuredly, it was not the residence of anyone in the government.

"I don't think anyone's set foot in there for ten years," she ventured.

"It looked like that ten years ago, too," Gil told her. "The old lady never was much for tidiness." He set his hand on the gate, turned to Anibal, who nodded. Gil pushed it open. For all its rust, its hinges were well oiled.

Ellen followed. They passed through the courtyard, then onto the shadowed patio. There was a large brass knocker on the door. Gil banged it three times. The hollow echo from within sounded ominous to Ellen, like Black Rod's rapping on the door of Commons. She looked in a window next to the door, but the drapes were pulled tight.

Gil tried the door. It swung inward. He did not seem surprised. His gaze swept from Anibal to her. "Come on," he said, then stepped inside.

There was a large room beyond the foyer. The sheets covering the furniture might once have been white; now, they appeared uniformly gray. Here and there, Ellen saw droppings; bat guano, by the look of it. "Pay no attention," Anibal advised. "The old woman rarely set foot in there. Claimed it was possessed by devils."

Devils? To whom had they entrusted their lives? Anibal and Gil set off down the hall to the right. Ellen remained behind. Slowly, she turned back to the large room. Something about it drew her toward it. She stepped inside.

It was darker than the foyer. What light it had took on the maroon hue of its drapes. The room felt like a Victorian parlor. She half expected velvet lampshades with maroon tassels, and starched lace antimacassars on the chairs under the sheets. A noise: a door slamming shut; Gil and Anibal searching the other wing.

They would find nothing. If Madam Gamba remained in the house, she was here. Ellen knew it. A human warmth hung in the air. She passed through an archway, entered what was once a dining room. The table, the chairs around it, and the sideboard were also shrouded.

On the sideboard stood a silver samovar, highly polished. The backs of the tabled chairs thrust the covering sheet up in eight peaks, like a snow-covered mountain range.

Ellen went on. A heavy, swinging door separated dining room from kitchen. She pushed it open. It swung quietly and smoothly. The kitchen was clean, but empty. There remained a low door on the far side of the kitchen. It led, she imagined, to the pantry. She hesitated, listening. Wherever Gil and Anibal were, they had passed out of earshot.

She pushed open the low door. The first slivered view revealed a candle burning on a table. Its smell of paraffin struck her.

"Hello, my dear," said a voice from inside. "You may enter."

Ellen stood, frozen into immobility. A comic song sung by a gravelly voiced American came to mind: *Have you ever had the feeling that you wanted to stay and the feeling that you wanted to go?* She opened the door more widely. The room was small, with a sloping ceiling.

"Yes," agreed the voice from within, "come in." The imperative was overlaid by a tone of civility. Ellen obeyed.

A small, wooden table and two wooden chairs. A woman sat on one; the other was empty. A mattress was crammed into the far side of the room where the ceiling sloped down toward the floor.

"Madam Gamba?" she asked.

The woman did not respond. The candlelight revealed deeply wrinkled skin. Shadows and embedded dirt made the lines seem deeper than they probably were. Still, she looked ancient, like some wizened matriarch of a long-forgotten tribe. Whether she was white or black was impossible to say.

At last, the woman nodded. "Yes, I am she," she said. The phrase revealed a trace of an accent, from somewhere in Southeastern or Eastern Europe. She motioned Ellen to the empty chair.

Ellen sat and returned the woman's gaze. The eyes which stared back were dark and alert, seemed filled with humor. The tight ringlets which poked from under her gray felt cloche were jet-black and shiny. Ellen waited, but the other said nothing, as if content to watch in silence.

The quiet unnerved Ellen. "My friends and I have come—" she began.

"I know why you've come." The woman leaned forward, her face close to the candle. There was a clicking sound, as if someone had brushed through a beaded curtain. It took a second before Ellen discovered its source. A dozen or more necklaces were strung around the old woman's neck. They cascaded down her bosom and then hung suspended in the air. The beads clicked as she moved. The space between the bosomy overhang and dangling strands reminded Ellen of a secret cave behind a waterfall. "You are here because you need help," the woman concluded.

Ellen would have preferred to be spared the fortune teller's cliché. Madam Gamba's darting eyes cued her toward the door. She heard footsteps. She turned and saw Gil stooping in the doorway.

His eyes swept the room, then locked in on Ellen. "We weren't sure where you'd gone off to," he said, before looking back to the old woman. "*Buenos días*, madam."

The woman showed no surprise. She acknowledged the greeting with a nod. "Señor Brant," she said, "Is Monsieur Dieudonné with you?"

How had the old woman recalled their names so readily, Ellen wondered.

"Here I am," said Anibal, entering the room. "You are staying in a different room than before."

"This is smaller," she said, "closer in size to my coffin."

Ellen could not hold back a smile; the old woman noticed and returned it, as if they shared a private joke. "Please," the woman continued, with a sweep of her arm. "Come in, sit. Anywhere."

More easily said than done, Ellen thought. But the gesture had been majestic. The old woman seemed not only impervious to the room's ratty appointments, but lost in times when her surroundings would have been equal to the invitation.

Whatever, it was Gil's and Anibal's task to obey. Anibal tugged the pallet out from the corner until he had headroom, then sank down, crossing his legs. Gil joined him, shouldering his friend off center to claim a share of the mattress. Gil had to bend his head to the side to avoid bumping against the ceiling. It gave him the appearance of having a broken neck.

"I was just telling your companion I know why you have come." She paused and let her eyes travel over her visitors. "You are wanted by the police," she said.

Gil and Anibal smiled. "We were *always* wanted by the police," Gil reminded her.

"This is worse than before," the old woman said. "Then, a few dollars in the hands of the right man was all you needed. Today, you need more than my telling you who to bribe."

Ellen found herself nodding in agreement. She stopped, embarrassed at having let the old woman's tactics draw her in. Madam Gamba noticed the change and shot her a sharp glance.

It was like a teacher's rap across the knuckles. Ellen sat back.

"Tell me what has happened," said Madam Gamba.

Gil glanced at Ellen, then explained, easily and thoroughly. Ellen was glad for the reprieve: being the sole object of Madam Gamba's attention had been unnerving. "And that's it," Gil concluded, "except to say that we need your help."

"I will be glad to offer it, as always," the woman agreed.

"But . . ." Ellen blurted. Three pairs of eyes focused on her.

"Yes, my dear," Madam Gamba said. "What is it?"

The elderly woman's gaze was disconcerting. Ellen was tempted to withdraw her objection, but did not. It was as if she were compelled to continue. She picked her words carefully, rolling each one around in her mind before uttering it. "My friends are confident you can assist us," she began, then halted. No one jumped into the ensuing silence. Ellen could hear Madam Gamba breathing. "Never did they explain their reasons," she continued. "It bothers me." Ellen looked up, saw Madam Gamba nodding. She rushed on. "Why will you help us, when no one else will, when no one else could?"

"Why?" Madam Gamba repeated, as if the word was unfamiliar to her. She turned her head to the men.

"I thought it best to tell her nothing of you," Anibal volunteered.

It was as if the old woman had been told a funny joke. Her laugh showed yellowed teeth. There were molars missing on both sides of her mouth. "Forgive me," she said after a moment. "You know nothing; no wonder you looked at me so strangely." For illustration, the woman turned down her lips and furrowed her eyebrows.

Ellen felt foolish. She imagined she had looked something like that. She was also relieved. All would be explained. The old woman cleared her throat.

"What do you know of theosophy?" Madam Gamba asked.

The woman had made a mistake. It was clarification, not obfucastion, Ellen needed. She looked across the table. Madam Gamba's bright eyes were trained on her. She expected an answer.

Theosophy. Ellen knew little of it: tidbits collected from sundry sources. Half truths, she assumed; information of that sort usually was. Interest in it had been revived late last century, she recollected. A woman had led its revival. She tried to think of her name, but it wouldn't come: a foreign name. Conan Doyle, among others, had been associated with theosophy if she was not mistaken. Theosophists believed in reincarnation, and its initiates had either always possessed the secrets of the universe or somehow received them at initiation. All preached nonsense. None of what she recalled was likely to please a true believer. She shook her head. "Very little, I'm afraid," she said at last.

"You know more than you pretend, my child," the woman chided. "I can see that. In its most recent manifestation," she prompted.

"Madam Blavatsky," Ellen suddenly said. That had been the woman. She had been an American, Ellen thought, or maybe a Russian, and had gone to Tibet. Ellen pressed back into her chair. She wanted to get as far from the old woman as possible.

Madam Gamba smiled and batted her eyes. Ellen remembered dropping a tomato into the gaping mouth of a hippopotamus once at the zoo. The old woman's grin brought the hippo's smile to mind.

"Well, then. There you have it," said the other.

Have it? Have what? "I don't understand."

"There is no need to pretend, my child," the woman replied. "You do understand; I can see it in your eyes. You simply are afraid to admit it. I am Madam Blavatsky."

Ellen's eyes swiveled to her associates. Their expressions were bland, revealing nothing, no hint of how to behave. She was on her own. It took an effort to look back at the woman. "Madam Blavatsky is dead," she said.

Madam Gamba was not to be deterred. "I am Madam Blavatsky's reincarnation," she said, in a tone of finality.

"Her reincarnation?" Ellen repeated.

"Exactly." Gamba's grin grew so broad that, for one wild second, Ellen thought it had been she and not Madam who had first said it: a humble acolyte acknowledging the old woman's divinity. Again, Ellen looked at the men. Anibal's gaze had not changed; if anything, Gil looked more innocent than before.

Ellen let Madam Gamba prattle on, permitting most of the words to slide directly into her subconscious, while she tried to make sense of what she had been told thus far. Madam Blavatsky had lived at least to the end of the last century, Ellen thought. Madam Gamba was at least seventy. She could have been no younger than thirty at the time of Blavatsky's death. Transmigration, not reincarnation? She wondered if Madam Gamba had ever stopped to consider the difference. She looked again at her hostess. If so, she would believe it was our problem, not hers.

". . . We have spent our lives seeking . . ."

Ellen scrambled to make sense of the collective plural,

then concluded it referred to Blavatsky and herself—not the royal "we" so much as the divine "we."

". . . Forces of evil and darkness have banded . . ."

She wished she were an expert on theosophy. Then, she might make sense out of the claptrap. *Had Blavatsky believed all that,* Ellen wondered, *or had Gamba contributed to the lore?* ". . . and Dieudonné are masters," finished Madam Gamba. "Because you are with them, you, too, are one."

Ellen had to scramble back over what she had heard to make sense of the conclusion. When she did, it stunned her. "No, I don't think—"

"Yes!" Madam Gamba insisted. "I saw it as soon as you entered this room. It is an occasion. Never before have I gathered with three of my masters. I am so happy I could cry."

Madam Gamba had not exaggerated. There were tears welling in the corner of her eyes. "No," Ellen implored, shaking her head. "Tell me what being a master means."

"It means you can rule the universe; you have transcended sin. You stand above the law, above ordinary rules of morality."

She had it all wrong, Ellen thought. They only wanted to get out of the country. "And that is why you will help us?" Ellen managed. "Because we are masters?"

"Why else?" the old woman answered, slapping the table and shaking her bosom. The beads tinkled. She rose, then added, "I need the money too, of course." She pulled Ellen from the chair, saying, "Let us go out front."

The old woman kept her arm through Ellen's as they walked through the house, yet it was not for support. Her step was sprightly. "I am losing my powers," Gamba whispered, nodding to indicate the covered furniture in the parlor. "As I do, others take control of my house. It is why I have retreated to the back.'' She seemed to attach no importance to the revelation.

It was like trying to figure out a foreign language. One knows there is a logic to it, but, until you have been initiated, it remains hidden. ''Is it wise to leave your room then?'' she whispered in return. It was as if she had become a partner in the conspiracy. Ellen thought about it. She supposed that was what had happened. She had fallen victim to the old woman's charm.

''I must do it every day, regardless,'' the woman said. ''A lad comes with food. And, today, I must give him a message. To escape, you need a guide. The child will get him for you.''

The woman stopped. Ellen sensed she had more to say. ''What is it?'' she asked.

The grin was wide. ''You read my thoughts,'' said Madam Gamba. ''Proof you are a master. I have something to give you. Come.''

There was but one escape route, Madam Gamba insisted. All coastal paths would be watched; they must make their way overland. Not even their combined powers would save them if they chose another route. Their guide would not arrive until after sundown. In the meantime, they must wait.

It was not uncomfortably hot in the room where they sat, probably because the walls were thick and the ceiling high. Gil had parted the drapes, and light poured in through the dusty window. Ellen wondered how long it had been since sunlight had last fallen on the sheeted furniture around her. She looked outside. There was not much to see—the same tangle of weeds, ferns, and trees as before.

La Gamba had no interest in what lay outside. She sat

in a rocking chair. The chair creaked and cracked, the sun grew lower, the shadows longer. The old woman appeared to age with the passage of time. Ellen remembered that Madam Gamba had planned to give something to her, concluded she had forgotten it, and did nothing to remind her of it.

Just before sunset, Madam Gamba spoke. "Please," she croaked, gesturing with an arm as she spoke, "help me."

All three sprang to their feet. The woman dismissed the men with a glance, but accepted Ellen's assistance. "Come," she said.

As they walked down the hall to the next room, Gamba spoke. "Men. They never see the truth. It is their strength that blinds them. It makes them think they are immortal."

She sank into a chair, and said, "They are wrong, of course. We women understand immortality. We are not the future, as men with their muscles pretend, but the future comes through us. The future needs us."

The room seemed cold. Ellen wished she had a shawl for Gamba's shoulders: a lace mantilla, such as the one her grandmother in Kingston once wore. What had happened to that shawl, she wondered.

"In there," the old woman said, and pointed to a chest of drawers, "the top one."

For a second, Ellen believed the woman had located her grandmother's shawl. She had to untangle her own thoughts from Madam Gamba's. The chest drawer slid open easily. Save for a pasteboard square, it was empty. She looked back at Madam Gamba. The old woman nodded and held out her hand. Ellen took out the square.

She flipped it over. A picture of a woman, dressed in a white gown, with a crown, and bedecked in jewelry. The colors of the print were bright and garish. Hardly a work of art, Ellen noted. She nearly missed the nimbus behind the woman's head. It identified the subject: the Virgin Mary. She handed it over, wondering why the old woman wanted it. Once it was out of her grasp, though, she wanted it back. The print merited a second look.

Gamba peered at the print for a few seconds, then lifted her eyes to Ellen. "Do you recognize her?" she asked.

"Mary," Ellen responded.

"You have not seen it with the inner eye of the master," said Madam Gamba. "Look again." She held the print up.

Ellen gazed at the picture. Madam Gamba was right. The Virgin Mother would never be depicted in such worldly ornaments. There was more. She stared, unable to pinpoint what disturbed her. "Then, who?" she asked.

"It is the Maitresse Erzulie," replied Madam Gamba.

That was a voodoo goddess, Ellen knew. Without lifting her eyes from the print, she shook her head. "I have never studied voodoo," she confessed.

"But you must," Madam Gamba informed her. "Such knowledge will prove important." She halted, as if to collect her thoughts, then proceeded. "Erzulie is goddess of the waters. She is very rich and very good. Our Haitian friends see her as white. They use her to intercede with the other *loa* on their behalf.

Loa. That meant "gods," Ellen remembered. The intercession part sounded as if she and the Virgin Mother were one and the same. Ellen was tempted to make the point, but did not. It was not an argument Gamba would appreciate. Instead, she asked, "Why have you shown her to me?"

"Keep looking," the woman urged. "View her with your inner eye."

Ellen did not know what she meant, but continued to

gaze on it. The malaise of a few minutes earlier returned. One minute passed. Ellen shook her head. "I'm sorry, I see nothing," she admitted.

"You are too young," Madam Gamba replied, shaking the print for emphasis. "Look at her! She is you!"

Ellen stared. The shape and color of the eyes, the mouth, the jawline, the lift of the cheekbones—even the hair coloring—were hers. It was like looking at a crude cartoon of herself.

Her reason fought back. The print was without subtlety. It depicted a type, not a person. One woman in ten might claim a resemblance. Ellen looked back at Madam Gamba.

The old woman said softly, "Do not deny it. That you resemble the Maitresse Erzulie is no accident." She pointed to another drawer. "Now," she said, "give me what you find there."

At least, Ellen thought, as she bent to her new task, Gamba had not claimed she was the Haitian water goddess's incarnation. The omission denoted progress in their relationship, she thought. There was a small carpetbag in the drawer. It caught on the edges of the drawer as she took it out. She had to pull to free it.

Madam Gamba took it on her lap. She worked to open it, but the clasp proved stubborn. At last, she succeeded. The bag yawned open. The woman dipped in her hand. When she took it out, dozens of strands of beads dangled from her fingers. Red beads, amber beads, imitation pearls: costume jewelry.

Ellen stepped back until she was against the open drawer. She wondered what else was in the bag, feared the other would demand she don it all.

The other smiled and shook her head. "I do not expect you to wear them," she said.

It was like receiving a reprieve. Ellen relaxed.

"Not now, at least," the woman amended. She let the necklaces slip back into the bag. "Take them. You will need them."

Only if Manhattan Island was put up for sale again, Ellen thought.

"You must learn to take all religions seriously," Madam Gamba intoned. "All exist as part of a divine scheme. You, as a master, can make them work for you." She closed the bag and held it out to Ellen.

Ellen took it. She did not know what else to do.

"Promise me you will keep it with you," the old woman asked. The look in her eyes was somber.

"I promise," Ellen replied.

The eyes brightened. "Good," Gamba said. "I am glad that is over. I was afraid you might resist."

How does one resist a tidal wave, Ellen wondered. "When will I need the jewelry?" she asked.

Madam Gamba held her hand out, indicating she wished to be helped from her chair. Ellen obeyed. "You are a master, my dear," the woman replied once she was on her feet. "When the time comes, you will know."

The guide was a small man with nervous eyes named Fabrizio. Ellen disliked him as soon as they were introduced. She told herself Madam Gamba had vouched for him; anyone who dared smuggle through wanted people was not likely to be an upright citizen. Her arguments lessened, but did not eliminate, her suspicions.

Speed was all important, Fabrizio said; they must travel lightly; food and water could be found along the way.

"How long will it take?" Ellen asked. She was thinking of carrying the carpetbag over the hills of Hispaniola.

"No less than ten days, señora," Fabrizio responded, "and possibly as long as three weeks."

That did it! She would ditch the bag as soon as they left the house.

Madam Gamba touched her on the forearm, and whispered, "You will need it. I guarantee it."

Ellen nodded.

It was nearly midnight before Fabrizio would let them leave. At the door, Anibal gave the old woman some money. He did it unobtrusively, as a restaurant-goer might slip a gratuity to a headwaiter. She took it coolly and slid it into her blouse without disturbing a bead.

La Gamba said to them, "Good luck. Remember, you have enemies everywhere. Trust no one. As for your boat, I will see that it gets to Port-au-Prince." She turned and disappeared into the house.

How had Madam Gamba known about the *Stardust*? As they filed through the gate, Ellen searched her memory. She had been with the old woman all evening. Neither Gil nor Anibal had mentioned the boat. Previous suspicions returned, festered. Madam Gamba was the same as Pombal in certain respects. Both dealt with the underworld; both profited from acquiring knowledge. She shook herself. The old woman might be crazy, but she was trustworthy. Ellen was certain of it.

She turned to Anibal, walking beside her. "What did she mean about you and Gil being masters?" she asked.

She could not make out the look on her friend's face, but he sounded embarrassed. "She believes all that, you know," he answered.

"But she thinks you do, too. Why?"

"Oh, Gil once told her we did."

"Why would he have done that?"

Anibal's embarrassment seemed to grow. "I'm not sure," he replied. "He thought it would make her happy, I think."

"And she accepted it?"

"Gil's a little strange, sometimes."

Ellen nodded grimly, and said, "She's really something, isn't she?"

"What was it you called her before you met her?" Anibal asked.

She had to think back. *A dance instructor,* it had been. "I can't remember," Ellen said. She lifted the carpetbag, testing its weight. It was not so heavy, not really.

CHAPTER 8

"**T**ell us again, general," Maria said, her words heavy with sarcasm, "how you lured them into the back country."

"It is true," Rosario admitted. "It did not go as planned. The switchboard operator reports a call to the woman's room only minutes before the attack. A man's voice, we were told. It was that which let her get away."

"A warning?" Maria queried. "Who could have given it?"

Rosario avoided glancing at Andre. "Few knew of it," he continued. "No one outside this room knew why I ordered it. Still, it happened."

"Perhaps one of your men is a British agent," Andre said.

Maria could not have reacted more quickly had she had an electric shock. She turned to Andre, saw defiance in his eyes, as if he were daring Rosario to voice his suspicions. It was an admission of guilt, Maria concluded, as convincing as a signed confession.

"Perhaps you are right," Rosario said in a tight voice.

Maria knew what the tightness meant. The general felt trapped in a position from which there was no exit. He was bound to follow Andre, however wrong he believed him. She shared the feeling. "Go on with your story," she told the Latin.

"There's no more to tell," he said. "She got away. Obviously, she made her way to their boat. Together with the Haitian, she freed the American. Bad luck, but we have taken steps—"

Maria turned her back on the both of them and peered out the window. It was raining. The city resembled its namesake himself: grander in conception than in reality. That was squalid, dirty. She sipped her champagne and grimaced. It was warm and flat. Why had Andre warned the Englishwoman? Women were not important to him. Certainly, Maria added, she wasn't. Necessary—essential, even—as a partner, but, as a woman, not important.

She tried to envisage the other woman, but no concrete image came to mind. That she would be beautiful was a certainty—Andre was incapable of being attracted to anyone other men would not deem desirable. It was the rest of it which mattered. Men like Andre picked women to love in the same way they picked dogs or horses. Breeding and bearing, pedigrees—outward signs of superiority—those were what mattered.

Did it matter why he had done it? Maria emptied her glass on a potted plant. Could plants get drunk? How could they? They had no brains. Like some men she knew.

She turned back to the room. "The American and his

associates are being watched," she said, "you are sure of that."

Rosario nodded. "Their guide is one of ours. He—"

"How did they find this guide?" Maria asked, interrupting.

"Through another of their former associates. An old woman."

"Is she one of yours, too?" Maria queried.

The general smiled. "Hardly. She's a crazy old gypsy." He waited, as if for more questions, then continued, "The guide will keep us informed of their whereabouts. When the moment is right, they will be eliminated. They've escaped, but this may work out better than we planned."

"Oh?" Maria thrust her glass at Andre, demanding he refill it. He unwound his legs, stood, and went to the table. "How?"

"They will be far from any American or British officials," Rosario answered. "There will be no one to ask any questions. It buys us time."

The answer did not make Maria feel better. A botch remained a botch, no matter how much one rationalized it. Only after she knew they had been eliminated would she relax. "There will be no second blunder," she told Rosario.

He nodded emphatically. "There cannot be. Police and military units will always know their whereabouts. Give us a week, perhaps a little longer. They will be killed, their bodies never found."

It was Maria's turn to nod. Suddenly she wanted to close her eyes and sleep. Perhaps, when she woke, all would be over. The admission of weakness frightened her. She shoved it aside and turned back to Andre. "What about you?" she asked. "Have you anything to add?"

The muscles in his jaw tightened, his eyes darkened.

Maria interpreted it as a warning. This remained his show; they were but paid subalterns. "It is as the general states: unfortunate, but we can turn it to our advantage. I am confident his men will accomplish the deed next time. In the meantime, we cannot let this sideshow interfere with our main task. There is still much to do."

Rosario looked as if he might disagree. "We are all in this," the Frenchman continued, his words heavy as lead. "None of us can back out."

Maria looked at Rosario, who refused to return her gaze. In a contest of machismo, she thought, the general had come out second best. In the silence, she heard autos passing by outside: the sizzle of tires on the wet street; occasionally, a horn honking.

"Good," Andre said at last. "We go forward." He swung his body to face Rosario directly. "General," he said, "Maria and I have more business to discuss."

Rosario rose, bowed to Maria, said, "In that case, I will leave." As he walked toward the door, his back was straighter than ever. Andre had made an enemy, Maria told herself.

After the door closed, Maria waited for a moment. "Why?" she then blurted.

"Why what?" Andre responded.

"The Englishwoman. Why did you warn her? You have endangered us all."

Andre's eyes blazed, then softened. He got up, came to her side, and gently stroked her arm. "It is not easy to run an operation like this," he purred. "There are facets you cannot see. This is one of them. It was important that the woman be permitted to live. Believe me."

How stupid did he think her? He still loved the woman, or believed he did. For a man like Andre, that might be all he was capable of. The conviction that he lied ran against the realization that she wanted to believe him, no matter how ludicrous his story. And that was the difference between them, Maria thought. He used her and probably would always use her; she loved him. Her love bound her to him as tightly as if they were shackled together. If love could persuade her to accept what was false and wrong, what good was it? It would turn her into something less than what she was. The conclusion made her feel grimy. Slowly, she nodded, a single lift and drop of her head.

The Frenchman smiled. "That is better. Now, how to permit our ship to remain inside the canal for a few days—you promised you would work on that problem. Have you found the answer?"

He had won and he knew it, Maria saw. Continuing on as if nothing had happened was his way of evincing dominance. Did she have the energy to contest it? Let him have his way. "There is a road-building project—the Pan American Highway—sponsored by the Americans," she answered. "Construction engineers are working on it in Panama. I can get a contract to carry blasting explosives to the work crews. We will contract to unload them at Gamboa; it is an old railhead inside the Canal Zone. The process will give you an excuse to remain within the Canal Zone for a few days."

"And if we need to stay longer than that?"

"When you enter the canal, you will inform the authorities at Colon that you intend to exit there. Since they will not know how much time it will take you to unload, and since your ship will not be tracked through the canal, you probably can delay your exit for a while longer." It was a recital of facts, reeled off without interest.

"Excellent," he said, smiling. "How much TNT does the Pan American crew need?"

"They are only surveying crews. Six tons, that is all.
And dynamite, not TNT. That you must carry under a
false manifest. All I have found is a reason for you to stay
inside the canal for a little while."

"No matter," Andre said. "You have done well." He
took her by the shoulders, pulled her close to him.

Maria accepted the embrace without enthusiasm. He
must have sensed her indifference, for he tightened his
grip, forced her body to meld more closely to his. Maria
closed her eyes, shut out the sight of Ciudad Trujillo and
imagined a view of Paris outside her window. It was for
that that she had agreed to help. That, and Andre himself.
She felt his strong hands along her flank, tracing her outline. She shuddered at the contact. *How bad a bargain
had she made?*

CHAPTER 9

October, 1941

Gil was suffocating. His ears throbbed. Everyone around him—his agent, the manager of the studio commissary—seemed all right; only he was afflicted. He opened his eyes. It was pitch-black. Someone's hand was cupped lightly over his mouth.

"Ssh," Anibal hissed, removing his hand.

He nodded to indicate he understood, then waited, breathing deeply, taking in the scene around them. The moon shone through the trees, speckling the forest floor with its glow. The effect was delicate, almost magical, like the filigreed silver earrings he had once purchased for Mona. She had thrown them in a drawer and had forgotten them, he remembered.

He sat up and tried to rub the stiffness from his neck. Sleeping on the ground had its drawbacks. Ellen stood behind Anibal. Fabrizio was not with them. He peered at the spot where their guide had been sleeping. He was not there, either. He turned back to Anibal.

The Haitian nodded. "He's gone," he confirmed. "Listen."

The air was filled with the sound of insects. Underlying the cacophony was something that sounded like water dripping into a tin cup. Gil concentrated. "A drum," he said. He had heard it in his dreams.

"Yes," Anibal agreed. "A *bula*."

Gil was tempted to ask what half a Yale man was doing in the Dominican forest, but skipped it. "What is that?"

"A voodoo drum. It is the first to be played. It wakes the gods."

That meant, Gil assumed, there was a Haitian encampment nearby. It was not good news. Where there were Haitians, there sometimes were soldiers. The government liked to keep its eye on foreign workers. After ten days of racing across sugar fields in the plains, of moving from one hiding place to another, he had hoped they might relax once they had hit the forest. He groaned and pushed himself to a full sitting position. "You're the expert, Anibal. Shall we get out of here?"

"It would be wise," Anibal agreed. "After . . ." He paused, listening.

A night bird of some sort, or perhaps a fruit bat, Gil thought. He did not like Anibal's qualification and looked at Ellen. She showed no surprise or puzzlement. She and Anibal had talked before they had waked him, he realized. They had already agreed and were ganging up on him, like they used to do on the boat. He came back to Anibal. "After what?"

"After we visit the encampment."

Had a screw worked loose somewhere in Anibal's head?

Running for their lives sounded like a better idea. "Why?" he asked.

"We could use some food," Anibal reminded him. "They might have some to sell. And we can't leave without Fabrizio. Maybe he went there."

The guide had proved a bust. As far as Gil was concerned, the Haitians could keep him. The food, though, that was different. It would be harder to find in the forest. He sighed. "You go along with this, Ellen?"

"Yes," she said.

"Hell," Gil said as he got up, "then I guess we'd better get started."

"Our gear?" Anibal asked.

"Leave it," Gil replied. "That way Fabrizio will know we've not gone off and left him."

They had come to a clearing. There were some lean-tos in front of them, the nearest hardly twenty feet away. None seemed occupied. Not surprising, Gil thought, in view of the din. The drum still played, its tattoo even harder on his ears from up close. There was a bonfire. Beyond it, a group of Haitians crowded around a large, open building. Moonlight washed away the colors on the top end of the spectrum, giving purple and blue hues to everything he saw.

"That is the *tonnelle*," Anibal whispered, pointing toward the large structure. "It is where the drums are."

Drums? Gil had heard only one.

"Seen enough?" Anibal asked.

No, Gil thought, he damned well hadn't. How did they know what kind of reception they would get? Anibal might not have to worry, but what about him and Ellen? "Think it's safe?"

Anibal nodded. "It's a voodoo ceremony," he explained. "What they're doing is no different from any other kind of religious ceremony."

Gil wanted to reply that he'd been to some pretty wild revivals in his time, but choked it back. "Maybe," he conceded. "Still, I'd feel better if Ellen stays here."

"I go with you," she protested.

"Make up your minds," Anibal said. "One way or another, we have to decide before the ceremony really begins."

"Ellen stays here," Gil insisted.

"It might not be a bad idea," Anibal agreed. "Sometimes women are not welcome."

"But—" Ellen began. She stopped.

It surprised Gil. It wasn't like Ellen to give in so easily. "We'll go in," he said. "If everything's all right, we'll come back for you."

"And if it isn't?" she asked, her face screwed up in an attitude of pugnacious defiance.

"If it's not, wait twenty minutes, then come in and rescue us." His attempt to be lighthearted fell flat. "Don't worry," he resumed. "Like Anibal says, it's probably only a weekly meeting of the elders." Anibal began walking. Gil got up before she could argue more. "We'll be okay," he said, starting after Anibal.

They threaded their way around the lean-tos and headed toward the *tonnelle*. A dog barked. Some Haitians turned. Gil slowed, only to quicken his pace again, lest he fall too far behind Anibal. The people did not seem menacing or overtly hostile, although Gil spotted no smiles of welcome. Wary, that would be a more apt description of their reaction.

Anibal waded into the crowd without hesitating. For the most part, the people parted easily enough. Anibal continued on, shouldering his way past those who did not. The drumming stopped. The dog, hanging close to Gil's leg, still yapped. A man lashed out with a foot. The dog yelped and slunk off.

They came to the *tonnelle*. The ground inside was decorated with corn meal markings, like a surrealistic infield. A young man sat with a small drum wedged between his thighs. Two others, the headman and one Gil assumed was the *hungan*, stood in the center. Anibal touched Gil on the arm. "Stay here," he whispered.

Gil turned. The mass of bodies through which they had passed had closed ranks again. Where did Anibal think he might go?

Ellen watched Gil and Anibal enter the crowd, but soon lost sight of them. They should not have left her behind. She had a right to share whatever difficulties they might find. It had been all Gil's doing; Anibal had had no objections to her coming. The anger was not strong enough to dispel another feeling. It was a sense of danger. And it was danger directed toward her friends, not herself. She rose, turned her back to the settlement, and started for their encampment. She picked up her pace and began to run. The bag.

Anibal rejoined Gil. "They're really pissed, aren't they?" Gil said, looking at the sea of faces around them.

"Seasonal laborers heading home," he said.

Gil saw the hard look in his friend's eyes, assumed Anibal was remembering his wife and son caught in a similar situation. "And?" he prompted.

"And their money's been stolen."

To be as poor as they, to work all season, only to have their wages stolen—it could mean starvation. "How?" Gil asked.

"Soldiers. They met them two days ago."

The response confirmed Gil's earlier fears. Whatever had happened, he thought, it made little sense to stay any longer than was necessary. "Fabrizio?" he asked.

Anibal shook his head. "They've seen no one, other than the troopers who robbed them."

Gil was going to ask about food, but thought better of it. Why complicate the issue? It would be best to get as far away as possible, as fast as possible. "Come on, let's get out of here," he told Anibal, turning to leave.

The people stood unmoving, shoulder to shoulder. Gil had a sinking feeling in his stomach. A decision had been made for them. "They're not going to let us go, are they?" he said.

"That's right," his friend agreed. "The headman fears we're with the soldiers and that we might lead them back now that they've been found again."

Gil felt his pulse speed up. "But we can't stay." Anibal offered no reply. "And what about them?" Gil continued, nodding at the Haitians. "What happens if the army finds them harboring us? Robbery will be the least of their worries."

"If the soldiers return, we'll all be killed," Anibal agreed. "But I don't know that we've a choice."

He was right, Gil conceded. "How long must we stay?"

"Until their ceremony is finished. The headman says they have angered a *loa*. They must identify him and pacify him before they move on."

That didn't sound so bad. "How long will it take?" Gil asked.

Anibal blinked. "It might take two days; even longer."

Two days? A lifetime. Literally. Gil struggled to appear calm. "Anything we can do to change their minds?" he asked, without much confidence. "We've got money. We can offer them some."

Anibal's head shake told the story. No dice.

"So what do we do?" asked Gil.

"That decision's been made for us. The question is: What about Ellen?"

Anibal was right. What about her?

Give them twenty minutes, Gil had said. Almost twice that had passed. Ellen sat, still staring across the clearing. The crowd of Haitians did not seem hostile.

That meant nothing, she reminded herself. They did not seem in a festive mood, either. And the drum was beating again. The ceremony had resumed. Obviously, Gil and Anibal had been unable to conduct their business and leave. If everything was all right, they would have sent for her; at the least, they would have got word to her. Since they had not, she concluded, they were in trouble.

But what to do about it? The drum's beat provided a rhythm for her thoughts. The *bula*, Anibal had called it. Its function was to alert the *loa* to an impending ceremony, something like an engraved invitation.

She stood up and opened the carpetbag. *I will need the bag*. Madam Gamba had promised. *And I will know when the time has come to use what it holds*. She had said that, too. Ellen pulled out the necklaces and set them on the ground. There was something under them. A garment. She pulled it free. She stood, shook it, and held it at arm's length. A white dress, one such as she had never laid eyes on outside a museum.

It had a flounce that angled down and around the skirt. Like a curtain ruffle, she thought. Puffed sleeves, with a pair of elbow-length white gloves pinned to one of them.

Hurriedly, she took off her slacks and blouse, then settled the dress over her head and pulled it down, straightening it at the waist, adjusting it elsewhere. The dress was loose at the bosom. Nothing could be done to correct that, short of stuffing the carpetbag in there, she decided.

The dress smelled of camphor. It made her want to sneeze. Ellen put on the necklaces, then the bracelets. She was done. She held out her skirt, trying to estimate what impact she would make. She was still wearing her tennis shoes, she saw. It was those or go barefoot. Ellen shook the skirt, then set out along the path Gil and Anibal had taken. If feeling a damned fool was a test of being a master, she decided, then she was one, no doubt.

Tonight, she thought, the *bula* was summoning one *loa* the Haitians might not have expected.

CHAPTER 10

The Haitians around her were whispering among themselves, half curious, half shy. Some mouthed Maitresse Erzulie's name. It didn't make Ellen feel any less a fool. She stopped in their midst, at a loss what to do next. Anibal and Gil remained inside the *tonnelle*. At least they looked unhurt.

A child stepped up, gathered a fistful of Ellen's skirt, and drew it out. The act evoked murmurs. From behind her, Ellen heard a woman's voice: "Emmaline, *arrête-toi!*" The child dropped the skirt and backed off, her large, round eyes still fixed on Ellen. Those eyes seemed to act as a conduit, drawing Ellen back to Jamaica. For an instant, the girl became Sara. Ellen tried to reorient herself, but only partially succeeded. It was as if she were a sleepwalker suddenly waked in a foreign environment, without the least notion of where she was or what she was doing.

She peered toward her friends, silently appealing for help. *I've come this far,* she tried to tell them. *The least you can do is help me the rest of the way.*

At last, Gil made his way toward her. She took two quick steps and reached for his outstretched hand. "Come to the prom alone?" he said, smiling.

The remark seemed to snap her back to reality. " 'Twenty minutes,' you told me; it's been almost an hour."

They worked their way back to the *tonnelle*. Anibal was conversing with two men—the headman and the priest, Gil informed her. Now and then, one would glance soberly her way, only to break off as soon as he knew she was aware of it. She moved half a step closer to Gil. "What's happening?" she asked.

He pressed her arm. "Damned if I know."

He was referring to Anibal's discussion with the men. It was not what she meant. And Gil knew it, she thought. His evasiveness frightened her. "I mean, are we in trouble?" she asked.

"Not really—" he began, then stopped. Anibal was returning. One glance at the two of them answered her question: There was trouble, no matter what Gil had been about to say. And, obviously, she had done nothing to alleviate it. So much for being a master.

"Is it that bad?" she asked when Anibal was close enough for conversation.

"It is not bad at all," Anibal said, looking at her, then at Gil. "The headman and his *hungan* have accepted you."

She didn't believe him. Anibal was tense; he seemed worried. "Then what is wrong?" she asked.

"What did they decide?" Gil asked at the same time.

Anibal spoke softly. "Take your arm from Ellen's elbow."

Gil's hand dropped. The loss of contact made Ellen all the more aware of herself. She peered down at her skirt and realized how silly she looked. She wanted to tear the dress off.

Anibal said, "One cannot approach the Maitresse Erzulie except with reverence."

It had worked, Ellen thought.

"You mean they bought it?" Gil asked. "They think she's a goddess? Erzulie, or whatever's her name?" His skepticism irritated Ellen.

A little smile broke across Anibal's lips, despite his tension. "These people don't think that way," he explained. "I've been assuring the *hungan* that this"—he paused and let his eyes run up and down Ellen's costume—"is not ordinary behavior for her. He agrees—"

"That's because he doesn't know her like we do," Gil said.

"You're only angry because I'm a better actor than you," Ellen suggested.

"The headman agreed with me," Anibal resumed. "As a matter of fact . . ." He paused.

"As a matter of fact, what?" Ellen asked.

"As a matter of fact," Anibal went on, "he said anyone would have to be crazy to walk through the forest dressed as you were." He paused again and glanced back at the headman and *hungan*. Ellen's eyes followed his. The pair were silent, seemed to be staring expectantly.

Anibal's gaze returned to her. "There is more—your look when you gazed at the child. Everyone saw it. 'There was love in her eyes, and the look was genuine'—his words. 'A soul with eyes like hers must be possessed by the Maitresse Erzulie,' that was what he told me."

Ellen thought back to that moment. There had been a feeling of loss of stamina, as if, in a second, it had all been flushed from her system. Something else had replaced it for an instant. What had it been? Nothing, she told herself: Only the recollection of her daughter, so real that, had she dared, she believed she could have reached out and touched her. So she had not needed Madam Gamba's costume to convince the assembly? Or had she? Was it possible the gown had triggered the response? If so, it would—

"The Maitresse Erzulie's presence is a good sign," Anibal said, returning her to the present. "You have been invited to remain during the ceremony."

"So what's changed?" Gil asked. "We still have to stay."

Ellen did not understand his remark and looked to him for enlightenment. She didn't get it.

"That is true," Anibal said, "but we must stay only for tonight. We can leave tomorrow as early as we want. And the headman trusts us. That's a change," he added, to Ellen. "In the meantime, we've been invited to share their food. Are either of you interested?"

The drumbeat was deep and hollow. Ellen felt it in her stomach. She leaned forward, asked Anibal, "And what is that one?"

"The *manman*," he explained. "It is that which stirs up the *loa*."

She could see why. It had already riled her up. All three drums were being beaten furiously: the *bula*, the *seconde*, and now this, the *manman*. They were accompanied by a man who played what looked like two short pieces torn from an automobile spring. A fifth musician shook a pair of dried gourds. No brass, strings, or woodwinds, Ellen thought, but a great rhythm section. She noticed little evidence of sorrow, and no symbols of guilt, such as she would expect in a ceremony of expiation. Instead, what was going on had all the trappings of a Mardi Gras celebration. .

"Ellen?"

Gil's voice. She leaned toward him, got a whiff of stale sweat and dirt. "What?" she asked, raising her voice above the sound of the drums.

"I've been thinking of what happened in Ciudad Trujillo."

In all this noise? Maybe he needed noise to think; maybe that explained why he hadn't done any before. "Yes?"

"About my conversation with Pombal."

She waited.

He was silent until a particularly fervent improvisation on the *manman* had ended. "Do you know the first thing Pombal asked?"

Ellen shook her head.

"If I still worked for Eric Gainsley."

She knew the name. Everyone in Jamaica did. She lifted an eyebrow.

"I keep going back to that," Gil went on. "Why would he have asked? He knew we'd stopped smuggling with the end of Prohibition."

She saw his point. "You think Gainsley might be involved in this and Pombal knew it?"

Gil's nod was emphatic. "What do you know about Gainsley?"

She glanced at the celebrants. Some were swaying; nearly all seemed to have been captured by the rhythmic patterns. She returned to Gil's question. "Not much," she offered. "An old family: It made its fortune in sugar in the eighteenth century, but I suppose you know that."

He nodded.

"Like the other planters, I assume he's fallen on bad times."

This time, Gil's nod betrayed impatience. "Anything you know specifically?"

Ellen searched her memory, but came up with little. "He hasn't been very active since coming down with polio," she said.

"Polio?"

"Yes," she affirmed. "A while ago, when I was in England." Another recollection. "And he married. I remember that."

Gil rejected that as of no importance. "Is he crippled?"

She had no idea and said so.

"And you say he's not doing well financially?" Gil queried.

"I would imagine that's so," she answered. "Times are bad for planters."

There were shouts. Ellen turned from Gil. A woman had fallen to her knees. She swayed, snapping her head so forcefully Ellen worried she might hurt herself. Others gathered around her, but the *hungan* remained seated. Apparently, he judged the woman's actions insufficient proof of possession. Ellen wondered what she would have to do to attract his ministrations.

Ellen spoke to Gil. "I don't know much about such things," she said. "If you want to learn about Jamaica's social leaders, find someone else. I've never had much interest in them."

Gil shook his head, scratched on the dirt floor with a twig. "I don't know," he confessed. "I can't picture old Gainsley involved in anything like this. He was always a patriot. He fought in the last war, was decorated for bravery. I saw his medals."

"But you fear he may be involved," she said.

He smiled. "I keep going back to Pombal's question."

She liked Gil's smile. It was open, honest, and admitted that he was in water too deep for him. "What are you going to tell your superior when we get out of here?" she asked.

"Exactly what we found out," he said. "That I have no idea if Duchesne is in the Dominican Republic, but that my questions about him damned near got our heads blown off; that every soldier and cop in the country were looking for us"—he paused—"but that I haven't the foggiest idea why."

But Duchesne was in Ciudad Trujillo. Ellen had all the proof she needed. She almost confessed it, but did not. "I'm sorry," she said lamely.

"I never promised McEachern I would succeed," Gil said, ignoring Ellen's sorrow. "I only told him I'd try."

A scream distracted them. Dust obscured their vision. Ellen could taste it, feel it in her nostrils. She peered into the crowd and saw a man on the ground, his body jerking in convulsions. Had he swallowed his tongue? No one else seemed concerned. They hovered about him, let him continue to writhe.

The man rose to his knees, then bent backward until his head brushed the ground. Through the dust and the forest of legs, he seemed to be thrusting his pelvis upward and was tearing at his clothing.

His screams rose above the noise of the drums, the people's murmurs. The man began to roll, raising more dust. Then he leaped and scaled a pole until he dangled from the top of the *tonnelle*. Sweat cut through the dust on his face and chest. The front of his shirt and trousers were shredded. Ellen saw streaks of torn flesh on his chest and thighs. It was as if he had been clawed by a tiger. But the wounds had been self-inflicted. She had watched him do it. She continued to stare.

His eyes were wild. If she had ever seen fright, this was it: unmasked, pure, total. "What is it, Anibal?" she asked.

"A possession," he responded, without taking his eyes from the scene. "See?" he added, nodding toward the *hungan* who had flung himself into the group standing under the man coiled around the crosspiece. Now, the people were silent. Only the drums and the *hungan's* voice were heard.

The *hungan* began to chant, then reached up and ran his hands over the man's calf. "What will he do?" she asked.

Anibal's smile seemed nervous and uncertain. "As with you, the *hungan* must decide if it is a true possession. If he judges it is, he will learn what *loa* it is. Then, he will rid him of it."

It sounded simple, automatic, like following the steps in *Mrs. Beeton's Cookery Book*. Her own skepticism wavered. She wondered why the priest had done nothing to rid her of her possession.

Anibal had read her thoughts. "Yours is a good possession. The presence of Maitresse Erzulie helps the people." He turned away, once again concentrating on the drama before them.

She followed suit. Whatever was happening, she thought, there was no playacting involved. Everyone was deadly serious. The conclusion startled her, made her realize it would not take much to turn her into a believer.

"You don't buy this stuff, do you?" Gil asked.

At first, Ellen feared the question was directed to her. Then, she saw he meant it for Anibal. She sighed with relief.

"You don't have to believe in voodoo to see its power," Anibal responded. "These people believe. It satisfies their needs, helps them survive."

Ellen could not tell how Gil took these words. For herself, she believed Anibal's mood matched hers: skeptical, but emotionally far more involved than he would admit.

The man possessed had been talked from his perch, was back writhing on the ground. The *hungan* stayed with him, head bent low, talking or preaching or chanting, she could not tell which.

The crowd gave a chorus of "ohs" and "ahs." "What's happened?" she asked.

"The *hungan* has decided he is possessed," Anibal said. "He has identified the *loa*."

"Who—which one is it?"

Anibal shrugged. "I don't know."

All the faces seemed solemn. The people stood in a tight group behind the *hungan* and the possessed, watching the two of them approach the central support of the *tonnelle*. Drums, rattles, and iron changed the rhythm. Again, Ellen glanced at Anibal.

"Each *loa* has its own music," he explained.

The *hungan* made the one possessed kneel before the central pole. The corn meal markings around the pole had long since been ground into the dirt, all evidence of design gone. The penitent crossed himself. He seemed weak, without spirit. The *hungan* handed him a calabash of water. The man poured some on the ground. A purifying ritual, Ellen imagined. The penitent was then led to kneel before the *manman*. Head lowered, the man waved a lighted candle in one hand and poured more water in front of the *manman* with the other.

The drums stopped. For a second, there was silence, as

if all were stunned. Suddenly all crowded around the *hungan*. Ellen glanced at Gil. He looked as perplexed as she.

As if by signal, the Haitians swung about and stared at the trio. No one said a word. The headman, *hungan* in tow, broke from the crowd and gestured that he wished to speak with Anibal. Anibal rose.

"They don't seem very happy, do they?" Gil whispered.

An understatement. Ellen did not respond, kept her eyes fixed on Anibal and the Haitian leaders.

CHAPTER 11

Anibal broke from his conference and started back their way. A single glance at the Haitian's face convinced Gil the news was not good. He stood and helped Ellen to her feet. Her gown was dusty and bedraggled: a reveler's attire at party's end.

The Haitian shook his head. "The *loa* has been identified as Ogun."

Gil expected him to go on, but he did not. "Tell us what that means."

"Ogun is god of war. The *hungan* thinks his presence means the soldiers are returning."

The *hungan*'s warning dovetailed with what Gil had been feeling since they learned soldiers were in the vicinity. It helped make a believer of him. "What will they do?" he asked.

"They are sending scouts out," Anibal said. "In the meantime, they are going to break camp."

Gil glanced around him, saw that it was already happening. The *tonnelle*, crowded only a minute ago, was almost empty. How could everyone have left so quietly? He should have noticed it. Only a few young men and women remained. Those stood in a tight group. Gil saw them occasionally glancing in their direction. The looks revealed curiosity, but no hostility. That could change quickly. He turned back to Anibal. "And us?" he asked.

"The headman suggests we stay until the scouts return. After that, we may leave."

A suggestion—or an order? Not that it made much difference, Gil thought. They would have to stay in either case. They had to find out whether the danger was real and, if so, from which direction it came. It would not do to stumble blindly into the soldiers. He touched his shirt pocket. No cigarettes, of course. He'd had none for over a week. He plucked a palmetto blade from the eave, shredded it, and stuck a length in his mouth.

An hour passed before a young man returned to camp. Anibal rose to join the Haitians collecting around the runner. Gil held out his hand to Ellen, intending to follow. "Come along," he said. "You might make some sense out of it."

She got to her feet and brushed her skirt, front and back. It was a civilized reflex, out of place in such surroundings. Perhaps that was why Gil was so charmed by it.

The group surrounding the messenger had already begun to thin out when they arrived. Anibal stood with the headman. "There are soldiers heading this way," he told them. "There is a man with them who might be Fabrizio."

"A prisoner?" Gil asked. He knew the answer as he spoke.

"Evidently not. He was seen walking freely among the soldiers."

Betrayed again. First by Pombal, now by a man of Madam Gamba's. The bastard had been leading them into a trap all along. Anger and fear merged into rage. The fury took in whoever stood in its path: Fabrizio, for his betrayal; McEachern, for employing him when he was clearly not equal to the job; even Anibal and Ellen, for not having countered his inclinations forcefully enough. Most, he reserved for himself.

He had to fight against the feeling, lest he be immobilized by it. "What will they do?" he asked, nodding at those Haitians who remained.

"What can they do but run?" Anibal responded.

Even if he and his friends escaped, Gil realized, the Haitians wouldn't. Their old people and children would slow them down. They would be caught and slaughtered—for having sheltered Gil and his friends. Another massacre, not as massive as that of four years ago, but just as merciless, just as final.

"You go," Gil said. "I'm staying."

Anibal's eyes widened, then narrowed. "What?" he asked.

"You heard me." Gil looked at Ellen and thought he saw comprehension in her eyes. "I'm going to fight them."

"You've lost your mind," Anibal protested. "How? They've got guns!"

"What are our chances if we run?" Gil saw the answer to his question in Anibal's eyes. He, too, knew how great were the odds against escape. "I'm the only one they really want. Maybe I can slow them up,'' he continued, ''or lead them off in another direction.''

He paused and looked at Anibal. ''People have died because of what I've done before,'' he said. ''I don't want any more killed because of me.'' He let his last words drift. His incoherence frustrated him. He wished he were better at explaining himself. ''I'm staying,'' he repeated, and turned away.

''Then we stay together,'' Anibal and Ellen chorused. Both spoke softly, but their words were resolute.

Gil turned and saw the determined look in their faces. He nodded.

Anibal bent over the steam and breathed deeply, ignoring the sting in his nostrils. He could feel the vapor cleansing his system. It was the lime leaves in the water which purified. He remembered that from his youth. The bodies of the dead were always bathed in water steeped in lime leaves before burial.

He lifted his head. Steam billowed around him. But this was a purification for the warrior, not for the dead. It had been so since before his people had been brought across the ocean. Sweat beaded on his forehead, flowed down, dripped from his chin. His bare chest was damp. He ran his hand around it. His skin felt clean in a way he had not known for years, as clean as it used to after bathing in a mountain stream.

He was at peace with himself. Tonight, he would avenge the death of his wife and son. One way or another, now, they too would find peace.

Gil was blameless. Anibal saw that now with a clarity which, at last, cut through all lingering doubts and questions. The only way his friend could have been responsible was if he could foretell the future. Anibal smiled. Gil was hardly able to interpret the present.

The American's sin was one he shared with most of his kind. He was too impetuous, too willing to act without thinking. Ten years ago, he had acted impulsively to save an old man's life. Now, he was doing the same thing to try to save a Haitian village. Anibal opened his eyes, shook his head. Water flew from it, as from a lion's mane. He ran his hands through his hair, felt the water stream down his neck. He had shed his man-smell. At night, without form and without smell, he would turn into a ghost, able to move without detection.

The flap to the hut opened. The *hungan* entered.

"It is time?" Anibal asked.

The priest nodded. "They are near." He took something from his pocket, held it out. "Here."

Anibal took it: a small pouch on a long loop of string. "A *drogue*," he said.

"It has been blessed. I have filled it with a *hoholi* plant."

The plant's many seeds made it a sign of life. Elders used to set the plant under the beds of newlyweds, but it was also thought it could ward off death. Before the Baron Samedi could claim you, he must first count your *hoholi* seeds. That gave you time to get away. He nodded at the priest, slipped the *drogue* over his neck, and stood.

A half-dozen warriors awaited him outside the hut, barechested, machetes in hand. The headman was there, too. "They wish to go with you," he told Anibal.

Anibal turned, saw Gil and Ellen together in the distance. He motioned them forward. "The soldiers are coming in two columns," he told his friends. "An advance guard, followed by the main body. We will take care of the advance. I want you to watch the others, but do nothing unless I ask it.''

Gil seemed about to protest, but kept silent.

Anibal pivoted, walked off to join those who would follow him. He felt whole again. The machete's wooden handle seemed to give under his fingers until it was molded to his hand. He waved; the men followed. In a few seconds, Anibal was under the cover of the trees, hidden from the moon. He had become invisible, like a panther padding through the Dahomean jungle in the dead of night. The *drogue* bounced on his chest as he walked.

"Did you feel it?" Ellen asked, watching Anibal and the warriors depart.

Gil shuddered. "He's changed."

An understatement, she thought. "So what do we do?" she asked.

"You heard him. We watch the main column." He pointed at her gown. "You'd better get back in your regular clothes."

Her time as Maitresse Erzulie was over. Somehow, the realization saddened her. "You don't mind my coming along?" she asked.

"Would you stay behind if I asked?"

She had done that once, she thought. It hadn't worked. "No."

"I didn't think so. Come on along. You've earned the right."

Ellen almost thanked him, but did not. If the right had been earned, no thanks were necessary. She looked around at the warriors Anibal had selected to accompany them. They were older than those Anibal led. These men, Ellen thought, would be observers. Those with Anibal were the flying squad. She went to shed the gown and put on her slacks and blouse.

There were no pickets, only a few soldiers lazing about, some polishing weapons near the bonfires, most simply chatting by the few tents. Now and then, one laughed. Obviously, they sensed no danger. In the center, Ellen spotted their commander. He wore riding boots and a Sam Browne belt.

Gil touched her shoulder, pointed into the clearing. There stood Fabrizio, dressed in clean clothing. He seemed to be laughing with the rest of them. The sound of cicadas and other insects overlaid the drone of men's voices.

Then, a scream rent the air. At first, Ellen thought it the cry of an animal. It came again, louder than before. Pain and fright. A human scream.

Those in the clearing heard, too. They froze in mid-motion, as if in a children's game, aimless chattering forgotten. None appeared more uncertain than the commander. He seemed paralyzed.

Another scream, not as piercing. Someone—not the officer—was trying to organize the troops. Men, immobilized a second ago, suddenly rushed for their weapons. She saw a sergeant shouting orders.

Too late. A rifle's report sounded from the far side of the clearing. A soldier dropped to his knees, holding his shoulder. She heard something behind her and whirled, thinking it might be one of Anibal's warriors. It was a bird, startled by the din. More shots. The sergeant fell. Ellen could no longer see Fabrizio. He had disappeared. She wondered where Anibal's men had found rifles. There was but one answer: from the advance guard.

Without the sergeant's guidance, the commander and

the soldiers seemed unable to anticipate what to do next. Ellen saw them flinching at the gunfire. It would not take much before they bolted.

Then, almost in the center of the clearing: Anibal, a rifle in hand. The sight jarred her. His black skin glistened in the firelight. There was blood on his face and smeared across his chest. The soldiers began to scatter, terrified.

The commander dug into his holster and leveled his gun at Anibal. There was a puff of smoke, then, instantly, a report. Anibal did not swerve. He kept coming, holding the rifle waist high, the bayonet centered on his target.

The officer fired a second time, this time from only a few feet. It was his last act. The bayonet caught him under the rib cage. Anibal drove it in and lifted him off the ground. The body folded down over the rifle. Anibal dropped man and gun and stood still in the center of the clearing.

It was too much for the remaining Dominicans. Demoralized, they fled, casting their weapons away, leaving dead and wounded behind. Anibal's men entered the clearing, dispatched the living with machetes. The sight forced Ellen to turn away. She felt sick.

"It's over." Gil's voice sounded strained. Ellen looked at him. "It's all done," he said, rising, offering to help her up. She accepted his aid, got to her feet, walked beside him into the clearing, fighting against the gorge which rose in her throat.

There were bodies. Pools of blood soaked into the ground around them. Some of the Haitians were collecting rifles, others were searching the corpses for valuables. Anibal loomed in their midst. He looked huge; she could see designs traced in the blood on his chest, like a child's finger painting . . . a reminder of his African warrior ancestors.

"We saw you out there," Gil said. "You almost got yourself killed." In the glare of the campfires, she saw the tension on his face. He had reacted to the carnage as she.

"I had the *drogue* to protect me," Anibal said.

Gil did not respond immediately. As for Ellen, she was not sure she could have spoken, had she wanted. "It worked, lucky for you," Gil acknowledged. "What's going on?" he added.

"The people have had their money stolen," Anibal said. "They want it back."

And whatever else they can find, Ellen thought. The plundering increased her malaise. She had come to like the Haitians. Now, the young warriors resembled scavengers perched on carrion. She no longer felt safe among them. It was because they had been blooded; that was said to change men. Would it change Anibal? She shivered. "When can we get out of here?" she managed weakly.

"Why leave them?" Anibal asked. "Why not go with them to Haiti?"

Gil stepped in. "Because our job is different from theirs," he said. The words were sharp, cutting. "Now, we must get on with our work."

"They may still need our help," Anibal insisted.

Gil shook his head. "We can do nothing more for them."

Ellen feared Anibal might defy Gil. Then, gradually, his face softened. "All right," he said at last. "Give me a minute. I must talk with the headman."

"You want them to build a shrine for your wife and son," Gil said.

Ellen looked at Gil, then at Anibal. Gil had guessed it. How?

"We call it a *hounfort*. I would like it built on the shores of Lake Enriquillo, near where they died." He turned. "I'll be back soon," he said over his shoulder.

"Take all the time you need," Gil told him, then looked at Ellen. "We've lost a guide. You're the geographer. Think you can get us to Port-au-Prince?"

Could she? The features they must cross before they reached their destination came to mind; they could skirt most of the mountainous terrain of the Cordillera Central and the Massif du Nord. They would have to cross some swamp; some arid land. Water would prove a problem: either too much or not enough. "Being a geographer is not the same as knowing the routes, but, yes, I can at least keep us going in the right direction."

Gil smiled. "That was more than our guide did, wasn't it? Come on, let's go back and get our gear. I think we'd better get out of here as soon as we can."

Ellen returned the smile. She was more than willing to leave. Sara came to mind. Soon, they would be reunited and the whole crazy adventure would be over. The conclusion had come unannounced, an unwanted coda. It dulled the warmth provided by her thoughts of Sara.

CHAPTER 12

Maria's head bounced against the rear of the seat. The jolt was like an electric shock, shivering up her legs and down her spine. She looked over at the driver. His face was lit up by the light from the dashboard. He was smiling, as if he had deliberately steered into the last pothole. The young man took his eyes from the road and rubbed his stomach in feigned sympathy. The headlights picked up a pothole as large as a crater. Maria grunted and pointed.

The driver saw it and swerved. Her shoulders and head bounced, as if unattached to the rest of her body. It was like being on the boat: she had to contend with roll as well as pitch. "Slower," she ordered. They could not afford an accident.

He glanced at her, as if he hadn't understood. She repeated the command, shouting above the engine's roar.

Obediently, the driver geared down; the truck slowed. Maria felt better. Careening down a road riven with pot-holes while carrying more than six tons of TNT was not her idea of fun. Andre had assured her that the explosive was passive unless electrically detonated. It was one thing to be told, another to believe. She saw the headlights of the truck following. Their glare was too close. Perhaps its driver had not noticed they had slowed. She wished their vehicle had a rearview mirror.

She wished for a lot of things. A smoother ride, more trucks. Rosario had been adamant: Four carriers was all he believed safe. The truck hit another pothole. Maria winced, suppressed a groan. The four vehicles could carry twenty-five tons of TNT. At one run a night, it would take sixteen nights to cart the four-hundred-ton load to Ocoa Bay. She would piss blood before it was done—if she were still alive to piss at all, she added, tensing for another jolt. The truck was overloaded; its springs were shot. Riding in it was like bouncing on rocks. Her tailbone was sore. Tomorrow, she vowed, she would bring a pillow. A stack of them.

She wondered if pillows would help. Maybe she was like the princess in the story about the pea. That might be the cause of her discomfort: She was an illegitimate daughter of royalty, the product of a secret tryst between old Alfonso of Spain and her mother. Maria could visu-alize it: King Alfonso, standing in line, a bar of soap and towel in one hand, ten pesos in the other. She shook her-self from the daydream and glanced at the speedometer. They were going nearly forty again. "Slow down, for Christ's sake!" she shouted.

The night was dark. Every so often, she glimpsed the sea out the driver's window. The moon shone on the water. It looked sparkling, fresh. By contrast, their road was lined by trees. It was like driving through a tunnel. Something was caught in the truck's headlights. The driver saw it, too, but did not slow. It was an old man leading a donkey along the side of the road. The driver veered a little to the left. Maria saw the man looking over his shoulder at them. He had a gray beard and eyes which shone like amber in the glare. Without thinking, she leaned to her left, as if to give the old man a little more room. Their truck sped past, missing him by no more than a few inches. The driver was smiling anew as she turned to him; it had been a game, seeing how close he could come.

The driver took his foot from the accelerator and began to brake. A few seconds later, Maria made out why: an armed patrol. The headlights picked up two men clearly: one standing in the road, signaling the truck to a halt, another on the verge next to him—thin, leaning to one side to counterbalance the Thompson submachine gun on his hip. They were not easily ignored.

The truck's brakes creaked; the vehicle stopped. The Thompson was leveled at them. The man in the road drew a pistol. A third man emerged from the shadows. All wore steel helmets, khaki shirts and trousers with puttees. Guardsmen. There were to be no roadblocks—Rosario said he had arranged it! Either these three had not heard the general's orders or had elected to ignore them.

The third man approached Maria's side of the cab. She found herself staring into a lighted flashlight. The glare blinded her. It held her eyes, then traveled down until the beam centered on her bosom. "You have papers?" the voice behind the flashlight asked.

Maria breathed a little easier. Only a routine search. "Yes," she replied and started to reach into the compartment of the door.

"Careful," the voice warned.

Maria moved more deliberately. She could no longer see the weapons, but was sure they were still trained on her. She took out an envelope. In full view of the man outside, she opened the flap and extracted Rosario's *laissez passer*. She remembered the general's words when he had given it to her: *"A formality; you will not need it."* She handed it through the window.

"Watch them," the voice said. The flashlight swung away. Maria could see the armed men again. The one with the submachine gun had mean eyes. "You carry food?" came back the voice.

Maria turned at his voice. He was a sergeant, she saw now. "Yes," she responded, "supplies for the garrison at Barahona."

"Ah," the sergeant said. "Food for the garrison at Barahona? My men are hungry, too."

It showed how far Rosario's power extended, Maria reflected. She swallowed her resentment. It was all part of the system: something for everyone, providing you were in a position to ask. These men were in such a position. "I imagine the garrison won't miss a few cases," she said and opened her door.

She stepped outside. The silence was stark, as if the trio had ceased breathing: their way of expressing appreciation for what they saw. "Please," she said, smiling. "Come with me." Followed by the sergeant, she sauntered to the rear of the truck, her elongated shadow silhouetted on the ground in front of her by the flashlight. She pointed to the canvas flaps. "Untie them."

One did. The flashlight played on the truck's interior. It was packed with crates. "Here, sergeant," Maria cooed, pointing to one. "Canned ham. Will one crate satisfy your hunger?"

There came a pause. The sergeant, she knew, was figuring how much he could safely ask. "We are three," he finally said.

"Three cases it is," she agreed. "Please, take them."

The sergeant shouted. The submachine gun was shouldered, the pistol holstered, and the men jumped to obey, carting the cases off to the side of the road. She was alone with the non-commissioned officer. "It is not usual for a woman to travel with a military convoy," he observed.

"That is so," she agreed. "But I am a friend of General Rosario. I have family in Barahona. The general sometimes lets me ride with his convoy."

"Ah, I see," the sergeant replied. The cases were gone. He ordered his men to secure the flaps, then walked her back to the cab. "In that case, we might meet again. I hope everyone in your family is well."

He hadn't believed her. She saw it in his eyes. She hadn't believed him, either. They would not meet again. If they did, the sergeant would wish he hadn't. "You are too kind," she answered. He opened the door and assisted her in. If his hand rested a little too long on her flank in doing so, it was only his way of telling her how beautiful he thought her. Her coccyx throbbed with pain as she settled on the hard seat. She leaned out the window. "Then our trucks are free to pass?"

The sergeant smiled and waved them on. Maria turned to her driver. "Go," she ordered. The driver double-clutched, the truck's gears clashed, and the vehicle was once more under way. Maria rested her head against the boarded rear of the cab. Mother of Christ, she thought. A ride that was likely to turn her kidneys into hamburger, guns pointed at her, being felt up by strangers. And fifteen more nights of it. She was pleased she had taken precautions. Food convoys, after all, should carry food. What a pain.

When the trips were done, she swore, when the TNT was safely stored, she would return to Jamaica and rest. Oh, she would get in touch with Andre to let him know that all was going well, but she was not to do that for a few more weeks. Until then, she could relax. The American and his colleagues were dead by now. Only Andre still had his work to do. The realization calmed her. Most everything had gone as planned; the unforeseen had been handled. What could go wrong?

PART THREE

•

CHAPTER 1

November, 1941

Sitting on the veranda was almost like lounging on deck, Gil thought, as he watched the water lap against the sand.

"It is nice, isn't it?"

Gil turned, startled. Olive Cooper, Ellen's mother, stood by the door. He began to scramble to his feet.

"Please don't get up," she told him.

He relaxed. "I didn't hear you come out. Yes, very."

"Ellen used to love it as a child."

Gil understood why. It was a child's world: sun, sand, trees, sky, and sea; yellow, white, green, and blue—stark as the colors in a box of crayons. "Does that mean she doesn't love it any longer?" he asked, then regretted the question. It seemed too personal.

If Mrs. Cooper took offense, it didn't show. "I suppose she still does," she conceded, "but it's different when you're an adult. It's hard not to take familiar sights for granted. You need to see them again through another's eyes."

He knew what she meant. "How far does your land go along the shore?" he asked, shading his eyes as he looked out from the veranda.

"It stretches around the point," she answered.

"That building is yours, then," he said, indicating a little structure almost hidden by the vegetation. It was strange-looking—square and boxy—like a motor court cabin on an American highway.

Olive laughed. "My husband's folly," she explained. "There was a time when we thought my mother might have to come live with us. He built it for her. She never made it, poor dear," Olive continued. "Since then, we've used it as a guest house."

He wondered why it had not been offered to him. She answered without his having to ask. "It's a long way off," she said, "and hard to keep up. It would be different if we had people dropping in more often, but we don't."

He nodded and waited for the question which must follow.

"How long do you think you will be here, Mr. Brant?" she asked.

It was easy to tell Ellen was her daughter: same hair, same eyes, same chin. The relationship was equally obvious with Sara, Mrs. Cooper's granddaughter. All might be thought different stages of the same person. Gil paused. That was what they were, in a way. "I don't know," he finally said. "I've contacted my superiors, but they've not yet got back to me. Meanwhile, I have work in Kingston. I am grateful you offered me your car."

Olive laughed. As she did, the resemblance to her daughter increased. It was the sparkle in her eyes, the ease with which she moved that did it. "I'm the grateful one," she said. "With petrol rationed, I can't use it much. At least you've kept our tank filled. I—"

There was a noise. Gil looked. Sara stood in the entry. "Mother said she needs your help," the girl told her grandmother.

"Fine, dear," the other replied. "You entertain Mr. Brant while I'm gone, won't you?" She looked up at Gil. "Would you excuse me?"

Gil smiled, then, belatedly, jumped to his feet. "Certainly."

She left. Sara hoisted herself up on the sofa, accommodating herself to the adult-sized piece by balancing on its edge, like a bird on a wire. There were pink bows in her hair, her legs were crossed at the ankles, her hands were folded in the lap of her gingham dress.

He tried to make conversation: playmates, where she went to school and whether she liked it, could she swim, whether she ever collected seashells or went surf-fishing. To each, Sara responded politely enough, but never with any enthusiasm. Gil began to think he was boring her. It was unsettling to be put in one's place by a seven-year-old.

A call from within. Ellen, informing them it was time for dinner. "Shall we go in?" he asked the girl.

Sara slid from her perch, reached out and took his hand, the reaction of a four-year-old innocent, not that of a seven-year-old sophisticate. Her hand was small and cool. Maybe he hadn't struck out with her, after all.

"Don't give me any of your excuses," Olive Cooper scolded. "All I'm telling you is that this is the first man you've looked at in almost five years."

"I'm not ready to think of men yet, Mother." Ellen

picked up a plate to dry. She wished her mother would drop the subject. How many times had she heard variations since she and Sara had come to live with her? Too many to count.

"There's a saying: 'Once you're dead, you can only get deader,' " responded her mother. "You've put life off too long. If you don't start thinking of men soon, you never will."

Would that be so bad? For the first time in years, an easy answer did not come. That was Gil's doing. Three weeks of crawling through the forests and fields of the Dominican Republic, of dodging armed patrols, shooing flies, killing bugs, and scratching bites in his company had had their effect. She had had to find a fall-back position. "He's a stubborn fool," she said. "And I really don't know much about him."

"What do you need to know?" her mother retorted, peeling off her rubber gloves. "Look at that," she said, pointing to one. "A hole. I don't know when we'll be able to get a new pair." She peered at Ellen. "I don't know if you saw it earlier this evening."

"Saw what?"

"Your daughter with him. I tell you, Sara knows more about human nature at seven than you ever did. And you know why?" She continued without taking a breath. "I'll tell you: She trusts her instincts. She took a shine to him and moved right toward him. But you!" She waved the sponge. "You'll argue with yourself and find reasons why you shouldn't do anything. I warn you: If you ever decide you want to know him a little better, you're likely to look up and find he's already back in California or wherever it is he lives." On that, she slapped the sponge down and left.

Ellen picked up a rag to dry the counter and sink. Was

her mother right? Did she always overthink things? It was a complaint she had heard all her life.

The answer was no. No one knew the depths of her hurt and guilt. Until those were resolved, there was no purpose in becoming interested in a man. The burden was too heavy to cart into a new relationship. It would not be fair to ask another to share it. She began to scrub the porcelain hard, as if to scour the problem from her mind.

"The breeze," Gil said, "I've never been able to figure it."

Ellen nodded, breathed in deeply, as if to test it. He imitated her, smelled the scent of flowers anew. Evening perfume.

"A doctor's wind, it's called," she replied. "It comes in every night. It's supposed to be health-giving."

"What is the one in the daytime called?" he asked.

"The undertaker's wind. It blows the stink of civilization to sea."

Health, sickness, death. Jamaicans seemed a pretty basic people, Gil thought. They walked on in silence. The moon, nearly full, shone brightly. Away from the moon's glow, the sky was black, the point at which sky ended and earth began apparent only by the line below which no stars were visible. The sand was firm; their feet barely made an impression in it. He felt the damp on the soles of his feet. Ellen's hip swung against his thigh. The moment's pressure lingered after the event. How often had they touched one another while in the forest?

Then, it had been a matter of survival. This was different; she was different. It was as if her past aloofness had been cut away. He moved closer, felt his hand brush the back of hers. She accepted the touch. Had she been as aware of the contact as he?

"So what will you do when your job is done?" she asked. There was evident tension in her voice. Their contact had affected her. The realization saddened him. He'd never had luck with women. When the time was right, the women were wrong, and vice versa. Never had his timing been as bad as now.

"When your job is done," she had said. Her question had a corollary. *Her part of it is already over. She has done what she promised; I've no right to ask for any more.* He grew further depressed. "I'm not a regular with the OCI. When this is over, I go back to my regular job."

"You mean the cinema?"

Did she lump him with ushers and popcorn sellers? Maybe she would be right to do so. A job, that's all it was to him; one he was not very good at. He wanted to tell her he was looking for a way out of his so-called career and into something which would bring him back to the Caribbean, but could not. Even if he spent no more of the funds McEachern had supplied, he still had less than half of what he needed for a boat. "The movies," he agreed, then added, "My wife is under contract to the same studio."

She stiffened. The distance returned, measured not so much in inches as in light-years. "How nice for you. Tell me about her," she said.

Her civility irritated him. He felt like stopping and turning her until she faced him, then telling her honestly what he felt, but he wasn't sure he could distinguish honesty from dishonesty. His words would be hollow; they would have nothing behind them.

"Mona Langer's her name," Gil said.

There was silence, then, "I'm sorry, should I recognize her name?"

"She's a star. Sid Grauman's already put her feet and hands in cement outside his theatre." The remark elicited no comment. " 'America's Girl Next Door,' she's called," he added.

"Then she's young," Ellen said.

Gil suppressed a laugh. "Not so very," he said, "but she photographs young: good skin, perky look."

"Do you enjoy acting?" she asked.

He told her, letting his feelings about Hollywood spill out, then, following other questions, telling her of Spain, of his time as a rumrunner, his year in Lewisburg. He wasn't sure of the impact of his revelations, only that whatever he said registered with her. They had walked about as far as they should go, he figured. He turned her around, noticed that, except for their last few steps, their footprints were already washed away. "What about you?" he said. He had talked enough about himself; it was her turn.

"What about me?" Her voice was soft. She was walking on the sea side of him. Now and then, the smell of her hair overrode the night's perfume and the air's salty tang.

"You were married. Were you happy?"

There was silence, then, "I'm not so sure I should tell you."

"I'm sorry. Don't."

Waves rolled to shore. He could hear his feet padding on the sand. "Happy enough," she finally said. "For a while."

"What happened?"

"We drifted apart, a little ways at a time. Eventually, the distance was so great there was no chance of bridging

243

it. We learned to tolerate one another—no big spats in public, smiling and supportive—an ideal couple, everyone believed. You know all about that, I'm sure.''

He did. She had not mentioned Andre Duchesne. It was not necessary. Gil knew where to insert him in her recitation of a marriage that was floundering. ''And then he went into the army?'' he asked.

''We had a fight,'' she confessed. ''We broke up. George quit the Foreign Service and I took Sara back with me to Jamaica. He told me he was going to divorce me, but never did. It's not as easy in Britain as it seems to be in the States. And it's much more public. George would have hated that.''

She paused. Gil said nothing, content to let her decide whether to continue or not.

''I don't know why he didn't obtain a divorce,'' she repeated. ''He just didn't. So, when he enlisted in the army, I was still legally his wife.''

''And you were legally his widow when he died,'' Gil said.

''Isn't it ironic? Wife of a fallen hero. I received condolences from the War Ministry. His personal effects were shipped to me, then, later, I received a medal, awarded posthumously. Letters from men with whom he'd served, from his commanding officer—colonel something-or-other—dribbled in for months. I get his pension.''

Ellen's snare seemed as tight as his: erring wife transformed into widow. ''Tough part to play,'' Gil said.

''Not at all. It's very easy. Everyone else does the acting, you see. All you must do is fill the space they have created for you. It's what goes on inside that is hard to take.''

''What is that?''

"The falsehood, the hypocrisy of your position. It hurts, like a little sore rubbed so often it never heals."

The house was only a short distance away. Gil slowed, wishing to prolong the evening, accepting the torment which went with the pleasure of her presence. The house loomed even nearer. He slowed still more.

"Do movie actors swim?" she asked.

"Some. Those who can't, have stand-ins."

"I swim every morning. If I invited you along tomorrow, who would show up, you or your stand-in?"

"I'll practice all night."

"Six o'clock?"

He agreed.

Ellen slipped into bed. Her daughter might be better at reading character than she, she told herself, but she was not yet old enough to tell whether a man was married or not. How old must one be before acquiring that skill? Lord knows she hadn't it. Nor, obviously, did her mother. Did it make a difference? She struggled for an answer. Ordinarily, yes, but these were not ordinary times. Everyone said that. She wondered whether her mother had words of wisdom to cover this situation. She should, since it was she who had urged her to let down her guard. Ellen stirred, swung her feet over the side of the bed and went to the window. It was a bright night. Through the palms she saw the beach and sea. Perhaps Madam Gamba would be a better person to consult than her mother. There might, after all, be special rules for masters.

Ellen sighed, tossed her head, felt the breeze against her skin. It was not something anyone else could solve, mothers or theosophists. She turned from the window and made her way back to bed. There was something comforting in the way she had led her life the past few years, she decided, as she slid under the sheet. It had carried no surprises, no dilemmas.

Swimsuits—wet, coiled into tight ringlets, and dappled with sand—lay amid dead wasps on a straw rug. Pale golden sun rays picked up motes of dust floating in the air. They gave substance to the air, made Gil think he should be able to feel it in his hand, as he had felt Ellen's skin a minute ago. The smells of dust and damp were overridden by that of furniture polish; Ellen's mother came to the guest house more frequently than she admitted. The observation raised ripples of guilt. He lifted his head. Ellen was beside him, lying on her stomach. Her hair seemed jet-black against the skin below her shoulders. The ends which had protruded below her swimming cap were still damp. He lifted his eyes and scanned the room, eager to fix his impressions. Her cap was lying beside the door. It and the swimsuits formed a trail leading to the bed, like an arrow.

How had it happened? All Gil knew was that it had been a mutual decision. He leaned over, brushed aside her hair, and kissed her shoulder. She had freckles on her shoulders. Her skin was dry, tasted salty. She murmured something. The muscles under her skin quivered.

He slipped from bed to retrieve his trunks. He unwound them and slipped them on, grimacing at their cloying wetness, then went onto the veranda, looking out at the water without seeing it. He had been right. Of all the times to have met Ellen, this was the worst. He halted. When would it have been better? After he had been released from Lewisburg and she was a diplomat's wife? After Spain, when he was trying to find work in Hollywood and she was revising her book on the Antilles? What difference was there between those times and now? Just one: He was married and she was not. Everything else was the same. He was the same bum he had always been; she, the same educated woman who got involved with men who did not appreciate her. Dreaming of going back in time to make something different of your life was useless.

"Hello."

Gil turned. Ellen stood in the doorway; she was wearing her swimsuit. It was sky blue, satin, he thought. The blue heightened the color of her eyes and hair, made both seem darker than they were. Never had he seen so lovely a woman. He looked carefully into her eyes, saw the same caution and sadness he had within him. "You feel as rotten as I do," he said.

She crossed her arms in front of her and hugged her shoulders. "Maybe rottener," she said, trying to smile.

Gil wanted to put his arm around her, but didn't.

"It's my feelings," she said. "I have to keep them in tight rein, otherwise they run away with me."

Gil saw the pain in Ellen's eyes.

"I'm not yet ready to leave my shell," she said.

"You've been hurt."

"Yes, but I've hurt others. That's the worst part. That's what's so hard to get over." She paused. "I have a favor to ask."

"What is it?"

"I want to keep working on this."

She had changed her mind. Why? Had she some private devils to exorcise, or was she as reluctant to part as he? "Are you sure?"

"Yes."

"You think we can work together after this?" he asked, nodding at the cottage behind her.

"I can, if you can."

Could he? It was asking a great deal. "Yes," he said, "if you promise one thing."

"What?"

"To let me know when you're ready to rejoin the living."

She smiled. "If you promise to let me know when you are ready to live honestly again."

How thoroughly she saw through him. "It's a deal," he agreed.

CHAPTER 2

"**A**hoy," Ellen said.

Anibal looked up; if she had surprised him, it didn't show. "I heard you'd signed on for the rest of the voyage," he said, grinning. "Come aboard." He turned back to his task.

There was a length of cable in his lap. "Bow strap needed replacing," he said as she knelt next to him. "Hand me the crimper."

She found it and gave it to him. "How'd you know?"

His forearms bulged as he levered down on the crimper. His skin shone under a film of sweat. He grunted, then: "Gil told me."

"Where is he?"

Anibal held up the repaired strap, snapped the cable. "Down at the Government House," he said. "Asking about Eric Gainsley.'' Anibal shifted to one knee. He was setting the bow strap in place. ''Stow those things.''

She gathered up the tools, wiped them with an oiled rag, then got up and replaced them in the chest. ''Anything else?'' she yelled.

''A couple beers, maybe,'' he suggested.

By the time she had returned, he was done and was wiping his brow. He took one of the bottles of Red Stripe and rested it against his temple before he took his first sip. ''Tastes good,'' he said. ''Too hot to work anymore.''

''What's he going to do?'' Ellen asked.

''What are we going to do, you mean,'' Anibal corrected. ''We're going to pay Mr. Gainsley a visit.''

She let the news roll around in her mind. It was logical, she supposed. It was the only lead they had.

''Why'd you change your mind?''

''What?'' she asked, although she knew what he had said, what he meant.

Anibal was aware of that. ''Was it him?''

Ellen wasn't sure what a proper reaction should be. A blush? A profession of ignorance? Either would be false. She shrugged. ''He has something to do with it,'' she admitted. ''It's me, mostly.'' She lifted her beer, drank, and took it from her lips. Foam poured over the bottle's neck and soaked her hand. It tickled.

''Life can be funny, can't it?'' Anibal observed. ''We sometimes work as hard as we can not to live it: We build walls around ourselves, try to shut it out, pretend it's not there. We put ourselves in the tomb long before le Baron Samedi is ready for us.''

Maybe Anibal had been talking to her mother. Ellen took another sip of beer; this time, she capped the bottle with the palm of her hand when she was done.

''Never works, though; not for long,'' Anibal continued. "Things keep slipping in between the cracks. It's best, I think, to knock the walls down and start living. I did that back there. At least I hope I did."

"You're not angry with Gil any longer?" she asked.

"Didn't know you knew about that."

"I'd have had to be blind or a fool not to. I don't know what caused it, but I could see it was there."

Anibal sat leaning against the mast, knees raised, forearms resting on them. He balanced his beer in his hands, seemed to speak to the bottle. "He did wrong back when he let the Coast Guard catch us," he mused. "It hurt me, hurt others, and I hated him for it. But I realized something when he told us he was going to hold up the soldiers."

He paused, seemed lost in thought. Ellen was willing to let him continue at his own speed. She waited. He resumed. "Gil doesn't have any walls around him, like you and me. He never has; I don't suppose he ever will. Something comes up, he does what he thinks is right. He makes mistakes sometimes, but not because he's mean or because he doesn't care."

"Then why?"

Anibal scratched his ear, then grinned. "I don't know. Maybe because he's the dumbest, most stubborn white man I've ever met."

She choked and coughed, noted Anibal's look of concern. "It's all right," she finally managed. "Beer just went down the wrong way."

He rose to his feet beside her. "Anything I can do?" he asked.

Ellen turned her bottle upside down, caught the last few drops in her hand. "You just did it," she said. "If you want to do anything else, how about going to the galley and bringing two more back?"

CHAPTER 3

Maria set her fingers around the stem of her glass. "Do you ride, Mr. Brant?" she asked. Her earlier tension was mostly gone, reflected now only in the care with which she picked her words. If any noticed her lack of spontaneity, she saw no sign of it. She had not been so confident of their reactions earlier. Then, she had felt as if she had been walking through a nightmare.

"Everyone in Hollywood can ride, Mrs. Gainsley," Gil responded, then wiped his lips. "Except, maybe, Mae West."

Eric Gainsley's guffaw was louder than the comment merited. Maria looked down the table at her husband. He was enjoying the evening, but then he had no idea how dangerous his former employee was. "Please, Eric, more wine for our guests," she said, then watched her husband pick up the bottle and offer it. Ellen Bainbridge smiled, but shook her head no. Gil Brant accepted and held his glass closer so Eric might reach it. Eric filled his own, as well. Maria knew he would.

During the respite, Maria went over her day: her peaceful return from Ciudad Trujillo, the ordinary automobile ride from the airport. The shock had come as soon as she had stepped into the sitting room, expecting to greet her husband, only to be introduced to two people she had been assured were dead.

What did they know of her? More than she had believed; why else would they be here? Had Pombal known more than he claimed? Had he, what could he have said? Certain knowledge or mere suspicion: both were equally dangerous. She eyed Gil. He had a typically American look to him: rugged, someone who moved with power rather than grace, more at ease in casual wear than dinner jacket. Handsome, but a man who was not necessarily comfortable around women, she thought. She must learn from him what the Americans suspected. Then she could decide what to do next.

The kitchen door opened, diverting her attention for a moment. It was Clovis, the butler Eric had recently hired, dressed in white jacket and gloves, black trousers. Tall, lean, with narrow slits for eyes, he reminded Maria of a stiletto. He made her feel uneasy. "We need nothing more for the evening," she said. "You may clean up when we are done."

Clovis bowed. As he turned from the table, Maria saw his gaze sweep over the American and Englishwoman. The look was cold, as if he were seeking chinks in their armor. It was the same way he looked at her, Maria thought.

Eric had launched into one of his interminable anecdotes. Their guests' attention was centered on him. Maria took advantage of it to study the woman. She was beautiful, Maria acknowledged, like an illustration for an English fairy tale. Her hands and wrists were thin, with long, tapering fingers. Delicate, fragile; those adjectives came to mind.

Maria stopped. Delicate? Fragile? This one had just traversed Hispaniola, had somehow evaded Rosario's entire army. She was as tough as leather, perhaps the only woman she'd ever met who might be as tough as she. Not beauty, but strength, that was what one knew was in her.

Ellen's head turned. Briefly their eyes met. The gaze was open and frank, containing an admission of who she was and why she had come. Then, just as quickly, the Englishwoman returned her attention to Eric and the conversation. The acknowledgment startled Maria. Strength and beauty, along with breeding and intelligence: no wonder Andre had warned her, back in Ciudad Trujillo. In his position, she might have done the same.

Ellen laughed and spoke to Eric. "From what Gil has told me, I gather he would rather be back working for you."

Maria had not followed the conversation. She saw that Eric was enchanted by her. She noted also how Ellen's hand had come to rest on the American's fingers as she spoke: a light, easy touch. It conveyed intimacy. Did Andre still love her? Why else would he have warned her? Whether he did or not, it was apparent the Englishwoman no longer shared his feelings.

Eric had begun another story. Maria retreated into her own thoughts. Andre would be in Galveston by now, picking up the dynamite for the highway surveyors she had arranged. In another week or ten days, he would be back in Ocoa Bay, ready to load the TNT. And after that, he and the German would set sail for Panama. The date was set, she knew. Andre had not had to tell her; she had seen it in his eyes. In four or five weeks, it would be over.

Everyone was looking at her: Eric must have finished his story. That she had become the center of attention unnerved her.

"Maria's heard my tales so many times, I fear she catnaps when I launch into one," Eric said.

"Eric, you know that's not true," she lied.

"I'm afraid our attention was diverted," Gil told her. "You had been saying something about riding," he prompted.

Had she? Maria backtracked in an effort to recall her words. "Oh, yes. I'm sorry for being so vacant. I'm afraid my day has suddenly caught up with me. An unfinished piece of business," she explained. "I was about to invite you riding. I'm sure we can find you some proper clothing if you need." She turned to Ellen. "And you, as well, my dear." She hoped she had hit the right tone: negative enough that she must refuse, but not so obvious that anyone could take offense.

Ellen glanced at Gil. He gave a barely perceptible negative head shake. *Does he want to be alone with me as much as I with him?* Maria asked herself. "Thank you, Mrs. Gainsley," Ellen said, "but I fear I would only slow you up."

"When?" Gil asked.

"What about ten o'clock tomorrow morning?"

"I look forward to it," the American said.

"No more than I," Maria replied. "I enjoy riding after a business trip. With company, it will be even more enjoyable." She looked at her husband. Eric was pouring the remainder of the claret into his glass. His complexion was flushed, his hand a little unsteady. He had been drinking more of late. Maria wondered if it was a reaction to her and her preoccupation with her work. There was nothing she could do about it.

"What do you think?" Gil asked.

"You were right," Ellen replied. "I don't think your old boss is involved, but she's in on it for sure. Did you hear her? 'Unfinished business.' That was us she was talking about."

"She's a cool customer," he agreed.

Far from cool, Ellen thought. "Those eyes," she said. "I caught her looking at me once. They shone like the dials of my clock." She shuddered in recollection. "If looks could kill . . ."

"Pretty, though."

She saw that he was teasing. "The woman's beautiful," she admitted, refusing the bait. She paused. "So what do we do?"

"Before she came in, Eric told us she often works at home. Her office is up in the corner of the east wing, he said. Could you sneak into it while we're out riding?"

Skulking along corridors and spying into other people's lives were not tasks for which she had been trained. "I'll try," she said.

"Good girl." Gil's smile provided reassurance.

"There's only one thing," she said.

"What?"

"What do I look for?"

The question stumped him. "Beats me," he finally admitted. "I'm as new at this as you. Use your imagination. See if you can find who she's been doing business with in the Dominican Republic: names, corporations, that sort of stuff. And . . ."

"Yes?"

"Be careful."

After all he'd put her through, it was a little late for that, she thought. "There's Anibal," she said. "If I get in trouble, I can find him." Anibal's having to stay in the servant's quarters might prove useful, she thought.

Gil shook his head. "Maybe, but don't count on it. He's going to be doing some snooping around on his own, remember. Just be careful."

Ellen agreed.

It defied reason, Ellen thought. They had been told that Maria worked night and day on her enterprises, but, beyond a few scraps of paper concerning household budget, she had found nothing: no correspondence, no ledgers, no sign of her being a businesswoman at all. She stood behind Maria's desk, perplexed. A scraping sound intruded on her thoughts. She looked up and saw Eric Gainsley's wheelchair bumping against the door. Its wheels were caught in the rug.

"Wouldn't believe I used to fly an airplane, would you?" he said. He finally extricated the wheels and entered. "When I bought this," he complained, "I was assured I would be able to operate it without help. Sometimes it doesn't work that way." He seemed neither surprised nor shocked to see her in his wife's office.

Ellen fought the guilt she felt. House guests, after all, were not expected to rifle through their hostess's belongings.

"I'm glad to catch you alone like this," he said, coming to rest beside the desk. "It gives us a chance to talk." He motioned her into a chair. "I'm old and crippled," he began, "and I know I drink too much, but my mind is not so far gone that I can believe your visit was made out of friendship." He stopped, as if in reflection.

Ellen wanted to protest, but Gainsley waved her to silence. "Yesterday," he continued, "after you arrived, I did some checking. I was told you are a noted scholar: 'A woman of sensibility and sensitivity as well as erudition,' they said. You might be pleased to know how you are regarded." He halted. "I loved Gil like a son . . ."

He lifted his eyes before resuming, ". . . almost like a son. One thing I'll tell you, however: Not even the most doting father in the world would believe someone like you could take up with a hothead like him. There's Anibal, too. In the old days, when the two of them were together, you could bet there would be trouble. Why are you with them?"

His pale eyes were watery, with the rheumy look of an aging alcoholic. His feet were twisted at unnatural angles against the footrest of his wheelchair. She imagined the soles of his shoes were still shiny. Ellen felt sorry for him, but could not let that interfere with her job. "We are interested in your wife's business activities," she confessed.

The old man nodded. "Are you with the Tax Authority?"

Her first inclination was to deny it, but she thought better of it. She said nothing.

"I thought so," he said, then, "I'm not sure how much I can tell you. I haven't been actively involved in the business for years."

"What is the nature of your wife's business in Cuidad Trujillo?"

Gainsley narrowed his eyes at the question. Ellen kept quiet and waited. "You know that," he said at last. "She operates Carib Shipping from there."

Ellen nodded. "How many ships?"

"Four. None larger than 1100 tons."

"Where does Carib Shipping trade?"

"Between the Greater Antilles and the United States, mainly. See here, this is all a matter of public record—"

"What cargo do your ships carry?" Ellen asked quickly.

"What they have always carried." This time he would not be interrupted. "Mrs. Bainbridge, I told you I knew very little of the business nowadays. I spoke the truth. As for my wife's dealings, she took over a business and an estate about to collapse. She has saved both. And she has broken none of our country's laws."

Ellen wondered whether to go on. She decided she must. "Do you know any of her associates in the Dominican Republic?"

Her question elicited a flare of anger. "You sound like a private investigator. Why should you care with whom she associates as long as I don't? I hold no illusions, Mrs. Bainbridge. I assume my wife has affairs. She is a young woman with needs I cannot satisfy."

"What about someone named Andre Duchesne?" she pressed. "Has she mentioned his name?"

"Not that I recall," he admitted, "but that is not surprising, is it? I would hardly expect her to boast of her romances."

Ellen shook her head. "This man is an official of Vichy," she asserted. "We believe he is in the Dominican Republic as an agent for his government, involved in business contrary to the interests of the British and American governments."

Had she reached over and slapped him, she could not have had a greater impact. Gainsley sat still, stunned. "Please understand we have no proof of their association," Ellen hastened to add, "nor, if they are associates, have we proof of her reasons for the relationship. It is only that we are compelled to investigate."

Her qualifications had made no difference. To a loyal

Britisher, Vichyites were as hated as Nazis. "Can you tell me anything of your wife and Duchesne?" she whispered.

"You are not with the Tax Authority." A statement, not a question.

"No," she admitted.

Other than a shake of his head, she got no more. It was as if Gainsley had aged ten years. Ellen rose from her chair. "I regret having had to ask these things," she said softly. She felt very dirty.

He waved a dismissal. Ellen left. One hope: that either Gil or Anibal had had more success than she. Then they might be done with this nasty business.

The air was still and heavy. Gil watched Maria cantering ahead of him. "Steady," he whispered to his stallion, fighting to keep him to a walk. The old manor to Gil's left had been destroyed in a hurricane early in the century, he remembered. The place had looked bad fifteen years ago; it seemed in greater disrepair now.

A man had been running around the corner of the ruin just now, as if trying to hide. Anibal? Why would he be nosing around the old manor?

Maria swung her roan mare back to rejoin him, then reined down to a walk beside him and leaned forward to pat the mare's neck. The roan's coat glistened from exertion. "She's nervous," Maria said. "She senses the storm."

The stretching had pulled Maria's jodhpurs tight over her rear. In a few years, Gil thought, she might get a little dumpy, but, for the moment, she was gorgeous. With her tawny skin and green eyes, dressed in blue coat and riding cap, she could pass for a wealthy maharani. "You ride well," he observed.

She smiled. "Thank you," she responded. "I've paid to learn: in money *and* bruises."

His laugh sounded strained, even to him. "The old place," he said, jerking his head toward the old manor, "must have been beautiful once."

"You strike me as an expert about beautiful things," she replied, looking back. Then, the flirtatiousness left her. "After Eric and I married, I thought of restoring it, but gave it up."

His horse snorted. The muscles around its shoulders twitched. He patted it. "Why?" he asked.

"Same old answer: money," she said. "It's too far gone."

Far gone it might be, but the furtive-looking figure of a minute ago had seemed interested enough in it. Might it have been Anibal, investigating how decrepit the place really was?

"We are near the sea," Maria said, rising in her stirrups and rocking forward. "Smell it?"

The aroma triggered a memory of sea hay on the Chesapeake Bay, one of the many places where he had lived as a child. It had been one of his happier times—before his parents' death.

Maria kicked. Her horse leaped forward. Gil's mount strained to catch up, but Gil kept him under tight rein. He looked back at the old manor, but could see nothing move there.

She was waiting for him at the crest of the next hill. Below stretched the sea. Dark waves pounded the shore, then spewed high in the air. The booming was like the *manman* back in the Dominican Republic. Out from under the hill's shelter, the wind was blowing hard. It would get worse, Gil reflected, looking up at the slate sky. He was happy to be ashore.

"It's beautiful, isn't it?" Maria asked.

Gil looked again. Beautiful was not a word he would have picked, but, yes, she was right. Frightening, too—like the woman next to him.

"We're going to be caught in the middle of a real storm if we're not careful," she said. "I think we'd better get back."

Gil nodded. The storm was coming up faster than he had figured it would. Still, Maria seemed unusually eager to return. He wondered what had caused the turnabout.

She must have sensed his puzzlement. "Perhaps another day," she suggested, looking at him.

Perhaps *what* another day?

CHAPTER 4

Windows, frames and all, were gone, leaving gaping holes in the walls. Sections of plaster sagged like an old white's skin, victim of age, the elements, and gravity. What paneling remained was water-soaked and insect-ridden, rotten to the touch. Anibal believed he could see slits of daylight high above him, but, with the sky getting darker every minute, it was hard to tell. The room's fixtures— chandeliers, sconces, even the fireplace mantel—had been removed, presumably to grace the new manor. Still, the floor seemed firm. He jounced a few times to test it. When he had been here in the old days, it had been soft and rubbery. Now, the joists had been reinforced.

The grand staircase had been replaced by a stairway of raw pine. It gleamed white, like a medical student's skeleton—a stark contrast to the ornate decay of the rest of the room. Under the stairs were a gas-powered electric generator and two jerricans of gasoline. The cook's tip had paid off. The repairs were recent; they had been made, furthermore, without any improvements to the exterior, as if the new Mrs. Gainsley wished to keep them secret.

A wire from the generator, stapled to the stringer, led up the stairs. The wind started blowing hard, whistling through the ruin's crevices. It was eerie. Anibal started up the stairs and heard thunder in the distance. It was late for a hurricane, he told himself, but there was a big storm brewing, regardless.

The wire led through a door. Inside, a desk, chair, and table. Anibal paused in reflection. The recent repairs, coupled with Maria Gainsley's Dominican birth and her frequent trips to that country—all pointed to her as the guilty one. Guilty of everything. She had been Gainsley's nurse at the time of Bettina's and young Anibal's deaths. She had taken control of Gainsley's life, he had been told. It was she who had stopped sending the money. *Her doing.* A flash of lightning brightened the room. Thunder cracked a few seconds later.

The desk was clear, but a book of charts lay on the table. Anibal looked at the topmost one. He knew the place. It was the Panama Canal. As a lad, he had stared at similar charts hundreds of times, always trying to put the lines on the map together with what he could see of the land. He bent over the chart, noted a spot encircled in red. He did not have to be able to read to recognize it. The railroad line and the hooked promontory of the harbor identified it as the town of Gamboa.

Another flash of lightning, followed almost immediately by thunder. The storm was coming up faster than he had figured. It was time to get out.

* * *

"Easy, boy," Gil cautioned, soothing his mount. The horse's ears were pinned back; it snuffled in fear. Gil looked up, saw that Maria was having as much trouble as he.

They arrived at the manor. Some of the servants were toting lawn furniture and closing shutters. Others were lashing down the palms. They were like circus workers putting up tents, except they were working harder and faster than he had ever seen circus people labor. A groom took Maria's horse by the halter. She dismounted and strode toward the manor without glancing back.

Gil watched her until she disappeared inside. Even at a distance, she was something. A raindrop landed on his hand: time to go. He walked his horse to the stable, handed him over, then ran to the manor to beat the rain.

Maria wrestled with her boots. She got the first off, threw it, then the second. She undid the leg buttons on her jodhpurs below the knees, stood, and peeled them off, leaving them where they fell. Who could the man poking around the old manor have been, but Brant's other associate? Her fingers kept slipping on the buttons of her shirt. It took forever to get it off.

She went to her chest, pulled out a chemise, put it on over her head, then stepped into a dress.

"Maria!"

It was Eric. She had not heard him enter. She turned. He was in his wheelchair, glowering. "What is it?" she asked, zipping her dress up under her arm.

"I want to talk to you."

She could tell he had been drinking. It was early in the day for it, even for him. She lowered her eyebrows and peered at him, trying to discern the cause of his anger. "Yes?" she answered.

"I want to know what you've been doing in Santo Domingo," he spat.

She caught her breath. "Nothing more than usual," she managed. "Later, I will fill you in on all the details, but—"

"Have you been involved with a Vichyite named Duchesne?"

It was as if a band of steel had tightened around her chest. "Who told—" she stopped, cursing herself.

"It's true, isn't it?" Gainsley shouted.

His hands tightened on the arms of his chair. His complexion was mottled, his eyes burned. Never had Maria seen him so angry. "You have never asked of my business before," she pointed out. "Why should you be interested now?"

"They are our enemy!"

Some of Maria's own fire returned. She stopped, turned to face him directly. He looked small. "Yours, perhaps, but not mine," she spat. "I am making us money. That is enough."

She brushed past the wheelchair. As she did, her husband reached out and grasped her wrist. There was power in his grip. "Let go my—"

He flung her back to the bed. His violence, his strength, brought on a shiver of fear. Maria lifted her head. "Eric, that's—"

She was struck dumb as she saw him struggle from his wheelchair, then lurch forward, grabbing the bedpost for support. He collapsed atop her, his hands around her shoulders. His fingers gripped hard. "Vichy is our enemy," he repeated from between clenched teeth.

His spittle sprayed her face as he spoke; she hardly recognized him. She reached up to pry his hands from her, but his grip was too strong for her. His dead weight threatened to drag them both to the floor. Maria braced her feet for support. Her husband had lost his glasses; his eyes looked wild. "Eric!" she shouted. She writhed in an effort to free herself.

It was as if he had lost all reason. "I'll teach you to do business with our enemy agents," he said. Slowly, his hands shifted from her shoulders to her neck. His thumbs pressed into her flesh.

"No," she squawked, and shifted her hands to his face, clawing, leaving bloody trails.

Maria felt her strength ebbing. She started to slide off the bed and grabbed the bedcovers, dragging them with her. She was going to die. She lost the strength to resist. His words, "Whore! Traitor!" grew fainter in her ears. The bedspread fell on top of her, blinding her.

Then, suddenly, it was over. For a second, she could not comprehend it. Someone removed the bedspread. She clutched her throat and rolled up on her elbow, fighting for air. Clovis stood there. He had saved her. Why?

He pulled her up. She had to lock her knees as she fought for strength. There, at her feet, Eric. He lay on his back in a pool of blood. She crossed herself. *Madre mia*, she thought, *it was not supposed to turn out like this*.

A tug on her elbow: Clovis, urging her from the room. She obeyed, too filled with her own fears to resist. Thoughts rocketed and exploded in her mind. It was no longer a question of her being under suspicion. Now, there could be no doubt. Treason and accessory to murder were both capital offenses. She had to get out of Jamaica and back to the Dominican Republic. There was work she must do there; she would be safe there. But first, she had to destroy any evidence linking her to the murder or her complicity in Andre's scheme. It would buy time, help ensure Andre's success.

She could no longer hide behind a husband and manage his shipping firm, could no longer reside in Jamaica—not, at least, until the war was over. All that had been swept aside. Andre's plan *must* succeed. She tried to clear her mind. Was there anything in the manor which might give it away? Nothing. But there were materials in the old manor: charts, some correspondence. She looked at Clovis. "I must get to the old manor. Will you help me?"

Clovis fixed his eyes on her. Slowly, he nodded. Maria touched her neck, then looked away. Whatever his reason for helping, she thought, he was not doing it for her. She had to be careful.

She glanced out the window. Black clouds tumbled overhead, the wind was blowing more fiercely than ever, but it was not yet raining hard. It would be a fiercer storm than the wireless had forecast, she knew. It might help her get away. She would do what must be done, then run, with or without Clovis's further help. The rest was up to Andre: the gold, the other promised rewards. Those were all she had left.

CHAPTER 5

Galveston harbor was crowded. Oil for Britain. Andre smiled at that. In six weeks, he told himself, the war will be all but over. The Americans will be powerless and Britain totally isolated. He glanced at Schatz down on deck. As if the German sensed Andre's attention, he turned and looked up, mopping his brow. "How much longer?" Andre shouted.

Schatz stuck his handkerchief back in his pocket and came up to the bridge. "*Verdammt* Americans," he said when they were together. He lit a Lucky Strike, blew his first puff of smoke from the corner of his mouth. "They and their regulations. It will take the rest of the afternoon. We won't be able to leave until tomorrow."

They had not been permitted to load the dynamite in dock. The harbor was too crowded, the danger of explosion and fire too great, the port authority claimed. It had to be transported from shore by lighter. The ruling trebled their loading time.

At least they were loading it in a regular port, Andre thought. When they got back to the Dominican Republic, they would have four hundred tons to take on board. And it would have to be done without port assistance or modern equipment. "Tomorrow," Alex mused. "That will still give us time to get the *Balboa* ready."

Schatz didn't respond; Andre was not sure he had heard. There *should* be time, he told himself, but they were cutting it close. He would not worry about that. If time grew short, they could load nights as well as days in Ocoa Bay. That was the nice thing about TNT; it didn't have to be treated as gently as the dynamite they were presently taking on.

The back of Schatz's shirt was soaked with perspiration. The German took one long, last drag on his cigarette, then crushed it out in a tin can. "I must get back," he said, more to himself, it seemed, than to Andre.

Alone once again, Andre left the bridge for his quarters. Familiar worries beset him, like a recurring nightmare. Two days at least—more, most likely—they would be on their own in Gatun Lake. The lake was large, Andre reminded himself. It had many islands off the main channel. Surely, they could hide behind one. Should they be discovered, they might plead engine trouble. But if the discovery came too soon, that would not help. There would be questions of why they hadn't radioed for assistance; the ship would become the center of attention. He had another thought: If found, there might be no questions; they might simply be blasted from the water.

How many times had the same fears plagued him? Discovery was unlikely. Once inside the canal, the odds were in their favor. All reports indicated the Americans were far more concerned with security at the approaches to the canal than with patrols of its inner waters. Those were infrequent and, by all information, more or less perfunctory. He rubbed his hands together, tried to think of something else.

Maria. She had been invaluable, well worth the money he promised. Too bad she was not more acceptable in other ways. If only Ellen . . . He could not let himself think of Ellen. He had done what he could. If he had failed to save her, it was her own fault. By now, she was dead. It served her right.

CHAPTER 6

Gil's eyes reflected disbelief.

"I'm telling you there was nothing," Ellen insisted, countering his silent criticism.

He bit his lip, apparently still unconvinced. "And Eric," he continued, "you think he has no knowledge of what's going on?"

"Yes," she agreed. "I'm sure of that."

He nodded. "Just the same, I want to go back to her office."

Ellen recoiled at the suggestion. "I'd far rather get out before the storm hits. And what about Maria?" she asked. "Mightn't she object to your snooping around?"

"Don't worry about that," Gil said. "You should have seen how anxious she was to get back home. She's outside somewhere supervising buttoning up the place by now." He met her gaze. "It's now or never." He turned to go.

Ellen sighed and followed him into the hall. It would be easier and quicker to show him the office than to argue about it.

The hall lights flickered off, came on again, then went off for good. Without them, the only light came from the stained-glass window in the staircase and the slivers of dim daylight which seeped from around the doors along the way. After a few steps, they were beyond the window's gleam. Hallway furniture grew gray and indistinct; the portraits on the walls were little more than black rectangles.

As they turned into the east wing, they passed by an open door. Gil stopped her with an outthrust arm. "What's the—"

Gil silenced her with a finger to his lips. "I heard something," he mouthed.

She pushed his arm away. It moved slowly, like a heavy gate. "What?" she whispered.

He shook his head. "I'm not sure." He nodded toward the door.

Ellen peeked inside. The curtains were pulled shut, the shadows were heavy. She saw the foot of a canopied bed and part of a dressing table. Other than that the bed was unmade, there seemed nothing unusual about it. Still, something made her skin grow cold. "I don't hear anything," she said. "Let's go."

"Wait here," he whispered, and stepped into the room. She debated whether to obey or follow. Then, from a far corner of the room, a shadowy blur rushed at Gil. Ellen shouted and, grabbing a vase from a hallway table, ran into the room. Gil swung his arm up and back, catching his attacker's thrust on the forearm. Something flew from the man's hand and skittered across the parqueted floor.

She brought the vase down on the man's head, then

stood, rooted in place, with a piece of the vase's base in one hand and the broken handle in the other. Gil drove a fist into the man's stomach, then hit him on the back of the head as he fell. Dazed, Ellen stumbled toward the window to retrieve what the man had dropped.

It was a revolver. She picked it up, moved the chamber, and heard it click. She lifted her eyes from the gun and saw Eric Gainsley's body: bulging eyes, mouth agape, bedspread coiled around him. A pool of black blood soaked one corner of it. "Gil," she managed, pointing.

"Jesus," Gil whispered. Sheets of lightning lit the crack between the curtains, gave life to the objects in the room. Ellen shuffled backward, stepped on something, and jumped at the contact. Gainsley's glasses. She watched Gil close Gainsley's eyes, wished something could be done with the mouth. She stooped to pick up the bedspread and put it over him.

"Poor bugger," Gil whispered, rising. There were bloodstains on his knees.

"What about him?" she asked, indicating the man who had attacked Gil.

Gil slipped the man's belt from his trousers and strapped his hands behind his back, then rolled him over on his back.

Ellen peered down at him: café au lait complexion, pockmarked, with short-sleeved white shirt and bib overalls.

"Doesn't look like one of the household staff, does he?" Gil commented, stuffing his handkerchief in the man's mouth. He shucked a pillowcase from a pillow, then tore a strip from it and looked around. "The drapery cord," he said, nodding toward the window. "Get it."

She went to the window and jerked the cord. It did not give. "Put some weight in it," Gil told her. Ellen coiled the cord around her right hand, took a deep breath, and pulled hard. She felt the drapery rod bending and pulled harder. At last, the cord came free. By the time she brought it to Gil, he had tied the strip of pillowcase around the man's mouth. Gil took the cord and bound him tightly. "There," he said at last, "he won't get out of that by himself for a while."

The qualifier, "by himself," worried her. What were the odds against his working alone? Somewhere between great and astronomical, she figured. Gil said something she did not catch. "What?"

"I just thanked you for saving my skin."

The sound of his voice helped bring her back to reality. "We're a team," she responded. "That's what teammates do for one another." She remembered the revolver in her hand. "Here," she said and handed it over to him.

Gil examined it, stuck it under his belt. "Let's get to that office," he said.

"Why?" Ellen asked. Every nerve in her body screamed in protest. "There'll be nothing there; not after this," she argued, nodding toward Eric's body.

"There'll be a phone there," Gil said. "I'm going to call the police in Kingston."

At last he was doing something which made sense.

In the office, Gil put the receiver to his ear, then jiggled the cradle. "Damn," he muttered. "Phone's out. Either the storm or . . ."

They retraced their steps and went down the stairs. Ellen could hear Gil breathing, could hear her own heartbeat. The house felt empty, as if with its master's death, it, too, had died. "Where are we going?" she asked.

"To pick up Anibal and get out of here," he answered. "Let's let the police take over."

It was the second sensible thing he had said. She followed him out the door. There was still little rain, but the wind was blowing harder than ever. Black clouds twisted in the sky. Hurricane? It couldn't be. Too late in the year, and there had been no news of one on the wireless. A big storm, though. No doubt of it. They'd have to hurry.

The servants' quarters were deserted. So was the garage. "What now?" she asked.

"Maybe he's at the old manor," Gil replied, staring into the gloom of the garage. Olive Cooper's Hillman was there, along with an old Packard sedan that had been converted into a truck. The center stall was empty. Ellen guessed what it meant: Maria was in the missing vehicle. *Doing what? Going where?*

"You game?" Gil asked.

"Can we take mother's auto out there?" she said in answer to his question.

"Not in this storm, I think. The road has some bridges I wouldn't trust if it rains hard."

He had another reason, Ellen believed. The man bound and gagged up in the manor—Gil suspected there were more around. So did she, now that she thought about it. Men Maria had hired; men looking for them. Gil was right. It was probably safer to stay off the road.

"Is it true that you don't ride very well?" he asked.

"Well enough," she admitted. "I just don't look very good doing it."

They set out for the stables. Ellen had to hunch her shoulders and lean forward against the wind. Gil took her arm. Even so, they had to shout to be heard. Everything was gray, as it if were twilight or later.

There was a light inside the stables. Crouched under the tin roof's overhang, Gil handed the revolver to her. "Ever use one?" he asked, his mouth to her ear.

She shook her head.

"The gun's ready to fire. Just aim and pull the trigger if you have to use it."

It seemed heavier than before. "What are you going to do?" she asked.

Gil pushed the barrel away from him. "Be careful where you point it," he said. "Not me, us. We're going inside."

He went to the stable door, pushed down the latch with his thumb, and pulled. The wind countered his efforts. He pulled harder, cracked it open. Suddenly the wind caught it, the large door began to swing on its own, while Gil fought to control it. He had to jump aside as it banged open. He stepped inside, Ellen followed behind, holding the revolver in both hands and away from her body. The wind whistled through the open door.

Gil peered into the stalls, then climbed the ladder to inspect the loft. Finally, he was satisfied and came down. "Give it to me," he said, indicating the gun. He snapped on the safety and tucked it under his belt. He took a saddle and went into one of the stalls. "Pick a horse and saddle up," he told her.

She found a gray gelding that looked tractable, chose a saddle and gear in the tack room, and went to work. The gelding *was* tractable, making no protest at her unskilled saddling. She checked the girth again, tightened it.

"Ready?" Gil asked.

"Ready," she echoed and led the gray into the storm.

Lightning turned the sky to silver. Palms snapped back and forth, like tortured animals. A few had snapped in half; some lay uprooted. As she mounted the gray, she had to fight to control it. The gelding calmed, but she could feel its fright. It was willing to let Ellen have her way for the moment, but its behavior made no promises should the storm get worse.

* * *

The old manor was outlined by lightning. Dark and incomplete, like the ruin of a ravaged monastery. Gil reined in his horse, cupped his hands about his mouth, and shouted. "No car. Going inside." He dismounted.

His declaration sent a shiver up Ellen's spine. It was raining harder. Wind-driven drops pelted her hands and face. She swallowed her fright and slid off the gelding. At least they would be out of the storm.

Gil opened the wooden door and led his horse into the ruin. Ellen followed behind with her gray, entering what must once have been called the great hall. It seemed vast. She waited while Gil wrestled to close the door behind them. "Shall we tie our horses up?" she asked when he had rejoined her.

"Where can they go?" he asked.

She looked about. It was true. Their mounts could not wander far. "Will they be safe?" she asked.

"As safe as us."

She would have preferred a more positive response. She let go her reins, wiped her eyes, and ran her fingers through her sopping hair.

Gil had gone over to the stairs. "Newly built," he commented. He bent and peered under them. "Something else," he told her.

At first, she saw nothing. Gradually, as her eyes grew accustomed to the shadowed space, helped by flashes of lightning, she made it out. "A generator," she replied at last, looking up at Gil.

"Someone's been making repairs," he said. "Let's get it going." He wound a cord around the flywheel and held it in his right hand. "Ready?" he asked, looking at her. His face was blue, his clothing black.

"Go ahead," she agreed. Her eyes darted from one

corner of the hall to another, as if their pursuers had already arrived.

He pulled. The engine sputtered, a light on the generator's side pulsed on and off; then the light steadied and intensified. In its glare, she saw a wire leading up the stairs.

Gil saw it, too. "Let's follow it up," he suggested. His words sounded hollow.

Ellen lagged behind. When she joined Gil on the balcony, he said, "There's a room with a light," as if he assumed that would please her.

If Anibal had been here, he would also have found the wire, Ellen thought. She remembered Gainsley's body in the manor and shuddered at the possibility of finding a second.

It was an office of sorts, with a lighted bulb dangling from a cord. Its glare increased Ellen's nervousness. At least, there was no body. Gil headed for a cabinet in the corner, while she opted for the desk. As she searched, she heard him sliding doors open and shut. By his manner, it was evident he was finding nothing. The office seemed nearly as bare as that in the manor had been. She glanced up, saw that Gil had transferred his attention to the table.

She opened the desk's center drawer. There was an envelope amid a pile of pencils, elastic bands, and paper clips. "Here's something," she said, taking it from the drawer. Gil joined her. The papers were in Spanish. A firm called Havana Shipping and Transfer was leasing a ship—the *Balboa*—to Inter-American Lines. Ellen had never heard of either. She looked at Gil. "What do you—"

The light went out. She stood frozen, trying to will it back on. "Time to go," Gil whispered and took her arm.

Ellen entered the dark hall, with Gil at her side. The

stairs, she knew, were to their right. She took one step in that direction when Gil stopped her. "Listen," he whispered. At first, the thunder, wind, and rain drowned out all other sounds. Then, in a lull, it came clearly. Voices. They were not alone. "This way," said Gil. He led her away from the stairs.

There had been a second staircase in the rear. It had been in bad shape, as Gil remembered. Was it still there? He pushed Ellen along the darkened halls, trusting to memory to find his way. There was a smell of fresh lumber; here and there, he trod on sawdust—signs of further repair. They gave him hope that the rear stairs had also been replaced.

Through the windows, lightning veined the black sky. With the light, Gil peered down at the stairwell. Half the balusters were missing; the railing was broken and useless. The stairs themselves seemed to hang loosely from the outside wall to which they were attached. He doubted they would support two people at the same time. "I'll go first," he said. "Wait until I'm down before you start. When you go, make sure you hug the outside wall."

He started down without another word. The steps creaked with each footfall, but they held. Finally, after what seemed hours, he was on the ground floor. He looked up to where he knew Ellen waited. "Okay," he said in a stage whisper. Amid lightning flashes, he saw her start down, shoulder tight against the outside wall.

Again, there came the sound of voices. A lightning flash: Ellen had stopped and was looking down. He motioned her to keep coming. Gil slipped the Colt from his belt and backed off. Lightning. Thunder rolled into the room. As it died, another sound registered: someone had kicked or knocked against something. It came from nearby.

Gil found a keg of nails and crouched behind it. Silently, he urged Ellen to hurry. She seemed always to lead off with her right foot. It was like watching a child coming downstairs.

He believed they might have a chance to get away. Lightning.

"Gil!" Ellen's shout rang in the empty space. "Look out!"

A gun roared above the din of the storm. Another flash of lightning. Gil hunched farther behind the keg, keenly aware Ellen was caught in the open. He didn't see their assailant. The room lit up, dimmed slightly, then flickered white. He glanced up at Ellen. In that instant, she stumbled and reeled to the side. She plunged through the railing, then pitched into the darkness. Gil heard the impact of her landing—then nothing. His gun's grip was wet with perspiration.

A flashlight snapped on not thirty feet away. Gil lifted his Colt. The beam swung on the floor, arching ever closer to Ellen. Then, she was caught in a cone of yellow light: lying on her back, left arm pinned under her, right arm stretched out on the floor. Gil saw a dark hand pointing a pistol at her head.

Gil fired. The man grunted, the beam wavered. Gil pulled the trigger again. Nothing happened. The gun had jammed.

The flashlight rolled on the floor. In its beam, Gil saw a man fall atop Ellen. Running to her, he kicked the flashlight and sent it spinning. Circles of light played against the walls.

The man had fallen across Ellen's shoulders, the back of his head a mass of blood and brains. Gil knelt, probing under the assailant to reach Ellen's neck. Quickly, he sought a pulse. It was strong, steady.

There came the sound of running feet. He straightened. The pursuers were closer. Gil sprinted to the window.

No one seemed to be following. For a moment, Gil remained still, debating whether to return or go on, staring back at the path he had just taken. It was raining too hard to enable him to make out the window from which he had escaped. *For once in your miserable life, don't go off half-cocked,* he advised himself. *Weigh the alternatives; consider their implications.* There was no choice, he finally admitted. Alone and unarmed, he could do nothing. It was best to get away and pick another time when the odds were better. *What if that time did not come?* It would come, he vowed. *It had to.*

A circle of steel pressed against the base of his skull. "Take it easy," came a man's voice. The pattern of speech identified him as Jamaican.

Energy flowed into Gil's muscles. He tensed, prepared to spin.

The circle of steel pressed harder against him. "Don't try," the other warned. "William!"

A second figure stepped from the darkness, carrying a shotgun. "That's better," the speaker crooned. "Now, lift them." He slapped Gil's arm.

Gil raised his hands in surrender. In a flash of lightning, he caught a glimpse of William: copper-colored, tall and thin. The man looked pleased with himself. "That's good," the first man said. "Turn around."

Gil obeyed. He was frisked, his hands were wrestled behind his back and tied. "You were here all the time?" Gil asked. The rain pelted his face. He was cold.

"That's right," the man said. "Waiting for you."

William pushed him in the small of the back. "Get going," he ordered. He had a deep voice.

"Where?" Gil asked.

The first laughed. "We've a car down the road. One of your friends is already in it."

Anibal. Gil slipped as he slid down a small embankment, but scrambled to his feet before either of his captors reached him. Only Ellen was left, Gil thought, and she was unconscious, pinned under a dead man.

CHAPTER 7

Her hair was clotted with blood; gore speckled her face. Nonetheless, it was Ellen. "My rival," Maria muttered. The competition for Andre's affections had ended. Maria had won. She did not feel like a winner.

Ellen's body was covered by the fallen bodyguard. It did not seem right. Maria knelt to roll him off. The lifeless bulk was heavy and resisted her efforts.

"What are you doing?"

Maria shaded her eyes from the flashlight's glare. It was Clovis. "Help me get him off the woman," she ordered.

"We've work to do." The refusal was flat, absolute.

It angered her. Maria stood. "You will do what I tell you," she spat. "Get him off her."

Clovis glared, mouth open, the tip of his tongue protruding. Then, he smiled and stuck his foot under the man, turning him on his side. "Through the head," he pronounced, holding the cadaver by the tip of his shoe. He let the body plop back. "Why bother?" he said. "Go." He pushed Maria to set her in motion.

Maria had to step back to regain her balance. She was about to protest, then stifled it. There was nothing she could do. The push, the ease with which he had ignored her, the look on his face—all confirmed that he was in control. She turned, began to walk back toward the great hall. The sound of rain against the ruin pounded in her ears.

The truth came. Clovis had been put on the estate to spy on her. Had Andre arranged it? She did not wish to think of it. It would only prove how false everything else he had said was.

Clovis took a grip on her arm. Maria permitted her captor to propel her into the hall. The generator was back on; its small bulb cast the room in a pale, golden light. Heavy shadows remained in the corners. Outside, flashes of lightning, peals of thunder. Inside, a fine mist hung in the air.

A pair of men were dousing the hall with fuel. She recognized neither. Clovis's men, doing his bidding. One, a young man still in his teens, was wrestling with a jerrican lodged underneath the stairs. "Mr. Watkins," he said, looking at Clovis, "it's stuck tight. Can you help?"

The grip loosened. Maria rubbed her arm as she watched him join his confederates. When the place was set afire, she realized, it would become an inferno, despite the rain. The manor, too, would be destroyed, she thought. They would leave nothing.

They would leave no one.

Tomorrow, perhaps the day after, searchers would find her body, burned to a cinder.

She stepped backward. Her right hand touched a sawhorse behind her. Something rested along its length. She glanced down. A large carpenter's level. She worked around the sawhorse. No one paid her any attention. She took another step, glanced at the entry. It was perhaps thirty feet away. A dozen strides, maybe fewer; a matter of a few seconds. The men were ten feet farther, spilling petrol on the floor.

"Thinking of running out?"

Clovis set his hands roughly on her shoulders. Maria recoiled at the touch, wresting herself free. She spun to face him, saw him laughing.

The laugh as much as the awareness of danger triggered her fury. She seized the level and brandished it as if it were a cricket bat. Its sharp edges pressed into the flesh of her hands. She gripped it even tighter. Clovis's eyes narrowed. "Put it down," he said.

Instead, she swung, aiming for his head. Clovis ducked. The metal struck his forearm. "Hey . . ." he managed before she struck again. This time she hit him across the side of the head. He fell in a heap. Maria dropped her weapon and bolted. There were shouts behind her. She kept running, burst out the door, and into the storm.

Water stung her arms, face, and legs. It was salty: sea spray mixed with rain. Lightning ripped open the sky, brightening the horizon. Palms danced, as if under a spell.

Behind her, a voice, yelling something. Water poured from her hair. Her eyes smarted. She ran blindly toward the palms.

Maria peered over the bank, but could see nothing. What she heard was frightening enough: the sound of rushing water. Weariness sucked at her. They were still searching for her. She had seen one of them only a minute ago, slithering through the trees behind her.

There was no retreat. She started down the bank, toward the swollen stream, slid in the mud, and fought to slow her descent. Suddenly her feet and calves were engulfed in the water. It threatened to sweep her out into the current and carry her off.

Her muscles ached, her skin was torn in a dozen places, and bruised everywhere else. Wearily, she scrabbled frantically, managed to get her feet under her, and fought for balance. She had crossed the stream many times, she remembered, not even having to lift the hem of her dress. But this was hardly the same stream. The noise told her that. It terrified her. She swung around, tempted to retreat, but knew what awaited her if she did: discovery, certain death. She had to cross. Slowly, she turned to face the stream. She took a tentative step; then, another.

The stream came to mid-calf after only a few steps. Its pressure was unrelenting, bone-crushing. It rose to her knees. With every step, she was pushed downstream, aware that, if she stumbled, she would never regain her balance. The water rose to above her waist. Her dress wrapped itself around her thighs, hobbling her. She swept an arm upstream. Almost immediately, weeds and grass were plastered to it, clinging like a thousand bracelets. With every step, there came a second of buoyancy before her lead foot touched bottom. In that second, she was powerless; the strength of the stream nearly irresistible.

Then the water reached only to her waist, and then only to her hips. She reached the far bank and started crawling up. It was like climbing a mountain of mud. No sooner did she set her hand down than mud covered it. The bankside moved beneath her. Maria slipped, crawled back, slid again. Below, the torrent seemed to be calling her back.

The sky lit up. She looked back: someone stood on the opposite bank. She kept crawling. Now she heard him, taunting her. The words were unintelligible, like those in a dream, but their meaning was unmistakable. Clovis was coming to kill her. Desperately, Maria renewed her efforts. Panting, her fingers rubbed raw, her knees sore and bleeding, Maria turned back to catch sight of her pursuer. It felt as if he were right behind her, poised to strike, but she could see nothing in the darkness of the storm.

Another flash of lightning. He was halfway through the water. He seemed naked, his teeth and eyes shone. Then, the grin vanished. Everything went black again. The only thing Maria could see was an image that had been burned onto her eye; Clovis swinging his torso to look upstream.

When next she could see, he was gone. A tree or other piece of flotsam had swept him away. If he escaped, he would be carried far downstream, but she thought that unlikely. There were too many snags in the flooded stream. One would catch him, hold him under. Perhaps he was already dead.

She drew her knees up, rested her head on her arm. Mud oozed over the arm; she could feel it in her hair. All was gone: her husband, the Gainsley estate, her hopes for Andre. Would it not be better to slip back into the water? Was not an instant death preferable to what faced her?

Santa Maria! Anything was better than death, even if it was only another minute of being wet and cold. She started crawling.

She dug for handholds—a root, a rock—and climbed, slowly, inch by inch. Port Antonio, on the other side of the island—she could go there. Her left foot slipped. Desperately, she clawed into the muck to stop from sliding. She waited for a few seconds, began to climb again. Cuba was only a few miles from Port Antonio. She would need money to get there. The wind plastered her shirt against her back. Was she out of the deepest part of the vale? She lifted her head, thought she saw the lip of the hill. Only a few feet more.

Eric's wall safe. There was some money there; not much, but enough. From Cuba, she could get back to the Dominican Republic. She had funds there. And the letter of marque was secure in a safety deposit box. She elbowed over the top, pulled herself to level ground, and lay there, panting, gasping.

She could wait out the war in the Dominican Republic. There were people there who would protect her. She would live to make the French government honor its agreement. Andre had not seen the last of her. But first, she had to get back to the manor.

CHAPTER 8

Ellen coughed. The air was filled with smoke. She tried to rise, but a heavy weight pinned her down. A body. Gil's? She pushed against it, then squirmed and kicked herself free. The exertion brought on new coughing spasms. It was as if a knife dug into her skull; each cough drove it deeper. The smoke was growing thicker. It crept down her throat toward her lungs.

She hugged the floor and sucked air in rapid, shallow sips. Lightning turned the air about her into a murky gray. The dead man's skin was black. Not Gil. Like a lizard, she swung to crawl away. Unable to think, blinded by smoke and darkness, Ellen relied on the sensation of heat for guidance, crawling away from where it seemed greatest. She prayed she would not end up in a cul-de-sac.

The smoke seemed to thin as she went. She reached a wall, felt rain falling on her. It was an outside wall; she was close to a window well. Ellen lifted herself up and scrambled out the opening. The rain came down in sheets. She welcomed it, stood still, breathing deeply with head raised and eyes closed while the rain washed the smoke from her. Then, she stumbled ahead, away from the old manor.

Two hundred yards later, she collapsed on a knoll, wrapped her arms around her stomach, and began to retch. The pain in her head returned with each contraction.

At last, she was done. She looked back at the ruin. Tongues of fire reached from every opening, striving to leap in the air, but beaten back by the rain. The wind was behind her. It drove the smoke away.

Gil: Had he been left in the ruin, too? She tried to recall those last few seconds before she had been knocked out. She remembered stumbling, grabbing the railing, sailing out into the darkness. Had someone shouted? She tried to think and decided the only shouts she had heard had been her own.

It made no difference. Until she had proof to the contrary, she had to assume Gil was still alive. Anibal, too—wherever he was. Her head hurt; she was weak. She pushed herself up and began to walk in the direction of the new manor. Water poured from her hair, down her forehead, and into her eyes.

Slowly, without the energy for either hope or despair, she continued walking, stumbling often. A noise caught her attention over the wind and rain. It came from far away. She heard it again: the whinnying of a horse.

Her first inclination was to hide, but she suppressed it. It could as easily be Gil or Anibal as any of the others. She moved along the trail toward the sound, slipping in the gumbo.

It was her gelding, its reins caught in the roots of a

downed palm. Its ears were pinned back. The beast was frightened half to death. At least the men had loosed the animals before they had fired the ruin.

She reached out to it. The gelding reared. Ellen clucked and cooed, grabbed its halter, petted its nose, then patted its flanks. It trembled under her hands.

It was heartening to have a living thing with her, Ellen thought. She freed the reins and led it back to the trail. It would not take her as long to get back to the manor as she had figured.

The worst of the storm was over. With the dying of the wind, the rain fell straight down. Lightning still crackled, but the accompanying thunder was faint and a full measure behind: distant timpani. Ellen's thighs were chafed from riding in wet clothing. Her head hurt; she was shivering, as much from uncertainty as from the cold.

She slid from the gelding and tied it to a tree at the edge of the woods. Steam rose from its flanks. Ellen patted it on the neck, whispered, ''Soon we'll get you where you can be warm and dry.'' She slipped around the tree to reconnoiter.

A truck was backed to the entrance of the manor and men were loading it with paintings and silver. Looting. Ellen looked over at the stables. A light shone through a window there. A guard knelt on the stable's lee side, cradling a pistol in his lap. His coat collar was turned up, his head was down. He looked as miserable as Ellen felt.

She set out on foot, keeping to the shelter of the trees, to circle the stables. No one else was outside. She darted across the open ground. The window was high in the wall; even on tiptoe, Ellen could not see all the interior.

But what she saw offered some reassurance: Gil and Anibal, trussed like a pair of rolled beef rumps, watched by a second guard. At least they were alive. She paused: voices in the distance. Men, laughing as they loaded the truck. They reentered the manor. She would have to hurry. The truck seemed nearly full.

The path to the stable door was lined with white-painted rocks. Ellen knelt and pried one up, then crept back around the corner. The guard was too engrossed in his discomfort to hear her and looked up only as she set her feet to drive the rock down on him. It landed on his forehead with a dull smack. The man fell against the wall without a sound, his mouth and eyes open. He lay motionless, a splotch of red the size of a shilling on his forehead. Gingerly, Ellen reached down for his gun, looked for the safety, and unsnapped it.

She slipped back for the horse and freed it. The gray trotted immediately to the stable door, whinnying and kicking. Seconds passed. At last, the latch was lifted. The door cracked open. As soon as it did, the gelding shoved its nose into the opening to force entrance. Ellen, pistol leveled, followed. The guard's eyes widened as he saw her. She pointed the gun at him, motioned him to precede her back into the stable. Silently, hands behind his head, he complied. He turned and walked slowly.

Gil was lying in a pile of straw; Anibal seemed tied to a post. Both were gagged. They saw her as soon as she saw them and lifted their eyes in warning.

There was a second guard, sitting on a bale of hay. *Maria Gainsley must have hired an army*, Ellen told herself. "Up," she said. He scrambled to his feet. She prodded the first guide in the small of his back, indicating she wanted him to join the second. Shuffling his feet, he did so.

"Turn around," she told the first man when the two were together. He obeyed. The two stood shoulder to shoulder. Both were young, not yet out of their teens, Ellen estimated. Dark-skinned, heavily muscled, and short, they could pass for brothers.

Gil was mumbling under his gag. Anibal remained still, but he was staring at her. "You," she said, pointing her revolver toward one of the guards. "Free them."

The man did not obey. Instead, he lowered his hands and took a step toward her. His skin glistened in the lamplight.

"That's far enough," Ellen warned.

He continued to advance.

"I don't think the lady wants to shoot," the other said. *He's right,* Ellen thought. *The lady doesn't want to shoot. But she will if she must.* The second guard had begun to sidle to his left. A shotgun rested against the wall, not far from him. Ellen aimed at the man's toe and pulled the trigger. The bullet spat dirt.

Before she could swing back, the first was on her. Ellen fired twice, point-blank, saw his face contort in pain and disbelief. With his hands wrapped around her weapon and pulling it from her grasp, he sagged, then fell, still clutching the gun. Ellen stared, then, willing herself to action, knelt to pry the gun free.

She looked up; the other was reaching for the shotgun. Desperately she reached for her pistol. It was as if time had stopped. She found the barrel, but could not loosen it. When she glanced back, she stared into the twin barrels of the shotgun.

The man holding it lurched. The shotgun's roar filled the stable as the guard toppled. Gil had rolled into the man from behind. Pieces of straw wafted down on Ellen's head and shoulders. The blast had gone awry. Wildly she looked for a weapon of some kind, then spied a hayfork. She scrambled to her feet, grabbed it, and spun back around. The guard had regained his feet. Shotgun still in hand, he reared back and kicked Gil in the face.

As he turned back to her, she drove the tines into his chest. Ellen let go and stepped back. The shotgun fell as the guard wrapped his hands around the fork handle. He fell to his knees, then forward, the hayfork his fulcrum. He was pinned to it. Like a specimen in a butterfly collection.

Gil lay on his side, blood streaming from under the gag and from his nose. He was unconscious. Ellen freed Anibal first. Together, they untied Gil. "I thought you were dead," Ellen said, working on Gil's legs.

"We would have been," Anibal agreed, "but the guards seemed leaderless."

What had happened to Maria Gainsley, Ellen wondered. She shrugged. It didn't matter.

Gil came to. He tried to grin, then sat up, holding the back of his hand to his nose. Ellen looked at Anibal. "I left one of them outside," she said.

Anibal nodded. He knelt beside the guard Ellen had shot and felt for a pulse on his neck. "He's dead," he said, pulling the pistol out from under him. He stood, retrieved the shotgun. There was a box of shells on a shelf. He took a handful, reloaded the gun, shoved the rest in his pocket. He saw Ellen staring at him and smiled, then left.

Gil mumbled something. He had difficulty pursing his lips; his nose was bent to one side.

"What did you say?" Ellen asked as she tried to stanch the bleeding.

Gil pushed her hand away. "I said 'ou 'ook 'ike a downed 'at," he repeated, refusing to purse his lips.

The remark sent her hand to her hair. It was wet, stringy, and, she was sure, filled with ashes and blood. "If you think I'm bad," she countered, "you should take a look at your nose. You could sneeze around corners."

She shouldn't have said it. Gil's hand flew to his nose. He said something. It took a second before she could assign meaning to the sounds. "Will it hurt my career?"

Ellen leaned back in disbelief. Then she saw what passed for a smile on his lips. He had been joking. Had he not, she might have tried shifting his nose to the other cheek.

She rolled up two ends of his handkerchief and thrust them as deep as possible into his nostrils. It was as if he were wearing a ring in his nose, like the wild man of Borneo. What a pathetic creature he seemed. Ellen felt a rush of sympathy, mixed with other, less neutral, emotions.

From outside came the sound of the truck careening along the lane, broken by the roar of the shotgun. Anibal came in. He moved easily, as if the threat of danger was gone. "What happened?"

"Couldn't find the guard you left. They came by in the truck, but left after I took a shot at them. The manor's on fire."

The fire seemed unimportant. "What about the guard?" Ellen asked.

Anibal shrugged. "He left with the others, I imagine."

"Why would they leave?" Gil asked.

"What would be their purpose in staying?" Anibal answered. "We've probably got all their guns."

That would mean they truly were out of danger. Ellen hardly dared accept it. "We can go?" she asked.

Anibal shook his head. "Nothing to leave with," he responded. "I checked the garage. All the cars are gone."

Ellen let it sink in. Someone had stolen the Hillman. *God*, she thought, *Mother's going to kill me.*

CHAPTER 9

"...**S**till hear me?"

Gil held the receiver tighter to his ear. "Barely," he shouted. "What's up?"

"... Trouble ... this end," McEachern responded.

Trouble with the report Gil had sent last week, or trouble hearing him? "What about it?"

"Navy brass ... didn't buy it. Canal ... well protected. Intelligence ... oil refineries ... and Aruba."

Gil had to fill in the missing pieces. Naval intelligence must have dismissed the possibility of an attack against the canal. Instead, some rumor about a plot to blow up the oil refineries in Aruba and somewhere else: Trinidad, he thought McEachern had said.

He wasn't sure he blamed the navy much. His report had been "a lot of potatoes and little meat," as his father used to say. Affirmation of Duchesne's probable presence in Ciudad Trujillo, a shipping firm's lease of a Cuban tramp steamer, and a map that had Gamboa encircled. That was the extent of the hard information. A chase halfway across Hispaniola, then murder and arson, still might not be convincing to the professional. Too many questions were unanswered, the conclusion still insufficiently obvious. "What?" he yelled. McEachern had said something Gil hadn't heard.

". . . said . . . stay . . . Jamaica . . . days?"

Gil smiled. His problem was getting off the island, not staying on it. "Sure," he shouted.

"Good. Keep . . . on job. All . . . help you . . . this end."

The line went dead. Gil held on to the receiver for a minute. He was still an OCI agent. Did that mean McEachern was more willing to accept Gil's interpretation of the information than the navy had been? It was nice to think not everyone believed him incompetent. He set the receiver back on the cradle and turned to Charles Strachey. "Thanks for letting me take the call in your office," he said.

Strachey seemed to be struggling against showing too much curiosity. "No problem at all, old boy. What's the word?"

"I might need your assistance."

"You've but to ask."

"Can you find out what the police have uncovered in their investigation of Gainsley's murder?"

Strachey nodded.

"And I'm not sure how long they'll want me to stick around, but I might have to leave. Can you square it with them?"

"Consider it done," Strachey replied. "I'll let you know how I come out tomorrow," he said, looking at his appointment book. "Morning's all booked up, I'm afraid. Afternoon? Two o'clock?"

"Two it is," Gil agreed.

"Anything else I can do?"

Gil shook his head gently, in order not to hurt his bandaged nose. "Nothing I can think of. Thanks for everything." He reached the door, paused, and turned back to Strachey. "There is one more thing. I need a car. Can you get one for me?"

"Already arranged. Do you want a driver?"

"I think I can manage. Thanks." Gil left. He had to go out and see Ellen. He'd put it off too long already.

Ellen's smile was quick enough when she greeted him in her mother's driveway, but her eyes gave her away. They had a haunted look to them, thought Gil. She was still in shock. The recognition sent new guilt through him. It was his fault.

He was tempted to climb back in the car and return to Kingston, but he remained, rooted in place. Ellen paused, too, halfway between the house and his auto. He saw Sara behind her mother, staring at him. Small wonder. He must look like a monster.

He'd come this far; it wouldn't do to drive off without a word. He closed the car door, breaking the silence. "Hello," he said. "I wanted to see how you were doing."

This time her gaze rested a little longer on him. The smile flickered back. "I'm fine," she replied. "And you?"

It was a start. He remained by the car door, hand still on the handle. "I'll make it."

"One wouldn't know from the look of you."

He raised his hand and gingerly bridged the plaster on his nose between thumb and forefinger. "The color's already begun to fade. You should have seen it a few days ago."

"Why didn't you come out before?"

The question's abruptness made it seem all the more harsh. "I was told you needed rest," he began. "After that, I got bogged down in the investigation." He wondered why he hadn't the courage to admit he'd been afraid to visit. "They've found your mother's car," he said.

She nodded. "We'd heard. Where was it?"

"On the other side of the island, at St. Ann's Bay. The police believe Gainsley's wife took it. She's probably in Cuba now."

"Good condition?"

"The car? Good enough, I guess. I've told the mechanics to go over it and get it in tip-top shape."

"Would you care for some tea?"

Why was that so hard to answer? "I don't want to put you to any trouble," he finally said.

The blue of her eyes grew darker. Then, the mood seemed to pass. "No trouble," she replied. "I was about to have some myself."

He followed her back to the veranda and nodded hello to Sara. Ellen sat him down and told him she'd be back in a moment. Sara did not return his smile. "How did your eyes get so black?" she asked.

"I had an accident," he told her. He had a feeling she knew he lied.

"Do they hurt?"

"Only if I sneeze." He figured that would stop her. It did.

Ellen returned, carrying a tray. She set it down, sat down herself, and began pouring. "Has Sara been grilling you? Milk?"

"Yes. Yes."

"Sugar? It, fortunately, is not rationed."

"Two spoons."

She put in the sugar, handed him the cup. "Children are so honest, aren't they? They've not had time to develop guile, or any other civilized tricks."

Gil lifted his cup and kept his eyes on it. However he responded, he was in for a tough time. He deserved it, he told himself. "You're probably right."

It was like watching a locomotive starting up: slowly, then growing more forceful with each stroke of the pistons. "Perhaps we should learn from them, rather than they from us," Ellen began. "Why didn't you come out? Anibal did," she blurted. "I waited three days, expecting to see you. After that, I wasn't sure I wanted to. Now, ten days later, here you are."

Gil hadn't known about Anibal's visit. They had talked about coming, but when Gil had refused, Anibal had not persisted. He picked up his spoon and stirred his tea, not looking up. "I wanted to," he admitted. "But after all I'd put you through, I didn't think I had the right."

He met her gaze. "In more ways than one," he continued. "I'm married. I've hurt you. What was the point?" He felt miserable.

"Then why did you come at all?"

"I had to." No embellishment.

"Anibal told me this is the way you were."

"He did?" Gil responded, not sure what she meant.

"He said you thought you were Christ. Know a few things, Mr. Brant: I'm an adult. I believe I'm reasonably intelligent. What I do, *I* do. And that goes for agreeing to accompany you on this crazy expedition as well as . . ." She paused and glanced over to her daughter. "It's almost time for you to get back to school. You must wash up."

Sara's eyes seemed suddenly to grow opaque. She did not move.

"Sara?" Ellen said.

With a sigh, the girl slid off her chair and went into the house.

Ellen waited until her daughter was gone, then returned to the subject. ". . . as well as for what happened between us. Do you understand?"

Guilt went, like molasses oozing from a bottle. Relief, mixed with embarrassment, replaced it. Slowly, he nodded.

"I'm glad you came," she said.

For the first time, he could look at her honestly. The hurt in her eyes remained, deep down, but there was something else in them: the assurance that she could cope. "I'm glad, too."

"Are you still on the job?" she asked.

"Yes." He pushed his full teacup aside.

"Why?"

A good question. "Some confusion in Washington, I gather. My boss has asked me to stay on it for a while longer."

"That's not the only reason, is it?"

No, it wasn't. Gil had no trouble identifying his other reasons. Putting them in order of importance was the hard part. Reluctance to return to Hollywood, certainly. His unwillingness to cut all traces connecting him to Ellen was even more important. But those were givens. Ellen was as aware of them as he. It was not what she meant. "I'm stubborn," he said. "I'd like to know for sure what's going on."

"Why?"

He looked at her, tried to smile. It was not returned. "I guess because, after all we've been through, it's become my private war," he said.

She leaned forward. Gil had the feeling she wanted to

touch him, but she did not. Instead, she sat back. "Mine too, then," she replied.

If Strachey was surprised at Ellen's and Anibal's presence, it did not show. The British intelligence agent rose and said, "Good of you to come. Please sit down."

Ellen and Anibal obeyed. Gil crossed the office for a third chair, came back with it, and joined them. "What have you got?" he asked.

The Englishman sighed at the American's rudeness. "Not a great deal. The police have sifted the ashes of both manors. Aside from Gainsley's remains and one other body, there was nothing."

"What about the three looters you arrested? Have they told you anything?"

"Nothing," Strachey confessed. "I doubt they know anything. Their leader might, but he has disappeared. A man named Clovis Watkins."

"Who is he?" Ellen's question.

"A troublemaker, according to the police," Strachey answered. "He and his associates pop up now and then, claiming to be fighting for Jamaican independence. During the troubles of '38, they tried to infiltrate Bustamente's union. He kicked them out. Since then, they've apparently been wandering from one part of the island to another, trying to set themselves up as modern Robin Hoods. No one seems to have bought it."

"The Hillman?" Gil said.

"The woman was driving it, no question. A fingerprint was found at last. We assume she went to Cuba. There's a warrant for her arrest. The Cuban police have been informed."

"Much likelihood of catching her?" Gil continued.

The Englishman shrugged. "It depends on how much

money she has. If it's enough, she might buy herself out of trouble. If not, we'll probably get her."

Somehow, Gil thought she wouldn't be found. "Encourage the police to keep working on it, that's all you can do. From your side of this, how much help can you give us?"

"London has made it abundantly clear," Strachey said. "All you ask for, short of lending you a battle cruiser." He paused. "I think we might even arrange that, if you wanted it badly enough."

"No battle cruiser," Gil responded. "What about the shipping lines?"

Strachey opened his folder and looked at his notes. "Nothing yet on Inter-American," he finally said. "Any idea where its home office is located?"

Gil looked at Ellen.

"We only found a single reference to it," Ellen said, "but I imagine its home office is in Ciudad Trujillo. Havana Shipping and Transfer should know. What about it?"

"We have a line on it," Strachey said. "It's owned by a man named Puentes. He was pretty important in the days when Machado ruled Cuba, but he's only a small-time businessman now."

"Is he honest?"

"Not any more than his peers, I gather. Rather less so, it would seem," Strachey replied.

"Has he given your people anything?"

Strachey shook his head. "Tight-lipped. And not much we can do to get the Cubans to help, I'm afraid. Your chaps might be a little more successful. Cuba's in your pocket, after all, not ours."

"Have you sent word about Puentes to Washington?"

"As you asked," Strachey said.

McEachern hadn't mentioned it. That probably meant

the navy wasn't doing anything about him, either. It was the OCI's weak point, Gil realized. It was empowered to gather information, but had no control of what was done with it. Operations belonged to the army, navy, and FBI. "What about the International Maritime Registry?" he asked. "Has it found out anything?"

"Nothing as yet," Strachey said.

So, in the meantime, they had to wait. For what? For the navy to get off its duff? For the International Maritime Registry to find out something about Inter-American Shipping? For the Cuban police to arrest Maria Gainsley? Why had McEachern asked him to stay on the job if there was nothing to do?

It could only be that he hoped Gil could come up with a new line of thought. And, if he did, McEachern was expecting him to follow it on his own. "Gamboa," he said.

He had the attention of all three. "The place Anibal saw encircled on the map," he reminded them. "What could be going on there that might have caught Maria's attention?"

There was silence. "Pan-American Highway," Anibal said. It was like being pricked by a needle. Gil turned to Anibal. "What about the Pan-American Highway?"

"I've been looking for a new job," Anibal said.

"And?"

"There's a Texas construction outfit—Maxwell's—that has a contract for the Pan-American Highway. Nothing big: surveying only, I think. But someone told me it's hiring. Workers report to Gamboa."

It wasn't anything definite, but Gil felt a chill of excitement nevertheless. "Do you know any more about it?" he asked Anibal.

"Only the jobs they want filled. They want blasters, among other things."

Blasters. Dynamite in the Panama Canal. Inter-American Shipping. One of its ships would be carrying the explosives. Gil would bet on it.

"It may not be anything," Anibal said.

Maybe not, Gil thought, *but it's a hell of a lot more than we had a minute earlier.* What more did he need to know: The name of the ship Gainsley's wife leased from the Cubans, that was all, then he could move. Then the navy would listen. It wouldn't dare not to.

PART FOUR

CHAPTER 1

November Twenty-sixth

Andre slid the knife under the heavy cardboard lid and tore open the box. He reached under a layer of waxed paper to lift out one of the bars. It was smooth, with the color, look, and texture of white chocolate. He turned it in his hands, examining it carefully. About twenty-five centimeters long, perhaps half that wide, the dimensions of a cigar box, except not as thick: no more than four centimeters. He set the bar back, then taped the lid shut.

TNT. Wonderful stuff. It could be dropped and broken, battered and abused, and nothing would happen to it. Heat didn't faze it, water didn't hurt it. One could do nearly anything with it and it remained passive. But put a charge to it and it became the deadliest force man had yet invented.

He sat back on his heels, savoring the moment, lingering over the steps which had led him to it. From engineering student to the foreign service; from the Dominican-German Scientific Institute to the *Balboa*. It was almost as if fate had determined his life.

Not almost, he told himself. Fate and nothing else. He could see that now. His destiny had forced him to reject his father's plans for a career in the military. And, later, when he had been at a crossroad, it had driven Ellen from him. Had they married, he would have left the Institute and gone back to Paris. His career would have taken a far less noble path. Fate had decided against Ellen. Fate was harsh, implacable, inexorable. Bountiful. He had been selected to lead his country back to glory. Anything which interfered with that mission had been brushed aside. One path, one choice. The choice was not, had never been, his to make.

He stood up, leaned his elbows on the railing and gazed toward the shore of Ocoa Bay. Only a few cases of TNT could be carted at a time in the canoes. Based on how much had been brought aboard in two days, the loading would take six more days, only just in time to let them keep to their December second sailing schedule.

It was not his only worry. Maria had not been in touch as she had promised. Had something gone wrong? He had picked up no indication of trouble on the wireless, but that was not proof there was none.

"Slow."

Andre jumped. It was Schatz. He had not heard the German come up beside him. "Too slow," he agreed.

"You, too, are nervous?" Schatz queried.

Was there any point in lying? "We have not heard from Maria."

"Just before the action begins, that is the hardest time," said Schatz.

An understatement, Andre thought.

"I am going to rig up some lights. If we load through the night, our loading time will be cut by one-third, perhaps more."

Andre turned to look at the naval captain. The sun shone directly into his eyes; he had to squint. The other's words echoed earlier thoughts of his own, yet he felt compelled to debate them. Faster loading might lead to the loss or damage of cargo. Andre's calculations had been precise, without much margin for error. They dared not lose much. It was November twenty-sixth. If they worked around the clock, they might finish before the end of the month. But what would they do with their saved time? Where would they go? "Here or there," Andre said, "we still would have to wait."

The German's glance was sharp, reminding Andre who was in charge. "But there is a difference in where we choose to wait. If we are found out, where would you rather be—here or in the canal?"

Andre could feel the vein in his temple pulse. God, the suggestion of discovery frightened him. "I don't understand," he said.

"If found out in the canal, we might still fulfill the mission, but if we're caught here, the entire effort would be wasted."

"But your instructions state that you are not to enter the canal too soon," Andre reminded him.

"Naval officers are trained to exercise independent judgment. It is enough to know my action fits into the overall plan of my superiors."

"Even at the risk of being hanged for piracy?" Andre queried.

The *Fregattenkapitän* grinned. "You should take *die*

Negerin's hair from between your teeth before you speak. Then maybe you will sound more like a man.''

Andre went cold. "I asked a question," he said.

"But you had not the right. We are aboard ship. I am now in command."

"As you say," Andre conceded, "you are in command."

Schatz gave a curt nod, then left.

Andre lifted his hand and saw it shaking. Fifty years ago, he would have challenged the *frisé* to a duel. Now, he could do nothing. *At least, not now,* he thought. *But later, after all was done, it might be different.*

November Thirtieth

From where Gil sat, Lieutenant Commander James Early's blond hair and crew cut made him look bald. He was writing something on a notepad, with a brusqueness Gil found annoying. It gave him the impression the chief of naval intelligence at Guantanamo was only going through the motions of cooperating with him. Finally, the man set his pencil aside and looked up. His smile was false. "I want to thank you for your efforts, Mr. Brant," Early said, forearms resting on the desk, hands folded. "I hope also you will convey our thanks to the British. They have gone to considerable effort to track down the location of Inter-American Shipping, to say nothing of flying you and your associates out here. We will take over from here on."

Gil had lived in Hollywood long enough to know a brushoff when he heard one. "What are your plans?" he asked.

Early's smile grew fixed. "Not your concern any longer,

is it?'' he answered. "It's a naval matter. You knew that before you came.''

"As a fellow intelligence officer, I'd like to know what you plan on doing,'' he said evenly, raising a hand to stifle Early's rejoinder. "I think I've earned that, at least.''

The lieutenant commander thumped his thick fingers on the desktop in frustration. He rose from his chair, walked to a wall map, turned to glare at Gil, and pointed over his meaty shoulder. "Recognize this?'' he said. "It's the Caribbean, plus a good bit of the South Atlantic: roughly a million square miles of water, along with a couple hundred islands. Do you know what we've got to patrol it?'' He stopped, as if pondering what to say. "Never mind. We had damned little to begin with; now that Roosevelt has handed over fifty destroyers to your limey friends, we have even less.''

"What's your point?''

"The point is you've come here with some bullshit about a Dominican plot against the Panama Canal. You don't know what it is, when it's supposed to take place, or how it will take place, except that the town of Gamboa is somehow involved.'' Early returned to his desk, still glowering at Gil. "Let me clue you in on a few things Washington might not have bothered to tell you,'' he said, lifting his right hand to tick off his points. "One, naval intelligence has the Caribbean covered like a blanket. Two, none of our people have even hinted at anything like what you've told me—and nothing like this could be planned without their getting an inkling of it. Three, Trujillo may be a pain in the ass, but he's a staunch ally. He would never permit anything as crazy as you've suggested.''

Early stopped, clamping his narrow lips shut.

"And four,'' Gil said. "You don't trust the OCI.''

"You said it, I didn't. But you're right. I don't. The navy doesn't. We predicted the OCI would come up with something as insane as this. Frankly . . ."

Gil fought to control his anger. The commander was beefier than he, but he had a roll of suet around his middle. *I could take him easy. Two chops to the midriff and one on the jaw. He'd never know what hit him.* "Frankly, what?" he asked.

"You're not trained," the man finally said. "You wouldn't recognize a valid piece of intelligence if it bit you in the ass. What in hell were you doing last year at this time: teaching history in some high school in Oregon?"

"So what are you going to do?" Gil repeated.

"Do? You're an American citizen; you've made a report. I'm going to treat it like any other unconfirmed report I get: fill it out in triplicate, send a copy to Washington, put another in my files, and give one to Admiral Wilson on base. It will be investigated, never fear. If we find any substance to it, we'll act on it."

"When?"

"In good time."

The navy would do what McEachern had predicted: nothing. Gil rose. "I see," he said. "Thank you for your time."

Now that Gil was ready to leave, some of the anger left Early's icy blue gaze. He ducked his head in dismissal.

Coldcocking him was not the way to handle it, Gil decided. He left the office, pulled out the pass he had been given at the main gate. The day's date was stamped in bold letters. The date rang a bell. Saturday, November thirtieth. The Army-Navy game was due to start in a little while. Maybe that explained why Early had given him the bum's rush: The son of a bitch wanted to run off and listen to it.

Gil walked faster. He knew what he had to do: get off base, back to Santiago, and wire McEachern. Everything depended on how much pull the OCI had in Washington.

CHAPTER 2

December, 1941

The First

Andre peered down at the gang of men scraping paint. Their efforts were lethargic—the motions of work with neither the interest nor the energy for the task. He felt a blister of rust under his fingers and took his hands off the railing. It was a filthy tub; it deserved to be blown into a thousand pieces. He rubbed his fingers free of the orange dust, then clasped his hands behind his back.

So what if he did not have Schatz's sangfroid? He was not a careerist naval officer. For him, this was a one-time operation. He could not be expected to keep his poise to the same extent as the *frisé*. For the hundredth time he peered shoreward. The town of Colon was to port; the canal's entrance lay directly ahead.

The canal did not interest him as much as did the dock by the office of the Canal Authority. Why wasn't there a launch heading toward them, carrying permission to enter the canal? It was two in the afternoon—over four hours since they had presented their application. What was taking the authorities so long? A dozen reasons suggested themselves. None were good. He leaned over the railing, yelling at the lazy crew.

It was the launch. Andre glanced down at the bucket. Three Lucky Strike butts rested there. A new way to measure time, he thought: by the accumulation of butts in a pail. The launch's engine sputtered; an ordinary seaman grabbed the *Balboa*'s ladder, an envelope jutting from the seaman's blouse pocket. Why only an ordinary seaman? As first mate and purser, he must meet the young man. He strode up the deck to greet him.

After a second's hesitation, the seaman saluted. Andre flicked his forefinger to his visor and waited. "Commander's compliments," the seaman said, handing over the long envelope. "He apologizes for the delay. Permission has been granted. I'm instructed to tell you to expect a pilot at first light tomorrow."

Andre suddenly needed to visit the head. "Thank you," he said. "Can you explain the delay? I've never waited this long before."

The seaman looked embarrassed through his acne. He stiffened and saluted. "Permission to leave, sir."

"Permission granted," Andre replied, returning the salute. He wondered what the seaman would think if he knew he had just saluted a commissioned officer of the German navy.

The Second

The corridor was deserted. It was one of the benefits of being on the top floor of police headquarters: no one walked its halls unless absolutely necessary. Maria caught her reflection in the glass of an office door and paused for a closer look. She fluffed her hair, checked her lipstick, and smoothed her white cotton jacket. It was a little tight at the bust, loose at the waist, but it would do.

It would have to. She was nearly out of money. Eric's safe had netted her less than two hundred pounds and half that she gave to the fisherman who took her to Cuba. Most of the rest had gone for the trip back to Ciudad Trujillo. She thought again of postponing this visit and going to her bank, instead. No. The British surely would have requested Dominican assurance in finding her. Her account might be red-tagged. It was best to see Rosario first. She checked her hose to make sure her seams were straight, sighed at the cheap black sandals with an ankle strap. They made her look like a tart on her day off, she thought. The first thing she would buy when she got her money would be a decent pair of shoes. She squared her shoulders and headed for Rosario's office.

White glass, with 412 painted in black on it, but no name, no title: Rosario did not believe in advertising. His line of work was dangerous enough, he always argued. Why assist his enemies any more than he had to? A private, secluded office at headquarters, reserved for when he was doing police business, that was all he wanted. She rapped on the glass.

"Entrar."

She stepped in. Rosario was seated at his desk, wearing

a gray business suit. His eyes showed a moment's surprise before he scowled and motioned her to shut the door.

"You should not have come here. It is dangerous," he said.

"What has happened?" she asked, sitting in a stiff wooden chair opposite him.

"We have a warrant for your arrest. An official from the British Consulate visits me daily. He seeks information about you, has demanded your photograph, reminds me always to be vigilant. I am thinking of moving in a cot so that he can stay at my office permanently."

Maria cut through the torrent. "Does he suspect we have been working together?"

"Would I be talking with you now, if that were so?" he answered. "No. He comes because I am head of the military district and commander of the national police."

"Have you followed Andre's progress?" she asked.

"The ship took on the materials at Ocoa Bay and left on the twenty-ninth—three days earlier than planned."

Why the change in timing? "Did you tell—?"

Rosario shook his head. "I told him nothing about your troubles. I made no effort to contact him at all."

Something else, then. Maybe Andre and the German had been skittish because she had not contacted them, or maybe they had become suspicious of Rosario. If the latter, they had been wise. Rosario was edgy enough that it would not take much to convince him to abandon the project. Had he, she knew, he would not have used halfway measures. All would have been killed; the ship would have been destroyed. He would not leave any evidence which might point to his involvement. That would include her, too.

She returned to the present. "The mission's chances for

success are as great as ever, then.'' She hoped her optimism would raise Rosario's spirits.

"I suppose you are right," he conceded.

"You know I am," she agreed. "It will succeed. We will receive the money promised us." Rosario did not look convinced. "In the meantime," she continued, "I need your help."

Rosario said nothing.

"As you have said, the British want me. I need a new identity."

Rosario's face went blank. "It will cost money," he said coolly.

"I can get no money until I have new papers," she said.

Rosario shook his head. "Payment cannot be put off that long. I will need cash, if I am expected to help. How much have you on deposit here?"

She was sure Rosario knew that better than she. He would have checked on deposits made in the last three weeks; she could only estimate them. "Somewhere around $7,000," she answered. That would be close enough to indicate she was not trying to hide anything.

"I will see what I can do. Have you a place to stay?"

"I hoped you could find me one." Perhaps she would have been better off staying in Cuba. But what would she have done there? How would she had gotten her money out of the Dominican Republic?

He rose from his chair. Offering his hand, he led her to the door. "I have an apartment in the Distrito San Carlos. You will be safe there." He told her the address and handed her a key.

Maria had heard of the apartment, a squalid hole he kept for dalliances. She was tempted to say she could do without his help, but bit her tongue. "Thank you," she said, taking the key.

A PRIVATE KIND OF WAR

"I will call on you later," Rosario replied.

"What about my photograph?" she asked. "Did you give one to the British Consulate?"

"I told him we had no file on you; he'll have to find one somewhere else."

Outside, she took a deep breath. She could smell the sea. No file on her, Rosario had said. But he would have one. A big one. "So, Maria," she muttered, "you have come full circle. You are now like your mother." She held no illusions about what her life with Rosario would be like. Unless she could regain a measure of control over him, he would take all she had. After that, once he tired of her, he would toss her out.

She could not let him do that. She had to find more money in order to wait out the war. A new thought chilled her. What if the war did not end as she and Andre had planned? She dared not dwell on that. Germany *had* to win.

CHAPTER 3

The Third

Lieutenant Commander Early was so red in the face he looked as if he might have a stroke. He glanced at Gil, averted his eyes, then looked back. "Sit down," he said.

Gil obeyed, wondering why he had been called back. Obviously, not because the man enjoyed his company. He kept his silence.

"Cigarette?" Early snarled.

Gil shook his head. "No." He had no more craving for them. The lieutenant commander slammed a pack of *Wings* against the extended forefinger of his left hand to jar one loose. Gil wondered if he saved the airplane pictures they put in every pack. Early tamped the cigarette down, shoved it in his mouth, lit it, then brushed tobacco shreds from his desktop.

He took a deep drag and barked, "All ships owned by Inter-American seeking passage through the Panama Canal will be detained. A sweep of the approaches to the canal will also be made for such a ship.''

Quite a turnabout from their last meeting, Gil thought. He glanced at the wall calendar with the Dionne Quintuplets' picture. They wore overcoats and fur muffs, he noticed, hardly appropriate for Guantanamo. Early drummed his fingers on his desk. For a second, Gil felt sorry for him. "Why the change?" he asked.

Early glared at him. "Don't ask. Just get in touch with that son of a bitch you work for and tell him I've stuck my ass out for him, now he's got to do what he promised.'' He crushed his cigarette into the ashtray. "If my superiors ever look too closely into this, I can kiss my career goodbye. Anyway, I'm giving you what you want. I hope you're frigging pleased about wasting the taxpayers' money.''

What had McEachern done to get such a reaction? Whatever it had been, Gil doubted it had been aboveboard. His respect for his boss went up. "*All* I want?" he asked.

The lieutenant commander furrowed his eyebrows, glowered at Gil from under them, as if fearing he had gone too far. "What've you got in mind?''

"For a start, quarters on base for me and my colleagues," Gil told him.

Early's lips curled into a sneer. "Can't be done," he said.

"Don't tell me you haven't any room."

"None for the nigger. There are rules. His kind can't be put up in officers' quarters. I might be able to get your search started, but I can't do that.''

Gil's anger lasted only a second. "Then we'll stay where we are," Gil answered, "but you learn something, you let us know. I don't care what time of day or night it is.'' He stood.

The other nodded grudgingly. "Got you," he said, and took another cigarette. "I'll let you know," he promised.

The Fifth

"Come in." Early held a paper in his hand.

"You've got something?" Gil asked.

The naval officer handed over the paper. The message was simple: A steamer named *Balboa* had entered the canal on the morning of the second. Gil looked up. "Inter-American?" he asked.

"Leased from a Cuban firm, like you said."

December second; today was the fifth: three days. Surely enough time to do whatever was planned. But nothing had happened. He wondered whether there might be a second Inter-American ship. It was not likely. "Why didn't you let me know earlier?" he asked when he looked up.

Early shrugged. "We were concentrating on ships approaching the canal: *your* suggestion, remember? This was already in it, had been for a couple days."

"When did it leave the canal?" The ship must have unloaded materials and men for a later attack.

"How in hell should I know? You'll have to talk to officials in the Canal Zone to find out."

"In Colon?"

Early nodded. "More likely at Gatun."

Gil paused a beat, then, "Can you get me there fast?"

"I've already set it up," Early answered sourly. "All our PBYs are out on patrol. You can get out on one tomorrow at dawn."

The Sixth: Early Afternoon

"Here it is," the Canal Zone clerk said, setting a folder on the desk for Gil. At first glance, the report meant nothing: a jumble of dates and figures. Gil slowed, began to decipher it. The *Balboa* had applied for permission to enter the canal at 10:05 on the morning of December 1. There followed a note Gil could not understand: *pb*, 6:02 *A.M.*, 12/2/41. "What's that?" he asked, pointing to the notation.

"Pilot boarded," the man replied. "All ships are guided through the locks by a licensed pilot."

"Does he stay with the ship through the canal?"

The man shook his head. He seemed impatient, a civil servant anxious to rid himself of an annoying intruder. "He leaves once he's through the Gatun Locks. Another pilot boards on the Pacific end."

Gil ran his finger down the report, came to a section which had not been filled in. "Here," he said, "why's this blank?"

The clerk turned the report so that he could read it, taking his time in doing so. The pace irritated Gil. "That's where we record the time of exit on the other end," the man answered at last. "But the *Balboa* didn't go through to the Pacific. It only went to Gamboa."

Was the clerk only acting stupid, or was he really that dumb? Gil dropped his line of investigation. Another thought had occurred to him. "Any reason why a ship's captain would tell you his destination was only Gamboa? Could he simply not say anything and let you assume he was going through to the Pacific?"

The look in the clerk's eyes revealed disbelief in the question. It passed. "Purser," he corrected. "In this case, it was the purser who gave us the information." He continued, "He'd have to tell us his destination, wouldn't he?"

"That's what I'm asking. Why?"

"It's simple," the clerk said. "A vessel enters here: name and time of entry are radioed to San Miguel on the Pacific side. If it doesn't exit within twenty-four hours of entry, we must search for it."

"So by telling you it was only going to Gamboa, he saw to it that you did not tell the people at the San Miguel Locks of its presence?"

"There was no reason to," the clerk agreed. His condescending tone indicated Gil should have grasped that elemental truth much more readily than he had.

Gil returned to his original question. "Okay, you've explained that, but this space is blank," he said, tapping the paper with his forefinger for emphasis. The clerk seemed about to repeat his explanation, but Gil did not give him time. "If the *Balboa* didn't exit through the San Miguel Locks on the Pacific side," he said, "then it damned well should have exited back through Gatun. It hasn't! Where is it? Four goddamn days it's been in there. Is the port of Gamboa so busy it would be still lying in wait?"

The clerk's eyes suddenly grew furtive. Reluctantly, he took the report and examined it, hoping to find an explanation he knew was not there. "I guess the ship's still inside," he answered at last. "It must still be at Gamboa."

"What was its cargo?" Gil asked.

The man flipped over the report. "Dynamite," he said, suddenly eager to help, "for Pan-American Highway work crews."

Jesus, Gil thought. "How much?" His voice sounded hollow, as if he spoke through a megaphone, like Rudy Vallee.

Again, a glance at the form. "Six tons."

Six tons? Not much. Still . . . "Have you a copy of the *Balboa*'s manifest?" he asked. "What else was it carrying?"

The other peered at the second sheet, flipped it over, flipped it back. It was obvious he knew the information was not there. "Nothing dangerous," he answered at last, bravado in his tone. He seemed to be sensing the gravity of the matter and was fearful he might be forced to shoulder some of the blame.

"How do you know?" Gil queried. "Did anybody inspect its cargo?"

"No. They asked." The clerk pointed to a question on the form.

Is your ship carrying any combustible or potentially explosive materials which might endanger the canal or its facilities? There, someone had written *No*. Gil wondered if it was Duchesne's handwriting. He turned the folder toward him, noted that the fee paid by the *Balboa*'s master to enter the canal was based on four hundred tons of cargo. "How is that figure arrived at? Is it accurate?" he asked.

"Water dispersal. Accurate enough, I guess," the man replied.

Four hundred tons: eight hundred thousand pounds. If six tons were dynamite, what were the other three hundred ninety-four? Out of nowhere a thought came. *How big a hole could he put in one of the locks with eight hundred thousand pounds of explosives?*

He looked up. "I'd like to talk to Gamboa," he told the clerk. "Can you call whoever's in charge of its dock?"

The man rubbed his chin. There were liver spots on the back of his hand. "I don't know that I can do that," he said.

"Why not?"

"It's Saturday afternoon," the other pointed out. "Nobody works full shifts on weekends. The telephone switchboard will be closed down. If you want to wait until Monday, I'll get them for you then."

It was all Gil needed. "Thanks, no," he said, starting to leave. He had to get back to Ellen and Anibal, then see the navy. He wondered if it would be any more helpful. *God help us if it isn't.*

The Sixth: Late Afternoon

The pilot was shouting and pointing off to port. Gil couldn't make out the words above the engine's roar, but he could see they were above Gamboa. The pilot pushed the stick forward. The controls seemed sluggish. Gil had known sailing ships like that—ones that took an eternity to respond to the rudder. Eventually, the Catalina nosed into a shallow dive. It made Gil's stomach jump into his throat. He swallowed twice. It didn't make him feel any better.

The airship skimmed the waters of Gamboa. There could be no doubt: The *Balboa* might have dropped anchor at Gamboa, but it was no longer there. Gil pointed up with his thumb. The pilot grinned, nodded, and pulled on the controls. This time, Gil's stomach sought shelter on the other end of his digestive system. The pilot was enjoying himself. He seemed about nineteen years old, hardly old enough for a driving license. Gil shouted at him. The lieutenant took off his headset, leaned closer to him. "I'm going aft for a minute," Gil said, enunciating carefully. "Let's prowl around Gatun Lake for a while."

The pilot nodded. Gil unbuckled his seat belt and rose

to join his colleagues. There wasn't a lot of headroom in the Catalina. He had to walk with a stoop.

They were gazing out one of the bubbles amidship. Ellen seemed to be enjoying herself, but Anibal looked gray, like a slice of roast beef left too long on the warming pan. Gil knew how he felt. It wasn't as noisy back where they were, but the ship shook more. Quivered was a better term, Gil thought, like a frightened puppy. "You said Gatun Lake was filled with islands?" he asked Anibal.

Anibal nodded, as if he didn't trust himself to talk.

"We're going to poke around to see if we spot the *Balboa*. Keep your eyes peeled." He returned to his copilot's seat, only bumping his head once on the craft's ribbing.

He sat, strapped himself back in. "They okay?" the lieutenant shouted.

Gil nodded. It was not so hard to hear now that the pilot had cut his engine speed. "As much as can be expected," he answered.

"Good," the pilot said with a grin. "How'd you like to take the controls?"

It was as if he'd been asked to stick his hand into a box filled with rattlesnakes. The metal wheel was warm to the touch. Slowly, using a mixture of gestures and words, the lieutenant familiarized Gil with the peculiarities of flight. It was not as difficult as he has assumed, something like sailing a ship, he decided.

"Got the hang of it?" asked the pilot.

Gil was beginning to relax. He smiled, nodded. "I think so."

"Good. Take over for a minute. I've got to take a leak." The pilot got up and left the cockpit. Gil's muscles tightened. He prayed Anibal wouldn't see the pilot. If he did, he'd faint.

* * *

They spotted it twenty minutes after sunset. "Think it's the one you want?" asked the pilot, banking for a second run.

From the way the small steamer was hugging the island, it looked like it was trying to escape detection. Gil focused the binoculars. On the bow, painted in white letters, almost obscured by streaks of rust, he made out its name: the *Balboa*. He nodded to the pilot and signaled he wanted the Catalina to swing away.

The pilot nodded and banked the ship. The PBY lumbered in a slow arc, until it was heading back in the direction from which they had come.

Gil waited until he was sure they were hidden from the eyes of anyone on the *Balboa*. "Okay," he said. "Put it down."

When the flying boat touched water, it seemed to skip, like a stone, before it finally settled. "What's up?" asked the pilot. The island was two miles, maybe more, behind them.

"We're taking a raft to the island to watch the ship," Gil replied. "You report its presence and tell your commander I'm requesting assistance. Got that?"

"Got it."

They left the cockpit. Gil and his friends waited while the pilot opened one of the bubbles, prepared the raft, then launched it. It bobbed in the water, with a yellow line connecting it to the aircraft, like an umbilical cord. "All set," said the lieutenant.

Gil went first. The evening was darker on the surface of the water than it had been in the air. The little raft was unsteady. He held on to a handgrip and waited for Ellen to come down. She made it easily. Anibal followed, looking happy to be out of the aircraft. "Okay?" the lieutenant said. He was shining a flashlight into the raft.

"Weapons. We might need them," Gil returned.

"Way ahead of you," said the pilot, reaching out. "Here."

Even in the dark, Gil knew what it was: a Thompson submachine gun. Holding it made him feel like John Dillinger. "There's more," the lieutenant said, passing over a Colt .45 and extra ammunition, then, finally, the flashlight. "Just don't lose them. They're inventoried out to me." He saluted, said, "Good luck," let loose the line, and closed the hatch. The island to which they were heading seemed a speck in the distance. Around it, hidden on the other side, lay the *Balboa*.

CHAPTER 4

The Sixth: Evening

"***H****erein*," said Schatz. His voice seemed strong. Andre stepped into the cabin. Schatz was at the table. A bottle of gin and a half-empty tumbler stood at the German's right hand. The cabin was steaming hot. "I am not drunk," the captain assured him. "I came here to escape the mosquitos; in a minute, I go face them to escape the heat. Life for us becomes a matter of choosing between two evils, *hein*?"

Andre winced. The half-whining interjection sounded like the grinding of an auto's gears. The captain tipped the bottle and raised an eyebrow. Andre rejected the offer. "We have to talk," he said.

"*Jawohl*," Schatz replied. "The flying boat."

Andre nodded. "They will investigate." His hands were clammy, his voice weak.

"Yes, they will investigate," Schatz replied, slurring

his words. "But, first, they will try to raise us on the radio. We still have a few hours, I think."

To do what? Find another island behind which to hide? Abandon ship and try to escape on foot? What could the airplane's presence mean but that they had been spotted. The operation was doomed. They had lost. France, the rewards, the fame—all Andre had worked for was suddenly out of reach.

"What do you propose?" Andre asked.

Schatz said nothing, but stared until Andre wanted to break eye contact. Finally, the German smiled.

The smile brought to mind their conversation in Ocoa Bay. Andre glanced at the captain's table. Stretched open, under the bottle, glass, and a pair of calipers, was a chart of the canal. "You are going through with it," he said.

"Yes."

"It is madness. It cannot succeed."

"There is a chance. I do not know what the American navy has on the Pacific side, but we saw no sign of naval vessels on the Caribbean. Even if they bring a destroyer into the canal, we might be able to evade it. The waters around the islands are shallow."

"There are patrol boats. And aircraft," Andre protested.

"Their patrol craft are too small to stop us once we are under way. As for the aircraft . . ." He stopped and took a drink. ". . . as for them," he said, "we must risk attack. It is what war is about, is it not?"

The *boche* was serious. Andre tried to envision it: a running fight all the way to Gatun Dam. In a tub held together by rust! Other than a few rifles they had no arms. Aircraft could pound them to pieces with impunity.

A thought budded. He need not share the crew's fate; he could get off the ship. That had been the bargain. Hope blossomed anew. As slight as the chance for success was, at least it remained. And he did not need to stay with the ship and be killed.

"It will take time to set the charges," he said. "When do you want me to start?" His voice was tight. Briefly, he contemplated reminding Schatz of his earlier promise. *Let it ride for the moment. That was best.*

Schatz took another drink. "I have ordered steam up. We shall leave at first light. Six o'clock tomorrow morning."

Andre checked his watch. It was after seven. The operation would begin in less than eleven hours—enough time to do his job. "And when do you anticipate reaching the dam?"

"The route is treacherous—shallow waters, narrow passages. Four hours."

Andre nodded. "Then I will set the charges to explode at two o'clock tomorrow afternoon. That will give the ship time to sink against the spillway."

"You are the expert," Schatz said. He paused, then: "And after the charges are set, what is your decision?"

The German's eyes shone in the poor light, revealing the contempt Andre had grown accustomed to. This time, they showed more. Malice, hatred. Andre suddenly grew as afraid of leaving as he had been of staying. "You're not going to let me off," he said.

Schatz nodded. "I would prefer you to remain, at least until we have rammed the spillway. Then, you and the rest of the crew can leave." His words were slurred.

Lies and evasions—*les frisés* were notorious for them. Stay with the ship! It was pointless. He had no duties for the final run. His only responsibility would be to die with them. A vision intruded: himself, dead, sinking into the water—his skin as white as a fish's belly. He fought for

336

control. There would be a way out. There had to be. "Very well," he said at last.

"Splendid!" Schatz said. "Germany and France, together. We will be comrades in arms. It is much better this way."

"This way?"

"Of course. Had you insisted on leaving, I would have had you shot," Schatz told him, smiling.

December 7: Predawn

Gil swatted his neck with his left hand, rubbed his cheek against his right shoulder. *Of all the damned places to spend a night,* he thought, *this has to be the worst.* Never had he seen so many bugs. "What time is it?" he asked. He was irritable, was sure it showed in his voice.

"A little after four," Ellen whispered, showing him the radium dials of her wristwatch. She sounded equally peevish.

"After four," he repeated to himself. *Where was the damned navy?* They should have sent something—a patrol boat, another Catalina, anything. He listened, half expecting, half hoping to hear the drone of a PBY's engines. Nothing. He looked back at the ship, bathed in the light of the moon, a black silhouette on the water. There was a smell of coal smoke in the air. The ship's furnaces had been firing for hours. "Anibal," he whispered. "What do you think?"

Anibal knelt silently, fingering something under his shirt. The *drogue,* Gil imagined. It had become a habit, he had noticed. "Steam's up," Anibal said.

"How long before they're ready to make way?"

"Ready now, that's my guess," Anibal answered. "They may be waiting for first light."

If the navy didn't come soon, it would be too late. Gil thought of Early, envisioned him gloating at their discomfort.

"What are we going to do?" Ellen's voice.

The question echoed his own doubts. The damned navy wasn't going to show. They were the only ones who could stop the ship. "We're going to board it," he said, surprised by his own assertion.

"Then what?" Ellen asked.

"You don't have to come along," he said, evading her question. "You can stay here."

"You'd like that, wouldn't you?" Ellen whispered. "Leaving me alone in this godforsaken place. I'm coming along."

Gil turned to Anibal. "Think we can take over the bridge?"

"If we're going to try," Anibal said, "we'd better start before it's light."

Gil nodded. They had moored their raft on the other side of the island. They would have to hurry if they were going to beat the dawn. He rose. The others followed.

Sweat dripped into Andre's eyes. He blinked and wiped them with his sleeve. The detonators were in place. All that was left was to hook up the timer and the batteries, then seal them to make sure they were waterproof.

The seaman holding the electric torch was shining it in his eyes. Andre looked up. "Down here," he said, gesturing toward his hands. The beam shifted. "That's better," Andre grunted. He set the timer and batteries in the box and ran the wires through the holes drilled in its side.

The still air seemed to press against him, stifling him. It was hard to move.

A noise distracted him. A rat. *You have a cousin up on the bridge,* Andre thought. "What time is it?"

The beam swung away as the seaman checked his watch. "Nearly five fifteen."

He had finished with time to spare. It would be good to get topside and breathe fresh air again, he told himself. Immediately came the thought that there might be only a limited number of breaths to take. How could that be? The idea of death was an absurdity.

He wiped his brow. Once again, he went over his decision to place the timer in the aft hold. There were drawbacks: aft hold was sealed from the hold forward it; the bulkhead separating them was thick—it had taken nearly an hour to drill a hole through which to run his wires. It had but two points of access: the loading hatch above and a passageway through the after deckhouse. Neither were convenient for opening the seacocks after it had rammed the spillway.

But it was farthest from the planned point of impact, and that was important. He did not want to jar the timing mechanism and the connecting wires any more than was necessary. Another thought, in counterpoint. If he was going to die anyway, what difference did it make?

He shook his head. He was alive now. There was a chance he might survive. He would, he vowed. The operation would succeed because it must succeed. He would live because he must live.

Ellen. The name came spontaneously. He regretted her death. It would have given him pleasure showing off his success to her. He set the timer in the box, connected the batteries, then the detonators. The box containing the timing device needed to be packed with sawdust. He told the seaman to do it.

Andre stood, put his hands in the small of his back, and arched his spine. He was stiff. He watched the young German pour the sawdust. "That's enough," he said. "Now, set the top and secure it." As the seaman did so, Andre tested the creosote. The box had to be waterproofed, then set firmly in place to prevent the collision from jarring the wires loose. After that, there would be nothing to do but double-check the connections.

Andre rubbed his neck with his handkerchief. The Americans might take him prisoner. If they did, he would be freed in no more than a few weeks. The war could end that quickly. The Japanese would soon be in the war: General Hibbert's theory. How long would the Americans fight if faced by both Germany and Japan? He snorted. How long did they do anything that did not make them money?

He glanced around him. A pail of creosote, some tools, pieces of rubber tape, bits of wire, sawdust, other clutter. "Clean up this mess," he ordered. "I'm going topside." He swung up the rungs, the young German beneath him swearing under his breath.

The raft bumped gently against the *Balboa*'s stern. Anibal walked his hands along the hull until he could grab the anchor chain. He steadied the craft. Gil and Ellen sat quietly, gazing up toward maindeck. Anibal listened. He could hear nothing beyond the lap of waves. "All right?" he whispered. The gray sky was getting lighter each moment.

"All right," Gil replied, and reached out to take the anchor chain. He tied the raft to it.

It was like scaling a ladder. Anibal mounted it easily, silently. He hooked his foot into the anchor port and raised an arm to grasp the open railing, then lifted himself cautiously until he could peer onto the deck. Quickly, he lowered his head. There was a guard. He was armed. The clump of the guard's shoes on deck came closer. Then the sound of feet faded.

Anibal took a breath and again peeked over the railing. It was as he thought. There was but the one on watch. His back to Anibal, the man had a foot on the lower railing and was looking out to sea. A rifle leaned against the railing next to him. Anibal reached into his shirt, pulled his knife from its sheath, kissed the blade, then slowly lifted himself up and swung his leg over the railing.

He crouched, motionless. He had not been seen. *Like a panther in the night.* He moved to gain the shadow of the after deckhouse, then slid toward the guard, coming within a step of him before the other began to turn.

Anibal was on him before he could make a sound. He grabbed the jaw and lifted it, drew his knife across the other's throat, digging it hard into the soft flesh where head and neck met. The man's hands flew to Anibal's arm, but there was no strength behind them. Hot blood gushed over Anibal's hand. Anibal held tightly as his victim thrashed. *Do it gently, man,* Anibal silently advised. *You're already dead.* He tightened his grip even more, prepared to hold up dead weight. There came a last shudder, then a clatter and splash.

Anibal looked down, saw that the rifle was gone. The man had kicked it over. The body went limp. Anibal lowered it slowly, cautious lest the noise had attracted attention. It seemed not to have. He came back to where he had climbed aboard. "It's all right," he whispered down. "Hurry!"

Ellen came aboard, Gil following a few seconds later. "Any trouble?" he asked.

"A guard," Anibal answered. "Help me get rid of him." Gil transferred the submachine gun, pistol, and ammunition to Ellen, with a whispered order to stay put, then joined Anibal. Anibal lifted the dead man's arms; Gil took his legs. "Where to?" Anibal asked.

"Under the dinghy," Gil whispered, nodding to the lifeboat a few feet away.

At the boat they stuffed the body between the chocks. *Like packing wadding into a hole,* Anibal thought.

"Good enough," Gil said. "Let's get back."

Ellen was waiting for them. Anibal took the Thompson from her and tested it for heft. It did not seem as heavy as he had imagined. He found the safety catch and slid it off.

"Ready?" Gil asked.

"As I'll ever be," Ellen responded.

Her words echoed Anibal's feelings. He said nothing.

In a deep crouch, with a .45 in hand, Gil moved a few feet, then paused by the after deckhouse. The deck was littered with bales of what felt like rags, crates, equipment, hawsers. The clutter seemed deliberate, as if to give a false impression of a ship whose officers had lost interest in maintaining it.

The forecastle lay approximately one hundred feet ahead, partially hidden by the funnel, a black shadow in the gray light. On the forecastle, jutting out on either side of the funnel, Anibal made out the bridge deck. He listened. All was quiet. Gil turned to him, lifting his head in a questioning way.

"Nothing," Anibal whispered in agreement.

"Let's head for the bridge."

It was then that Anibal heard metal scraping. They were next to the aft hold hatch. The hatch cover was partly off. The sound came from within. A white face popped up, not five feet away. For a second, the man only stared, then, *"Wer da?"*

The man's eyes widened as Anibal lunged for him. *"Hilfe-ruf,"* the man shouted, then ducked back into the hold. He dropped from sight.

From the bridge deck, on the far starboard side, a beam of light caught them.

"Back," Gil shouted.

Anibal needed no urging. He headed for the shadow of the funnel, pulling Ellen with him. As they reached a bale by the after deckhouse, there came a rifle shot, followed by the ping of the bullet against metal. Gil was scrambling behind them, dove the last few feet to the bale. Shouts in German came from the depths of the after hold. The seaman, outlined in the searchlight's beam, flew up out of it and ran for the forecastle, arms flailing wildly.

Anibal raised his Thompson, trained it on the light, and pulled the trigger. The gun pulled up and to the right. He fired a second volley. The searchlight went out.

"So much for sneaking up on them," Gil whispered beside him.

"What do we do?" Anibal asked.

The capstan engine sputtered, then took. Chain began clattering through the anchor port. They were weighing anchor.

"There goes our raft," Gil whispered. "Let's get some of these bales together," he said. "We'll be safe enough behind them for a while."

Bon Dieu bon, Anibal thought, as he helped Ellen wrestle a bale into position, *what have we let ourselves in for?* The three of them alone on a steamer, facing a crew of hostile Nazis, and with no certainty the navy would come to their aid. The ship shuddered as its screw began to revolve. The *Balboa* was under way.

CHAPTER 5

The Seventh: Morning

Ellen leaned against the bale and stared back at the after deckhouse. The ship had picked up speed. She ran her fingers along the deck. There was a thin film of water on it. Slick, like oil. When she turned back, she saw Gil looking at her. She knew what he wanted to say, shook her head to stop him. He needn't be sorry. He had done what he had to. She started to look at her watch, but remembered that she had broken it somewhere between leaving the island and building their rampart of old rags. She turned her eyes to the sky. About seven o'clock, she thought. The sun was still a little low, but was shining brightly. In a few hours, it would heat up the deck.

What would she be doing back in Jamaica? Getting ready to teach her sixth form geography class at St. Elizabeth's. No, it was Sunday. She would be having breakfast with Sara and her mother. Then they would go to church. The two would be going without her today.

Anibal was to Ellen's right, peering out between two bales. "What is it?"

"The bridge deck, something's going on," he said, then moved away from the opening to give her a look.

It took a second to focus. A dark-haired man was looking at them from around the funnel. Then he ducked back. Ellen caught her breath. Andre. Unmistakably he. His presence among German sailors was ironic. He might have admired German National Socialism, she recalled, but he had never liked the Germans. She had often wondered what would happen if she ever met up with him again. She searched her own feelings toward him and found nothing—neither love nor loathing.

A seaman with a rifle appeared where Andre had been. There was a puff of smoke as the man fired. Two riflemen popped up on main deck amidship and joined in. Some bullets thudded into the baled rags, others plunked into the structure behind her. "Get your head down before it's blown off," Gil said. He grabbed her, pulled her down. When she looked back, there were a half-dozen round dents in the deckhouse, paint and rust knocked free in a two-inch circumference around each. The bare steel glistened. Anibal poked his submachine gun over the bales and raked the forward section. Wood chips flew from the cargo boom. Hollow thuds—bullets striking a lifeboat. The two riflemen on main deck and the one on the bridge beat a retreat.

"How many are there?" Schatz asked.

Andre wondered whether the *boche* had finished the bottle. He seemed sober enough. He had met men before who could drink for hours and not show it. "I counted two, for sure, and possibly a third." he replied.

"From the flying boat," Schatz said. *"Das Unglück."* His eyes were red-rimmed.

Bad luck? That was the best the kraut could manage? Andre clenched his fists. "What do we do?" he croaked.

The captain closed one eye and glared at him. Then, suddenly, he laughed. "We take them along for the ride, yes? A little cruise through the canal. As long as we keep them where they are, they cannot stop us."

Andre shook his head. "You cannot do that."

"And why not?" the captain asked. "You told me that you were done in the after hold. Did you lie?"

The *frisé* was drunker than he seemed. "I did not lie," Andre began. "There is nothing more to do, as far as the charges are concerned, but we must get down into the after hold after we ram the spillway." The *boche* did not know how to drink; Germans always took too much. "If we don't open the seacocks," he explained, "there is no guarantee the ship will sink deeply enough to blow up the spillway."

Schatz nodded slowly. "We get rid of them," he said. "How?"

"Through the propellor shaft alley. It has a repair hatch in the stern. We can sneak up on them from their rear."

Andre tried to visualize the alley. It was large enough to crawl through, he thought, but it had no entry from the engine room or the midships hold. "How—" he began.

"We cut into it from the engine room," Schatz told him.

"You will remain under way while you do it?" Andre asked.

"That depends on you," Schatz said, smiling.

Fear returned, stabbing him in the chest. "I don't—"

"I give you the honor of leading the attack," Schatz said. "It is up to you to decide whether we should stop the engine."

Andre tried to convince himself that Schatz was joking, but knew he was not. The man would like nothing more than to see him refuse. Schatz could shoot him and take pleasure in doing it. "Very well," he whispered, "but why . . ."

"I have always heard how brave you *Franzosen* are," Schatz said, sneering. "It would be unfair not to give you this opportunity to prove it. So, you go through the alley. Do you wish the engine stopped or not?"

A vision of crawling through the alley while the shaft was turning came to mind. It would be foolhardy to try. "You will stop the engines," he said, glaring at the German.

The engines had been stopped for at least an hour, Gil figured. No clouds, no breeze, and the ship was dead in the water. Gil's throat was dry. He turned to Anibal. "What do you suppose they're planning?" he asked.

"You mean why they have stopped the engines?"

"That, too," Gil said, "but what do they intend to do with four hundred tons of explosives?"

The Haitian shrugged. "Try to blow up the locks, maybe."

"Think they could do that?" It didn't sound possible.

"Andre was an engineer," Ellen said. "If he thinks they can, they probably can."

Gil looked at them. "I've put us in a hell of a spot."

"Don't exaggerate," Ellen replied. "You did what you thought you had to. And we're still alive."

They had no food or water, and they were in danger of getting their heads blown off whenever they peeked out.

If that wasn't bad enough, they could be blasted sky high any minute. He went over her words: *"did what you thought you had to"*—not exactly a ringing testimonial. *The story of my life,* he concluded, *a man of impulse.*

"Anibal," he said.

"Yes?"

"If you're right, what can we do to stop them?"

"What do you mean?" the Haitian asked.

"You've worked on steamships. Suppose they're getting ready to ram the locks. Any way we can prevent it?"

Anibal looked toward the bridge, then turned and stared at the after deckhouse. "There might be," he said at last.

Gil: "How?"

Ellen: "What do we do?"

"The wheel's up on the bridge," Anibal began. "It controls the rudder electrically."

"Yes?" Gil whispered.

"You have to know how it works. Wires run from the wheel to the motor which operates the rudder. If we cut them . . ."

If the wires were cut, Gil thought, the bridge would lose control of the rudder. "Won't they still be able to control the rudder mechanically?"

"Not from the bridge," he said. "Too long a run for cables from there to the rudder: the torque would be impossible. That wheel will be over the rudder."

Before he had finished, Gil and Ellen had turned aft, looking at the deckhouse.

"Yes. In there."

It was a small, steel structure, hardly larger than ten feet square, rust streaks trailing from nearly every rivet, peppered with round dents like a car hood after a hailstorm. It had closed portholes to port and starboard, and, as Gil recalled, a door abaft. "You sure?"

"No," Anibal admitted, "but I can't think of any other reason for that after deckhouse."

"So if we cut the wires, then we control the rudder," Gil said slowly.

"We don't even need it. What's important is that *they* won't be able to use it."

"How can we get at the wires?"

" 'Tween decks, most likely. There will be entry from inside the deckhouse."

"You willing to give it a go?" Gil asked.

"Willing to try." Anibal handed Gil the submachine gun, then checked to make sure he still had his knife. "Cover me."

Gil estimated his friend would be exposed for no more than five or six strides. He nodded. "Ready?"

Anibal licked his lips. "Yes."

Gil lifted the gun over the top of their redoubt and pulled the trigger. It released a blur of bullets. From the corner of his eye, he saw Anibal, bending low, race around the deckhouse. He had made it.

It seemed to take forever, cutting this opening into the propellor shaft alley. Andre looked at his watch: after eleven. A shower of sparks flew in the air. He flinched, although they fell nowhere near him. They had to get rid of the boarders; he must reset the timer. At least the American navy had not put in an appearance. There was only the trio on board to worry about and, at last report, they were still pinned down, only firing short bursts now and then. Annoying, but nothing more. There remained a chance—if they hurried.

The torch was extinguished. One of the men approached and saluted. "Chief says they can pound in the rest. He'll finish the job after you're inside."

Andre turned to the three selected to accompany him, wondered how they had earned Schatz's displeasure. "Are you ready?" he asked. His words were drowned by the sledge hammer's banging, but the men understood. Each began a last minute check of his weapons. The banging stopped; the opening was wide enough. Andre took a deep breath and tried to swallow, but his throat was dry. He pulled out his pistol, flicked on his flashlight, and stepped forward, handing the flashlight to the chief. "Hold this until I get inside," he said. His chest felt tight, forcing him to breathe in short gasps.

He was in. He reached back for the flashlight. The alley was over a meter high: he could crawl without bumping his head. It smelled of stale air and grease, and of dead vermin. The screw shaft ran down the middle, supported every five meters by bearing foundations through which he had to squeeze. The flashlight illuminated only the section immediately ahead. He began to sweat more than before. Grease oozed between his fingers as he crept forward.

Gil shifted to catch the thin line of shade cast by the boom. "How long has he been gone?" he asked Ellen. Her eyes were red, her clothing drenched with perspiration. He wished he had some water to offer her, but they had brought none. Another example of sterling leadership, Gil thought.

"Your guess is as good as mine," Ellen replied. "Maybe an hour."

"He might be having trouble finding it. Think you could check?" It would be close below deck, but at least she would be shielded from the direct sunlight.

"Anything's better than baking in the sun," she returned.

"Take the pistol," he told her.

Her smile was tentative. Nevertheless, she tucked it under her belt.

Gil nodded. "Okay," he said, "like before. Wait until I start firing before you take off." He put on a new drum of ammunition. Seconds ticked by. Still, he did not move. He glanced at Ellen, saw her staring back at him, waiting for him. *Do it,* he urged himself. *Don't give yourself time to think.* Twice, he permitted the initial surge of energy to flow into his muscles, only to block it at the last second. Then, almost as if the impulse came from outside him, he popped up and began to fire. He fought to keep the gun level, raking the forecastle. He looked off to his left. Ellen was gone.

The deckhouse door was unlatched, its hinges creaking in tune to the imperceptible motion of the ship. Ellen pushed the door open all the way and peered inside. It was dark. There was the after wheel, as Anibal had predicted. From below came a hollow echo, like someone pounding on pipe. There was a gaping hole in the deckhouse deck, surrounded by railing, the top of a ladder. Ellen grabbed the barely visible railing and started down the rungs.

The echoes grew louder. Her foot hit deck. Lights glowed faintly, painting the large, open space in sepiatone, broken by long, shadowed lines of ducts. She tested the headroom, found she had to walk with a stoop. Aside from the metallic echoes, all was quiet. Then she saw Anibal. He was on his knees and reaching overhead, in the pose of a supplicant.

He turned in her direction. "Gil?" he said.

"No, me," she responded as she came up to him. "Gil sent me to make sure everything was all right. How are you doing?"

He grunted. Ellen crouched beside him. He was separating some wires.

She sensed some nearby presence, but she could not tell what. Listening for that which was not there, trying to see what was invisible, was painful.

Ellen straightened her back and extracted the gun from under her belt. "See anything?" she whispered.

Anibal stopped working and looked at her. His shirt was drenched with perspiration.

"Look out!" she screamed.

Shadows slipped along the duct. Ellen raised her weapon, clicked off the safety, and fired. The gun roared, there came a smell of powder and a succession of pings as the bullet ricocheted from one angle to another. She ducked to avoid her own bullet.

They came in a rush. Four that she could make out. Anibal, still on his knees, swung a wrench, smashing an attacker at the knee. Ellen fired a second time, thought she hit someone. It was hard to tell. Her eyes were so watery from the gunpowder she could hardly see. A pair of their attackers had backed off. One of them raised a pistol and emptied its chambers. Bullets flew all over the place, pinging and ringing. It was like being caught inside a pinball machine. Ellen fired again, blindly.

Anibal wrenched the pistol from her. "They've gone," he said.

"Where did they come from?" she asked.

"Nothing to do but find out," Anibal said. "Let's look." Ellen followed, her pistol at the ready. For the first time, she realized what having an itchy trigger finger meant. She had fired three times. It meant she had four bullets left. They found no one. Ellen was sure she had hit one of them and Anibal had smashed a second. The others must have helped them get away.

Anibal knelt and peered at a hatch, then ran his finger along the edge. "It's been opened," he said. "They came from in there."

"What is it?"

"Propellor shaft alley. Shaft runs from the engine out to the screw," he explained.

They were in the stern. Beyond the bulkhead, only a thin sheet of plating separated them from the water. It gave her an eerie feeling, something, she imagined, like waking to find yourself in a casket.

"Here," Anibal said, "help me with this." He held a length of timber.

They jammed it between the hatch and a hold pillar. Once they could no longer budge it, Anibal muttered, "They won't use that any longer. Let's get out of this hole."

"The wire?"

"Already cut," he said. "The only way they can steer this tub now is from the rear wheel, and they're going to have to go through us to get to it."

CHAPTER 6

The Seventh: Afternoon

"Take him," Andre barked in the engine room, transferring the wounded man into the hands of the chief engineer. He waited until the man was taken from him, then squeezed out the opening. A seaman knelt beside the wounded man, two others stood gaping at him. The wounded man groaned, clutching his shoulder. The two others who had been with Andre stumbled from the alley. One seemed unable to plant his foot firmly on deck, but looked otherwise all right. Andre addressed the chief. "Where's the captain?"

"On the bridge."

Andre took the ladder's rungs two at a time. He felt feverish, muscles in his arms and chest twitched. *It had been she. Ellen! Why?* He loved her, he knew, and always had. He had risked his future to save her life. And this was how she repaid him. *Bitch!*

He emerged from below deck and raced to the forward companionway. *And siccing those mongrels she was with onto him.* Andre had seen who she had been with. It was like gongs banging in his mind. *Un nègre. She prefers a nigger to me. Whore . . . filthy slut.* An image of Ellen in a black's embrace blossomed in his imagination: kissed by a big-lipped, kinky-headed animal, white skin pawed by an ape's fingers, she was gasping, begging . . .

He burst onto the bridge. "Schatz," he said, then halted. The German was standing with folded arms. He was in uniform. Slowly, the man turned and fixed his gaze on Andre. "You are back," he said. "Report, *Herr Kapitänleutnant.*" The words were slurred.

The idiot's still drunk, Andre thought. The use of rank confused him further.

"The attack failed," Schatz spat accusingly.

"They were waiting for us," Andre said. "Your plan was anticipated. I had two wounded. I brought both back."

"It would have been just as well had you left them," Schatz replied.

Another seaman stood on the bridge, peering out to sea, refusing to meet Andre's gaze.

"They have fucked us," Schatz finally said.

Andre still said nothing.

"The wires connecting the wheel to the rudder motor have been severed," the German screamed, grabbing the wheel and spinning it. "We are adrift in the middle of the canal."

Drunk or not, Schatz was not one to lose control in front of an enlisted man. And why the uniform? It was not quite one in the afternoon. They had not yet run out of time. They could eliminate the boarders. Attack them, throw them overboard. It was a simple operation. Then he could reset the timer while the steering mechanism was repaired. They could fulfill the mission. "An assault," Andre insisted. "Pin them down from the bridge. We outnumber them. They cannot have brought much ammunition on board."

Schatz's grin showed neither humor nor camaraderie. "Our French pussycat has become a tiger." He paused, then, as if it were of little importance: "The radioman has picked up a message."

Andre waited.

"The Japanese have attacked the American naval base in Hawaii."

War! That meant Schatz had even less reason to back down. Suddenly, Andre's skin seemed to become extra sensitive, his hearing capable of identifying sounds which previously would have eluded him. He felt strong. It was what going to battle meant, he thought, what his father must have felt so often in the last war. "Then we *must* attack," he pressed. "This has been promised your Japanese allies. You cannot let them down." Privately, he added, *And Ellen must be forced to see how wrong she was*. He would make her cringe before she died.

Gil put his hand on the deck, then lifted it. The sun had begun to bake into the metal. Anibal and Ellen were beside him, their mission accomplished. But if anything, they were in even graver danger than before. Duchesne and his German buddies would try something. And whatever it was, they would have to do it soon. They wouldn't dare wait for the navy to show up.

Where in hell *was* the damned navy? Gil took his eyes from the bridge deck and scanned the skies. Nothing in sight. *Come on*, he thought. *Hurry up.*

"I see something," Ellen said.

"What?"

"To port," she whispered.

Gil looked, saw a man's back poking over a packing crate. "See that?" he asked Anibal.

"Starboard, too," the Haitian replied. "They're getting ready to come."

It was silent. There was no breeze. Gil checked the Colt to make sure it contained a full clip.

"I think—" Ellen's words were punctuated by a volley of gunfire. Gil peeked from between two bales and saw men working their way nearer. "I count six," he said.

"Six, at least," Anibal replied.

Another volley from the bridge deck. Bullets thudded into the bales, raising little clouds of dust. "Watch the bridge," Gil told Anibal. The nearest seaman was crouched behind the funnel. Gil figured he would make for the hatch cover next. He aimed his weapon and waited.

The man darted out. Gil's gun kicked. The seaman grabbed his thigh and sank to the deck. He began to crawl back to the funnel. Gil let him go.

"The bridge," Anibal shouted. Gil ducked while Anibal poked the snout of the Thompson over his bale and let loose a burst. There followed the sound of glass shattering, of bullets pinging against steel. Quickly Gil lifted his head, spotted another man moving toward them. Without aiming, he snapped a shot. A second victim. It was like Spain, he reminded himself, the battle for the University of Madrid.

Five minutes passed; then there was more fire from the bridge. Gil peered out the slit between two bales and fired a single shot to remind them they were still there. The smell of cordite was embedded in the rags, irritating his nose. He looked down at his last spare clip on the deck beside him. "How much ammunition have you got?" he asked Anibal.

Anibal glanced at him and shook his head. *Outnumbered and out of ammunition,* Gil thought. *That was like Spain, too.*

Gil was sweating, the grip on his pistol wet. A minute passed without any shots. On the deck, thirty feet in front of him, the lifeless body of a seaman, but he could see no one else. Why? Ellen was concentrating on the sky off to starboard. "Hear that?" she said.

Gil heard nothing at first, then faintly, the drone of a Catalina's twin Pratt and Whitney engines. It took a few more seconds before he was able to locate the PBY low on the horizon. The navy had come to their rescue. At last.

"There is a flying boat circling the horizon," Schatz said. "Our ship is rudderless. The boarders control both the wheel and access to the explosives. We cannot complete our mission. It is impossible." The German's breath was foul.

"No. There is still time," Andre protested. "It takes only a few seconds to reset the timer. Attack now and we can still carry it out."

He glanced around him. The German crew stared silently with round eyes, like so many marbles, revealing their lack of comprehension. He faced them. "You are sailors of the Third Reich," he screamed. "Death is your business. You have sworn to do your duty, regardless of consequences."

The circle widened as the men backed away from him. They thought he was crazy, he realized. But he wasn't. Never had he been more sane. "You are expected to die for your country. So die!"

A buzz of conversation followed. It was because he had been speaking French. Those who understood him were translating for the others. Andre could not let Ellen win. The English cunt would laugh in his face. He tore a rifle from the closest sailor's grasp and leveled it at Schatz. "We have not been defeated," he insisted. "It is not too late. Order these men to attack again."

Schatz's eyes glanced back and forth between Andre's face and the rifle he was holding. Finally, he spat. A blob of phlegm landed at Andre's feet. "It is over," the German said and turned away.

Andre fired. Schatz's back arched at the impact, like a bow drawn back. He fired again, then turned to the mass of seamen rushing him. A hand circled his wrist, forcing the rifle from his grasp. A knee crushed into his groin. He fell, retching, under a kick in the ribs.

"Let's get off this time bomb," he heard one say. Their retreating feet beat in counterpoint to the throb in his head. The men were heading for the rafts stored by the forward hold, he knew. They were leaving him. He lost consciousness.

The PBY circled overhead. "Better late than never, I guess," Gil said.

Ellen was staring off to starboard. "Look."

He followed her gaze: Two rafts appeared from under the bow. They were crowded with seamen, all pulling hard for shore. Gil squinted at the PBY Catalina, then back at the rafts. "What do you think?" he asked. "Have they left the ship to us?"

"If they have, I'm not so sure we want it," replied Ellen. She rose; the others did likewise. For a moment, Gil stood tensed, anticipating the sound of gunfire, prepared to dive back to shelter. None came.

"Let's see what we've captured," he suggested. He

checked his Colt to make sure it was ready to fire. Anibal, he saw, was cradling the Thompson.

They came to the aft hold hatch, still slightly ajar. "Let's take a look," Gil suggested, bending to slide it all the way off. Anibal set the Thompson down and assisted him. Iron scraped against iron, then the cover fell free. Sunlight poured into the hold, illuminating its contents. Crates, all with the same markings:

> Property United States Army
> Danger
> TNT

"Think it's set?" Gil asked.

"Think those Germans are rowing for exercise?" Ellen responded.

Gil sat with his legs dangling over the edge of the hatch opening. He reached for the ladder fixed to the hatch. "Quick, let's defuse it."

"Are you out of your mind?" Ellen shouted.

She didn't understand, Gil realized. This was his chance at last, his ticket out of Hollywood. A deserted ship in the middle of Gatun Lake, stuffed to the gunwales with valuable cargo. The salvage rights would set him up for life. Hell, it would set them *all* up for life. He grabbed the rung and swung down on the ladder, then looked at his mates.

They hadn't budged. "What's wrong?" he asked.

"What do you know about TNT?" Anibal asked, eyes wide open.

What did that have to do with it? He shifted his gaze from one to the other. Anibal grabbed him under the arm and started pulling him back. Gil resisted, flung off the restraining hand. "What in hell—" he shouted.

"We're not alone," Ellen said, in a level tone.

Gil poked his head out of the hatch and saw a lone figure, in the uniform of a German naval lieutenant, running toward them, rifle in hand.

"Merde," breathed Anibal, and retreated for the Thompson leaning on the hatch opening.

"Arrêtez," said the man, raising his rifle. Anibal froze. *Damn,* thought Gil. He was stuck halfway in, halfway out, of a hold filled with explosives, unable to move. A saying of old Ned Walker's came to mind, something about there being a world of difference between greed and ambition and no one ever amounted to a damn until he knew what that difference was.

"Andre!" Ellen shouted.

The man's eyes widened. He pointed his weapon at Ellen, then paused and, as if driven by an alien will, shifted it once again.

In that instant, Anibal dived for his weapon, seized it, and rolled on the deck, while Duchesne shifted his arm, aiming the gun directly at Anibal. He squeezed the trigger. Gil saw the flash, heard the report.

Anibal rolled onto one knee and fired. The burst caught the Frenchman across the stomach, sent him twirling, hands outstretched, the rifle flying free.

Gil came out of the hold at a run and knelt beside the Frenchman. He turned him over. Duchesne's eyes were open, blood seeped from his mouth. He said something, the words popping out from bloody bubbles. Gil could not make them out, looked up, saw Ellen standing over him, sadness in her eyes. "What did he say?" Gil asked.

She shrugged. "Something about the French Academy. It made no sense."

Gil turned back to the fallen man. *Greed and ambition,*

he thought, then, aloud, to the Frenchman: "Can you understand me?"

Nothing. Then, slowly, a nod.

"Is the TNT fused?"

The other nodded.

"Can we get to the detonator?"

Duchesne coughed.

The cough splattered Gil's face with blood. "When will it explode?" he pressed.

The Frenchman's gaze shifted, focusing on one, then another, until it found Ellen. He smiled.

"He's dead," said Anibal, feeling for a pulse on the Frenchman's neck.

It was enough for Gil. "Let's get out of here," he said, noting the relief which spread across Anibal's and Ellen's faces. "The dinghy astern," he said. It was behind the after deckhouse and would have escaped the damaging gunfire. "How did the Frenchman manage to miss you?" Gil asked.

Anibal smiled. "I have a *drogue*, remember?"

They came to the dinghy. It was, as Gil expected, intact. Underneath was the guard, stiff with rigor mortis. Anibal started knocking out the chocks with the butt of the submachine gun. Gil checked the davits. They seemed sturdy. He looked at Anibal. The Haitian nodded, and threw the Thompson into the boat. "You work that line," Anibal said. "I'll take this. Now, on command. Ready?"

It proved easier than Gil had anticipated. The dinghy swung out on its davits. Anibal told Ellen to get in. She climbed the railing and crawled in headfirst.

Gil and Anibal lowered the boat with a series of jerks. It hit the lake bow first, but Ellen was still in it, and it shipped only a little water. "All right, my friend," Anibal suggested. "Let's go." He jumped. Gil went right after him.

The roar was deafening. Gil stopped rowing, looked up. A few seconds later, he felt the heat. Shock waves rocked the boat. A mile or more behind him, smoke and flame towered in the air, all he could see of the *Balboa*. Eight hundred thousand pounds of TNT, Gil reminded himself. A fat lot of good salvage rights would have done him.

Something plopped in the water beside them. Other objects followed. Debris from the ship. "Cover your heads," Gil shouted, bending over and covering his own, even as he knew how useless that would be should a section of boiler fall on them. The submachine gun was lying in the scuppers. When, finally, he judged it safe to straighten up, he retrieved the weapon and showed it to Anibal. The stock was cracked. A bullet was lodged in the crack. "You may have a *drogue*," he said, "but it doesn't hurt to be lucky, either."

Anibal grinned. "*Bon Dieu bon* works in strange ways," he said.

The Catalina was rocking in the water, a quarter of a mile away. If he and Anibal ever managed to synchronize their strokes, he thought, they might reach it by nightfall.

CHAPTER 7

It was the same hotrodder who had piloted them yesterday, but yesterday's grin and nonchalance were gone. The lieutenant stuck his hand out of the bubble to help Ellen. Anibal went next. Gil gathered up the Thompson and handed it to the lieutenant, along with his Colt. "We can't account for the ammunition," he said. "I hope that doesn't screw up your inventory."

The other did not crack a smile. He set the weapons to the side, then reached back to give Gil a hand. Once aboard, his last vestiges of anger at the navy's delay gave way to his curiosity. "Something's happened," he said. "What?"

"So you haven't heard," the lieutenant commented. "I had wondered about that. The Japanese attacked Pearl Harbor a few hours ago. We're at war."

Gil's mind refused to absorb the news. He'd beaten his

country to war by a good three months, he figured. He peered out the airship's bubble. The cloud of smoke in the air had begun to dissipate. The lifeboat was bobbing in the water, stern first, a few feet away, the only tangible reminder of the *Balboa*. "Get on the radio. There was a German crew on board ship. We need some men over there," he said, nodding toward the far shore, "before they have a chance to get away."

The pilot turned without a word and went for the cockpit.

"And water," Gil shouted. "We need some."

The pilot leaned over, picked up a canteen and pitched it underhanded.

Gil caught it, unscrewed the cap, and handed it to Ellen. She drank, then handed it to Anibal. "Your country's now at war, too," she whispered. She looked frightened.

Gil nodded. "Looks like it."

"The whole world's at war," she said. She leaned against him, her softness against his shoulder. She, too, was gazing out at the lake.

McEachern assured me the task would be a simple one, he remembered. *Thank God he didn't give me anything hard.*

CHAPTER 8

The Eleventh

As Gil entered the anteroom, Ellen looked up from the old copy of *Punch* she had been pretending to read. "You talked with McEachern," she said.

"Thanks for meeting me," he said. "Let's get out of here."

She probed his eyes, sought a spark, but found none. There were questions she wanted to ask: *What now? What will you do?* Later, she told herself. They walked down the corridor and out the door, then stepped from the shaded ambulatory of the Jamaican government building into the sun. A bronze cannon perched to her right. It was polished to a bright sheen, but green patina lurked in its crevices. An antique instrument of death, now purely decorative, like a flowerpot, or a huge teakettle.

They walked toward her mother's Hillman. It was hot inside. Her bare knee touched the emergency brake. It burned. She jerked it away and rubbed the tender spot. Four days ago she had been sitting on a metal deck under a raging sun; now the heat of a brake burned her skin. Not only do never-ending adventures end, but they have no permanent effect.

"Are you done with what you had to do?" she asked Gil, once he was in the driver's seat. Surely the question was safe, neutral.

He looked at her. "For a day or so," he answered. "Your people want me to stick around for a while. They're still interested in what happened out at Gainsley's place. McEachern says it's okay. He says I need a rest, anyway." He turned on the ignition, shifted into low, and let out the clutch.

At least they would have a little more time together. *One day at a time*, she told herself. "Where are you heading?"

"Down to the marina. I have to see Anibal."

"He's not there."

The news surprised him. "He's here in Spanish Town?"

She shook her head. "Wrong again. He's in East Kingston, visiting friends. I have their address. We invited him to stay with us, but he said no."

Gil pulled over to the side of the street and stopped. "Then—"

"Why don't you stay with us?" she broke in. "Just because Anibal doesn't accept our hospitality, there's no reason for you to turn us down."

"I don't—" he began.

"Mother and Sara would love to have you. You can stay in the guest cottage."

"Ellen," he said. "I'm sorry if I'm out of line, but I'm not very good with women . . ."

There are many things you're not very good at, she

thought. *But you try, and I've never met a man before who did.* "Yes?" she said.

". . . and I'm married," he said. As if she needed reminding.

"I know," she said. "What I also know, however, is that we're friends." What if that was only a part of it? It wasn't really a lie. "Accept. Please."

He smiled, threw the car back into gear. "I'd be happy to," he answered.

"So what did you find out?" Ellen asked, once they were on their way again.

"It's worse than we've heard," he said. "The Japanese have sunk damned near the entire Pacific Fleet. What's more, they've smashed most of our aircraft in the Philippines."

She digested his news. "Think what would have happened had they carried out their mission against the canal," she offered.

Gil kept his eyes on the road. "That's what McEachern said. We've 'prevented a disaster from turning into a catastrophe': his words."

"And you," she asked. "What about your plans?" She dreaded his answer.

"I talked with McEachern about that. He wants to keep me on. Told me to think about it."

"Would you stay with the OCI?"

He shrugged. "One thing I know: No one else is going to want a thirty-two-year-old man with a metal plate in his leg. It's either that or go back to Hollywood and make serials."

There was silence. "Funny thing," Gil said. "Six months ago, this is what I prayed for: being 4F in Hollywood with all the other actors going off to war. Now that we're in it, it doesn't sound so appealing."

Was it only the fact of war which made the prospect of life in Hollywood pale for him? It would be nice to think he had other reasons to change his mind.

"Anyway," Gil said, "we're going to turn *Stardust* over to Anibal. It's the least we can do. Look what he's done for a country that's never done anything for him but throw him in jail. I told McEachern we had to do it."

"What did he say?"

"He yelled, said the boat was government property."

"What did you say?"

" 'So were all the ships in Pearl Harbor,' I told him. Besides, I reminded him it was beyond his control. They had to give me the ownership papers, remember. I could give it away or sell it and no one could do a thing about it."

"Anibal deserves it," Ellen commented.

"That's what McEachern finally said." He glanced at her. "I've never been friends with a woman I love before. Let's stop somewhere for lunch before we go to your mother's place. Agreed?"

His words took the breath from her. It took time before she was able to respond. "Agreed," she finally said.

The Eighteenth

The whoop came from the beach. Ellen looked up. Gil was racing for the house, holding some papers in his hand. He ran with a slight limp. She had never noticed that before. "What is it?" she asked as he came panting up the veranda stairs.

"First, a cup of coffee," he said and sank down in the

chair beside her. The grin on his face made him look almost boyish. She poured the coffee.

"So what is it?" she repeated. She tried not to catch his enthusiasm, lest the letdown prove too painful.

"It's the mail McEachern forwarded," he said, waving a letter at her. "It's from Mona. Or, rather, from her shyster lawyer. She's suing me for divorce. Desertion, she claimed. And in wartime, yet. Christ, she could have me shot, if she wanted."

Ellen struggled to restrain her feelings: it was like trying to rein in a team of wild horses. "How can she do that?" she asked. She was proud of her cool, detached tone.

"She can't. Not if I protest. It's all a part of the agreement we signed before we married. If I divorced her, I'd get nothing, but if she divorced me, except under certain circumstances, I'd be entitled to some money. It was a way to get around community property laws."

A coldness crept into Ellen's chest. Money? Was that why Gil had stayed married? "Desertion is one of the circumstances?" she said.

"Desertion, adultery, kicking the cat off the bed—a couple dozen other things."

"Will you contest it?"

Gil looked at her. "I couldn't, even if I wanted to. I wrote her four days ago asking for a divorce. Our letters must have crossed."

It was as if the sun had come out from behind a cloud. "Poor Mona," she said. "America's sweetheart will be crushed."

"Not for long. There's a story about her and a navy pilot in the *Variety* McEachern forwarded. Poor Mona has already found some way of doing her bit for the war effort."

"What does it mean for you?" she asked. *Don't show him how you feel.* "I mean," she continued, "does the letter also mean you've made a decision about what you want to do?"

"Maybe," he admitted. "I told you McEachern wants me to stay with the OCI?"

Ellen nodded.

"I don't think you know he offered to let me stay in the Caribbean, though."

She hadn't known that. "Do you want that?" she asked. *Don't sound desperate. Don't let the longing show.*

"It all depends on you," he said.

Ellen took a deep breath. *At last.* Somehow, the air seemed sweeter than it had in years. "You asked me once to let you know when I wanted to rejoin the living."

Gil stared hard into her eyes. He nodded.

"Well," she breathed. "Don't lock your door tonight."

He kissed her. Ellen returned it, broke reluctantly away. "And if I do?" he said after he released her.

"Locked doors can't stop me any longer, not after all I've been through," she said. "Go ahead and try. I'll climb in a window, break through the door, blow down walls."

Gil laughed. "When you decide to start living, it sounds like there's not much that can stop you."

Her smile couldn't get any broader. "Don't even try," she said.

CHAPTER 9

January, 1942

The stairs seemed forbidding, like steps leading to a gallows. Maria took a deep breath and mounted them.

Carlos, the maître d', was at his old post. She saw his eyes widen as he recognized her. She shook her head, and he understood. "Señora . . . ?" he queried.

"Peton," she replied. She had been practicing the name for days. It did not yet sound natural. She wished Rosario had found a different one for her. "I am expected. A Mr. William Burrows, from the United States. Has he arrived?"

The maître d'hôtel's eyes lit up in amusement. Ah yes, señora, the gentleman from the Department of Agriculture. He is here." He lowered his voice. "Would you like to take a look at him before I show you to his table?"

"It is not necessary," she said. The request triggered memories of Andre and the great scheme. It had collapsed totally. What wasn't gone was in shambles: Carib Shipping, the prospect of a quick Axis victory, her bank balance, Andre. Eric, too. Strange, she reflected, she did not miss Andre, but she missed Eric terribly. What was left? A letter of marque, wrinkled and waterstained, worth either $1,500,000 in gold or whatever Marchal Pétain's signature might bring in the postwar autograph market. Fifty cents? Something like that. She let the memories pass. They were all *disparu*, as Andre might say, like last night's dream—images without substance or cohesion.

Burrows had broad shoulders, heavy jowls, a mass of white hair. His eyes grew wider, the closer she came to his table. Carlos drew out a chair for Maria. The American rose hastily. He looked like a child who had been given a pony for Christmas. "Señora Peton," he said. "It is good to meet you." He had a paunch.

"Please," she said, sitting, motioning him back in his chair. He looked better that way. He sat, still staring. Maria averted her eyes.

It was not hard to get him to relax. She was good at it. A few opening comments, a little flirting to let him know she thought him clever and attractive, that was all it took. By the time dinner was over, Burrows was leaning back and boasting. He reached into his pocket and pulled out a cigarette case. "Would you care for one?" he asked, grinning at her.

She took one. He leaned across the table to light it. The manner in which his gaze lingered at her bosom did not escape her. She would have little trouble with the man, she concluded, and drew deeply on the cigarette. "Now, Mr. Burrows," she told him, "to business."

He nodded. "Business," he said, "then pleasure."

He was an idiot. She smiled. "You are here because your government is interested in seeing if we would like to grow—how do you say it?—cryptostoria.'' She simpered prettily.

Burrows leaned back with a condescending smirk. ''Cryptostegia, dear.''

''My government and our people are interested in doing all we can to assist you in this war,'' she said, ''so, of course, we will help you in this, if it is what you want. I know nothing of the plant,'' she lied. ''Tell me about it.''

He took a sip of wine, then set his glass down. ''It's a vine,'' he explained. ''It grows wild in some parts of this island. My department has done some experimenting with it. Its sap contains a relatively high amount of latex . . .'' He paused, looked at her. ''That's what rubber is made of, honey,'' he added. ''The British have damned near lost Malaya and, frankly, I wouldn't give a tinker's damn for our chances of keeping the Dutch East Indies. We lose them, we lose most of our rubber supply.''

''And so you are thinking of beginning a rubber industry here,'' she concluded.

''That's it in a nutshell,'' Burrows agreed.

Experiment here instead of in your own country, she added silently. *When the war ends, all you'll have to do is pack up and go home. You won't have to deal with American farmers screaming about fields filled with worthless weeds.* Such thoughts were counterproductive. She put out her cigarette, refused another glass of champagne with a shake of her head. ''Tell me what your department is prepared to spend to start up this operation,'' she said.

The appreciative look left his eyes. ''Well, now, pretty miss, I'm not sure—''

''Reluctant? Then, perhaps, I should tell you,'' Maria said. ''Your Department of Agriculture has allocated funds for converting a sugar mill into a plant for extracting latex from the cryptostegia vine. You, furthermore, have funds leasing of land and the construction of a plant for producing latex. You, of course, will supervise all my dealings, but I am the one who will handle all transactions."

His grin broadened. "And what will be your cut?"

"Eight percent of every transaction," she told him, meeting his gaze evenly, refusing to smile in return.

"The dragon lady!"

"Pardon?"

"Nothing. You just reminded me of someone, with you green eyes and all," he explained. "I admire your nerve, sneaking in like this under Trujillo's nose, then trying to cut him out of the deal."

He couldn't know how much pleasure she took in cutting Trujillo and all his cronies out, she reflected. She had her papers, her new identity, but nothing else. Rosario and Trujillo had taken everything: all her money in the bank, even Carib Shipping: nationalized, Trujillo's newest trick. The satin cocktail dress she wore—sheath skirt, sleeveless, with sweetheart neck, fashioned from one of Rosario's bedsheets by a Dominican seamstress and dyed black—constituted half her entire wardrobe.

There was a double irony in Rosario having furnished the material for the dress. It marked the beginning of her way back. She touched her hair. She had combed it into a tight bun to show off her earrings, made from the baguettes of her engagement ring. Her look was severe, classic, sleek—like that of a jungle cat.

"Eight percent amounts to an awful lot of money."

She smiled, batted her eyes. "It is not much if it is split with a partner," she said.

His eyebrows shot up. A look Maria interpreted as budding greed touched his face. "Partner?" he asked.

She said nothing, only continued to look at him. The poor man didn't know what to think of first: the money or you are willing to disburse to anyone willing to tear up their sugar crop and convert to the vine. Altogether, you have budgeted $2,000,000 to start this program.''

The look of stupefaction on Burrows's fat face was what she wanted. She had been right to cultivate the young man at the American Consulate. His information was accurate, invaluable. "It is all very well," she continued, "but let me assure you, your money will get you nowhere if you choose to work with *El Presidente*. He and his brothers will eat it up and be back for more before a single vine is planted."

"Tell me more. I am interested," Burrows said.

Maria nodded. "Cryptostegia grows wild in the Haitian district of Gonaïves. You are reluctant to deal with the Haitians because you fear their government is unstable. Still, that is where your chances of production are best, am I not correct?"

"Go on, I'm listening," he said. He was even more unattractive when he thought he was being shrewd.

"It would be wise to take a second look at Haiti," Maria said. "If you work through me, you will not have to deal with the Haitian government, nor will you have to deal with any Haitians. But you must work through me only. No one else. I will get you what you want and I will do it at a fraction of what you would have to expend in the Dominican Republic."

The American downed the rest of his champagne in a single toss, set down his glass, and said: "Pardon my French, honey, but you've got balls." When she made no protest at his vulgarity, he continued, "How much do you expect to get personally from this?"

"I expect an initial payment of five percent—$100,000— of the funds under your control. That will be transferred to me immediately. Once I have it, I will arrange for the knew but what she would not be able to do both at once? It would mean a little more work, but it carried the promise of even greater reward. It was exciting, like being at a race and knowing that, whichever horse wins, you own the winning ticket. That came from the second lesson she had learned: always back the winner.

her. At last, she sipped her wine. She looked over the top of the glass at him as she did so. Then, putting the glass back down, she nodded.

"Fifty-fifty?"

"Fifty-fifty," she agreed. "And your government will still get a better deal than if it chose to work here."

"Who cooks the books?"

"That will be my affair. They will contain no hint of your involvement, I assure you."

"And what kind of working arrangement do you expect us to have?"

"We will be partners. You will be free to examine our books and question me about business affairs at any time." She carefully licked a drop of champagne from the corner of her mouth, never dropping her eyes from his.

"That's not all we'll be, though, is it?" His face was ﾠd.

ﾠhy could the Americans not send a different sort to ﾠtheir dirty work? "I have learned one lesson in life," ﾠbegan. "It is that I cannot mix business and romance. ﾠat least, in the beginning."

ﾠs face fell, but only for a moment. She had hit the ﾠnote, of course. Burrows was not going to give up ﾠpromise of money or her favors. Now it was time to start thinking of other matters, most notably how she was going to deliver what she had promised.

It would fall in place once she put her mind to it. Making deals, working with people, she was good at such things. And, if it failed, there was the other proposition the young man at the consulate had mentioned: bauxite. The United States suffered a shortage of aluminum. The War Department was handing out exploration and development contracts on a cost-plus-ten-percent basis all over the Caribbean. She should be able to swing one. Who

Meat Turnovers

Ingredients	Total Calories	Starch Calories (Blocked by Starch-Blocker)	Non-Starch Calories Remaining (After Starch-Blocker Use)
½ lb. ground round steak	405	0	405
1 c. bean sprouts, drained	40	0	40
1 c. cabbage, chopped fine	20	0	20
1 T. onion, chopped	10	0	10
salt and pepper	0	0	0
1 pkg. refrigerator crescent rolls	600	540	60
Totals per Recipe	1,075	540	535
Totals per Serving	215	108	107

Directions: Brown the ground round steak with the chopped onion. Add sprouts, cabbage, salt and pepper and cool. Divide the meat and vegetable mixture on top of the flattened rolls. Fold dough up over mixture and pinch shut. Let rise 10 minutes. Place in pre-heated 375° oven and bake 15-20 minutes, or until golden brown. Makes 5.

Shrimp Stuffed Peppers

Ingredients	Total Calories	Starch Calories (Blocked by Blocker?)	Non-starch Calories Remaining After Starch-Blocker Use
¼ lb. fresh shrimp, cooked and shredded	240	0	240
6 medium green peppers	96	0	96
1 c. uncooked rice	600	540	60
1 10-oz. can mushroom soup	130	0	130
1 T. onion, grated	10	0	10
1 tsp. parsley, chopped	0	0	0
½ c. Swiss cheese, grated	210	0	210
sea salt, pepper and paprika	0	0	0
Totals per Recipe	1,286	540	746
Totals per Serving	215	90	125

Directions: Cut tops from green peppers and remove seeds and fibers. Cook peppers in salted water for about 10 minutes and drain. Cook the rice. Drain rice (if necessary) and mix it with the soup, onion, parsley, salt, and pepper. Add shrimp to rice mix and use to fill the green peppers to within about ½ inch of their tops. Divide the grated cheese among the stuffed peppers, placing it on top of the rice and shrimp mix. Sprinkle all with paprika. Place in baking dish which has a cover, and pour about 1 cup of water around the stuffed peppers. Cover and bake at 350° for 50 minutes. Remove cover and bake 20 minutes more. If you have extra shrimp and rice mixture, this can be placed around the peppers instead of water, or baked in a separate dish. Stuffed peppers freeze well. Serves 6.